THE TERROR
&
WHITE FACE

'THE DETECTIVE STORY CLUB is a clearing house for the best detective and mystery stories chosen for you by a select committee of experts. Only the most ingenious crime stories will be published under the THE DETECTIVE STORY CLUB imprint. A special distinguishing stamp appears on the wrapper and title page of every THE DETECTIVE STORY CLUB book—the Man with the Gun. Always look for the Man with the Gun when buying a Crime book.'

Wm. Collins Sons & Co. Ltd., 1929

Now the Man with the Gun is back in this series of COLLINS CRIME CLUB reprints, and with him the chance to experience the classic books that influenced the Golden Age of crime fiction.

THE DETECTIVE STORY CLUB

THE TERROR & WHITE FACE

STORIES OF CRIME BY
EDGAR WALLACE

WITH AN INTRODUCTION BY
MARTIN EDWARDS

COLLINS
CRIME
CLUB

COLLINS CRIME CLUB
An imprint of HarperCollins*Publishers*
1 London Bridge Street
London SE1 9GF
www.harpercollins.co.uk

This edition 2016

The Terror first published in Great Britain
by The Detective Story Club Ltd
for Wm Collins Sons & Co. Ltd 1929
White Face first published in Great Britain
by Hodder & Stoughton 1930

Introduction © Martin Edwards 2016

A catalogue record for this book is
available from the British Library

ISBN 978-0-00-813757-1

Printed and bound in Great Britain by
Clays Ltd, St Ives plc

INTRODUCTION

In July 1929, Edgar Wallace's *The Terror* headed the list of the first half dozen titles published by Collins in their Detective Story Club, the only one which was not a reissue. This lively, melodramatic thriller does not outstay its welcome—its brevity is such that some bibliographies describe it as a short story, although in fact it is a novella with an unusual history. On its first appearance, *The Terror* was published on its own, its modest length bulked out to 192 pages thanks to the cunning use of a conspicuously large type-face. Rather than resort to the same tactic to achieve its page count, this reissued edition includes the bonus of a second Wallace book published in the following year, and *White Face* is rather more than twice as long as *The Terror*.

An enthusiastic preface to the Detective Story Club edition hailed *The Terror* as 'a masterpiece of its kind', and, nearly ninety years later, there is no denying that it displays the characteristics that made Edgar Wallace a literary phenomenon. Margaret Lane, his first major biographer, summarised the lurid plot ingredients: 'an old mysterious house built over hidden dungeons . . . hidden treasure . . . the hooded figure appearing on moonlit nights and leaving a trail of murder in its wake, the shrieking heroine trapped in the dungeon with a sinister madman'. Add to that both a master criminal and ace detective masquerading as someone else, and you have a classic slice of Twenties popular culture.

Just like the early whodunits of Agatha Christie and Dorothy L. Sayers, *The Terror* belongs to an age when people craved escapism at least as much as they had ever done. Memories of the First World War, which in one way or another touched almost every family in the land, were still raw. Edgar Wallace's

v

thrillers met a particular need, and met it better than any of his peers. He was, G. K. Chesterton said, 'a huge furnace and factory of fiction', and the popularity of his books made him a fortune, which he spent as quickly as he earned it.

An intriguing facet of *The Terror* is the story's genesis in the theatre. The idea for the story came during the course of an extravagant holiday in Caux in late 1926. Wallace met Bertie Meyer, a theatrical manager, who suggested that Wallace write a play for two prominent actors, Mary Glynne and Dennis Nielsen-Terry. It took Wallace a mere 'five nervous and preoccupied days', as Margaret Lane perhaps euphemistically described them, to rise to the challenge. Even more impressive was the result of his frantic labours: the play ran for almost seven months at the Lyceum, and having cost just £1,000 to stage, made £35,000 in profits.

Success in the theatre led to *The Terror* being filmed; it became Warner Brothers' second 'all-talking picture' before Wallace produced this book version. A more notable screen adaptation came in 1938; the cast included such luminaries as Alastair Sim, in characteristic scene-stealing form as Soapy Marks, and Bernard Lee, best remembered today as 'M' in *Dr No* and ten subsequent James Bond films, as Freddy Fane.

White Face appears to be the only other example of an original book that Wallace based on an earlier stage play, *Persons Unknown*, although his productivity was so astonishing that his bibiliography is as convoluted as a thriller plot, and it is hard to be sure about such things: *The British Bibliography of Edgar Wallace* by W. O. G. Lofts and Derek Adley is a full-length work, yet even its industrious authors admitted that, after four years' research, they were far from confident they had traced all his stories published in Britain, let alone anywhere else. In 1932, *White Face* was turned into a film, but like the original film version of *The Terror*, it is now considered officially to be lost, unless any prints turn up in archives or the hands of private collectors.

This tale of a white-masked villain who terrorises London boasts a neat 'least likely person' twist, and also some snappy snatches of dialogue, as when a detective opines: 'Policemen and reporters get their living out of other people's misfortunes.' Another police officer expresses the view: 'The jury is a body or institution which gives everybody the benefit of the doubt except the police.' A later passage, which has something of a timeless quality, notes: 'Parliament had been playing too inter-fering a part in the police force lately ... The Home Office had issued new instructions which, if they were faithfully carried out, would prevent the police from asking vital questions. Every step that the crank and the busybody could devise to interfere with the administration of justice had assumed official shape.'

Wallace never pretended to be a literary stylist, but the energy of his writing and the slickness of his plot twists earned him countless readers. At one time, his publishers claimed that he was responsible for one in every four British novels read. If this was an exaggeration, it did at least have the merit of seeming plausible. A Detective Story Club advertisement for *The Terror* said the tale proved once again 'that there are many imitators, but only one Edgar Wallace'. This was perfectly true. Richard Horatio Edgar Wallace (1875–1932) was extraordinary among authors in that his life was as extraordinary as his books. He was one of a kind, and the latest biography, written by Neil Clark and published in 2014, is called fittingly *Stranger than Fiction*.

Wallace's work had a universal appeal. As Clark says, 'Among his millions of fans were King George V ... Stanley Baldwin, a president of the United States, and a certain Adolf Hitler.' Writing in 1969, Penelope Wallace, his daughter, suggested that an underlying reason for his popularity was 'his lack of bitterness':

'There are occasions when he is angry, particularly on such subjects as "baby farming" but none where hatred ...

obscures the text. His villains are usually English and on the rare occasions when they are not home-grown they are imported impartially . . . There is no trace of racial or religious prejudice and it is rare for the villain to be completely bad. Those who say that his characters are either black or white can never have read his books. Few of his bad men are disallowed a redeeming feature or two.'

Reading tastes fluctuate as time passes, and the world has changed a great deal since Wallace adapted *The Terror* and *White Face* from his plays. Fortunately, good story-telling never goes completely out of fashion. Edgar Wallace was a gifted story-teller, and it is a pleasure to introduce these two lively tales to a new generation of readers.

MARTIN EDWARDS
May 2015
www.martinedwardsbooks.com

THE TERROR

THE TERROR

EDITOR'S PREFACE

POST-WAR fiction has produced hundreds of clever detective novels and not a few really first-class writers, but there is only one Edgar Wallace. His supremacy we feel sure cannot be challenged. His name has become a household word throughout the English-speaking world, and many of his 'thrillers' have already found their way in translations into the libraries of every country in Europe.

While we make a superlative statement about the man without any fear of criticism, we hesitate to say which of the novels of his very prolific pen is the best! Perhaps, taking popularity as a guide, we may put *The Terror* in the place of honour. This wonderful story has thrilled the London theatre world in its dramatised form; it has been made into a super film, which was one of the first 'talkies' shown to the public, and which will long be pronounced one of the best, and now in book form the Detective Story Club presents it to the world.

The Terror is a masterpiece of its kind, and the Edgar Wallace enthusiast will delight in tracing a hundred and one clever devices from subtleties in plot to fine consistency in the characters. The plot speaks for itself, but as an example of a cleverly drawn character take Soapy Marks, a man of secondary importance in the story. In the opening scene we see him chided by his confederate, Connor: ('Don't try swank on me, Soapy—use words I can understand') but this characteristic does not obtrude—in fact, it is only well on in the book that we see Soapy in his true light, spoken of by Scotland Yard as 'so clever that one of these days we'll find him in Oxford or Cambridge'. And so with each and every one of the characters.

The atmosphere of terror suggested by the very title of the book is handled with that care which makes real melodrama—a word, by the way, which should not have become degraded in meaning, had all the novels and plays so called been of the Edgar Wallace standard! He never overdoes it. His thrills are relieved by flashes of real humour and the love element introduced with Mary Redmayne and the drunken Ferdie Fane is so slightly suggested that when she admits in the closing chapter, 'Yes—I—I'm awfully fond of—of Mr Fane,' we only then realise that the unknown something which gave the story its charm was indeed love!

CHAPTER I

O'SHEA was in his maddest mood, had been like it all night. Stalking up and down the grassy slope, muttering to himself, waving his hands at some invisible audience, cackling with laughter at his own mysterious jokes; and at dawn he had fallen upon little Lipski, who had dared light a cigarette in defiance of instructions, and had beaten him with savage brutality, and the other two men had not dared interfere.

Joe Connor sprawled on the ground, chewing a blade of grass, and watching with sombre eyes the restless figure. Marks, who sat cross-legged by his side, watched too, but there was a twisted and sneering smile on his thin lips.

'Mad as a coot,' said Joe Connor in a low voice. 'If he pulls this job off without getting us in gaol for the rest of our lives we'll be lucky.'

Soapy Marks licked his dry lips.

'He's cleverest when he's mad.' He spoke like a man of culture. Some said that Soapy was intended for the church before a desire for an easier and more illicit method of living made him one of the most skilful, and nearly the most dangerous, gangster in England.

'Lunacy, my dear fellow, does not mean stupidity. Can't you stop that fellow blubbering?'

Joe Connor did not rise; he turned his eyes in the direction of the prostrate figure of Lipski, who was groaning and swearing sobbingly.

'He'll get over it,' he said indifferently. 'The bigger beating he gets the more he respects O'Shea.'

He wriggled a little closer to his confederate.

'Have you ever seen O'Shea—his face, I mean?' he asked, dropping his voice a note lower. 'I never have, and I've done two—' he thought '—three,' he corrected, 'jobs with him. He's always had that coat on he's got now, with the collar right up to his nose, the same old hat over his eyes. I never used to believe there was that kind of crook—thought they were only seen on the stage. First time I ever heard of him was when he sent for me—met him on the St Albans Road about twelve o'clock, but never saw his face. He knew all about me; told me how many convictions I'd had, and the kind of work he wanted me for—'

'And paid you well,' said Marks lazily, when the other paused. 'He always pays well; he always picks up his 'staff' in the same way.'

He pursed his lips as though he were going to whistle, examined the restless figure of the master thoughtfully.

'He's mad—and he pays well. He will pay better this time.'

Connor looked up sharply.

'Two hundred and fifty quid and fifty getaway money—that's fair, ain't it?'

'He will pay better,' said Marks suavely. 'This little job deserves it. Am I to drive a motor-lorry containing three tons of Australian sovereigns through the streets of London, possibly risk hanging, for two hundred and fifty pounds—and getaway money? I think not.'

He rose to his feet and dusted his knees daintily. O'Shea had disappeared over the crest of the hill, was possibly behind the hedge line which swept round in a semi-circle till it came within half a dozen feet of where the men were talking of him.

'Three tons of gold; nearly half a million pounds. At least I think we're entitled to ten per cent.'

Connor grinned, jerked his head towards the whimpering Lipski.

'And him?'

Marks bit his lip.

'I don't think we could include him.'

He glanced round again for some sign of O'Shea, and dropped down beside his companion.

'We've got the whole thing in our hands,' he said in a voice that was little more than a whisper. 'He'll be sane tomorrow. These fits only come on him at rare intervals; and a sane man will listen to reason. We're holding up this gold convoy—that's one of O'Shea's oldest tricks, to fill a deep cutting full of gas. I wonder he dare repeat it. I am driving the lorry to town and hiding it. Would O'Shea give us our share if he had to decide between an unpleasant interview with us and a more unpleasant interview with Inspector Bradley?'

Connor plucked another blade of grass and chewed on it gloomily.

'He's clever,' he began, and again Marks' lips curled.

'Aren't they all?' he demanded. 'Isn't Dartmoor full of clever people? That's old Hallick's great joke—he calls all the prisoners collegers. No, my dear Connor, believe me, cleverness is a relative term—'

'What does that mean?' growled Connor with a frown. 'Don't try swank on me, Soapy—use words I can understand.'

He looked around again a little anxiously for the vanished O'Shea. Behind the hill crest, in a narrow lane, O'Shea's big car was parked that would carry him to safety after the job. His confederates would be left to take all the risks, face the real dangers which would follow, however cleverly the coup was organised.

A little distance away to the left, on the edge of the deep cutting, four big steel gas cylinders lay in line. Even from where he sprawled he could see the long white road leading into the cutting, on which presently would appear the flickering lights of the gold convoy. His gas mask lay under his hand; Marks had his sticking out of his coat pocket.

'He must have a lot of stuff,' he said.

'Who—O'Shea?' Marks shrugged his shoulders. 'I don't know. He spends money like a lunatic. I should think he was broke. It's nearly twelve months since he had a big haul.'

'What does he do with the money?' asked Connor curiously.

'Spends it, as we all do,' was the laconic answer. 'He talked about buying a big country house last time I saw him; he was going to settle down and live the life of a gentleman. Last night, when I had a chat with him, he said it would take half this loot to pay his debts.'

Marks examined his well-manicured nails.

'Amongst other things he's a liar,' he said lightly. 'What's that?'

He looked towards the line of bushes a few yards distant. He had heard a rustle, the snap of a twig, and was on his feet instantly. Crossing the short intervening space, he peered over the bushes. There was nobody in sight. He came back thoughtfully to Connor.

'I wonder if the devil was listening,' he said, 'and how long he's been listening!'

'Who—O'Shea?' asked the startled Connor.

Marks did not reply, but drew a deep breath. Obviously he was uncomfortable.

'If he'd heard anything he would have come for me. He's moody—he's been moody all night.'

At this point Connor got up and stretched himself.

'I'd like to know how he lives. I'll bet he's got a wife and family tucked away somewhere—that kind of bird always has. There he is!'

The figure of O'Shea had appeared across the rise; he was coming towards them.

'Get your masks ready. You don't want any further instructions, Soapy?' The voice, muffled by the high collar which reached to the tip of his nose, was rational, almost amiable.

'Pick that fellow up.' He pointed to Lipski, and, when the order had been obeyed, he called the cringing man before him. 'You'll go to the end of the road, put your red lantern on and stop them. By stop them I mean slow them down. Don't let yourself be seen; there are ten armed men on the lorry.'

He examined the cylinders; from the nozzle of each a thick rubber pipe trailed down into the cutting. With a spanner he opened the valve of each, and the silence was broken by the deep hissing of the gas as it escaped.

'It'll lie in the bottom, so you needn't put on your masks till we're ready,' he said.

He followed Lipski to the end of the cutting, watched the red lamp lit, and pointed out the place where the man was to hide. Then he came back to Marks. Not by word or sign did he betray the fact that he had overheard the two men talking. If there was to be a quarrel this was not the moment for it. O'Shea was intensely sane at that moment.

They heard the sound of the incoming trolley before they saw the flicker of its lights emerge from the cover of Felsted Wood.

'Now,' said O'Shea sharply.

He made no attempt to draw on a mask, as did his two assistants.

'You won't have to use your guns, but keep them handy in case anything goes wrong—don't forget that if the guard isn't knocked out immediately it will shoot at sight. You know where to meet me tomorrow?'

The shrouded head of Soapy nodded.

Nearer and nearer came the gold convoy. Evidently the driver had seen the red light at the end of the cutting, for his siren sounded. From where O'Shea crouched he commanded a complete view of the road.

The trolley was within fifty yards of the cutting and had slowed perceptibly when he saw a man leap up, not from the place where he had posted him, but a dozen yards farther up the road. It was Lipski, and as he ran towards the moving trolley his hand went up, there was a flash and a report. He was firing to attract attention. O'Shea's eyes glowed like coals. Lipski had betrayed him.

'Stand by to run!' His voice was like a rasp.

And then the miracle happened. From the trolley leapt two pencils of flame, and Lipski crumpled up and fell by the side of the road as the lorry rumbled past. The guard had misunderstood his action; thought he was attempting to hold them up.

'Glorious,' whispered O'Shea huskily, and at that instant the lorry went down into the gas-filled cutting.

It was all over in a second. The driver fell forward in his seat, and, released of his guidance, the front wheels of the lorry jammed into a bank.

O'Shea thought of everything. But for that warning red light the trolley would have been wrecked and his plans brought to naught. As it was, Marks had only to climb into the driver's seat, and reverse the engine, to extricate it from the temporary block.

A minute later the gold convoy had climbed up to the other side of the depression. The unconscious guard and driver had been bundled out and laid on the side of the road. The final preparations took no more than five minutes. Marks stripped his mask, pulled on a uniform cap, and Connor took his place in the trolley where the gold was stored in small white boxes.

'Go on,' said O'Shea, and the trolley moved forward and four minutes later was out of sight.

O'Shea went back to his big, high-powered car and drove off in the opposite direction, leaving only the unconscious figures of the guard to testify to his ruthlessness.

CHAPTER II

It was a rainy night in London. Connor, who had preferred it so, turned into the side door of a little restaurant in Soho, mounted the narrow stairs and knocked on a door. He heard a chair move and the snap of the lock as the door was opened.

Soapy Marks was there alone.

'Did you see him?' asked Connor eagerly.

'O'Shea? Yes, I met him on the Embankment. Have you seen the newspapers?'

Connor grinned.

'I'm glad those birds didn't die,' he said.

Mr Marks sneered.

'Your humanity is very creditable, my dear friend,' he said.

On the table was a newspaper, and the big headlines stared out, almost shouted their excitement.

GREATEST GOLD ROBBERY OF OUR TIME.
THREE TONS OF GOLD DISAPPEAR BETWEEN SOUTHAMPTON
AND LONDON.
DEAD ROBBER FOUND BY THE ROADSIDE.
THE VANISHED LORRY.

In the early hours of yesterday morning a daring outrage was committed which might have led to the death of six members of the C.I.D., and resulted in the loss to the Bank of England of gold valued at half a million pounds.

The *Aritania*, which arrived in Southampton last night, brought a heavy consignment of gold from Australia, and in order that this should be removed to London with the least possible ostentation, it was arranged that a lorry carrying the treasure should leave Southampton at three o'clock in the morning, arriving in London before the normal flow of traffic started. At a spot near Felsted Wood the road runs down into a depression and through a deep cutting. Evidently this had been laid with gas, and the car dashed into what was practically a lethal chamber without warning.

That an attack was projected, however, was revealed to the guard before they reached the fatal spot. A man sprang out from a hedge and shot at the trolley. The detectives in charge of the convoy immediately replied, and the man was later found in a dying condition. He made no statement except to mention a name which is believed to be that of the leader of the gang.

Sub-Inspectors Bradley and Hallick of Scotland Yard are in charge of the case ...

There followed a more detailed account, together with an official statement issued by the police, containing a brief narrative by one of the guards.

'It seems to have created something of a sensation,' smiled Marks, as he folded up the paper.

'What about O'Shea?' asked the other impatiently. 'Did he agree to split?' Marks nodded.

'He was a little annoyed—naturally. But in his sane moments our friend, O'Shea, is a very intelligent man. What really annoyed him was the fact that we had parked the lorry in another place than where he ordered it to be taken. He was most anxious to discover our little secret, and I think his ignorance of the whereabouts of the gold was our biggest pull with him.'

'What's going to happen?' asked Connor in a troubled tone.

'We're taking the lorry tonight to Barnes Common. He doesn't realise, though he will, that we've transferred the gold to a small three-ton van. He ought to be very grateful to me for my foresight, for the real van was discovered this evening by Hallick in the place where O'Shea told me to park it. And of course it was empty.'

Connor rubbed his hand across his unshaven chin.

'O'Shea won't let us get away with it,' he said, with a worried frown. 'You know him, Soapy.'

'We shall see,' said Mr Marks, with a confident smile.

He poured out a whisky and soda.

'Drink up and we'll go.' He glanced at his watch. 'We've got plenty of time—thank God there's a war on, and the active and intelligent constabulary are looking for spies, the streets are nicely darkened, and all is favourable to our little arrangement. By the way, I've had a red cross painted on the tilt of our van—it looks almost official!'

That there was a war on, they discovered soon after they turned into the Embankment. Warning maroons were banging from a dozen stations; the darkened tram which carried them to the south had hardly reached Kennington Oval before the anti-aircraft guns were blazing at the unseen marauders of the skies. A bomb dropped all too close for the comfort of the nervous Connor. The car had stopped.

'We had better get out here,' whispered Marks. 'They won't move till the raid is over.'

The two men descended to the deserted street and walked southward. The beams of giant searchlights swept the skies; from somewhere up above came the rattle of a machine-gun.

'This should keep the police thoroughly occupied,' said Marks, as they turned into a narrow street in a poor neighbourhood. 'I don't think we need miss our date, and our little ambulance should pass unchallenged.'

'I wish to God you'd speak English!' growled Connor irritably.

Marks had stopped before the gates of a stable yard, pushing them. One yielded to his touch and they walked down the uneven drive to the small building where the car was housed. Soapy put his key into the gate of the lock-up and turned it.

'Here we are,' he said, as he stepped inside.

And then a hand gripped him, and he reached for his gun.

'Don't make any fuss,' said the hated voice of Inspector Hallick. 'I want you, Soapy. Perhaps you'll tell me what's happened to this ambulance of yours?'

Soapy Marks stared towards the man he could not see, and for a moment was thrown off his guard.

'The lorry?' he gasped. 'Isn't it here?'

'Been gone an hour,' said a second voice. 'Come across, Soapy; what have you done with it?'

Soapy said nothing; he heard the steel handcuffs click on the wrist of Joe Connor, heard that man's babble of incoherent rage and blasphemy as he was hustled towards the car which had drawn up silently at the gate, and knew that Mr O'Shea was indeed very sane on that particular day.

CHAPTER III

To Mary Redmayne life had been a series of inequalities. She could remember the alternate prosperity and depression of her father; had lived in beautiful hotel suites and cheap lodgings, one following the other with extraordinary rapidity; and had grown so accustomed to the violent changes of his fortune that she would never have been surprised to have been taken from the pretentious school where she was educated, and planted amongst county school scholars at any moment.

People who knew him called him Colonel, but he himself preferred his civilian title, and volunteered no information to her as to his military career. It was after he had taken Monkshall that he permitted 'Colonel' to appear on his cards. It was a grand-sounding name, but even as a child Mary Redmayne had accepted such appellations with the greatest caution. She had once been brought back from her preparatory school to a 'Mortimer Lodge', to discover it was a tiny semi-detached villa in a Wimbledon by-street.

But Monkshall had fulfilled all her dreams of magnificence; a veritable relic of Tudor times, and possibly of an earlier period, it stood in forty acres of timbered ground, a dignified and venerable pile, which had such association with antiquity that, until Colonel Redmayne forbade the practice, charabancs full of American visitors used to come up the broad drive and gaze upon the ruins of what had been a veritable abbey.

Fortune had come to Colonel Redmayne when she was about eleven. It came unexpectedly, almost violently. Whence it came, she could not even guess; she only knew that one week he was poor, harassed by debt-collectors, moving through side streets in order to avoid his creditors; the next week—or was

15

it month?—he was master of Monkshall, ordering furniture worth thousands of pounds.

When she went to live at Monkshall she had reached that gracious period of interregnum between child and woman. A slim girl above middle height, straight of back, free of limb, she held the eye of men to whom more mature charms would have had no appeal.

Ferdie Fane, the young man who came to the Red Lion so often, summer and winter, and who drank so much more than was good for him, watched her passing along the road with her father. She was hatless; the golden-brown hair had a glory of its own; the faultless face, the proud little lift of her chin.

'Spring is here, Adolphus,' he addressed the landlord gravely. 'I have seen it pass.'

He was a man of thirty-five, long-faced, rather good-looking in spite of his huge horn-rimmed spectacles. He had a large tankard of beer in his hand now, which was unusual, for he did most of his drinking secretly in his room. He used to come down to the Red Lion at all sorts of odd and some-times inconvenient moments. He was, in a way, rather a bore, and the apparition of Mary Redmayne and her grim-looking father offered the landlord an opportunity for which he had been seeking.

'I wonder you don't go and stay at Monkshall, Mr Fane,' he suggested.

Mr Fane stared at him reproachfully.

'Are you tired of me, mine host?' he asked gently. 'That you should shuffle me into other hands?' He shook his head. 'I am no paying guest—besides which, I am not respectable. Why does Redmayne take paying guests at all?'

The landlord could offer no satisfactory solution to this mystery.

'I'm blessed if I know. The colonel's got plenty of money. I think it is because he's lonely, but he's had paying guests at Monkshall this past ten years. Of course, it's very select.'

'Exactly,' said Ferdie Fane with great gravity. 'And that is why I should not be selected! No, I fear you will have to endure my erratic visits.'

'I don't mind your being here, sir,' said the landlord, anxious to assure him. 'You never give me any trouble, only—'

'Only you'd like somebody more regular in his habits—good luck!'

He lifted the foaming pewter to his lips, took a long drink, and then he began to laugh softly, as though at some joke. In another minute he was serious again, frowning down into the tankard.

'Pretty girl, that. Mary Redmayne, eh?'

'She's only been back from school a month—or college, rather,' said the landlord. 'She's the nicest young lady that ever drew the breath of life.'

'They all are,' said the other vaguely. He went away the next day with his fishing rod that he hadn't used, and his golf bag which had remained unstrapped throughout his stay.

Life at Monkshall promised so well that Mary Redmayne was prepared to love the place. She liked Mr Goodman, the grey-haired, slow-spoken gentleman who was the first of her father's boarders; she loved the grounds, the quaint old house; could even contemplate, without any great uneasiness, the growing taciturnity of her father. He was older, much older than he had been; his face had a new pallor; he seldom smiled. He was a nervous man, too; she had found him walking about in the middle of the night, and once had surprised him in his room, suspiciously thick of speech, with an empty whisky bottle a silent witness to his peculiar weakness.

It was the house that began to get on her nerves. Sometimes she would wake up in the middle of the night suddenly and sit up in bed, trying to recall the horror that had snatched her from sleep and brought her through a dread cloud of fear to wakefulness. Once she had heard peculiar sounds that had sent cold shivers down her spine. Not once, but many times, she thought she heard the faint sound of a distant organ.

She asked Cotton, the dour butler, but he had heard nothing. Other servants had been more sensitive, however; there came a constant procession of cooks and housemaids giving notice. She interviewed one or two of these, but afterwards her father forbade her seeing them, and himself accepted their hasty resignations.

'This place gives me the creeps, miss,' a weeping housemaid had told her. 'Do you hear them screams at night? I do; I sleep in the east wing. The place is haunted—'

'Nonsense, Anna!' scoffed the girl, concealing a shudder. 'How can you believe such things!'

'It is, miss,' persisted the girl. 'I've seen a ghost on the lawn, walking about in the moonlight.'

Later, Mary herself began to see things; and a guest who came and stayed two nights had departed a nervous wreck.

'Imagination,' said the colonel testily. 'My dear Mary, you're getting the mentality of a housemaid!'

He was very apologetic afterwards for his rudeness, but Mary continued to hear, and presently to listen; and finally she saw ... Sights that made her doubt her own wisdom, her own intelligence, her own sanity.

One day, when she was walking alone through the village, she saw a man in a golf suit; he was very tall and wore horn-rimmed spectacles, and greeted her with a friendly smile. It was the first time she had seen Ferdie Fane. She was to see very much of him in the strenuous months that followed.

CHAPTER IV

SUPERINTENDENT HALLICK went down to Princetown in Devonshire to make his final appeal—an appeal which, he knew, was foredoomed to failure. The Deputy-Governor met him as the iron gates closed upon the burly superintendent.

'I don't think you're going to get very much out of these fellows, superintendent,' he said. 'I think they're too near to the end of their sentence.'

'You never know,' said Hallick, with a smile. 'I once had the best information in the world from a prisoner on the day he was released.'

He went down to the low-roofed building which constitutes the Deputy-Governor's office.

'My head warder says they'll never talk, and he has a knack of getting into their confidence,' said the Deputy. 'If you remember, superintendent, you did your best to make them speak ten years ago, when they first came here. There's a lot of people in this prison who'd like to know where the gold is hidden. Personally, I don't think they had it at all, and the story they told at the trial, that O'Shea had got away with it, is probably true.'

The superintendent pursed his lips.

'I wonder,' he said thoughtfully. 'That was the impression I had the night I arrested them, but I've changed my opinion since.'

The chief warder came in at that moment and gave a friendly nod to the superintendent.

'I've kept those two men in their cells this morning. You want to see them both, don't you, superintendent?'

'I'd like to see Connor first.'

'Now?' asked the warder. 'I'll bring him down.'

He went out, passed across the asphalt yard to the entrance of the big, ugly building. A steel grille covered the door, and this he unlocked, opening the wooden door behind, and passed into the hall, lined on each side with galleries from which opened narrow cell doors. He went to one of these on the lower tier, snapped back the lock and pulled open the door. The man in convict garb who was sitting on the edge of the bed, his face in his hands, rose and eyed him sullenly.

'Connor, a gentleman from Scotland Yard has come down to see you. If you're sensible you'll give him the information he asks.'

Connor glowered at him.

'I've nothing to tell, sir,' he said sullenly. 'Why don't they leave me alone? If I knew where the stuff was I wouldn't tell 'em.'

'Don't be a fool,' said the chief good-humouredly. 'What have you to gain by hiding up—?'

'A fool, sir?' interrupted Connor. 'I've had all the fool knocked out of me here!' His hand swept round the cell. 'I've been in this same cell for seven years; I know every brick of it—who is it wants to see me?'

'Superintendent Hallick.'

Connor made a wry face.

'Is he seeing Marks too? Hallick, eh? I thought he was dead.'

'He's alive enough.'

The chief beckoned him out into the hall, and, accompanied by a warder, Connor was taken to the Deputy's office. He recognised Hallick with a nod. He bore no malice; between these two men, thief-taker and thief, was that curious camaraderie which exists between the police and the criminal classes.

'You're wasting your time with me, Mr Hallick,' said Connor. And then, with a sudden burst of anger: 'I've got nothing to give you. Find O'Shea—he'll tell you! And find him before I do, if you want him to talk.'

'We want to find him, Connor,' said Hallick soothingly.

'You want the money,' sneered Connor; 'that's what you want. You want to find the money for the bank and pull in the reward.' He laughed harshly. 'Try Soapy Marks—maybe he'll sit in your game and take his corner.'

The lock turned at that moment and another convict was ushered into the room. Soapy Marks had not changed in his ten years of incarceration. The gaunt, ascetic face had perhaps grown a little harder; the thin lips were firmer, and the deep-set eyes had sunk a little more into his head. But his cultured voice, his exaggerated politeness, and that oiliness which had earned him his nickname, remained constant.

'Why, it's Mr Hallick!' His voice was a gentle drawl. 'Come down to see us at our country house!'

He saw Connor and nodded, almost bowed to him.

'Well, this is most kind of you, Mr Hallick. You haven't seen the park or the garage? Nor our beautiful billiard-room?'

'That'll do, Marks,' said the warder sternly.

'I beg your pardon, sir, I'm sure.' The bow to the warder was a little deeper, a little more sarcastic. 'Just badinage—nothing wrong intended. Fancy meeting you on the moor, Mr Hallick! I suppose this is only a brief visit? You're not staying with us, are you?'

Hallick accepted the insult with a little smile.

'I'm sorry,' said Marks. 'Even the police make little errors of judgment sometimes. It's deplorable, but it's true. We once had an ex-inspector in the hall where I am living.'

'You know why I've come?' said Hallick.

Marks shook his head, and then a look of simulated surprise and consternation came to his face.

'You haven't come to ask me and my poor friend about that horrible gold robbery? I see you have. Dear me, how very unfortunate! You want to know where the money was hidden? I wish I could tell you. I wish my poor friend could tell you, or even your old friend, Mr Leonard O'Shea.' He smiled blandly. 'But I can't!'

Connor was chafing under the strain of the interview.

'You don't want me any more—'

Marks waved his hand.

'Be patient with dear Mr Hallick.'

'Now look here, Soapy,' said Connor angrily, and a look of pain came to Marks' face.

'Not Soapy—that's vulgar. Don't you agree, Mr Hallick?'

'I'm going to answer no questions. You can do as you like,' said Connor. 'If you haven't found O'Shea, I will, and the day I get my hands on him he'll know all about it! There's another thing you've got to know, Hallick; I'm on my own from the day I get out of this hell. I'm not asking Soapy to help me to find O'Shea. I've seen Marks every day for ten years, and I hate the sight of him. I'm working single-handed to find the man who shopped me.'

'You think you'll find him, do you?' said Hallick quickly. 'Do you know where he is?'

'I only know one thing,' said Connor huskily, 'and Soapy knows it too. He let it out that morning we were waiting for the gold lorry. It just slipped out—what O'Shea's idea was of a quiet hiding-place. But I'm not going to tell you. I've got four months to serve, and when that time is up I'll find O'Shea.'

'You poor fool!' said Hallick roughly. 'The police have been looking for him for ten years.'

'Looking for what?' demanded Connor, ignoring Marks' warning look.

'For Len O'Shea,' said Hallick.

There came a burst of laughter from the convict.

'You're looking for a sane man, and that's where you went wrong! I didn't tell you before why you'll never find him. It's because he's mad! You didn't know that, but Soapy knows. O'Shea was crazy ten years ago. God knows what he is now! Got the cunning of a madman. Ask Soapy.'

It was news to Hallick. His eyes questioned Marks, and the little man smiled.

'I'm afraid our dear friend is right,' said Marks suavely. 'A cunning madman! Even in Dartmoor we get news, Mr Hallick, and a rumour has reached me that some years ago three officers of Scotland Yard disappeared in the space of a few minutes—just vanished as though they had evaporated like dew before the morning sun! Forgive me if I am poetical; Dartmoor makes you that way. And would you be betraying an official secret if you told me these men were looking for O'Shea?'

He saw Hallick's face change, and chuckled.

'I see they were. The story was that they had left England and they sent their resignations—from Paris, wasn't it? O'Shea could copy anybody's handwriting—they never left England.' Hallick's face was white.

'By God, if I thought that—' he began.

'They never left England,' said Marks remorselessly. 'They were looking for O'Shea—and O'Shea found them first.'

'You mean they're dead?' asked the other.

Marks nodded slowly.

'For twenty-two hours a day he is a sane, reasonable man. For two hours—' He shrugged his shoulders. 'Mr Hallick, your men must have met him in one of his bad moments.'

'When I meet him—' interrupted Connor, and Marks turned on him in a flash.

'When you meet him you will die!' he hissed. 'When *I* meet him—' That mild face of his became suddenly contorted, and Hallick looked into the eyes of a demon.

'When you meet him?' challenged Hallick. 'Where will you meet him?'

Marks' arm shot out stiffly; his long fingers gripped an invisible enemy.

'I know just where I can put my hand on him,' he breathed. 'That hand!'

Hallick went back to London that afternoon, a baffled man. He had gone to make his last effort to secure information about the missing gold, and had learned nothing—except that O'Shea was sane for twenty-two hours in the day.

CHAPTER V

It was a beautiful spring morning. There was a tang in the air which melted in the yellow sunlight.

Mr Goodman had not gone to the city that morning, though it was his day, for he made a practice of attending at his office for two or three days every month. Mrs Elvery, that garrulous woman, was engaged in putting the final touches to her complexion; and Veronica, her gawkish daughter, was struggling, by the aid of a dictionary, with a recalcitrant poem—for she wooed the gentler muse in her own gentler moments.

Mr Goodman sat on a sofa, dozing over his newspaper. No sound broke the silence but the scratching of Veronica's pen and the ticking of the big grandfather's clock.

This vaulted chamber, which was the lounge of Monkshall, had changed very little since the days when it was the ante-room to a veritable refectory. The columns that monkish hands had chiselled had crumbled a little, but their chiselled piety, hidden now behind the oak panelling, was almost as legible as on the day the holy men had written them.

Through the open French window there was a view of the broad, green park, with its clumps of trees and its little heap of ruins that had once been the Mecca of the antiquarian.

Mr Goodman did not hear the excited chattering of the birds, but Miss Veronica, in that irritable frame of mind which a young poet can so readily reach, turned her head once or twice in mute protest.

'Mr Goodman,' she said softly.

There was no answer, and she repeated his name impatiently. 'Mr Goodman!'

'Eh?' He looked up, startled.

24

'What rhymes with "supercilious"?' asked Veronica sweetly.

Mr Goodman considered, stroking chin reflectively.

'Bilious?' he suggested.

Miss Elvery gave a despairing cluck.

'That won't do at all. It's such an ugly word.'

'And such an ugly feeling,' shuddered Mr Goodman. Then: 'What are you writing?' he asked.

She confessed to her task.

'Good heavens!' he said despairingly. 'Fancy writing poetry at this time in the morning! It's almost like drinking before lunch. Who is it about?'

She favoured him with an arch smile. 'You'll think I'm an awful cat if I tell you.' And, as he reached out to take her manuscript: 'Oh, I really couldn't—it's about somebody you know.'

Mr Goodman frowned.

'"Supercilious" was the word you used. Who on earth is supercilious?'

Veronica sniffed—she always sniffed when she was being unpleasant.

'Don't you think she is—a little bit? After all, her father only keeps a boarding house.'

'Oh, you mean Miss Redmayne?' asked Goodman quietly. He put down his paper. 'A very nice girl. A boarding house, eh? Well, I was the first boarder her father ever had, and I've never regarded this place as a boarding house.'

There was a silence, which the girl broke. 'Mr Goodman, do you mind if I say something?'

'Well, I haven't objected so far, have I?' he smiled.

'I suppose I'm naturally romantic,' she said. 'I see mystery in almost everything. Even you are mysterious.' And, when he looked alarmed: 'Oh, I don't mean sinister!'

He was glad she did not.

'But Colonel Redmayne is sinister,' she said emphatically.

He considered this.

'He never struck me that way,' he said slowly.

'But he is,' she persisted. 'Why did he buy this place miles from everywhere and turn it into a boarding house?'

'To make money, I suppose.'

She smiled triumphantly and shook her head.

'But he doesn't. Mamma says that he must lose an awful lot of money. Monkshall is very beautiful, but it has got an awful reputation. You know that it is haunted, don't you?'

He laughed good-naturedly at this. Mr Goodman was an old boarder and had heard this story before.

'*I've* heard things and seen things. Mamma says that there must have been a terrible crime committed here. It is!' She was more emphatic.

Mr Goodman thought that her mother let her mind dwell too much on murders and crimes. For the stout and fussy Mrs Elvery wallowed in the latest tragedies which filled the columns of the Sunday newspapers.

'She *does* love a good murder,' agreed Veronica. 'We had to put off our trip to Switzerland last year because of the River Bicycle Mystery. Do you think Colonel Redmayne ever committed a murder?'

'What a perfectly awful thing to say!' said her shocked audience.

'Why is he so nervous?' asked Veronica intensely. 'What is he afraid of? He is always refusing boarders. He refused that nice young man who came yesterday.'

'Well, we've got a new boarder coming tomorrow,' said Goodman, finding his newspaper again.

'A parson!' said Veronica contemptuously. 'Everybody knows that parsons have no money.'

He could chuckle at this innocent revelation of Veronica's mind.

'The colonel could make this place pay, but he won't.' She grew confidential. 'And I'll tell you something more. Mamma knew Colonel Redmayne before he bought this place. He got into terrible trouble over some money—Mamma doesn't exactly know what it was. But he had no money at all. How did he buy this house?'

Mr Goodman beamed.

'Now that I happen to know all about! He came into a legacy.'

Veronica was disappointed and made no effort to hide the fact. What comment she might have offered was silenced by the arrival of her mother.

Not that Mrs Elvery ever 'arrived'. She bustled or exploded into a room, according to the measure of her exuberance. She came straight across to the settee where Mr Goodman was unfolding his paper again.

'Did you hear anything last night?' she asked dramatically.

He nodded.

'Somebody in the next room to me was snoring like the devil,' he began.

'I occupy the next room to you, Mr Goodman,' said the lady icily. 'Did you hear a shriek?'

'Shriek?' He was startled.

'And I heard the organ again last night!'

Goodman sighed.

'Fortunately I am a little deaf. I never hear any organs or shrieks. The only thing I can hear distinctly is the dinner gong.'

'There is a mystery here.' Mrs Elvery was even more intense than her daughter. 'I saw that the day I came. Originally I intended staying a week; now I remain here until the mystery is solved.'

He smiled good-humouredly.

'You're a permanent fixture, Mrs Elvery.'

'It rather reminds me,' Mrs Elvery recited rapidly, but with evident relish, 'of Pangleton Abbey, where John Roehampton cut the throats of his three nieces, aged respectively, nineteen, twenty-two and twenty-four, afterwards burying them in cement, for which crime he was executed at Exeter Gaol. He had to be supported to the scaffold, and left a full confession admitting his guilt!'

Mr Goodman rose hastily to fly from the gruesome recital. Happily, rescue came in the shape of the tall, soldierly person of Colonel Redmayne. He was a man of fifty-five, rather nervous and absent of manner and address. His attire was careless and somewhat slovenly. Goodman had seen this carelessness of appearance grow from day to day.

The colonel looked from one to the other.

'Good-morning. Is everything all right?'

'Comparatively, I think,' said Goodman with a smile. He hoped that Mrs Elvery would find another topic of conversation, but she was not to be denied.

'Colonel, did you hear anything in the night?'

'Hear anything?' he frowned. 'What was there to hear?'

She ticked off the events of the night on her podgy fingers.

'First of all the organ, and then a most awful, blood-curdling shriek. It came from the grounds—from the direction of the Monk's Tomb.'

She waited, but he shook his head.

'No, I heard nothing. I was asleep,' he said in a low voice.

Veronica, an interested listener, broke in.

'Oh, what a fib! I saw your light burning long after Mamma and I heard the noise. I can see your room by looking out of my window.'

He scowled at her.

'Can you? I went to sleep with the light on. Has anyone seen Mary?'

Goodman pointed across the park.

'I saw her half an hour ago,' he said.

Colonel Redmayne stood hesitating, then, without a word, strode from the room, and they watched him crossing the park with long strides.

'There's a mystery here!' Mrs Elvery drew a long breath. 'He's mad. Mr Goodman, do you know that awfully nice-looking man who came yesterday morning? He wanted a room, and when I asked the colonel why he didn't let him stay he turned on me like a fiend! Said he was not the kind of man he wanted to have in the house; said he dared—"dared" was the word he used—to try to scrape acquaintance with his daughter, and that he didn't want any good-for-nothing drunkards under the same roof.'

'In fact,' said Mr Goodman, 'he was annoyed! You mustn't take the colonel too seriously—he's a little upset this morning.'

He took up the letters that had come to him by the morning post and began to open them.

'The airs he gives himself!' she went on. 'And his daughter is no better. I must say it, Mr Goodman. It may sound awfully uncharitable, but she's got just as much—' She hesitated.

'Swank?' suggested Veronica, and her mother was shocked. 'It's a common expression,' said Veronica.

'But we aren't common people,' protested Mrs Elvery. 'You may say that she gives herself airs. She certainly does. And her manners are deplorable. I was telling her the other day about the Grange Road murder. You remember, the man who poisoned his mother-in-law to get the insurance money—a most interesting case—when she simply turned her back on me and said she wasn't interested in horrors.'

Cotton, the butler, came in at that moment with the mail. He was a gloomy man who seldom spoke. He was leaving the room when Mrs Elvery called him back.

'Did you hear any noise last night, Cotton?'

He turned sourly.

'No, ma'am. I don't get a long time to sleep—you couldn't wake me with a gun.'

'Didn't you hear the organ?' she insisted.

'I never hear anything.'

'I think the man's a fool,' said the exasperated lady.

'I think so too, ma'am,' agreed Cotton, and went out.

CHAPTER VI

MARY went to the village that morning to buy a week's supply of stamps. She barely noticed the young man in plus-fours who sat on a bench outside the Red Lion, though she was conscious of his presence; conscious, too, of the stories she had heard about him.

She had ceased being sorry for him. He was the type of man, she decided, who had gone over the margin of redemption; and, besides, she was annoyed with him because he had irritated her father, for Mr Ferdie Fane had had the temerity to apply for lodging at Monkshall.

Until that morning she had never spoken to him, nor had she any idea that such a misfortune would overtake her, until she came back through the village and turned into the little lane whence ran a footpath across Monkshall Park.

He was sitting on a stile, his long hands tightly clasped between his knees, a drooping cigarette in his mouth, gazing mournfully through his horn-rimmed spectacles into vacancy. She stood for a moment, thinking he had not seen her, and hesitating whether she should take a more round-about route in order to avoid him. At that moment he got down lazily, took off his cap with a flourish.

'Pass, friend; all's well,' he said.

He had rather a delightful smile, she noticed, but at the moment she was far from being delighted.

'If I accompany you to your ancestral home, does your revered father take a gun or loose a dog?'

She faced him squarely.

'You're Mr Fane, aren't you?'

He bowed; the gesture was a little extravagant, and she went hot at his impertinence.

'I think in the circumstances, Mr Fane, it is hardly the act of a gentleman to attempt to get into conversation with me.'

'It may not be the act of a gentleman, but it is the act of an intelligent human being who loves all that is lovely,' he smiled. 'Have you ever noticed how few really pleasant-looking people there are in the world? I once stood at the corner of a street—'

'At present you're standing in my way,' she interrupted him.

She was not feeling at her best that morning; her nerves were tense and on edge. She had spent a night of terror, listening to strange whispers, to sounds that made her go cold, to that booming note of a distant organ which made her head tingle. Otherwise, she might have handled the situation more commandingly. And she had seen something, too—something she had never seen before; a wild, mouthing shape that had darted across the lawn under her window and had vanished.

He was looking at her keenly, this man who swayed slightly on his feet.

'Does your father love you?' he asked, in a gentle, caressing tone.

She was too startled to answer.

'If he does he can refuse you nothing, my dear Miss Redmayne. If you said to him, "Here is a young man who requires board and lodging"—'

'Will you let me pass, please?' She was trembling with anger.

Again he stepped aside with elaborate courtesy, and without a word she stepped over the stile, feeling singularly undignified. She was half-way across the park before she looked back. To her indignation, he was following, at a respectful distance, it was true, but undoubtedly following.

Neither saw the other unwanted visitor. He had arrived soon after Mrs Elvery and Goodman had gone out with their golf clubs to practise putting on the smooth lawn to the south of the house. He was a rough looking man, with a leather apron, and carried under his arm a number of broken umbrellas. He did not go to the kitchen, but after making a stealthy reconnaissance, had passed round to the lawn and was standing in the open doorway, watching Cotton as he gathered up the debris which the poetess had left behind.

Cotton was suddenly aware of the newcomer and jerked his head round.

'Hallo, what do you want?' he asked roughly.

'Got any umbrellas or chairs to mend—any old kettles or pans?' asked the man mechanically.

Cotton pointed in his lordliest manner. 'Outside! Who let you in?'

'The lodge-keeper said you wanted something mended,' growled the tinker.

'Couldn't you come to the service door? Hop it.'

But the man did not move.

'Who lives here?' he asked.

'Colonel Redmayne, if you want to know—and the kitchen door is round the corner. Don't argue!'

The tinker looked over the room with approval.

'Pretty snug place this, eh?'

Mr Cotton's sallow face grew red.

'Can't you understand plain English? The kitchen door's round the corner. If you don't want to go there, push off!'

Instead, the man came farther into the room.

'How long has he been living here—this feller you call Redmayne?'

'Ten years,' said the exasperated butler. 'Is that all you want to know? You don't know how near to trouble you are.'

'Ten years, eh?' The man nodded. 'I want to see this colonel.'

'I'll give you an introduction to him,' said Cotton sarcastically. 'He loves tinkers!'

It was then that Mary came in breathlessly.

'Will you send that young man away?' She pointed to the oncoming Ferdie; for the moment she did not see the tinker.

'Young man, miss?' Cotton went to the window, 'Why, it's the gent who came yesterday—a very nice young gentleman he is, too.'

'I don't care who he is or what he is,' she said angrily. 'He is to be sent away.'

'Can I be of any help, miss?'

She was startled to see the tinker, and looked from him to the butler.

'No, you can't,' snapped Cotton.

'Who are you?' asked Mary.

'Just a tinker, miss.' He was eyeing her thoughtfully, and something in his gaze frightened her.

'He—he came in here, and I told him to go to the kitchen,' explained Cotton in a flurry. 'If you hadn't come he'd have been chucked out!'

'I don't care who he is—he must help you to get rid of this wretched young man,' said Mary desperately. 'He—'

She became suddenly dumb. Mr Ferdinand Fane was surveying her from the open window.

'How d'ye do, everybody? *Comment ça va?*'

'How dare you follow me!' She stamped her foot in her fury, but he was unperturbed.

'You told me to keep out of your sight, so I walked behind. It's all perfectly clear.'

It would have been dignified to have left the room in silence—he had the curious faculty of compelling her to be undignified.

'Don't you understand that your presence is objectionable to me and to my father? We don't want you here. We don't wish to know you.'

'You *don't* know me.' He was hurt. 'I'll bet you don't even know that my Christian name is Ferdie.'

'You've tried to force your acquaintance on me, and I've told you plainly that I have no desire to know you—'

'I wan' to stay here,' he interrupted. 'Why shouldn't I?'

'You don't need a room here—you have a room at the Red Lion, and it seems a very appropriate lodging.'

It was then that the watchful tinker took a hand.

'Look here, governor, this lady doesn't want you here—get out.'

But he was ignored.

'I'm not going back to the Red Lion,' said Mr Fane gravely. 'I don't like the beer—I can see through it—'

A hand dropped on his shoulder.

'Are you going quietly?'

Mr Fane looked round into the tinker's face.

'Don't do that, old boy—that's rude. Never be rude, old boy. The presence of a lady—'

'Come on,' began the tinker.

And then a hand like a steel vice gripped his wrist; he was swung from his feet and fell to the floor with a crash.

'Ju-juishoo,' said Mr Fane very gently.

He heard an angry exclamation and turned to face Colonel Redmayne.

'What is the meaning of this?'

He heard his daughter's incoherent explanation.

'Take that man to the kitchen,' he said. When they were gone: 'Now, sir, what do you want?'

Her father's tone was milder than Mary had expected.

'Food an' comfort for man an' beast,' said the younger man coolly, and with an effort the colonel restrained his temper.

'You can't stay here—I told you that yesterday. I've no room for you, and I don't want you.'

He nodded to the door, and Mary left hurriedly. Now his voice changed.

'Do you think I'd let you contaminate this house? A drunken beast without a sense of chivalry or decency—with nothing to do with his money but spend it in drink?'

'I thought you might,' said Ferdie.

A touch of the bell brought Cotton.

'Show this—gentleman out of the house—and well off the estate,' he said.

It looked as though his visitor would prove truculent, but to his relief Mr Fane obeyed, waving aside the butler's escort.

He had left the house when a man stepped from the cover of a clump of bushes and barred his way. It was the tinker. For a few seconds they looked at one another in silence.

'There's only one man who could ever put that grip on me, and I want to have a look at you,' said the tinker.

He peered into the immobile face of Ferdie Fane, and then stepped back.

'God! It is you! I haven't seen you for ten years, and I wouldn't have known you but for that grip!' he breathed.

'I wear very well.' There was no slur in the voice of Fane now. Every sentence rang like steel. 'You've seen a great deal more than you ought to have seen, Mr Connor!'

'I'm not afraid of you!' growled the man. 'Don't try to scare me. The old trick, eh? Made up like a boozy mug!'

'Connor, I'm going to give you a chance for your life.' Fane spoke slowly and deliberately. 'Get away from this place as quickly as you can. If you're here tonight, you're a dead man!' Neither saw the girl who, from a window above, had watched—and heard.

CHAPTER VII

MRS ELVERY described herself as an observant woman. Less charitable people complained bitterly of her spying. Cotton disliked her most intensely for that reason, and had a special grievance by reason of the fact that she had surprised him that afternoon when he was deeply engaged in conversation with a certain tinker who had called that morning, and who now held him fascinated by stories of immense wealth that might be stored within the cellars and vaults of Monkshall.

She came with her news to Colonel Redmayne, and found that gentleman a little dazed and certainly apathetic. He had got into the habit of retiring to his small study and locking the door. There was a cupboard there, just big enough for a bottle and two glasses, handy enough to hide them away when somebody knocked.

He was not favourably disposed towards Mrs Elvery, and this may have been the reason why he gave such scant attention to her story.

'He's like a bear, my dear,' said that good lady to her daughter.

She pulled aside the blind nervously and peered out into the dark grounds.

'I am sure we're going to have a visitation tonight,' she said. 'I told Mr Goodman so. He said "Stuff and nonsense!"'

'I wish to heaven you wouldn't do that, mother,' snapped the girl. 'You give me the jumps.'

Mrs Elvery looked in the glass and patted her hair.

'I've seen it twice,' she said, with a certain uneasy complacency.

Veronica shivered.

For a little while Mrs Elvery said nothing, then, turning dramatically, she lifted her fat forefinger.

'Cotton!' she said mysteriously. 'If that butler's a butler, I've never seen a butler.'

Veronica stared at her aghast.

'Good lord, Ma, what do you mean?'

'He's been snooping around all day. I caught him coming up those stairs from the cellars, and when he saw me he was so taken aback he didn't know whether he was on his head or his heels.'

'How do you know he didn't know?' asked the practical Veronica, and Mrs Elvery's testy reply was perhaps justifiable.

Veronica looked at her mother thoughtfully.

'What *did* you see, mother—when you squealed the other night?'

'I wish to goodness you wouldn't say "squeal",' snapped Mrs Elvery. 'It's not a word you should use to your mother. I screamed—so would you have. There it was, running about the lawn, waving its hands—ugh!'

'What was it?' asked Veronica faintly.

Mrs Elvery turned round in her chair.

'A monk,' she said; 'all black; his face hidden behind a cowl or something. Hark at that!'

It was a night of wind and rain, and the rattle of the lattice had made Mrs Elvery jump.

'Let's go downstairs for heaven's sake,' she said.

The cheerful Mr Goodman was alone when they reached the lounge, and he gave a little groan at the sight of her and hoped that she had not heard him.

'Mr Goodman'—he was not prepared for Veronica's attack— 'did mother tell you what she saw?'

Goodman looked over his glasses with a pained expression.

'If you're going to talk about ghosts—'

'Monks!' said Veronica, in a hollow voice.

'One monk,' corrected Mrs Elvery. 'I never said I saw more than one.'

Goodman's eyebrows rose.

'A monk?' He began to laugh softly, and, rising from the settee which formed his invariable resting place, he walked across the room and tapped at the panelled wall. 'If it was a monk, this is the way he should come.'

Mrs Elvery stared at him open-mouthed.

'Which way?' she asked.

'This is the monk's door,' explained Mr Goodman with some relish. 'It is part of the original panelling.'

Mrs Elvery fixed her glasses and looked. She saw now that what she had thought was part of the panelling was indeed a door. The oak was warped and in places worm-eaten.

'This is the way the old monks came in,' said Mr Goodman. 'The legend is that it communicated with an underground chapel which was used in the days of the Reformation. This lounge was the lobby that opened on to the refectory. Of course, it's all been altered—probably the old passage to the monks' chapel has been bricked up. The monks used to pass through that chapel every day, two by two—part of their ritual, I suppose, to remind them that life was a very short business.'

Veronica drew a deep breath.

'On the whole I prefer to talk about mother's murders,' she said.

'A chapel,' repeated Mrs Elvery intensely. 'That would explain the organ, wouldn't it?'

Goodman shook his head.

'Nothing explains the organ,' he said. 'Rich foods, poor digestion.'

And then, to change the subject:

'You told me that that young man, Fane, was coming here.'

'He isn't,' said Mrs Elvery emphatically. 'He's too inter-esting. They don't want anybody here but old fogies,' and, as he smiled, she added hastily: 'I don't mean you, Mr Goodman.'

She heard the door open and looked round. It was Mary Redmayne.

'We were talking about Mr Fane,' she said.

'Were you?' said Mary, a little coldly. 'It must have been a very dismal conversation.'

All kind of conversation languished after that. The evening seemed an interminable time before the three guests of the house said good-night and went to bed. Her father had not put in an appearance all the evening. He had been sitting behind the locked door of his study. She waited till the last guest had gone and then went and knocked at the door. She heard the cupboard close before the door unlocked.

'Good-night, my dear,' he said thickly.

'I want to talk to you, father.'

He threw out his arms with a weary gesture.

'I wish you wouldn't, I'm all nerves tonight.'

She closed the door behind her and came to where he was sitting, resting her hand upon his shoulder.

'Daddy, can't we get away from this place? Can't you sell it?'

He did not look up, but mumbled something about it being dull for her.

'It isn't more dull than it was at School,' she said; 'but'—she shivered—'it's awful! There's something vile about this place.'

He did not meet her eyes.

'I don't understand—'

'Father, you know that there's something horrible. No, no, it isn't my nerves. I heard it last night—first the organ and then that scream!' She covered her face with her hands. 'I can't bear it! I saw him running across the lawn—a terrifying thing in black. Mrs Elvery heard it too—what's that?'

He saw her start and her face go white. She was listening.

'Can you hear?' she whispered.

'It's the wind,' he said hoarsely; 'nothing but the wind.'

'Listen!'

Even he must have heard the faint, low tones of an organ as they rose and fell.

'Can your hear?'

'I hear nothing,' he said stolidly.

She bent towards the floor and listened.

'Do you hear?' she asked again.

'The sound of feet shuffling on stones, and—my God, what's that?'

It was the sound of knocking, heavy and persistent.

'Somebody is at the door,' she whispered, white to the lips.

Redmayne opened a drawer and took out something which he slipped into the pocket of his dressing-gown.

'Go up to your room,' he said.

He passed through the darkened lounge, stopped to switch on a light, and, as he did so, Cotton appeared from the servants' quarters. He was fully dressed.

'What is that?' asked Redmayne.

'Someone at the door, I think. Shall I open it?'

For a second the colonel hesitated.

'Yes,' he said at last.

Cotton took off the chain, and, turning the key, jerked the door open. A lank figure stood on the doorstep; a figure that swayed uneasily.

'Sorry to disturb you.' Ferdie Fane, his coat drenched and soaking, lurched into the room. He stared from one to the other. 'I'm the second visitor you've had tonight.'

'What do you want?' asked Redmayne.

In a queer, indefinable way the sight of this contemptible man gave him a certain amount of relief.

'They've turned me out of the Red Lion.' Ferdie's glassy eyes were fixed on him. 'I want to stay here.'

'Let him stay, Daddy.'

Redmayne turned; it was the girl.

'Please let him stay. He can sleep in number seven.'

A slow smile dawned on Mr Fane's good-looking face.

'Thanks for invitation,' he said, 'which is accepted.'

She looked at him in wonder. The rain had soaked his coat, and, as he stood, the drops were dripping from it, forming pools on the floor. He must have been out in the storm for hours—where had he been? And he was strangely untalkative; allowed himself to be led away by Cotton to room No. 7, which was in the farther wing. Mary's own pretty little bedroom was above the lounge. After taking leave of her father, she locked and bolted the door of her room, slowly undressed and went to bed. Her mind was too much alive to make sleep possible, and she turned from side to side restlessly.

She was dozing off when she heard a sound and sat up in bed. The wind was shrieking round the corners of the house, the patter of the rain came fitfully against her window, but that had not wakened her up. It was the sound of low voices in the room below. She thought she heard Cotton—or was it her father? They both had the same deep tone.

Then she heard a sound which made her blood freeze— a maniacal burst of laughter from the room below. For a second she sat paralysed, and then, springing out of bed, she seized her dressing-gown and went pattering down the stairs, and she saw over the banisters a figure moving in the hall below.

'Who is that?'

'It's all right, my dear.'

It was her father. His room adjoined his study on the ground floor.

'Did you hear anything, Daddy?'

'Nothing—nothing,' he said harshly, 'Go to bed.'

But Mary Redmayne was not deficient in courage.

'I will not go to bed,' she said, and came down the stairs. 'There was somebody in the lounge—I heard them,' Her hand was on the lounge door when he gripped her arm.

'For God's sake, Mary, don't go in!' She shook him off impatiently, and threw open the door.

No light burned; she reached out for the switch and turned it. For a second she saw nothing, and then—

Sprawling in the middle of the room lay the body of a man, a terrifying grin on his dead face.

It was the tinker, the man who had quarrelled with Ferdie Fane that morning—the man whom Fane had threatened!

CHAPTER VIII

SUPERINTENDENT HALLICK came down by car with his photographer and assistants, saw the body with the local chief of police, and instantly recognised the dead man.

Connor! Connor, the convict, who said he would follow O'Shea to the end of the world—dead, with his neck broken, in that neat way which was O'Shea's speciality.

One by one Hallick interviewed the guests and the servants. Cotton was voluble; he remembered the man, but had no idea how he came into the room. The doors were locked and barred, none of the windows had been forced. Goodman apparently was a heavy sleeper and lived in the distant wing. Mrs Elvery was full of theories and clues, but singularly deficient in information.

'Fane—who is Fane?' asked Hallick.

Cotton explained Mr Fane's peculiar position and the hour of his arrival.

'I'll see him later. You have another guest on the books?' He turned the pages of the visitors' ledger.

'He doesn't come till today. He's a parson, sir,' said Cotton.

Hallick scrutinised the ill-favoured face.

'Have I seen you before?'

'Not me, sir.' Cotton was pardonably agitated.

'Humph!' said Hallick. 'That will do. I'll see Miss Redmayne.'

Goodman was in the room and now came forward.

'I hope you are not going to bother Miss Redmayne, superintendent. She is an extremely nice girl. I may say I am—fond of her. If I were a younger man—' He smiled. 'You see, even tea merchants have their romances.'

'And detectives,' said Hallick dryly. He looked at Mr Goodman with a new interest. He had betrayed from this middle-aged man

43

a romance which none suspected. Goodman was in love with the girl and had probably concealed the fact from everybody in the house.

'I suppose you think I am a sentimental jackass—'

Hallick shook his head.

'Being in love isn't a crime, Mr Goodman,' he said quietly.

Goodman pursed his lips thoughtfully. 'I suppose it isn't— imbecility isn't a crime, anyway,' he said.

He was going in the direction whence Mary would come, when Hallick stopped him, and obediently the favoured guest shuffled out of another door.

Mary had been waiting for the summons, and her heart was cold within her as she followed the detective to Hallick's presence. She had not seen him before and was agreeably surprised. She had expected a hectoring, bullying police officer and found a very stout and genial man with a kindly face. He was talking to Cotton when she came in, and for a moment he took no notice of her.

'You're sure you've no idea how this man got in last night?'

'No, sir,' said Cotton.

'No window was forced, the door was locked and bolted, wasn't it?'

Cotton nodded.

'I never let him in,' he said.

Hallick's eyelids narrowed.

'Twice you've said that. When I arrived this morning you volunteered the same statement. You also said you passed Mr Fane's room on your way in, that the door was open and the room was empty.'

Cotton nodded.

'You also said that the man who rung up the police and gave the name of Cotton was not you.'

'That's true, sir.'

It was then that the detective became aware of the girl's presence and signalled Cotton to leave the room.

'Now, Miss Redmayne; you didn't see this man, I suppose?'

'Only for a moment.'

'Did you recognise him?'

She nodded.

Hallick looked down at the floor, considering.

'Where do you sleep?' he asked.

'In the room above this hall.'

She was aware that the second detective was writing down all that she said.

'You must have heard something—the sound of a struggle— a cry?' suggested Hallick, and, when she shook her head: 'Do you know what time the murder occurred?'

'My father said it was about one o'clock.'

'You were in bed? Where was your father—anywhere near this room?'

'No.' Her tone was emphatic.

'Why are you so sure?' he asked keenly.

'Because when I heard the door close—'

'Which door?' quickly.

He confused her for a moment.

'This door.' She pointed to the entrance of the lounge. 'Then I looked over the landing and saw my father in the passage.'

'Yes. He was coming from or going to this room. How was he dressed?'

'I didn't see him,' she answered desperately. 'There was no light in the passage. I'm not even certain that it was his door.'

Hallick smiled.

'Don't get rattled, Miss Redmayne. This man, Connor, was a well-known burglar; it is quite possible that your father might have tackled him and accidentally killed him. I mean, such a thing might occur.'

Mary shook her head.

'You don't think that happened? You don't think that he got frightened when he found the man was dead, and said he knew nothing about it?'

'No,' she said.

'You heard nothing last night of a terrifying or startling nature?'

She did not answer.

'Have you ever seen anything at Monkshall?'

'It was all imagination,' she said in a low voice; 'but once I thought I saw a figure on the lawn—a figure in the robes of a monk.'

'A ghost, in fact?' he smiled, and she nodded.

'You see, I'm rather nervous,' she went on. 'I imagine things. Sometimes when I've been in my room I've heard the sound of feet moving here—and the sound of an organ.'

'Does the noise seem distinct?'

'Yes. You see, the floor isn't very thick.'

'I see,' he said dryly. 'And yet you heard no struggle last night? Come, come, Miss Redmayne, try to remember.'

She was in a panic.

'I don't remember anything—I heard nothing.'

'Nothing at all?' He was gently insistent. 'I mean, the man must have fallen with a terrific thud. It would have wakened you if you had been asleep—and you weren't asleep. Come now, Miss Redmayne. I think you're making a mystery of nothing. You were terribly frightened by this monk you saw, or thought you saw, and your nerves were all jagged. You heard a sound and opened your door, and your father's voice said "It's all right", or something like that. Isn't that what occurred?'

He was so kindly that she was deceived. 'Yes.'

'He was in his dressing-gown, I suppose—ready for bed?'

'Yes,' she said again.

He nodded.

'Just now you told me you didn't see him—that there was no light in the passage!'

She sprang up and confronted him.

'You're trying to catch me out. I won't answer you. I heard nothing, I saw nothing. My father was never in this room—it wasn't his voice—'

'My voice, old son!'

Hallick turned quickly. A smiling man was standing in the doorway.

'How d'ye do? My name's Fane—Ferdie Fane. How's the late departed?'

'Fane, eh?' Hallick was interested in this lank man.

'My voice, old son,' said Fane again. 'Indeed!' Then the detective did an unaccountable thing. He broke off the cross-examination, and, beckoning his assistant, the two men went out of the room together.

Mary stared at the new boarder wonderingly.

'It was not your voice,' she said. 'Why did you say it was? Can't you see that they are suspecting everybody? Are you mad? They will think you and I are in collusion.'

He beamed at her.

'C'lusion's a good word. I can say that quite distinctly, but it's a good word.'

She went to the door and looked out. Hallick and his assistant were in earnest consultation on the lawn, and her heart sank.

Fane was helping himself to a whisky when she returned to him.

'They'll come back soon, and then what questions will they ask me? Oh, I wish you were somebody I could talk to, somebody I could ask to help! It's so horrible to see a man like you—a drunken weakling.'

'Don't call me names,' he said severely. 'You ought to be ashamed of yourself. Tell me anything you like.'

If only she could!

It was Cotton who interrupted her confidence. He came in that sly, furtive way of his.

'The new boarder's arrived, miss—the parson gentleman,' he said, and stood aside to allow the newcomer to enter the lounge.

It was a slim and aged clergyman, white-haired, bespectacled. His tone was gentle, a little unctuous perhaps; his manner that of a man who lavished friendliness.

'Have I the pleasure of speaking to dear Miss Redmayne? I am the Reverend Ernest Partridge. I've had to walk up. I thought I was to be met at the station.'

He gave her a limp hand to shake.

The last thing in the world she craved at that moment was the distraction of a new boarder. 'I'm very sorry, Mr Partridge—we are all rather upset this morning. Cotton, take the bag to number three.'

Mr Partridge was mildly shocked.

'Upset? I hope that no untoward incident has marred the perfect beauty of this wonderful spot?'

'My father will tell you all about it. This is Mr Fane.'

She had to force herself to this act of common politeness.

At this moment Hallick came in hurriedly.

'Have you any actors in the grounds, Miss Redmayne?' he asked quickly.

'Actors?' She stared at him.

'Anybody dressed up.' He was impatient. 'Film actors—they come to these old places. My man tells me he's just seen a man in a black habit come out of the monk's tomb—he had a rifle in his hand. By God, there he is!'

He pointed through the lawn window, and at that moment Mary felt a pair of strong arms clasped about her, and she was swung round. It was Fane who held her, and she struggled, speechless with indignation. And then—

'*Ping!*'

The staccato crack of a rifle, and a bullet zipped past her and smashed the mirror above the fireplace. So close it came that she thought at first it had struck her, and in that fractional space of time realised that only Ferdinand Fane's embrace had saved her life.

CHAPTER IX

HALLICK, after an extensive search of the grounds which produced no other clue than an expended cartridge case, went up to town, leaving Sergeant Dobie in charge.

Mary never distinctly remembered how that dreadful day dragged to its end. The presence of the Scotland Yard man in the house gave her a little confidence, though it seemed to irritate her father. Happily, the detective kept himself unobtrusively in the background.

The two people who seemed unaffected by the drama of the morning were Mr Fane and the new clerical boarder. He was a loquacious man, primed with all kinds of uninteresting anecdotes; but Mrs Elvery found him a fascinating relief.

Ferdie Fane puzzled Mary. There was so much about him that she liked, and, but for this horrid tippling practice of his she might have liked him more—how much more she did not dare admit to herself. He alone remained completely unperturbed by that shot which had nearly ended her life and his.

In the afternoon she had a little talk with him and found him singularly coherent.

'Shooting at me? Good Lord, no!' He scoffed. 'It must have been a Nonconformist—we High Church parsons have all sorts of enemies.'

'Have you?' she asked quietly, and there was an odd look in his eyes when he answered:

'Maybe. There are quite a number of people who want to get even with me for my past misdeeds.'

'Mrs Elvery said they were going to send Bradley down.'

'Bradley!' he said contemptuously. 'That back number at Scotland Yard!' And then, as though he could read her thoughts, he asked quickly: 'Did that interesting old lady say anything else?'

49

They were walking through the long avenue of elms that stretched down to the main gates of the park. Two days ago she would have fled from him, but now she found a strange comfort in his society. She could not understand herself; found it equally difficult to recover a sense of her old aversion.

'Mrs Elvery's a criminologist.' She smiled whimsically, though she never felt less like smiling in her life. 'She keeps press cuttings of all the horrors of the past years, and she says she's sure that that poor man Connor was connected with a big gold robbery during the war. She said there was a man named O'Shea in it—'

'O'Shea?' said Fane quickly, and she saw his face change. 'What the devil is she talking about O'Shea for? She had better be careful—I beg your pardon.' He was all smiles again.

'Have you heard of him?'

'The merest rumour,' he said almost gaily. 'Tell me what Mrs Elvery said.'

'She said that a lot of gold disappeared and was buried some-where, and she's got a theory that it was buried in Monkshall or in the grounds; that Connor was looking for it, and that he got Cotton, the butler, to let him in—that's how he came to be in the house. I heard her telling Mr Partridge the story. She doesn't like me well enough to tell me.' They paced in silence for a while.

'Do you like him—Partridge, I mean?' asked Ferdie.

She thought he was very nice.

'That means he bores you.' He chuckled softly to himself. And then: 'Why don't you go up to town?'

She stopped dead and stared at him.

'Leave Monkshall? Why?'

He looked at her steadily.

'I don't think Monkshall is very healthy; in fact, it's a little dangerous.'

'To me?' she said incredulously, and he nodded.

'To you, in spite of the fact that there are people living at Monkshall who adore you, who would probably give their own lives to save you from hurt.'

'You mean my father?' She tried to pass off what might easily develop into an embarrassing conversation.

'I mean two people—for example, Mr Goodman.'

At first she was inclined to be angry and then she laughed. 'How absurd! Mr Goodman is old enough to be my father.'

'And young enough to love you,' said Fane quietly. 'That middle-aged gentleman is genuinely fond of you, Miss Redmayne. There is one who is not so middle-aged who is equally fond of you—'

'In sober moments?' she challenged.

And then Mary thought it expedient to remember an engagement she had in the house. He did not attempt to stop her. They walked back towards Monkshall a little more quickly.

Inspector Hallick went back to London a very puzzled man, though he was not as hopelessly baffled as his immediate subordinates thought. He was satisfied in his mind that behind the mystery of Monkshall was the more definite mystery of O'Shea.

When he reached his office he rang for his clerk, and when the officer appeared:

'Get me the record of the O'Shea gold robbery, will you?' he said. 'And data of any kind we have about O'Shea.'

It was not the first time he had made the last request and the response had been more or less valueless, but the Record Department of Scotland Yard had a trick of securing new evidence from day to day from unexpected sources. The sordid life histories that were compiled in that business-like room touched life at many points; the political branch that dealt with foreign anarchists had once exposed the biggest plot of modern times through a chance remark made by an old woman arrested for begging.

When the clerk had gone Hallick opened his notebook and jotted down the meagre facts he had compiled. Undoubtedly the shot had been fired from the ruins which, he discovered, were those of an old chapel in the grounds, now covered with ivy and almost hidden by sturdy chestnut trees. How the assassin had made his escape was a mystery. He did not preclude the possibility that some of these wizened slabs of stone hidden under thickets of elderberry and hawthorn trees might conceal the entrance to an underground passage.

He offered that solution to one of the inspectors who strolled in to gossip. It was the famous Inspector Elk, saturnine and sceptical.

'Underground passages!' scoffed Elk. 'Why, that's the last resource, or resort—I am not certain which—of the novel writer. Underground passages and secret panels! I never pick up a book which isn't full of 'em!'

'I don't rule out either possibility,' said Hallick quietly. 'Monkshall was one of the oldest inhabited buildings in England. I looked it up in the library. It flourished even in the days of Elizabeth—'

Elk groaned.

'That woman! There's nothing we didn't have in her days!'

Inspector Elk had a genuine grievance against Queen Elizabeth; for years he had sought to pass an education test which would have secured him promotion, but always it was the reign of the virgin queen and the many unrememberable incidents which, from his point of view, disfigured that reign, that had brought about his undoing.

'She would have secret panels *and* underground passages!'

And then a thought struck Hallick.

'Sit down, Elk,' he said. 'I want to ask you something.'

'If it's history save yourself the trouble. I know no more about that woman except that she was not in any way a virgin. Whoever started this silly idea about the Virgin Queen?'

'Have you ever met O'Shea?' asked Hallick.

Elk stared at him.

'O'Shea—the bank smasher? No, I never met him. He is in America, isn't he?'

'I think he is very much in England,' said Hallick, and the other man shook his head.

'I doubt it.' Then after a moment's thought: 'There's no reason why he should be in England. I am only going on the fact that he has been very quiet these years, but then a man who made the money he did can afford to sit quiet. As a rule, a crook who gets money takes it to the nearest spieling club and does it in, and as he is a natural lunatic—'

'How do you know that?' asked Hallick sharply.

Before he answered, Elk took a ragged cigar from his pocket and lit it.

'O'Shea is a madman,' he said deliberately. 'It is one of the facts that is not disputed.'

'One of the facts that I knew nothing about till I interviewed old Connor in prison, and I don't remember that I put it on record,' said Hallick. 'How did you know?'

Elk had an explanation which was new to his superior.

'I went into the case years ago. We could never get O'Shea or any particulars about him except a scrap of his writing. I am talking about the days before the gold robbery and before you came into the case. I was just a plain detective officer at the time and if I couldn't get his picture and his fingerprints I got on to his family. His father died in a lunatic asylum, his sister committed suicide, his grandfather was a homicide who died whilst he was awaiting his trial for murder. I've often wondered why one of these clever fellows didn't write a history of the family.'

This was indeed news to John Hallick, but it tallied with the information that Connor had given to him.

The clerk came back at this moment with a formidable dossier and one thin folder. The contents of the latter showed the inspector that nothing further had been added to the sketchy details he had read before concerning O'Shea. Elk watched him curiously.

'Refreshing your mind about the gold robbery? Doesn't it make your mouth water to think that all these golden sovereigns are hidden somewhere. Pity Bradley isn't on this job. He knows the case like I know the back of my hand, and if you think this murder has got anything to do with O'Shea, I'd cable him to come back if I were you.'

Hallick was turning the pages of the typewritten sheets slowly.

'As far as Connor is concerned, he only got what was coming to him. He squealed a lot at the time of his conviction about being double-crossed, but Connor double-crossed more crooks than any man on the records, and Soapy Marks. I happened to know both of them. They were quite prepared to squeak about O'Shea just before the gold robbery. Where is Soapy?'

Hallick shook his head and closed the folder.

'I don't know. I wish you would put the word round to the divisions that I'd like to see Soapy Marks,' he said. 'He usually hangs out in Hammersmith, and I should like to give him a word of warning.'

Elk grinned.

'You couldn't warn Soapy,' he said. 'He knows too much. Soapy is so clever that one of these days we'll find him at Oxford or Cambridge. Personally,' he ruminated reflectively, 'I prefer clever crooks. They don't take much catching; they catch themselves.'

'I am not worrying about his catching himself,' said Hallick. 'But I am a little anxious as to whether O'Shea will catch him first. That is by no means outside the bounds of possibility.'

And here he spoke prophetically.

He got through by 'phone to Monkshall, but Sergeant Dobie, who had been left in charge, had no information.

'Has that woman, Elvery, left?' asked Hallick.

'Not she!' came the reply. 'She will hang on to the last minute. That woman is a regular crime hound. And, Mr Hallick, that fellow Fane is tight again.'

'Is he ever sober?' asked Hallick.

He did not trouble about Fane's insobriety, but he was interested to learn that life in Monkshall, despite the tragedy and the startling event of the morning, was going on as though nothing had happened. Reporters had called in the course of the day and had tried to interview the colonel.

'But I shunted them off. The general theory here is that Connor had somebody with him, that they got hold of the money and quarrelled about it. The other fellow killed Connor and got away with the stuff. When I said "The general idea",' said Dobie carefully, 'I meant it is my idea. What do you think of that, sir?'

'Rotten,' said Hallick, and hung up the receiver.

CHAPTER X

ALL the machinery of Scotland Yard was at work. Inquiries had gone out in every direction and not even Mrs Elvery and her daughter had been spared. By midnight Hallick learned the private history, as far as it could be ascertained, of every inmate of Monkshall.

Mrs Elvery was a woman in fairly comfortable circumstances, and, since her husband's death had released her from a gloomy house in Devonshire, she had no permanent home. She was more than comfortably off, by certain standards she was a wealthy woman, one of that mysterious band of middle-aged women who move from one hotel to another, and live frugally in fashionable resorts in the season. You find them on the Lido in August, in Deauville in July, on the Riviera or in Egypt in the winter.

Mr Goodman held a sleeping partnership in an old-established and not too prosperous firm of tea importers. Probably, thought Hallick, the days of its prosperity expired before Goodman retired from business.

Cotton, the butler, had the least savoury record. He was a man who had been discharged from three jobs under suspicion of pilfering, but no conviction could be traced against him. (Hallick wrote in his notebook: 'Find some way of getting Cotton's fingerprints.') In every case Cotton had been employed at boarding houses and always small articles of jewellery had disappeared in circumstances which suggested that he was not entirely ignorant of the reason for such disappearance.

Colonel Redmayne's record occupied a sheet of foolscap. He had been an impecunious officer in the Auxiliary Medical Staff, had been court-martialled in the last week of the war for drunkenness and severely reprimanded. He had, by some

56

miracle, been appointed to a responsible position in a military charity. The disappearance of funds had led to an investigation, there had been some talk of prosecution, and Scotland Yard had actually been consulted, but had been advised against such a prosecution in the absence of direct proof that the colonel was guilty of anything but culpable negligence. The missing money had been refunded and the matter was dropped. He was next heard of when he bought Monkshall.

The information concerning Redmayne's military career was news to Hallick.

'A doctor, eh?'

Elk nodded. He had been charged with collecting the information.

'He joined up in the beginning of the war and got his rank towards the finish,' he said. 'Funny how these birds hang on to their military rank—"doctor" would be good enough for me.'

'Was he ever in the regular army?'

Elk shook his head.

'So far as I could find out, no. Owing to the trouble he got into at the end of the war he was not offered a permanent commission.'

Hallick spent the evening studying a large plan of Monkshall and its grounds, and even a larger one of the room in which Connor had been found. There was one thing certain: Connor had not 'broken and entered'. It was, in a sense, an inside job, he must have been admitted by—whom? Not by Redmayne, certainly not by his daughter. By a servant, and that servant was Cotton. The house was almost impossible to burgle from outside without inside assistance; there were alarms in all the windows and he had seen electric controls on the doors. Monkshall was almost prepared for a siege. Indeed, it seemed as though Colonel Redmayne expected sooner or later the visitation of a burglar.

Hallick went to bed a very tired man that night, fully expecting to be called by telephone, but nothing happened.

He 'phoned Monkshall before he left his house and Dobie reported 'All is well.' He had not been to bed that night, and nothing untoward had occurred. There was neither sound or sight of the ghostly visitor.

'Ghosts!' scoffed Hallick. 'Did you expect to see one?'

'Well,' said Dobie's half-apologetic voice, 'I am really beginning to believe there is something here that isn't quite natural.'

'There is nothing anywhere that is not natural, sergeant,' said Hallick sharply.

There was another case in which he was engaged, and he spent two unprofitable hours interviewing a particularly stupid servant girl concerning the mysterious disappearance of a large quantity of jewellery. It was nearly noon when he got back to his office and his clerk greeted him with a piece of unexpected information.

'Mr Goodman is waiting to see you, sir. I put him in the reception-room.'

'Goodman?' Hallick frowned. At the moment he could not recall the name. 'Oh, yes, from Monkshall? What does he want?'

'He said he wished to see you. He was quite willing to wait.'

'Bring him in,' said Hallick.

Mr Goodman came into the tidy office a rather timid and diffident man.

'I quite expected you to throw me out for I realise how busy you are, inspector,' he said, putting down his hat and umbrella very carefully; 'but as I had some business in town I thought I'd come along and see you.'

'I am very glad to see you, Mr Goodman.' Hallick placed a chair for him. 'Are you coming to enlarge on your theories?'

Goodman smiled.

'I think I told you before I had no theories. I am terribly worried about Miss Redmayne, though.' He hesitated. 'You cross-examined her. She was distressed about it.' He paused a little helplessly, but Hallick did not help him. 'I think I told you that I am—fond of Mary Redmayne. I would do anything to clear up this matter so that you would see, what I am sure is a fact, that her father had nothing whatever to do with this terrible affair.'

'I never said he had,' interrupted Hallick.

Mr Goodman nodded.

'That I realise. But I am not as foolish as, perhaps, I appear to be; I know that he is under suspicion. In fact, I imagine that everybody in the house, including myself, must of necessity be suspected.'

Again he waited and again Hallick was wilfully silent. He was wondering what was coming next.

'I am a fairly wealthy man,' Goodman went on at last. He gave the impression that it required a desperate effort on his part to put his proposition into words. 'And I would be quite willing to spend a very considerable sum, not necessarily to help the police, but to clear Redmayne from all suspicion. I don't understand the methods of Scotland Yard and I feel I needn't tell you this'—he smiled—'and probably I am exposing my ignorance with every word I utter. But what I came to see you about is this—is it possible for me to engage a Scotland Yard detective?'

Hallick shook his head.

'If you mean in the same way as you engage a private detective—no,' he said. Goodman's face fell.

'That's a pity. I had heard so much from Mrs Elvery—a very loquacious and trying lady, but with an extraordinary knowledge of—er—criminality, that there is a gentleman at Scotland Yard who would have been of the greatest assistance to me—Inspector Bradley.'

Hallick laughed.

'Inspector Bradley is at the moment abroad,' he said.

'Oh,' replied Mr Goodman, getting glum. 'That is a great pity. Mrs Elvery says—'

'I am afraid she says a great deal that is not very helpful,' said Hallick good-humouredly. 'No, Mr Goodman, it is impossible to oblige you and I am afraid you will have to leave the matter in our hands. I don't think you will be a loser by that. We have no other desire than to get the truth. We are just as anxious to clear any person who is wrongfully suspected as we are to convict any person who comes under suspicion and who justifies that suspicion.'

That should have finished the matter, but Mr Goodman sat on looking very embarrassed.

'It is a thousand pities,' he said at last. 'Mr Bradley is abroad? So I shan't be able even to satisfy my curiosity. You see, Mr Hallick, the lady in question was talking so much about this superman—I suppose he is clever?'

'Very,' said Hallick. 'One of the ablest men we have had at the Yard.'

'Ah.' Goodman nodded. 'That makes my disappointment a little more keen. I would have liked to have seen what he looked like. When one hears so much about a person—'

Hallick looked at him for a second, then turning his back upon the visitor he scanned the wall where were hanging three framed portrait groups. One of these he lifted down from the hook and laid on the table. It was a conventional group of about thirty men sitting or standing in three rows and beneath were the words 'H.Q. Staff.'

'I can satisfy your curiosity,' he said. 'The fourth man on the left from the commissioner who is seated in the centre is Inspector Bradley.'

Mr Goodman adjusted his glasses and looked. He saw a large, florid-looking man of fifty, heavy-featured, heavily built. The last person in the group he would have picked out.

'That's Bradley; he isn't much to look at, is he?' smiled Hallick.

'He is the livest wire in this department.' Goodman stared at the photograph rather nervously, and then he smiled.

'That's very good of you, Mr Hallick,' he said. 'He doesn't look like a detective, but then no detective ever does. That is the peculiar thing about them. They look rather—er—'

'A commonplace lot, eh?' said Hallick, his eyes twinkling. 'So they are.'

He hung up the portrait on the wall.

'Don't bother about Miss Redmayne,' he said, 'and for heaven's sake don't think that the employment of a detective, private or public, on her behalf will be of the slightest use to her or her father. Innocent people have nothing to fear. Guilty people have a great deal. You have known Colonel Redmayne for a long time, I think?'

'All my life.'

'You know about his past?'

The old tea merchant hesitated.

'Yes, I think I know,' he said quietly. 'There were one or two incidents which were a little discreditable, were there not? He told me himself. He drinks a great deal too much, which is unfortunate. I think he was drinking more heavily at the time these unfortunate incidents occurred.'

He picked up his hat and umbrella, took out his pipe with a mechanical gesture, looked at it, rubbed the bowl, and replaced it hastily.

'You can smoke, Mr Goodman, we shan't hang you for it,' chuckled Hallick.

He himself walked through the long corridor and down the stairs to the entrance hall with his visitor, and saw him off the premises. He hoped and believed that he had sent Goodman away feeling a little happier, and his hope was not without reason.

CHAPTER XI

It was four o'clock when Goodman reached the little station which is some four miles distant from Monkshall, and, declining the offer of the solitary fly, started to walk across to the village. He had gone a mile when he heard the whir of a motor behind him. He did not attempt to turn his head, and was surprised when he heard the car slacken speed and a voice hailing him. It was Ferdie Fane who sat at the wheel.

'Hop in, brother. Why waste your own shoe leather when somebody else's rubber tyres are available?'

The face was flushed and the eyes behind the horn-rimmed spectacles glistened. Mr Goodman feared the worst.

'No, no, thank you. I'd rather walk,' he said.

'Stuff! Get in,' scoffed Ferdie. 'I am a better driver when I am tight than when I am sober, but I am not tight.'

Very reluctantly the tea merchant climbed into the seat beside the driver.

'I'll go very slowly,' the new inmate of Monkshall went on. 'There's nothing to be afraid of.'

'You think I am afraid?' said Mr Goodman with a certain asperity.

'I'm certain,' said the other cheerfully. 'Where have you been this fine day?'

'I went up to London,' said Mr Goodman.

'An interesting place to go to,' said Fane; 'but a deuced uncomfortable place to live in.'

He was keeping his word and driving with remarkable care, Mr Goodman discovered to his relief.

He was puzzled as to where Ferdie had obtained the car and ventured upon an inquiry.

'I hired it from a brigand in the village,' said Ferdie. 'Do you drive a car?'

Mr Goodman shook his head.

'It is an easy road for a car, but a pretty poisonous one for a lorry, especially a lorry with a lot of weight in it. You know Lark Hill?'

Mr Goodman nodded.

'A lorry was stuck there. I guess it will be there still even though the road is as dry as a bone. What it must be like to run up that hill with a heavy load on a wet and slippery night heaven knows. I bet that hill has broken more hearts than any other in the county.'

He rumbled on aimlessly about nothing until they reached the foot of the redoubtable hill where the heavy lorry was still standing disconsolate by the side of the road.

'There she is,' said Ferdie with the satisfaction of one who is responsible. 'And it will take a bit of haulage to get her to the top, eh? Only a super-driver could have got her there. Only a man with a brain and imagination could have nursed her.'

Goodman smiled.

'I didn't know there were such things as super-brains amongst lorry drivers,' he said. 'But I suppose every trade, however humble, has its Napoleon.'

'You bet,' said Ferdie.

He brought the car up the long drive to Monkshall, paid the garage hand who was waiting to take it from him, and disappeared into the house.

Goodman looked round. In spite of his age his eyesight was remarkably good, and he noticed the slim figure walking on the far side of the ruins. Handing his umbrella to Cotton he walked across to Mary. She recognised and turned to meet him. Her father was in his study and she was going back for tea. He thought that she looked a little peaked and paler than usual.

'Nothing has happened today?' he asked quickly.

She shook her head.

'Nothing. Mr Goodman, I am dreading the night.'

He patted her gently on the shoulder. 'My dear, you ought to get away out of this. I will speak to the colonel.'

'Please don't,' she said quickly. 'Father does not want me to go. My nerves are a little on edge.'

'Has that young man been—?' he began.

'No, no. You mean Mr Fane? He has been quite nice. I have only seen him for a few minutes today. He is out driving a motor car. He asked me—'

She stopped.

'To go with him? That young man is certainly not troubled with nerves!'

'He was quite nice,' she said quickly; 'only I didn't feel like motoring. I thought it was he who had just come back, but I suppose it was you who came in the car.' He explained the circumstances of his meeting with Ferdie Fane. She smiled for the first time that day.

'He is—rather queer,' she said. 'Sometimes he is quite sensible and nice. Cotton hates him for some reason or other. He told me today that unless Mr Fane left he would.'

Mr Goodman smiled.

'You seem to have a very troublesome household,' he said; 'except myself—oh, I beg his pardon, the new guest. What is his name? Mr Partridge? I hope he is behaving himself.'

She smiled faintly.

'Yes, he's quite charming. I don't think I have seen him today,' she added inconsequently.

'You can see him now.' Mr Goodman nodded towards the lawn.

The slim, black figure of Mr Partridge was not easily discernible against the dark background of the foliage. He was strolling slowly up and down, reading a book as he walked; but evidently his eyes and attention were not entirely for the literature which he studied, for he closed his book and walked towards them.

'A delightful place, my dear Miss Redmayne,' he said. 'A most charming place! A little heaven upon earth, if I may use a sacred expression to describe terrestrial beauties.'

In the light of day, and without the softening effect of curtains, his face was not too pleasant, she thought. It was a hard face, angular, wasted. The dark eyes which surveyed her were not his least unpleasant feature. His voice was gentle enough—gentle to the point of unctuousness. Instinctively she had disliked him the first time they had met; her second impression of him did not help her to overcome her prejudice.

'I saw you come up. Mr Fane was driving you.' There was a gentle reproach in his tone. 'A curious young man, Mr Fane—given, I fear, to the inordinate consumption of alcoholic beverage. "Oh," as the prophet said, "that a man should put an enemy into his mouth to steal away his brains!"'

'I can testify,' interrupted Mr Goodman staunchly, 'that Mr Fane is perfectly sober. He drove me with the greatest care and skill. I think he is a very excitable young man, and one may often do him an injustice because of his peculiar mannerisms.'

The reverend gentleman sniffed. He was obviously no lover of Fane, and sceptical of his virtues. Yet he might find no fault with Ferdie, who came into the lounge soon after tea was served, and would have sat alone if Goodman had not invited him to the little circle which included himself, Mrs Elvery and Mary. He was unusually quiet, and though many opportunities presented themselves he was neither flippant nor aggressive.

Mary watched him furtively, more than interested in the normal man. He was older than she had thought; her father had made the same discovery. There was a touch of grey in his hair, and though the face was unlined it had the setness of a man who was well past his thirties, and possibly his forties.

His voice was deep, rather brusque. She thought she detected signs of nervousness, for once or twice, when he was addressed, he started so violently as to spill from the cup of tea which he held in his hand.

She saw him after the party had dispersed. 'You're very subdued today, Mr Fane.'

'Am I?' He made an attempt at gaiety and failed. 'It's funny, parsons always depress me. I suppose my conscience gets to work, and there's nothing more depressing than conscience.'

'What have you been doing all day?' she asked.

She told herself she was not really interested. The question was one of the commonplaces of speech that she had employed a dozen times with guests.

'Ghost-hunting,' he said, and when he saw her pale he was instantly penitent. 'Sorry—terribly sorry! I was being funny.'

But he had been very much in earnest; she realised that when she was in the privacy of her own room, where she could think without distraction. Ferdie Fane had spent that day looking for the Terror. Was he himself the Terror? That she could not believe.

CHAPTER XII

NIGHT came—the dreary night with its black mysteries and its suggestive horrors.

The telephone in the deserted lounge rang shrilly. Cotton came from some mysterious recess in a hurry to answer it. He heard Hallick's voice and winced painfully. He did not like Hallick, and wondered how soon this officer of Scotland Yard, with the resources at his disposal, would discover his own unsavoury antecedents.

'I want to speak to Dobie,' said Hallick's voice.

'Yes, sir; I'll call him.'

There was no need to call Sergeant Dobie; he was at Cotton's elbow.

'Is that for me?'

Cotton passed him across the instrument.

'Yes, sir? . . .' He glanced out of the corner of his eye and saw the interested Cotton. 'Hop it,' he said under his breath, and Cotton withdrew reluctantly.

'Have you found anything further?' asked Hallick.

'Nothing, sir. Another spent cartridge—you saw one of them before you left.'

There was a long pause at the other end of the wire, and then Hallick spoke again.

'I've got an idea something may happen tonight. You have my private telephone number? . . . Good! Call me if anything happens that has an unusual appearance. Don't be afraid of bringing me down on a fool's errand. I shall have a car waiting, and I can be with you in an hour.'

Dobie hung up the receiver as Mr Goodman came ambling into the lounge. He wore his black velvet smoking jacket; his old pipe was gripped between his teeth. Dobie was on his way to the door when the tea merchant called him back.

'You're staying with us tonight, aren't you, Mr Dobie? . . . Thank goodness for that!'

'You're nervous, are you, sir?' smiled Dobie, and Goodman's good-natured face reflected the smile.

'Why, yes, I am a little—raw. If anybody had told me I should get jumpy I should have laughed.'

He took out his cigar case and offered it to the detective, who chose one with considerable care.

'There's no new clue, I suppose?' said Goodman, making himself comfortable at the end of the settee.

'No, sir,' said Dobie.

Goodman chuckled.

'If you had any you wouldn't tell me, eh? That isn't one of the peculiar weaknesses of Scotland Yard officers, that they wear their—I won't say hearts, but their brains, upon their sleeves. You didn't find the gentleman who did the shooting yesterday? I ask you because I have been in town all day, and was a little disappointed when I came back to find that apparently nothing had happened.'

'No, we haven't found the shooter,' said Dobie.

Neither of them saw the door open, nor the pale face of Mr Partridge peeping through.

'I was at Scotland Yard today,' said Goodman; 'and I had a chat with Mr Hallick. A nice man.'

'Very,' agreed Dobie heartily.

John Hallick was one of the few men at the Yard who had no enemies amongst his subordinate staff. He was the type who placed the service first and individual kudos second, so that it was a tradition that any officer who deserved praise invariably received his full meed of recognition.

'The whole thing is really extraordinary,' said Goodman thoughtfully; 'in fact, the most extraordinary thing that has ever happened. Do you know, I am developing a theory?'

Dobie paused in the act of lighting his cigar.

'You're like Mrs Elvery,' he said, and Goodman groaned.

'That's the rudest thing that's been said to me today! No, it is about this unfortunate man, Connor, who was found dead in this room yesterday morning. The moment I heard the name I remembered the case—the gold robbery during the war. There were three men in it—O'Shea, the gang leader; a man named Marks—Soapy Marks; and Connor. I wouldn't like to confess as much to Mrs Elvery for fear she never left me to myself, but I was tremendously interested in war crimes, and I am pretty sure that this dead man was Connor.'

'Do you think so, sir?'

Mr Goodman smiled.

'No, I am perfectly sure now, from your badly simulated innocence! That was Connor, wasn't it?'

'Did you ask Mr Hallick?' asked Dobie, and, when the other shook his head: 'Well, Scotland Yard is issuing a statement tonight, so you might as well know that it was Connor.'

'H'm!' Goodman frowned. 'I am trying to reckon up how long he was in prison. He must have been released very recently?'

'A month ago,' said Dobie. 'He and Marks came out within a few hours of each other.'

Mr Goodman was beaming.

'I knew that I was right! I've got rather a good memory for names.'

Dobie lingered. There was nothing for him to do, but he had a human weakness for human society.

'I suppose you're not staying on after tonight?' he suggested. 'All these boarding house murders clear out the tenants and generally ruin the man or woman who's running the show.'

Goodman shook his head.

'I don't know. I'm an old bachelor and I hate change. I suppose I must be a little callous, but I am not as affected as some of the other people are.'

And then he went back to his original thesis.

'Now, suppose this crime is in connection with the gold robbery—'

But here he came across the official policeman. It was not a matter which Dobie could discuss, and he said so.

'Certainly—perfectly correct,' said Goodman hurriedly. 'I am sorry I was so indiscreet.'

'Not at all,' replied Dobie, and Goodman saw that he was aching to tell him all he knew. 'Perhaps you're nearer the truth than you imagine.'

Whatever revelation he might have made after that was interrupted by the arrival of Mrs Elvery and her daughter. The Rev. Mr Partridge followed, carrying in his hand a skein of wool.

Mrs Elvery at any rate was not so reticent. She was trembling with excitement, had information to give to the bored tea merchant.

'I'm going to give you a surprise, Mr Goodman,' she said, and Goodman closed his book with an expression of resignation. 'Do you know that Mr Partridge is an authority on spiritualism?'

'And I am an authority on good coffee,' said Mr Goodman. Cotton had come in with a tray full of little cups, and Goodman selected one. 'And if this coffee is good you can thank me, for I have taught the cook, after many years, how to prepare coffee that doesn't taste like dish-water. Spiritualism, eh? B-r-r! I don't want to know anything about spirits!'

Mr Partridge was all apologies.

'You rather exaggerate, I fear, my dear friend. Do you mind my saying that? I certainly have studied the science from an outsider's point of view, but I am no authority.'

'Then you won't object to a few spooks?' said Goodman, smiling.

'Spooks?' The reverend gentleman was puzzled. 'Ah, you mean—thank you, Cotton.' He took his coffee. 'I know what you mean.'

Mary came in at this uncomfortable moment, when Mr Partridge chose to discuss the tragedy of the previous day.

'How terrible it must have been for all you poor souls! How staggering! How—'

Mary was looking at the girl, saw her suddenly stare towards the window and turn pale. Veronica leapt to her feet and screamed.

'I saw a face at the window!' she gasped.

'Draw the curtains,' said Mr Goodman testily.

A few minutes later Fane strolled into the room, and Mary saw there were raindrops on his shoulders.

'Have you been out?'

'Yes, I've been strolling around,' he said.

Mary thought he had been drinking; his speech was slurred and he walked none too steadily.

'Did you see the monk?' asked Veronica spitefully.

Ferdie smiled broadly.

'If I had I'd have called his reverence to lay the ghost.'

Mr Partridge looked up, reproach in his eyes.

'It is all very dreadful. I only heard by accident of the tragedy that occurred here last night.'

'Don't talk about it, please!' wailed Veronica.

'A fellow creature cut off in his prime,' said the Reverend Partridge sonorously. 'I confess that I had a cold shiver run through me when I heard of this awful happening. The man's name is not known, I understand?'

He was reaching for a cup of coffee.

'Oh, yes, it is.' It was Fane who spoke. 'I wonder somebody didn't tell you.'

Their eyes met.

'The name of the murdered man,' said Fane deliberately, 'was Connor—Joe Connor.'

The coffee cup slipped from the parson's hand and was shattered on the parquet floor. The yellow face turned a dirty white.

'Connor!' he faltered. 'Joe Connor!'

Ferdie, watching him, nodded.

'You know the name?'

'I—I have heard it.'

Mr Partridge was talking with difficulty; he was a little breathless.

'Joe Connor!' he muttered again, and soon after went out of the room.

Mary noticed this and was puzzled. She wondered if Goodman had seen, but apparently he was unobservant, and he was more interested in another inmate of Monkshall. The first moment they were together he opened his heart on the subject.

'You may not believe me, my dear, but Mrs Elvery has been very interesting tonight. She showed me her press-cutting book—about this man Connor. There is no doubt it was he—I saw a picture in one of the cuttings. And I saw another photograph which rather interested me—had you ever met Mr Fane before he came here?'

'Was it his?' she asked.

He hesitated.

'Yes, I think it was.'

And then she remembered. She had been in the village that afternoon and had seen Goodman at the post office, in the little private telephone booth, and the postmistress had volunteered the information, rather proudly, that he was speaking to Scotland Yard. She had thought no more of this than that Goodman was getting further details about the crime of last night, and she realised that his call had a deeper significance when he went on:

'I have been making a few inquiries, and I think there is no doubt that Mr Fane is—um—well, Mr Fane is not all that he appears to be.' And then, earnestly: 'I beg of you not to mention this to him in any circumstances.'

She was amazed by his vehemence, and laughed.

'Why, of course I won't.'

'Mary'—he glanced over his shoulder; the rest of the company were engaged in their own affairs, and he dropped his hand timidly upon hers—'Mary, my dear, why don't you leave this place—go to London?'

'How curious!' she laughed. 'That is exactly what Mr Fane suggested.'

'Mr Fane made the suggestion for another reason,' he said, with a touch of grimness in his usually mild voice. 'I suggest it because—well, because I am very fond of you. Don't think I'm stupid or sentimental. In spite of the disparity in our ages, I love you as I have never loved any woman in my life.'

She was unprepared for the declaration, and could only look at him wonderingly.

'Think it over, my dear; and if you say "No"—well, I shall understand.'

She was glad when Cotton came in at that moment and told her her father wished to see her about some domestic trifle. She did not go back to the room until Cotton came to the study with the request that he should be allowed to lock up.

'They're all in bed except Mr Fane,' he said. 'I've got an idea he's waiting for you, miss.'

'Why should he be?' demanded Redmayne wrathfully.

Cotton did not know.

It was a shrewd guess on his part. Ferdie Fane sat on the sofa, hoping against hope that the girl would return. There was something he wanted to tell her, an urgent message of warning he wished to give to her. He heard the door click and turned quickly. It was the Reverend Mr Partridge.

'Pardon me,' said the clergyman, who seemed to have recovered something of his equilibrium; 'I left a book here.'

Fane did not speak until the white-haired man was turning to leave the room. Then:

'You were awfully rattled, Mr Partridge.'

'Rattled?' The parson frowned. 'That is a strange term to employ. I was naturally distressed to hear of this poor man's death.'

Fane grinned.

'Cotton was more distressed—he had to pick up the pieces of your coffee cup,' he said. 'Will you sit down for a second?'

The clergyman hesitated, and then sat down on the settee by Ferdie's side.

'What a terrible fate—poor soul!' he muttered.

'Silly—that was what was the matter with Connor,' said Fane coolly. 'You see, he wasn't as clever as his pal—the other fellow wouldn't have been so crude.'

'The other fellow?' Mr Partridge appeared to be puzzled.

'Soapy Marks—you've never heard of him? O'Shea's right-hand man. You've never heard of O'Shea? I'll bet you've not only heard of him, but if you haven't recognised him you'll know him pretty soon.'

The other man shook his head.

'This is Greek to me. Whom am I to recognise?'

'Soapy's got brains,' Fane went on. 'I'm going to give them a chance.'

Suddenly he reached out, gripped the white hair of the clergyman and pulled. The wig came away in his hand.

'Soapy!'

Soapy Marks leapt up.

'What the hell—' he began, but the face of Fane thrust into his.

'Go whilst the going's good,' he said deliberately. 'Go whilst there's life in you. I'm telling you, as I told Connor. You're asking for death—and you'll get it!'

'Well, I'll take it,' said Marks savagely. 'That's what! I'll take anything that's going.'

Ferdie Fane nodded.

'You never could take a warning, could you? Clever Mr Soapy—all brain and confidence!'

'You can't frighten me.' Marks was breathing heavily. 'You know what I've come for? My share of the swag—and I'm not going away till I get it!'

'You're going out feet first,' said Fane sombrely.

'I am, am I? You think you're damned clever, but I'll tell you something. I knew you the moment you told me about Connor. And there's somebody else in this house who knows you—that guy Goodman. He's no fool—he's knocked about the world. I saw him looking at you.'

Fane was startled.

'Goodman? You're crazy mad!'

'Mad, am I? I was down in the village this afternoon, and he was putting calls through to London—making inquiries about you. That girl, Redmayne, was in the post office too. That's made you sit up. What'll you do now, my dear friend? Get Goodman out of the way. I know your methods—I know that old drunk trick of yours too.'

Fane had recovered from his consternation.

'Whether he knows or whether he doesn't, I'm warning you,' he said sternly. 'You'll go the way of Connor.'

Marks moved to the door.

'That's fair warning. The man who gets me has got to be quick.'

In another second he passed through the curtains which hid the long French windows. Fane heard the click of them as the man opened them and stepped into the night.

Fane waited some time; he heard a step outside in the hall and slipped out through a door which would bring him to the lawn by another route.

He saw the door open slowly. It was Mr Goodman. He came in, grumbling to himself, looking from table to table for his pipe. Presently he found it. He put it in his pocket and was walking slowly back to the door when he saw something on the ground, and, stopping, picked it up. It was the wig that Marks had dropped in his flight. He looked at this for a long time, and then, conscious of the draught which came through the open French windows, moved towards the closed curtains.

His hand was on the point of drawing them back when two hands shot out, gripped him by the throat and drew him into the alcove.

Mary was half undressed when she heard the struggle below; heard the cry of a man in pain, and, pulling on her gown, fled down the stairs. She pushed open the door of the hall; it was in darkness, as it had been the night before.

'All right,' said a voice, and the lights came on suddenly.

Ferdie Fane was standing by the window, his coat and hair dishevelled.

'Mr Goodman!' she gasped. 'I heard his voice—where is he?'

'I haven't the slightest idea,' he said.

And then she saw the smear of blood across the white expanse of his shirt front ... As she fell fainting to the ground he caught her in his arms and the blood of a murdered man stained her kimono.

CHAPTER XIII

IT was half-past two in the morning, and Monkshall was awake. Hallick's mud-stained car stood at the door; the carpets were rolled up, in the search for hidden traps; and Mrs Elvery, in a pink dressing-gown, dozed and snored in the most comfortable arm-chair. There Hallick found her when he came in from a search of the grounds.

'Take my advice and go to bed,' he said, shaking her to wakefulness. 'It's nearly three o'clock.'

Mrs Elvery blinked herself awake and began to cry softly.

'Poor Mr Goodman! He was such a nice man, and there are so few bachelors left!' she wailed.

'We don't even know that he's dead yet,' snapped Hallick.

'There was blood all over the floor,' she whimpered. 'And that nice Mr Partridge—have you found him?'

'That nice Mr Partridge,' said Mr Hallick irritably, 'is on his way to London. You needn't worry about him; he's an old lag, and his name is Soapy Marks.'

Suddenly Mrs Elvery became galvanised to life.

'Have you questioned Cotton? He's been behaving very strangely this evening. Twice he's been down to the cellar, and when he came up the last time his knees were covered with dust—and do you know why?'

'I don't want to know why,' said the weary Hallick.

'He's searching for the gold that's hidden in this house. Ah, that makes you jump, Mr Inspector.'

'Superintendent,' said Hallick coldly. 'The gold in this house, eh? So you've got that O'Shea story, have you? Where did you get it?'

'Out of my press cuttings,' said Elvery triumphantly.

'Will you kindly go to bed?' snapped Hallick, and succeeded in hustling her from the room.

His assistant, Sergeant Dobie, had a theory that needed a little investigation, and now that they were alone for a minute Dobie stated his views.

'Redmayne? Nonsense! Why should he—?'

'That's what I was going to tell you, sir. Redmayne is broke; he borrowed all his money from Goodman. The first thing he did after the disappearance of Goodman was to go up into the old man's room, open a box and take out a promissory note. Here it is.'

Hallick examined the slip of paper thoughtfully.

'Get Redmayne here.'

The colonel almost staggered into the room. His nerve was gone, he was the wreck of the man he had been.

'I want to ask you a few questions,' said Hallick brusquely, and Redmayne scowled at him.

'I'm tired of answering questions,' he snapped.

'I'm sure you are,' said the other sarcastically. 'There's a ghost in Monkshall.' He produced the promissory note and held it out for the colonel to see. 'Is that the secret of all the queer happenings in this house? Is that the real explanation of the Terror?'

'It was money I borrowed,' said Redmayne in a low voice.

Hallick nodded.

'Ten years ago you were the secretary of a military fund. There was an audit and a large sum was missing. You were almost on the point of being arrested when you found the money—you borrowed it from Goodman?'

'Yes.'

'An hour or two ago you were searching Goodman's papers. Was it to find this?' asked the detective sternly.

'I refuse to be cross-examined by you,' said Redmayne, with something of his old spirit. 'You have no right to question me as to my private affairs.'

Hallick shook his head.

'Colonel Redmayne,' he said quietly, 'last night a man was murdered in your house; tonight a gentleman has disappeared in circumstances which suggest murder. I have every right to question you. I have even the right of arresting you, if I wish.'

'Then arrest me.' The colonel's voice quavered.

'I want you to realise the position you are in. There is somebody in this house whom no man has seen—somebody you are sheltering!'

'What do you mean?' The shaft had struck home.

'I am suggesting,' Hallick went on, 'that this loan of yours from Goodman was a blind; that at the time you borrowed it you had command of immense sums of money; that you bought this house to protect a desperate criminal wanted by the police—Leonard O'Shea!'

'It's a lie,' said the other hoarsely.

'Then I'll tell you another,' retorted Hallick. 'Somewhere in this house there is hidden hundreds of thousands of pounds in gold, the proceeds of the Aritania robbery; somewhere in these underground rooms of yours is a man half-sane, half-mad.'

The colonel cringed back.

'I did my best to keep him away. Do you think I wanted him here—where my daughter is?' he whined.

'We'll get the truth about this,' said Hallick.

He signalled to Dobie, who led the unresisting man to his study. Hallick followed, and, as the door closed behind them, Mr Ferdinand Fane came through the closed curtains. He had changed his clothes and was wearing a golfing suit.

Going back to the window, he called softly and Mary came out of the darkness.

'The coast is clear,' he said extravagantly, 'and nobody need ever know that you have committed the indiscretion of walking in the dark with me.'

She pulled off her raincoat and dropped wearily into a chair.

'It is part of the night's madness,' she said; 'and yet I felt safer there than in the house.'

'I never feel safe anywhere,' said Ferdie. 'I'm going to sleep in this room tonight—where's Cotton?'

'What do you want?'

'A drink,' he said, and rang the bell. Cotton came in so quickly that he might have been standing outside the door. His coat was wet, his boots muddy.

'Hallo!' Fane eyed him keenly. 'Why have you been sneaking about the grounds, my young friend?'

'Just looking round, sir. There's no harm in that, is there?' the man's voice was hollow and tremulous.

Then Mary remembered.

'Cotton, you have been with the detectives. What do they say?'

Fane laughed softly, and she interpreted his scorn.

'I want to know,' she said impatiently.

'I'll tell you what they say.' He stared at her. 'They think Mr Goodman's dead—somewhere in this room.' He leered at her. 'That's a queer idea, ain't it?'

She shuddered.

'And they think that old parson's dead too,' he went on with relish. 'I heard Dobie telling the superintendent that the parson must have come into the room when the fight was goin' on and that the Terror killed 'em both!'

'The Terror?' she repeated.

'That's what they call him. They say he goes mad two hours every day. That's a queer thing to happen, ain't it, miss? Fancy havin' a lunatic around, and nobody knows who he is. It might be you, sir—it might be me.'

'Most likely you, I should think,' said Fane sharply. 'Cotton, bring me a pint of champagne.'

'Haven't you had enough tonight?' pleaded Mary.

He shook his head.

'There's no such thing.'

She waited till Cotton was out of the room, then:

'Mr Fane, what happened to Mr Goodman?'

He made no attempt to answer her until Cotton had brought the wine and gone away again.

'This really is champagne,' he said as he poured out the foaming liquor. 'Gosh, I've got a headache.'

'I wish you'd have such a headache that you'd never drink again,' she said passionately.

'In other words, you wish I were dead?' he suggested.

He was disappointing her terribly; she had thought that in a time like this he would have been a help.

And then a thought struck her.

'What do you mean by "this really is champagne"?' she asked.

'I mean that this is the first drink of wine I've had for a week,' he said. 'Don't ask me any more about my habits—I'm a modest man.'

Was he serious? Was this drunkenness of his affected?

'What happened tonight when I found you in this room?' she asked. 'When that terrible fight was going on?'

He shook his head.

'I don't know. Some feller hit me in the jaw. I began to feel that I wasn't amongst friends.'

Then suddenly he became unexpectedly embarrassed.

'I say, would you really like me to—sort of—well, you know, look after you?'

'I don't know what you mean,' she said. And yet she knew well enough.

'I mean, to be around when you want somebody to protect you.'

He had come closer to her, but he did not touch her.

'Do you think you're in a fit state to protect anybody?' she asked, and knew that she was begging the question.

'Do you know, Mary, that I'd do a tremendous lot for you? You see, Mary—'

'Must you call me Mary?' she asked.

'Unless your name's Jemima. You can call me Ferdie if you like.'

'I don't like—not at the moment,' she said, a little out of breath.

'Did Goodman tell you he was awfully keen on you?'

She nodded.

'Poor Mr Goodman! Yes, he was very fond of me, and I liked him too.'

She looked round suddenly and he saw her face.

'What is the matter?' he asked quickly.

She shook her head.

'I don't know, but I've got a horrible feeling that somebody is listening. I wish that man would come,' she added inconsequently.

'Expecting somebody?' He was surprised.

'Yes, another detective—Mrs Elvery calls him the great Bradley. He is coming tomorrow morning.'

'Poor old blighter!' he chuckled. 'What's the use of bringing in a feller like that? I'm as good as a thousand detectives. I'm as good as O'Shea.' He laughed. 'O'Shea! There's a lad!'

She stepped back from him.

'I've heard of O'Shea,' she said slowly. 'What does he look like?'

He laughed again.

'Something like me—only not so good looking.'

She nodded and her voice sank to a whisper.

'You know too well who O'Shea is.'

The accusation took him aback.

'Yesterday, when you spoke to that man Connor, I was at the window and I heard you threaten him.'

He was silent.

'I warned him,' he said at last.

As though to put an end to the conversation he wheeled an easy-chair until it faced the panelled wall, and dragged forward a screen which he placed at its back.

'What are you going to do?' she asked.

'Sleep,' was the laconic answer.

'But why do you put the chair there?' she asked in amazement.

'Old monks' door!' he smiled. 'Any ghost of a monk is bound to come through the monks' door! If it was a ghost of a cook-general, she'd come through the kitchen door. You can't tell me anything about ghosts.'

She was compelled to laugh at the absurdity.

Hallick came back at that moment with the colonel.

'What the dickens are you doing?' he asked.

Ferdie had found a rug, left behind by Mrs Elvery, and this he was wrapping about himself.

'I'm going to sleep.'

'Sleep in your room,' said Redmayne harshly.

'Let him alone.' Hallick was rather indulgent to this eccentric man.

He felt a draught and pulled back the curtains. The windows were open.

'Bolt this after we go out, Miss Redmayne, and don't let anybody in unless you hear your father's voice. We're going into the grounds.'

'You'd better go to your room, my darling,' said the colonel, but she shook her head.

'I'll wait here.'

'But, my dear—'

'Leave her, leave her,' said Hallick impatiently. 'He'll do her no harm.' Ferdie, wrapped in the rug, had ensconced himself in the chair. He thought he heard her go out, but she was still there, and presently she peeped round the corner, and, seeing that his eyes were closed, switched out all the lights save one. She thought that she would speak to him, but changed her mind, tiptoed softly to the door and pulled it open. Her head was turned towards where Ferdie sat behind the screen. She did not see the man who suddenly appeared in the doorway, within inches of her. A tall shape, draped from head to foot in black, two eyes gleaming through the slits of the cowl.

She had no warning, no premonition of her danger, till an arm like steel slipped round her waist and a great hand covered her mouth.

She looked round, frozen with horror; saw the gleam of those gloomy eyes and went limp in the arms of the black monk.

Without a sound he lifted her into the passage, closed the door softly behind him, and carried her, as though she had no weight, past the door of her father's study to a little room that was used as a store. Had she been conscious, she would have remembered the big trap-door in the middle of the room which was always fastened. Stooping, he pulled the trap open, and, hoisting her to his shoulder, descended a flight of stone stairs. He left her for a moment, came back and fastened the trap from the inside.

CHAPTER XIV

HALLICK and the colonel visited the men they had stationed in the grounds, but nothing had been seen of the mysterious apparition, nor had any trace been found of Goodman or Marks.

'Marks is in London by now,' said Hallick as they squelched across the sodden grass to the house. 'He won't take much finding.'

'Why did he come here?'

'To get the stuff that's hidden here—the gold your friend, O'Shea, has cached somewhere in this house,' said Hallick. 'I am taking O'Shea tonight, and I advise you to keep out of the way, because I have an idea somebody is going to be badly hurt. My suggestion to you is that you take your daughter to London tonight; use one of my cars.'

'She will not go. How can I explain to her—?' began the colonel.

'There's no need for explanations,' said the other shortly. 'You can tell her the truth, or you can wait till the case comes for trial. O'Shea, I presume, gave you the money to buy this house.'

'He had already bought it, before the robbery,' said the colonel. 'I was in a terrible state of mind, expecting arrest at any moment. I can't tell you how he got to know of my situation. I'd never heard of the man before. But when he offered me a loan, a fixed income, and a decent house over my head, I jumped at it. You see, I'm not a fighting soldier—I'm an army doctor; and when he explained that he had these little troubles I very naturally thought he'd be easy to deal with. I didn't even know he was O'Shea till a year or so ago.'

They trudged on in silence, and then Hallick said:

'Have other men been here—other boarders?' He mentioned two names, and the colonel nodded.

'Yes, they came for a day or two, and then disappeared without paying their bills.'

'They died here,' said Hallick grimly; 'and died at O'Shea's hands—if they'd had the sense to tell me that they'd located O'Shea I could have saved them. But they wanted all the credit for themselves, I suppose, poor chaps!'

'Killed them—here!' gasped the colonel.

By this time they had come to the house, and Hallick tapped gently on the French windows. There was no response. He tapped again, but there was no answer.

'We'd better come to the door and wake Cotton,' he said.

It was a long time before Cotton heard the knocking, and a longer time before he opened the door.

'Where's Miss Redmayne?' asked Hallick.

The man shook his head.

'Haven't seen her, sir. There's somebody sleeping here—he's covered up with a blanket—gave me quite a start when I peeped round the screen.'

'That's Fane; leave him alone.'

He turned on all the lights.

And then suddenly a cold feeling came to this hardened detective, a sense of impending disaster.

'Go and find your daughter,' he said. Redmayne went out, and the detective heard his feet on the floor above. He came back in five minutes, white and shaking.

'She's not in her room and I don't think she's in the house. I've looked everywhere.'

'Have you seen her, Cotton?'

'No, sir, I haven't seen the young lady at all.'

'What's that?' said Hallick.

He picked up something from the floor; it was a girdle. The two men looked at one another.

'He's been here—the monk!' said Redmayne in horror.

Hallick had turned back the screen and dragged the chair, with its slumbering form, into the middle of the room.

'Wake up, Fane—Miss Redmayne has disappeared.'

With a quick movement he jerked away the corner of the rug that covered the sleeper's face, and started back with a cry. For the man who lay in that chair was not Fane. He looked down at the dead face of Soapy Marks!

CHAPTER XV

MARY came to consciousness with a curious sensation of discomfort. She was lying on something hard and cold. She looked up and her eyes were attracted by a pale blue lantern which hung from a vaulted roof; and to her ears came the sound of music; the deep, bass notes of an organ.

She struggled to a sitting position, and looked round. She was in a tiny chapel. In a recess stood a white-draped altar. Great wooden pillars supported the roof, and between these she saw a small organ, at which there was seated a black-robed monk.

He heard her move and, looking round, came stealthily towards her. She was paralysed with fear and could not move.

'Don't be afraid,' he whispered. 'There is nothing to be afraid of, my little lamb.' The voice was muffled by the thick cowl that hid the face.

'Who are you?' she whispered.

'Your friend—your lover—your worshipper!'

Was she dreaming? Was this some hideous nightmare? No, it was real enough.

She saw now that there were two entrances to the vault, one on either side. Two recesses whence stone steps wound upward.

'Who are you?' she asked again, and slowly he pulled back the hood.

She could not believe her eyes. It was Goodman. The grey hair was ruffled, the keen face less serene than she had known it. His eyes were like burning fires.

'Mr Goodman!' she whispered.

'Leonard, you shall call me,' he said in the same tone.

He reached his trembling hands down and caught her by the shoulders.

'Mary, my love, I have waited—oh, so long—for this glorious moment. For you are to me as a divinity.'

She came to her feet and shrank back from him.

'You're not afraid of me, Mary?' She drew to herself all her reserves of courage and strength, and shook her head.

'No, Mr Goodman. Why should I be afraid of you? I'm glad that you're alive. I was afraid—something had happened to you.'

'Nothing could happen to me, my lamb.' His smile was full of confidence. 'Nothing could happen to your lover. The very gods protected him and reserved him for this glorious reward.'

Her knees were trembling under her. She was sick, and would have fainted again, but by force of will maintained her consciousness.

'Your lover,' he was saying. 'I've loved you all this time. Sometimes I've wanted you so that there was a fire in my heart and in my brain that was beyond my control.'

He took her cold hand in his and brought it to his lips. She tried to pull it away, but he held it firmly, and his eyes smiled into hers. They were bigger than she had ever seen them—wide, glowing eyes that transfigured his face.

'You're not afraid of me?' he breathed. 'Not afraid of the lover who can give you all your heart's desire?'

Suddenly he caught her arm, and waved his hand about the room.

'There's money here; gold—thousands and thousands of golden pieces. Beautiful golden pieces, all hidden away. I hid them with my own hands.'

And then he waxed confidential, and was more like his normal self.

'This chapel is full of hollow places. I found deep cavities where the bodies of the dead monks lay. I took them out and purified their charnel houses with beautiful gold.' He pointed. 'That wall behind that old seat, these wooden pillars, are packed tight with it.'

She tried to keep him in that saner mood.

'What is this place, Mr Goodman? I've never seen it before.'

He looked at her strangely, and a slow smile dawned on his face.

'This is a sanctuary for my bride.' His arms went round her, and she steeled herself to offer no resistance. 'Men and women have been married here,' he said. 'Can't you smell the fragrance of the bride's hair? We will be married here,' he nodded. 'And men have died here—hundreds of years ago. We may die here too.'

He laughed. She had heard that laugh in the night, and the horror of it turned her blood to ice.

'I've buried men here—there!' He pointed. 'And there!' He pointed again. 'They came in search of me—clever men from Scotland Yard!'

He knelt down on the floor and put his face to the joints of a stone slab.

'There's one there. Do you hear me, you dead man—you who came, so full of life, to catch O'Shea? Do you hear me? I am alive. And you—what are you?'

'Please, please don't!' she gasped. 'You are terrifying me!'

He chuckled at this.

'The Terror—ah! That is what they call me—the Terror that walks by night. Biblical—a strange thing to call poor old Goodman. I used to sit, smoking my pipe, in that room of ours'—he pointed up—'and hear that stupid old woman talk of the Terror. And inside me my heart was laughing. She never knew how near she was.' He reached out his long hand, and it clenched horribly.

'Mr Goodman!' She strove to bring him back to a rational level. 'You'll let me go now, won't you? My father will give you anything you want, will do anything for you—he has been a doctor, you know.'

Not once did his hand release the grip on her arm.

'Your father?' He was amused, and chuckled for a long time. 'He'll do as I tell him, because he's afraid of me. You never thought he was afraid of me, but he is. He thinks I'm mad. That's why he's looking after me. I know he's a doctor—of course he's a doctor. Sometimes he used to lock me up in a cell. I used to scream and tear at the walls, but he kept me there. He's mad—they're all mad!'

She was swooning with fright, and with a superhuman effort tore her arm from his grip and fled to the stairs. Before one foot was on the lowest step he had caught her and dragged her back again.

'Not yet—not yet.'

'Let me go.' She did not struggle. 'I swear I won't attempt to run away again. You can believe me, can't you?' He nodded and released her. She crouched down on the stone seat before the altar.

'I'll play to you,' he said, with sudden inspiration. 'Lovely music—'

As his fingers wandered over the keys he was talking disjointedly to himself, presently he began to play, so softly that his voice sounded harsh against that wonderful background of melody.

'You've heard this old organ?' He looked round over his shoulder at her. 'I play to the dead and make them live! Old monks walk here—long lines of them, marching two and two. And people bring young brides to wed and old men to die. And sometimes I see men here that I know—dead men—'

He dropped again into a conversational tone. Suddenly the music stopped, and he pointed to an invisible shape.

'Look—Joe Connor!'

She tried to pierce the gloom but saw nothing. Goodman was talking now, beckoning to the invisible shape.

'Come here, Connor; I want to talk to you. Been to prison, have you? Poor fellow! And all because of that wicked man O'Shea. Come for your share of the swag? You shall have it, my boy.'

The organ ceased. He went across and put his arm around something that was invisible to Mary, but was plain to his crazy eyes. And so he led the thing he saw to the stone seat she had vacated.

'You shall have it, my boy. It's all here, Connor—the good red gold that I got away with. Sit down, Connor—I want to tell you all about it. I'd bought this old house months before—you see, Connor? And I brought the gold here in the lorry by night, and I hid it in the hollow places. Weeks and months I worked, filling hollow pillars and the graves of old monks. Clever, eh, Connor? No wonder you smile.'

He rose and stood behind the ghostly shape he saw.

'I tell you this because you're dead—and dead men never tell. And then I got Redmayne as a blind, put him in charge of the house. He had to do it, Connor'—he lowered his voice to a confidential note—'because I had a hold on him. I used to go a little queer and he looked after me—that's what I paid him for. I was nothing—he was the master of Monkshall. He, he—that's how I fooled the police. Nobody dreamed that I was O'Shea. You want your share—damn you! You dog! I'll choke the life out of you, you hound!'

His voice rose to a yell as he gripped the spirit throat and, in his imagination, hurled it to the ground. He was kneeling on the floor now, his face demoniacal in its fury.

And then he remembered the girl and looked round.

'I'm frightening you.' His voice was soft. He came nearer to her and suddenly clasped her in his arms.

She screamed, but he hushed her.

'I don't want to frighten you. Don't scream. I love you too much to frighten you.' His lips sought hers, but she avoided them.

'No, not yet—give me a little time.' He loosed his hold on her.

'But you will love me? Did you see those little doors in the passage walls? The old monks lived there. You and I will find a bridal suite there.'

She was fighting desperately for time. At any moment this madness might pass. She knew now he was O'Shea—sane for twenty-two hours a day.

'Wait. I want to talk to you, Mr Goodman. You said you loved me.'

'You are God to me,' he said reverently.

'You would not want me to love you if I loved someone else, would you?' His face changed at this.

'Loved someone else? No, no. I would not ask it. But do you love someone else?'

'Yes—I—I'm awfully fond of—of Mr Fane.'

For a second he neither spoke nor moved, then his hand shot out to her throat. She thought she was doomed, but at that moment she was gripped by the arm and swung aside, and O'Shea looked into the levelled muzzle of an automatic.

'I want you, O'Shea!'

It was Fane's voice, Fane's arm that encircled her.

'Come away from that switch. That's right. I don't want to be in the dark. Farther. Now stand still.'

'Who are you?' O'Shea's voice was surprisingly gentle.

'My name's Bradley!' said Fane quietly. 'Inspector Bradley of Scotland Yard. I want you, O'Shea. For three years I have been waiting for this opportunity, and now I know all that I want to know.'

O'Shea nodded.

'You know what I have done to Marks?'

'You killed him—yes.'

'He tried to strangle me—I think he must have recognised me. His body—'

'I found it behind the monks' door and left it in my place. If he and Connor had taken my advice they would have been alive today.'

O'Shea gave a deep sigh and smiled.

'I'm afraid I've given everybody a lot of trouble,' he said blandly. 'So you're Bradley, the man who arrested Connor and the man who arrested our old friend, Soapy Marks, and now you have done the hat trick! Really, I deserve everything for not recognising you. Miss Redmayne, will you accept my apologies? I am afraid at times I get a little out of hand—a mere passing folly—um. May I take off this ridiculous robe?' He stripped the black robe from him, slowly.

'Be careful. He is not sane yet,' said Mary in a low voice. He heard her.

'Oh, my dear Miss Redmayne'—he smiled—'you must be a very poor judge of sanity. And now, I suppose, inspector—or is it superintendent?—you will marry this charming young lady who has so touchingly declared her love for you? I wish I could find you a little wedding present.'

So quickly did he move that Bradley could not have escaped death had not the foot of the assassin slipped. The knife struck one of the pillars, and in the impact the rotting wood broke and a stream of gold flowed from its hollow depth.

O'Shea glared at the gold that had cost him so much, and then he began to laugh.

'A wedding present,' he chuckled.

He was still laughing when Hallick and three detectives took him by car to London.

THE END

WHITE FACE

DEDICATED
TO MY DEAR FRIEND
GEORGE DORAN

CHAPTER I

MICHAEL QUIGLEY had a fair working knowledge of perverse humanity, having acquaintance with burglars, the better class of confidence man, professional forgers, long firm operators, swindlers, ingenious and naïve, bank workers, bucket shop keepers and pickpockets. He did not know White Face because nobody knew him, but that was a pleasure deferred. Sooner or later, the lone operator would make a mistake and come within the purview of a crime reporter.

Michael knew almost everybody at Scotland Yard and addressed chief constables by their first names. He had spent weekends with Dumont, the hangman, and had helped him through an attack of delirium tremens. He had in his room signed photographs of *ci-devant* royalties, heavy-weight champions and leading ladies. He knew just how normal and abnormal people would behave in almost any circumstances. But personal experience failed him in the case of Janice Harman, although he had heard of such cases.

He could understand why a girl with no responsibilities (since she was an orphan) and three thousand pounds a year should want to do something useful in life and should choose to become a nurse in an East End clinic; other girls had allowed their enthusiasm for humanity to lead them into similar vocations, and Janice only differed from the majority in that she had not wearied of her philanthropy.

She was very lovely, though he could never analyse the qualities which made for loveliness. She had amazingly clear eyes and a mouth that was red and sensitive—perhaps it was the quality of her skin. He was never sure—the only thing he was certain about was that he could look at her for hours and wanted to look at her for ever.

The one quality in her which made him wriggle uncomfortably was her cursed motherliness. He could never bridge the gulf which separated her from his twenty-seven years.

She was twenty-three and, as she often told him, a woman of twenty-three was at least twenty years older than a man of the same age. But twenty-three can be motherly or cruel. One night she told him something that struck all the colour out of life. It was the night they went to supper at the Howdah Club—the night of Michael's pay-day.

He knew, of course, about her romantic correspondent. Had sneered at him, raved at him, grown wearily amused about it all. The correspondence started in the most innocent fashion. One day a letter had come to Janice's flat in Bury Street, asking if she would be kind enough to place the writer in touch with his old nurse, who had fallen on evil times. This was a few months after she had begun her work in Dr Marford's clinic and one of the newspapers had found a good story in the 'rich young society woman' who had given her life to good works. The letter was written from South Africa and enclosed five pounds, which the writer begged her to hand to his old nurse if she found her, or to the funds of the clinic if she did not.

'How do you know this fellow isn't working a confidence trick on you?' demanded Michael.

'Don't be stupid,' said Janice scornfully. 'Because you are a wretched crime reporter you think that the world is made up of criminals.'

'And I'm right,' said Michael.

That the unknown stranger had arrived in England Michael did not know until ten days later. She called him up, asked him to take her to supper: she had some important things to tell him.

'You're one of the oldest friends I have, Michael,' she said, speaking rather breathlessly. 'And I feel that I ought to tell you.'

He listened, stunned.

She might have seen how pale his face was, but she purposely did not look at him, fixing her eyes on the dancing couples on the floor.

'I want you to meet him—you may not think he is wonderful, but I've always known . . . from his letters, I mean . . . he has lived a terrible life in the wilds of Africa; I'll be terribly sorry to leave Dr Marford . . . I shall have to tell him, of course . . .'

She was incoherent, a little hysterical.

'Let me get this right, Janice. I'll try to forget that I love you and that I was only waiting until I got my salary raised before I told you.' His voice was very steady, so unemotional that there was every encouragement to look at him. Nevertheless she kept her eyes steadily averted.

'This isn't unusual—I have heard of such cases. A girl starts a correspondence with a man she has never seen. The correspondence grows more intimate, more friendly. She weaves around him a net of romance. And then she meets him and is either—disillusioned, or else falls for him. I've heard of happy marriages which started that way—I've heard of others. I can't believe it is true—but obviously it is, and I don't exactly know what to do or say.'

It was at this moment that he missed something from her hand—a long oval-shaped ruby ring that she had worn since he had first known her.

Instantly she knew what he was looking for and dropped her hand out of sight.

'Where is your ring?' he asked bluntly.

She had gone very red: the question was almost unnecessary.

'I've—I don't see what it has to do with you?'

He drew a long breath.

'Nothing has to do with me—but I'm curious. An exchange of love tokens?'

He was very tactless tonight.

'It was my ring and I refuse to be cross-examined by a—by somebody who hasn't any right. You're being horrible.'

'Am I?' He nodded slowly. 'I suppose I am, and I know I've no right to be horrid or anything else. I won't ask you to show me what you got in exchange. A bead necklace perhaps—'

She started at this chance shot.

'How did you know? I mean, it is very valuable.'

He looked long and earnestly at the girl.

'I want to vet this fellow, Janice.'

She saw his face now and was in a panic—not on his behalf, but on her own.

'Vet—I don't know what you mean?'

He tried, with a smile, to minimise the offensiveness of what he had to say.

'Well, make inquiries about him. You vet a horse before you buy him—'

'I'm not buying him—he is a rich man—well, he has two farms.' Her manner was cold. There was a touch of resentment in her voice. 'Vet him! You'll find he is a criminal, of course; if you can't find this, your fertile imagination will invent something. Perhaps he is White Face! He is one of your specialities, isn't he?'

He groaned miserably. Yet here was an opportunity to escape from a maddening topic.

'He is not an invention; he's a fact. Ask Gasso.'

Gasso, the slim *maître d'hôtel*, was near the table. Mike beckoned him.

'Ah! That White Face! Where is your so-called police? My poor friend Bussini has his restaurant ruined by the fellow.'

It was to Bussini's restaurant that White Face had come in the early hours of a morning and, stepping to the side of Miss Angela Hillingcote, had relieved her of six thousand pounds' worth of jewels before the dancers realised that the man in the white mask, who had appeared from nowhere, was not a guest in fancy dress. It was all over in a second or two and he was gone. A policeman at the corner of Leicester Square saw a man fly past on a motor-cycle. The cycle had been seen on the Embankment going eastward. It was the third and most spectacular appearance of White Face in the West End of London.

'My patrons are nervous—who is not?' Gasso apparently shared their nervousness. 'Fortunately they are refined people—' He stopped suddenly and stared at the entrance of the room. 'She should not come!' he almost shrieked and darted forward to meet an unwanted guest.

This was a blonde lady who called herself Dolly de Val. It was found for her by an imaginative film agent, who thought—and rightly—that it sounded more pretentious than Annie Gootch, which name she had borne in the days of her poverty. She was not a good actress, because she could never quite remember all that the producer told her, and more often than not she was the only girl in the front line who kicked with her right leg when she should have kicked with her left. And frequently she was not in the line at all.

But there were quite a lot of people who found her attractive, and in the course of the years she became very rich, and packed a considerable amount of her fortune into platinum settings, so that in all the fashionable nightclubs of London she was known as 'Diamond Dolly'.

Managers of such clubs and fashionable cabaret restaurants grew a little nervous after the Hillingcote affair, and when Dolly booked a supper table table they rang up Scotland Yard and Superintendent Mason, who was in control of 'C' area but had an executive post at headquarters, would delegate a couple of detectives arrayed like festive gentlemen, but looking remarkably like detectives, to the club or restaurant favoured by her dazzling display, and these were generally to be found lounging in the vestibule or drinking surreptitious glasses of beer in the manager's office.

But sometimes Dolly did not notify her intentions before-hand. And she would glitter into the club surrounded by handsome young men, and a hasty table would be wedged impossibly on the packed floor and waiters would lay the table with extraordinary enthusiasm, conveying the impression that this was a favoured position for a table.

She came this night unheralded into the Howdah Club and Gasso, who was Latin and entirely without self-control, threw up his hands to the ceiling, stiff with cupids, and said things in Italian which sounded very romantic to people who only understood English.

'No room—don't be stupid, Gasso! Of course there's room. Anywhere will do, won't it, boys?'

So they put a table near the door, and Dolly sat and ordered *consommé Julienne*, chicken *à la* Maryland.

'I don't like you to seet here, madam,' said Gasso fearfully, 'with so much beautiful jewellery . . . Miss 'Illingcote—ah, what a disaster! This fellow with the white face—'

'Oh, shut up, Gasso!' Dolly snapped. 'And, after that, we'll have *coupe Jacques* and coffee . . .'

The Russian dancers had taken the floor and had made their exit after the third encore, when: 'Bail up—you!'

Dolly, who had seen the face of her escort suddenly blanch, half turned in her chair.

The man in the doorway wore a long black coat that reached to his heels, his face was covered by a white cloth in which two eye-holes had been cut.

He carried an automatic in his gloved hand; with the other, which was bare, he reached out.

There was a 'snick'—the long diamond chain about Dolly's neck parted. She stood frozen with fear and saw the glittering thing vanish into his pocket.

Men had risen from the tables, women were screaming, the band stood ludicrously grouped.

'After him!' yelled a voice.

But the man in the white mask was gone and the cowering footmen, who had bolted on his entrance, came out from cover.

'Don't move—I'll get you out in a minute.' Mike's voice was urgent, but she heard him like one in a dream. 'I'll take you home; I must get through to my paper. If you faint, I'll be rough with you!'

'I'm not going to faint,' she quavered.

He got her out before the police came, and found a cab.

'It was dreadful; who is he?'

'I don't know,' he answered shortly. Then: 'What's this romantic lover's name—you've never told me?'

Her nerves were on edge; she needed the stimulant of righteous anger to recover her poise and here was an excuse.

Mike Quigley listened unmoved to her tirade.

'A good looker, I'll bet; not a gaunt-faced, tow-haired brute like me,' he said savagely. 'O God, what a fool you are, Janice! I'm going to meet him. Where is he staying?'

'You'll not meet him.' She could have wept. 'And I won't tell you where he is staying. I hope I never see you again!'

She declined the hand he offered to assist her out of the cab; did not answer his 'good-night'.

Mr Quigley went raging back to Fleet Street, and all the vicious things he wrote about White Face he meant for the handsome and romantic stranger from South Africa.

CHAPTER II

A SLOVENLY description of Janice Harman would be that she was the product of her generation. She had inherited the eternal qualities of womanhood as she enjoyed a freedom of development which was unknown in the formal age when guardians were restrictive and gloomy figures looming behind the young and beautiful heiress.

Janice had attained independence almost unconsciously; had her own banking account when she was seventeen, and left behind the tangibilities of discipline when she passed from the tutelage of the venerable headmistress of her school.

A bachelor uncle was the only relative she had possessed. In a spasmodic and jolly way he was interested in his niece, made her a lavish allowance, sent her beautiful and useless presents at Christmas and on her birthday, which he invariably remembered a month after. When he was killed in a motor accident (the three chorus girls who were driving with him escaped with a shaking) she found herself a comparatively rich young woman.

He had appointed as trustee a friend whose sole claim to his confidence lay in the fact that he was the best judge of hunters in England, and was one of the few men who could drink half a dozen glasses of port blindfolded and unerringly distinguish the vintage of each.

Janice left school with an exalted code of values and certain ideals which she religiously maintained. She had in her bedroom a framed portrait of the Prince of Wales, and she took the Sacrament on Christmas mornings.

At eighteen all men were heroes or dreadful; at nineteen she recognised a middle class which were neither heroic nor unspeakable. At twenty the highlights had receded and some of the duller tones were taking shape and perspective.

Donald Bateman belonged to the old regime of idealism. In his handsome face and athletic figure she recaptured some of the enthusiasm of the classroom. He was Romance and Adventure, the living receptacle in which were stored all the desirable virtues of the perfect man. His modesty—he no more than inferred his excellent qualities—his robust personality, his good humour, his childish views about money, his naïveté, were all adorable. He accepted her judgments and estimates of people and events, giving to her a sense of superiority which was very delightful.

In one respect he pleased her: he did not embarrass her more than once. He never forgot that their acquaintance was of the slightest, and the word 'love' had never been uttered. The second time they had met he had kissed her, and she was ridiculously uncomfortable. He must have seen this, for he did not repeat the experiment. But they talked of marriage and their home and the wonders of South Africa; she could even discuss in a prim way the problem of children's education. A breezy figure of a man, delightfully boyish.

She was taking afternoon duty at the clinic and had been worrying about him all the morning—he had been a little depressed when she had seen him last.

'Did your money come?' she asked, with a smile.

He took out his pocket-book and drew forth two crisp notes. She saw they were each for a hundred pounds.

'It arrived this morning. I drew out these in case of emergency—I hate being without money when I'm in London. Angel, if the money hadn't turned up, I should have been borrowing from you this morning, and then what would you have thought of me?'

She smiled again. Men were so silly about money. Michael, for instance. She had wanted him to have a little car, and he had been almost churlish when she offered to help him.

He sat down and lit a cigarette, blowing a cloud of smoke to the ceiling.

'Did you enjoy your dinner?'

She made a little face.

'Not very much.'

'He's a reporter, isn't he? I know a reporter on the *Cape Times*—quite a good chap—'

'It wasn't Michael who made the dinner a failure,' she intervened loyally. 'It was a man who came into the club with a white mask.'

'Oh!' He raised his eyebrows. 'The Howdah Club—White Face? I've been reading about it in this morning's papers. I wish I'd been there. What is happening to the men in this country that they allow a fellow like that to get away with it? If I'd been within reach of him one of us would have been on the floor. The trouble with you people in England is that you're scared of firearms. I know from my own experience . . .'

He told a story of a prospector's camp in Rhodesia; it was a story which did not place him in an unfavourable light.

He sat facing the window, and during the narrative she had time to scrutinise him—not critically, but with indiscriminate approval. He was older than she had thought; forty, perhaps. There were little lines round his eyes, and harder ones near his mouth. That he had led a difficult and a dangerous life, she knew. One cannot starve and thirst in the desert of the Kalahari, or lie alone racked with fever on the banks of the Tuli River, or find oneself unarmed and deserted by carriers in the lion country west of Massikassi, and present an unlined and boyish face to the world. He still bore beneath his chin the long scar which a leopard's claw had left.

'Living in Africa nowadays is like living in Bond Street,' he sighed. 'All the old mystery has departed. I don't believe there's a lion left between Salisbury and Bulawayo. In the old days you used to find them lying in the middle of the road . . .'

She could listen to him for hours, but, as she explained, there was work to do.

'I'll come down and bring you home—where is it?' he asked.

She explained the exact location of Tidal Basin.

'Dr Marford—what sort of a man is he?'

'He's a darling,' said Janice enthusiastically.

'We'll have him out at the Cape.' He echoed her enthusiasm. 'It's very easy. There's an extraordinary amount of work to be done, especially with the coloured children. If I can buy that farm next to mine, we might turn the farm building into a sort of convalescent home. It's one of those big, rambling Dutch houses and, as I've rather a nice house of my own, I shouldn't have use for the other.'

She laughed at this.

'You're suffering from land hunger, Donald,' she said. 'I shall have to write and get particulars of this desirable property!'

He frowned.

'Have you any friends at the Cape?' he asked.

She shook her head.

'I know a boy there—he was a Rhodes scholar—but I haven't written to him since he left England.'

'H'm!' He was rather serious now. 'When strangers come into the property market they soak 'em! Let me give you a word of advice: never try to buy land in South Africa through an agent—half of 'em are robbers, the other half an incompetent lot. One thing is certain, that the property at Paarl—that is where my farm is—will double itself in value in a couple of years. They are running a new railway through—it passes at the end of my land—and that will make an immense difference. If I had a lot of money to invest I should put every cent of it in land.'

He explained, however, that the Cape Dutch, who were the largest landowners in the country, were a suspicious folk who never did business with an Englishman, except to the latter's disadvantage.

He took out the two hundred pound notes and looked at them again, rustling them affectionately.

'Why don't you put it back in the bank?' she asked.

'Because I like the feel of it,' he said gaily. 'These English notes are so clean-looking.'

He returned the case to his pocket, and suddenly caught her by both arms. She saw a light in his eyes which she had never seen before. She was breathless and a little frightened.

'How long are we going to wait?' he asked in a low voice. 'I can get a special licence; we can be married and on the Continent in two days.'

She disengaged herself; discovered, to her amazement, that she was trembling, and that the prospect of an immediate marriage filled her with a sense of consternation.

'That is impossible,' she said breathlessly. 'I've ever such a lot of work to do, and I've got to finish up my work at the clinic. And, Donald, you said you didn't want to be married for months.'

He smiled down at her.

'I can wait months or years,' he said lightly, 'but I can't wait for my lunch. Come along!'

She had only half an hour to give to him, but he promised to meet her and take her to dinner that night. The prospect did not arouse in her any sense of pleasurable anticipation. She told herself she loved him. He was everything that she would have him be. But immediate marriage? She shook her head.

'What are you shaking your head about?' he asked.

They were at Pussini's, and, as it was before one o'clock, the restaurant was empty save for themselves.

'I was just thinking,' she said.

'About my farm?' He was looking at her searchingly. 'No? About me?'

And then suddenly she asked: 'What is your bank, Donald?'

He was completely surprised at the question.

'My bank? Well, the Standard Bank—not exactly the Standard Bank, but a bank that is affiliated with it. Why do you ask?'

She had a good and benevolent reason for putting the question, but this she was not prepared to reveal.

'I will tell you later,' she said, and when she saw that she had worried him she was on the point of making her revelation. 'It's really nothing, Donald.'

He drove down with her to Tidal Basin, but refused the offer of her car to take him back, his excuse being that he felt nervous of the London traffic. She was secretly glad that there was some feature of London life of which he stood in awe.

Mr Donald Bateman came back to town in a taxi and spent the afternoon in the City office of a tourist agency, examining Continental routes. He would like to have stayed in London; but then, he would like to have stayed in so many places from which expediency had dragged him. There was Inez. She had grown into quite a beautiful woman. He had seen her, though she was not aware of the fact. It was curious how women developed. He remembered her—rather sharp-featured, a gawk of a girl who had bored him utterly. In what way would Janice grow? For the moment she was very delectable, though she had qualities which exasperated him. Perfect women, he decided, were difficult to find.

When he had caught her by the shoulders that morning and looked down into her eyes, he had expected some other reaction than that fit of shivering. She had shown her alarm too clearly for him to carry the matter any further. It must be marriage, of course. But marriage was rather dangerous in a country like this. That reporter friend of hers? He hated reporters; they were a prying, unscrupulous lot. And crime reporters were the worst.

He began to feel uncomfortable, and turned relief to a contemplation of the physical perfection of Inez. From Inez his mind strayed to other women. What had become of Lorna, for example? Tommy had found her, probably, and forgiven everything. Tommy was always a weak-willed sap. But Inez! ...

He and Janice dined together that night, and most resolutely he chose the Howdah Club. Already the outrage had had effect upon the attendance: the dining-room was half empty, and Gasso stalked up and down, a picture of gloom.

'This has ruined me, young miss,' he said brokenly. 'You were here last night with the newspaper gentleman. People will not come unless they have no jewels. And I particularly desire jewelled people here, but not jewelled as Miss Dolly!'

'I hope he comes tonight,' said Donald with a quiet smile.

'You 'ope so, eh?' asked the agitated Gasso. 'You desire me to be thrown into the street with only my shirt on my back? That is good for business!'

Janice was laughing, but she succeeded in pacifying the outraged *maître d'hôtel*.

'It certainly is empty, but I don't suppose we shall see our white-faced gentleman.' said Donald. 'It's rather like old times. I remember when I was in Australia there was a gang which held up a bank—they wore white masks, too. They got away with some money, by Jove! Ever heard of the Furses? They were brothers—the cleverest hold-up men in Australia.'

'Perhaps this is one of them,' she said thoughtlessly.

'Eh?'

She could have sworn he was frightened at that moment. Something she saw in his eyes. It was absurd, of course, for Donald Bateman was afraid of nothing.

'I shouldn't think so,' he said.

Half-way through dinner, when they were discussing some amiable nothing, he dropped his knife and fork on the plate. Again she saw that frightened look intensified. He was staring at somebody, and she followed the direction of his eyes.

A man had come in. He must have been nearly sixty, was slim, dandified, rather fussy. He had a small party with him, and they were surrounded by waiters. Curiously enough, she knew him: curious, because she had made his acquaintance in a slum.

'Who—who is that?' His voice was strained. 'That man there, with the girls? Do you—do you know him?'

'That is Dr Rudd,' she said.

'Rudd!'

'He's the police surgeon of our division—I've often seen

him. In fact, he once came to the clinic. Quite an unpleasant man—he had nothing at all nice to say about our work.'

'Dr Rudd!'

The colour was coming back to his face. He had gone pale! She was astounded.

'Do you know him?' she asked in surprise.

He smiled with difficulty.

'No; he reminds me of somebody—an old friend of mine in—er—Rhodesia.'

She noticed that when on their way out he passed the doctor's group Donald was patting his face with a handkerchief as though he were healing a scratch.

'Are you hurt?' she asked.

'A little neuralgia.' He laughed cheerily. 'That is the penalty one pays for sleeping out night after night in the rain.'

He told her a story of a rainfall in Northern Rhodesia that had lasted four weeks on end.

'And all that time,' he said, 'I had not so much as a tent.'

She left him at the door of the flat in Bury Street, and he was frankly disappointed, for he had expected to be asked up to her apartment. There was consolation on the way back to the hotel, certain anticipations of an interview he had arranged for the morrow. It was not with Janice.

CHAPTER III

In his rare moments of leisure Dr Marford was wont to stand in his surgery, behind the red calico curtains which were stretched across the big window level with the bridge of his thin, aristocratic nose, and muse, a little sourly, upon Tidal Basin, its people and its future.

He had material for speculation on those summer evenings, when the light of the brazen day still persisted in the western skies, and when every dive and tenement spilt the things that were so decently hidden in the cold days and nights of winter. On such nights the sweltering heat forced into the open the strangest beings, creatures which even the oldest inhabitants could not remember having seen before and the most hardened could hardly wish to see again.

The red calico curtain was strung across the window of the large room which was his surgery. It had been a boot store and a confectioner's parlour. Loucilensky, of infamous memory, had housed his 'club' in it and found the side door which led to the little yard a convenient exit for his squalid patrons.

It was a derelict property when Dr Marford came to found his practice here. All Tidal Basin knew that the doctor was so poor that he had painted, distempered and scrubbed the place from top to bottom with his own hands. He had probably sewn his own curtains, had certainly collected from the Caledonian Market, where you may furnish a house for a few pounds, such domestic equipment as was necessary for his well-being. Tidal Basin, which favoured those cinemas which featured pictures of high life, had despised him for his poverty. A consumptive plumber had fixed the huge sink, which was an unsightly feature of one corner of the surgery, and had received, in return, free treatment and medicine until he went the dingy way of all consumptive plumbers.

Tidal Basin had known and still knew Dr Marford as the 'penny doctor'. They knew him better as the 'baby doctor', for, after he had been in Tidal Basin a year, by some miracle he succeeded in founding a free clinic, where he gave ray treatment to children. He must have had influential friends, for on top of his other activities he founded a small convalescent home at the seaside.

His work was his obsession, and not a penny of the money which came to him went to his own advantage. The drab surgery remained as shabby as it had always been—a very dreary place compared with the spick and span little palace of white enamel and glass where the children of Tidal Basin were made acquainted with artificial sunlight and the beneficent quality of strange rays.

He saw Janice Harman pass the window and went to open the door to her. It was not true that this preoccupied man was hardly aware of her loveliness. He used to sit at his desk and think about her for hours on end. What strange dreams came to disorder the tidiness of his methodical mind was known only to Dr Marford; and now, when she told him awkwardly, a little disjointedly, of her future plans, he showed no evidence of the sudden desolation and despair that crushed him.

('The oddest people fall in love with Janice,' said her best friend.)

'Oh!' he said, and bit his thin lip thoughtfully. 'That is very unfortunate—for the clinic. What does Mr Quigley say to all this?'

Hitherto he had felt an unreasonable antipathy to the young reporter, who had been a too frequent visitor to the clinic, and had written too much and too enthusiastically about Dr Marford's ventures to please a man who shrank instinctively from publicity.

'Mr Quigley has no right to raise any objections whatever.' There was a note of defiance in her voice. 'He is a very good friend—or was.'

There was an embarrassing pause.

'But isn't any longer,' said Dr Marford gently.

He experienced an inexplicable sense of kinship with Michael Quigley.

Her native loyalty made her modify her attitude.

'I like Michael—he is extraordinarily nice, but very domineering. He was awfully good to me the other night, and I was a beast to him. I was in the Howdah Club when that dreadful man came.'

He turned an inquiring face to her.

'Which dreadful man?'

'The robber—White Face.'

He nodded.

'Yes, I know. I read the newspapers. I was talking to Sergeant Elk about him. There is a theory that he lives in this neighbourhood, a theory for which I am afraid your young friend is responsible. Are you wise?'

He asked the question suddenly.

'About—my marriage? Is any girl wise, Dr Marford? Suppose I'd met this man every day of my life for years, should I know him—I mean, as one knows one's husband? Men always put on their best appearance for women, and unless one lives in the same house with them it is impossible to be absolutely sure.'

Marford nodded, fondling his bony chin.

There was a long silence, which he broke.

'I shall be sorry to lose you; you have been a most enthusiastic helper.'

Now she came to a delicate stage of the interview—delicate because she knew how sensitive he was on the point.

'I'd like to give the Institute a little present,' she said jerkily. 'A thousand pounds—'

He raised his hand; his expression was genuinely pained.

'No, no, no; I couldn't hear of it. You asked me once before if I would. No, I am satisfied that I have not paid you for the help you have given us. That is your splendid contribution to the clinic.'

She knew he would be adamant on this point and had already decided that if he refused her gift it should take the form of an anonymous donation on her wedding day. Michael, in one of his more cynical moods, had once accused her of being theatrical, and the charge was so ridiculous that she had laughed. Yet there is a touch of theatricality in every senti-mentalist, and Janice Harman was not without that weakness.

Unexpectedly the doctor put out his thin hand and took hers.

'I hope you will be happy,' he said, and this was at once a benediction and a dismissal.

She crossed the road at Endley Street. At the corner stood a tall, good-looking man, with greying hair at his temples. To her surprise he was talking to a woman, talking confidentially it seemed. Presently the woman walked away and he came, smiling, to meet the girl.

'What a ghastly place, darling! I am so happy you're leaving it.'

'Who was that woman you were speaking to?' she asked curiously.

He laughed—she loved that laugh of his.

'Woman? Oh, yes.' He looked round and nodded towards a slim figure walking ahead of them on the opposite side of the road. 'It was rather odd—she thought I was her brother, and when she saw she'd made a mistake she was a little embar-rassed. Rather a pretty girl.'

Her car was in a nearby garage—in the early days she had driven up to the clinic, which was at the far end of Endley Street, but the doctor had advised her against the practice—advice well justified, for in a week everything that was movable in the car had been stolen by the parents of the children she cared for.

She seated herself at the wheel, a radiant figure of youth, he thought, more beautiful than even he in his wildest imaginings had dreamed. The car came down the slope of the road; she saw the shabby figure of the doctor watching them, and waved her hand to him.

'Who was that?' he asked carelessly.

'That was Dr Marford.'

'Your boss, eh? I'd like to have had a look at him. He's a big noise around here, isn't he?'

She laughed at this.

'There isn't a tinier murmur in Tidal Basin,' she said. 'But he's marvellous! I sometimes think he starves himself to keep his clinic going.'

She rhapsodised all the way through the City. In Cranbourn Street they were held up by a traffic block. By this time he had gained command of the conversation and the excellences of Dr Marford were relegated to a second place. He was talking of South Africa and his two farms, one in the wilds of Rhodesia, the other amidst the beauties of Paarl. He liked talking of the Paarl property.

'It's going to be terribly slow for you, though there is some sort of social life at the Cape. I'm pretty well known—'

'There's somebody who knows you,' she laughed.

He turned his head quickly, but could distinguish amongst the hurrying throng on the sidewalk no familiar face.

'Where?' he asked.

'There—that dark man.' She looked back. 'He is standing by the hosiers.'

He looked round and frowned.

'Oh, yes, I know him—not very well, though; I got the better of him in a business deal, and he hasn't forgiven me.' He uttered an exclamation. 'Darling, I can't take you to the theatre tonight: I've just remembered. Will you forgive me?'

She was too happy, too completely under the fascination of this exalted adventure, to resent the missed engagement. This good-looking stranger who had come from the blue, whose name she could hardly use without an unaccountable sense of shyness, was Romance—the fulfilment of vague and delightful dreams. He was still outside the realms of reality.

She had known him for ten days; it seemed that it was a lifetime. Once or twice during the journey she was on the point of telling him of the surprise she had for him. He was a great home-lover; his self-confessed sin was that he coveted his neighbour's land. There was a farm adjoining his at Paarl that had come into the market, could be had for a mere £8,000. He waxed enthusiastic on the advantage of having this additional property—vineyards and orange groves, new pastures for his cattle.

He returned to the subject as the car was crossing Piccadilly Circus.

'You've made me ambitious, you angel,' he said. 'I'm a poor farmer and can't lay my hands on a fortune, so the farm will have to go.'

Again she was nearly telling him. She had a friend in Cape Town, a young lawyer, a Rhodes scholar, whom she had met at Oxford. That very morning she had wired to him, asking him to buy the property.

He parted from her at the door of her flat in Bury Street, and her chauffeur, who was waiting, drove him to his modest hotel. At parting: 'I hate the thought of losing that farm—if I could cable four thousand pounds tomorrow morning I could clinch the bargain.'

She smiled demurely and went up to her room to daydream of green slopes and high, sun-baked mountains where the little baboons chatter all day and night.

At ten o'clock that night, when she was undressing for bed, came a cablegram which left her white and shaking. It was in one sense remarkable that the first person she thought of to help her in her necessity was Michael Quigley; but when she reached for the telephone with a trembling hand it was to learn that Michael had left the office on a hurry call. She looked at the clock; it was by then half-past ten. She changed her mind about going to bed and began to dress quickly.

CHAPTER IV

AFTER Janice had left, Dr Marford walked slowly to that corner of the surgery where his drugs were stocked and began to dispense the medicines he had prescribed in the course of the day. This was generally his afternoon task, but he had spent most of the day at the clinic.

He wearied of the task very soon and went to his desk. There was a heap of papers to go through—the accounts from the clinic showed a heavy deficit. The place ate money: there was always new apparatus to buy, new equipment to furnish. The daily report from the convalescent home in Eastbourne, which maintained the progress of a dozen small hooligans of Tidal Basin, was as cheerless; but it brought no sense of depression to Dr Marford. He grudged nothing to these ventures of his—neither time nor exertion.

He was expecting a remittance almost any day. There was a man in Antwerp who sent him money regularly, and another in Birmingham—he pushed the papers aside, looked at his watch and went out by the side door into the yard.

It was a fairly large yard. At one end was the big shed in which old Gregory Wicks kept his taxicab, paying a small weekly rent.

Old Gregory Wicks had been a famous driver even in the days of the festive hansom. And always he had housed his horses and his resplendent cab in Tidal Basin, where he was born and where he hoped to end his days. In his advanced middle age came the taxicab. Gregory refused to regard motor vehicles as new-fangled crazes that would soon go out of fashion. He was one of the first to sit at a driving wheel at a motor school and solve the mysteries of clutches and gears. He found his lameness no obstacle in obtaining a cab-driver's licence—he limped from a thirty-year-old injury to his ankle.

Always he was a night bird; even in the horse cab he went clop-clopping along Piccadilly in the early hours of the morning, picking up swells from the clubs and driving them unimaginable distances to their country houses. And when the taxi came he continued his nocturnal wanderings. A silent, taciturn man, who never stood on a rank or invited the confidence of his brother drivers, he was known locally and abroad for his rigid honesty. It was he who restored to a certain Austrian baron a million kroners in hard paper cash, left in the cab by the Herr Baron in a moment of temporary aberration caused by a quarrel with a lady friend. Old Gregory had returned thousands of pounds' worth of goods left by absent-minded riders. In the police books he was marked 'Reliable; honest; very excellent record.'

You could see him and his cab on certain nights prowling along Regent Street, his long, white hair hanging over the collar of his coat, his fierce white moustache bristling from his pink, emaciated face, choosing his fares with a nice discrimination. He had no respect for any man save one. In his more than seventy-year-old arms he packed a punch that was disconcerting to the punchee.

The doctor unfastened a door and passed through into Gallows Court. That narrow and unsavoury passage was alive with children—bare-legged, unwashed and happy. Nobody offered the doctor a friendly greeting. The frowsy men and women lounging in the doorways or at the upstairs windows favoured him with incurious glances. He was part of the bricks and mortar and mud of the place, one with the brick wall which separated his yard from this human sty. He belonged there, had a right in Gallows Court, and, that being so, might pass without notice or comment.

The last house in the court was No. 9; smaller than the others; the windows were clean, and even the lower one, which was heavily shuttered, had a strip of chintz curtain. He knocked at the door—three short quick raps, a pause and a fourth. This signal had been agreed as between himself and old man Wicks; for Gregory had been annoyed by runaway knocks and by the appearance on his doorstep of unwelcome visitors. He knew the regular hour at which the milkman called and the baker, and could cope with them. Whosoever else knocked at the door during the daytime received no answer. Marford heard the shuffle of feet on uncarpeted stairs and the door was opened.

'Come in, doctor.' Gregory's voice was loud and hearty. He had been a shouter all his life, and age had not diminished the volume of his tone. 'Don't make a row; I expect the lodger's asleep,' he said as he closed the door with a slam.

'He must be a very good sleeper if you don't wake him, you noisy old man!' said Marford, with his quiet smile.

Gregory guffawed all the way up the stairs, opened the door of his room and the doctor passed in.

'How are you?'

'Fit as a flea, except this other little trouble, and I'm not going to mention that. I'm doing fine, doctor. Sit down. Where's a chair? Here we are! What I owe to you, doctor! If the people in Tidal Basin knew what you've done for me—'

'Yes, yes,' said Marford good-humouredly. 'Now let me have a look at you.'

He turned the old man's face to the light and made a careful examination.

'You're no better and no worse. If anything you're a little better, I should think. I'll test your heart.'

'My heart!' said the other scornfully. 'I've got the heart of a lion! There was an Irish family moved in here and the woman wanted to borrow a saucepan, and when I told her just what I thought of people who borrow saucepans, along came her husband—a new fellow, full of brag and bluster! I gave him one smack in the jaw and that was his finish!'

'You shouldn't do it, Gregory. It was a stupid thing to do. I heard about it from one of my other patients.'

The old man was chuckling gleefully.

'I needn't have done it at all,' he said. 'Any of the boys round here would have put him out if I'd said the word. I dare say the lodger would, but of course I wouldn't have wakened him up.'

'Is he here today?'

Gregory shook his head.

'The Lord knows! I never hear him come in or go out, except sometimes. I've never known a quieter fellow. Reformed, eh, doctor? I'll bet you I know who reformed him! You'd never dream'—he lowered his voice—'that he was a man who'd spent half his life in stir—'

'You're giving him a chance,' said Marford.

He was going, when the old man called him back.

'Doctor, I want to tell you something. I made my will today—not exactly a will, but I wrote down what I wanted doing with my money.'

'Have you got a lot, Gregory?' asked the other good-humouredly.

'More than you think.' There was a significance in the old man's voice. 'A lot more! It's not money that makes me do what I'm doing—it's pride—swank!'

To most men who had known him for years, Gregory Wicks was a taciturn and uncommunicative man. Marford was one of the few who knew him. He often thought that this loquacity which Gregory displayed at home was his natural reaction to the hours of silence on the box. Night after night for nearly half a century this old cabman had placed himself under a vow of silence. Once he explained why, and the reason was so inadequate that Marford, who was not easily amused, laughed in spite of himself. Gregory had in a talkative moment allowed a client—he always called his fares 'clients'—to wish a counterfeit half-crown upon him. It was a lesson never to be forgotten.

The doctor often came in to chat with the old man, to hear stories of dead and forgotten celebrities whose names were famous in the eighties and the late seventies. As he was leaving, Gregory referred again to his lodger.

'It was a good idea putting up that shutter to keep out the noise, though personally there's nothing that would stop me sleeping. I sometimes wish he'd be a bit more lively—'

'And come up and have a little chat with you at times?' suggested Marford.

Gregory almost shuddered.

'Not that! I don't want to chat with anybody, especially strangers. I chat with you because you've been God's-brother-Bill to me, to use a vulgar expression. I don't say I'd have starved, because I shouldn't have done. But I'd have lost something that I'd rather die than lose.'

He came down to the door and stood looking out after the doctor, even when Marford was out of sight. The noisy children did not gibe at him, and none of these frowsy ones hurled their inevitable and unprintable jests in his direction. A wandering policeman they would have covered with derision. Only the doctor and Gregory Wicks escaped their grimy humour; the latter because of that ready fist of his, the doctor—well, you never know when the doctor will be called in, and if he's got a grudge against you who knows what he'll slip into your medicine? Or suppose he had to use the knife, eh? Nice so-and-so fool you'd look, lying under chloroform with your inn'ards at his mercy! Fear was a governing factor of life in Gallows Court.

CHAPTER V

THAT he had no other friends was good and sufficient reason why Mr Elk should drop in at odd minutes to discuss with Dr Marford the criminal tendencies and depravities of that section of the British Empire which lies between the northern end of Victoria Dock Road and the smelly drabness of Silvertown.

Elk called on the evening Janice Harman took her farewell, and found Dr Marford's melancholy eyes fixed upon the dreary pageant of Endley Street. They were working overtime in the shipyard, which was almost opposite his surgery, and the din of mechanical riveters would go on during the night. Dr Marford was so accustomed to this noise that it was hardly noticeable. The sound of drunken songsters, the pandemonium which accompanied amateur pugilism, the shrill din of children playing in the streets—hereabouts they played till midnight—the rumbling of heavy lorries on the way to the Eastern Trading Company's yard which went on day and night never disturbed his sleep.

'If I was sure this was hell'—Mr Elk nodded his own gloomy face towards the thoroughfare—'I'd get religion. Not that I don't say my prayers every night—I do. I pray for the Divisional Inspector, the Area Inspector, the Big Five and the Chief Commissioner; I pray for the Examining Board and all other members of the criminal classes.'

The ghost of a smile illuminated the thin face of Dr Marford. He was a man of thirty-five who looked older. Spare of build, his greying hair was thin on the top. He wore absurd little side-whiskers half-way down his cheek, and gold-rimmed spectacles, one lens of which was usually cracked.

For a long time they stood in silence behind the calico curtains, attracting no attention from the passers-by, for there was no light in the surgery.

'My idea of hell,' said Elk again.

Dr Marford laughed softly.

'With its own particular devil, by all accounts,' he said.

Detective-Sergeant Elk permitted himself to guffaw.

'*That* bunk! Listen, these people believe anything. Funny thing, they don't read, so they couldn't have got the idea out of books. It's one of the—what do you call the word—um—damn it! I've got it on the end of my tongue . . .'

'Legends?'

'That's it—it's like the Russians passing through England with the snow on their boots. Everybody's met the man who saw 'em, but *you* never meet him. Every time there's a murder nobody can explain, *you* see it in the newspaper bills: "The Devil of Tidal Basin", an' even after you've pinched the murderer an' all the earth knows that he never heard of Tidal Basin, or thinks it's a patent wash-bowl, they still hang on to the idea. These newspapers! Next summer you'll have joy-wagons full of American trippers comin' here. Limehouse has had it, why shouldn't we?'

A bright young newspaper man had invented the Devil of the Basin. It was the general opinion in Tidal Basin that he wasn't any too bright either.

'There is a devil—hundreds of 'em! The waterside crowd wouldn't think twice of putting me out. They tried one night—Dan Salligan. The flowers I sent to the man when he was in hospital is nobody's business.'

Dr Marford moved uncomfortably.

'I'm afraid I helped that legend to grow. The reporter saw me and very—er—indiscreetly, I told him of the patient who used to come to me—he hasn't been for months, by the way—always came at midnight with his face covered with a mask. It wasn't good to see—the face, I mean. Explosion in a steel works.'

Elk was interested.

'Where does he live?'

The doctor shook his head.

'I don't know. The reporter tried to find out but couldn't. He always paid me in gold—a pound a visit, which is forty times more than I get from my regulars.'

Mr Elk was not impressed. His eyes were fixed upon the squalling larrikins in the roadway.

'Weeds!' he said, and the doctor laughed softly.

'Those ugly little boys are probably great political leaders of the future, or literary geniuses. Tidal Basin may be stiff with mute, inglorious Miltons,' he said.

Sergeant Elk of the Criminal Investigation Department made a noise that expressed his contempt.

'Nine-tenths of that crowd will pass through the hands of me and my successors,' he said drearily, 'and all your electric rays won't stop um! And such of them as don't finish in Dartmoor will end their days in the workhouse. Why they call it a workhouse, God knows. I've never known anybody to work in a workhouse except the staff. You know Mrs Weston?' he asked suddenly. 'A pretty woman. She's got the only respectable apartment in the Basin. All Ritzy—I went up there when some kids broke her windows. She's not much good.'

'If she's not much good,' said Marford, and again that ghost of a smile came and went, 'if she's not much good, I probably know her. If she's the kind of woman who doesn't pay her doctor's bills, I certainly know her. Why do you ask?'

Elk took a cigar from his pocket and bit off the end. It was obviously a good cigar. He had hoarded it so long that it had irregular fringes of leaf. He lit it with great deliberation and puffed enjoyably.

'She was saying that she knew you,' he said, fully two minutes after the question had been asked. 'Naturally I said a good word for you.'

'Say a few good words for the clinic,' said the doctor.

'I'm always doing it,' said Sergeant Elk complacently. 'You're wasting your time and other people's money, but I do it. That's a pretty nurse you've got—Miss Harman. Quigley the reporter's all gooey about her.'

'Yes,' said Dr Marford quietly.

He rose and pulled down the blind, went to a cupboard, took out a whisky bottle, a siphon and two glasses, and looked inquiringly at the detective.

'I'm off duty,' said Elk, 'if a detective is ever off duty.'

He pulled up a chair to the writing table. The doctor was already in his worn leather chair. 'Ever read detective stories?' asked Elk.

Dr Marford shook his head.

At that moment the telephone rang. He took up the instrument, listened for a while, asked a few questions, and put down the receiver.

'That's why I don't read detective or any other kind of stories,' he said. 'The population of Tidal Basin increases at a terrific rate, but not so rapidly as some people expect.'

He jotted a note down on a little pad.

'That's a come-at-once call, but I don't suppose they will require my attention till three o'clock tomorrow morning. Why detective stories?'

Sergeant Elk sipped at his whisky. He was not a man to be rushed into explanation.

'Because,' he said eventually, 'I'd like some of these clever Mikes to take my patrol for a couple of months. I saw an American crook play up in the West End the other night. It was all about who-did-it. First of all they introduced you to about twenty characters, told you where they were born and who their fathers were, and what money they wanted and who they were in love with—you couldn't help knowing that the fellow who did the murder was the red-nosed waiter. But that's not police work, Dr Marford. We're not introduced to the characters in the story; we don't know one. All we've got in a murder case is the dead man. What he is, who his relations are, where he came from, what was his private business—we've got to work all that out. We make inquiries here, there and everywhere, digging into slums, asking questions of people who've got something to hide.'

'Something to hide?' repeated the doctor.

Elk nodded.

'Everybody's got something to hide. Suppose you were a married man—'

'Which I am not,' interrupted Marford.

'We've got to suppose that,' insisted Elk. 'Your wife is abroad. You take a girl into the country . . .'

The doctor made faint noises of protest.

'We're supposin' all this,' conceded Elk. 'Such things have happened. And in the morning you look out of your window an' see a feller cut another feller's throat. You are a doctor and cannot afford to get your name into the papers. Are you going to the police and tell them what you saw? And are you going to stand up in court and tell them what you were doing out of town and the name of the lady you were with, and take the chance of it getting into all the papers? Or are you going to say nothing? Of course you are! That happens every day. In a murder case everybody has got something to hide, and that's why it's harder to get the truth about murder than any other kind of crime. Murder is a spot-light. You've got to take the stand and face a defending counsel who's out to prove that you're the sort of fellow that no decent jurywoman could ask to meet her young daughter.'

The detective sucked at his cigar for a long time in silence. Then he asked:

'Bit of a mystery, this woman Lorna Weston?'

The doctor's tired eyes surveyed him thoughtfully.

'I suppose so. They're all mysteries to me. I can't remember their names. God, what names they've got! Like the patterns of a dull wallpaper—one running into the other. Jackson,

Johnson, Thompson, Beckett, Dockett, Duckett, Roon, Doon, Boon . . . eh? And some without any names at all. I attended a young woman for three months—she was just "the young woman upstairs", or "Miss What's-her-name". Her landlady didn't know it. She was a waitress working nobody knew where. If she had died I couldn't have certified her. I called her Miss Smith—had to put some sort of name on the books. What does Mrs Weston do for a living?'

Mr Elk made a little grimace.

'Well, you know, she's . . . well, she goes West every night all dolled up.'

The doctor nodded.

'There are lots of 'em—a whole colony. Why do they live in this hell shoot? I suppose it's cheap. And their earnings are not what they were. One girl told me—but you can't believe 'em.'

He sighed heavily and sighed again.

'You can't believe anybody.'

Elk got up, drained his glass and reached for his hat.

'She wanted to know if you were an easy man to get on with. I got an idea she's a dope-getter. I don't know why, but I've just got that idea. There was a doctor in Silvertown who made a fortune out of it: he spent over a thousand on his defence when I got him to the Old Bailey . . .'

The doctor went out with him, and they arrived at the street door at an opportune moment.

The earlier sound of the battle had come to them in a confused hubbub of sound as they passed through the disinfected passage. As Marford opened the door he saw two men fighting, surrounded by a crowd. It was a fair fight, both men being well matched in point of physique and equally drunk. But they were too close to the granite kerb of the sidewalk. One of the combatants went down suddenly, and the grey, dusty kerbstone went red.

'Here—you!'

Elk made a grab at the victor and swung him round. The policemen came running and plunged through the crowd.

'Take this man.'

Elk handed over his dazed prisoner and shouldered his way through the tightly packed knot of people that surrounded the man on the kerb.

'Get him inside the doctor's shop. Lift him . . .'

They carried the limp thing into the surgery and Dr Marford made a brief examination whilst Mr Elk bustled the bearers into the street.

'Well?' he asked when he came back. 'Hospital case, isn't it?'

Marford was fixing an enormous pad of gauze and cotton-wool to the head of the white-faced man.

'Yes. Do you mind ringing the ambulance? Two shillings' worth of surgical dressings and I don't get a cent for it. You can't sue their relations—they need the money for a swell funeral. Everybody has to go into black, and that costs money.'

Elk screwed up his lips painfully.

'Is he booked?' he asked, looking at the figure with the awed curiosity which the living have for the dead.

'I should think so: compound fracture of the occiput. Get him to the London and they may do something. It costs me ten shillings a week just for surgical dressings. I'll tell you something, and you can arrest me. If I get 'em alone, I go through their pockets and take the cost of the dressing. But usually they've got some howling women with 'em who won't leave 'em. "When pain and anguish wring the brow," eh?'

The ambulance came noisily and the patient was taken away.

It was an incident not worth remembering—except for two shillings' worth of dressing that would never be liquidated.

The doctor closed the door upon Mr Elk, and went back to his books and his thoughts. Two inconvenient new lives were coming to Tidal Basin. The district nurses would call him in good time. Inconvenient . . . the children of an unemployable labourer and a father who was resting in one of His Majesty's prisons.

As to this Lorna Weston . . .

He knew her, of course. She often passed the surgery on her way to the provisions store next door, and once or twice she had come in to see him. A pretty woman, though her mouth was a trifle hard and straight. He never confessed to Elk that he knew anybody. Elk was a detective and respected no confidences.

There was a 'phone call from Elk. The fighter had died on admission to hospital. The doctor was not surprised. An inquest, of course.

'We shall want you as a witness,' said Elk's voice. 'He's a dock labourer from Poplar—a man named Stephens.'

'How thrilling!' said the doctor, hung up the receiver and went back to his book—the intrigues of Louis's court, the scheming Polignacs and the profitable machinations of Madame de Lamballe.

He heard the shrill call of the door-bell, looked plaintively round, finally rose and went to the door. The night had come down blackly; the pavement outside was glistening: you do not hear the rain falling in the East End.

'Are you Dr Marford?'

The woman who stood in the doorway exhaled the faint fragrance of some peculiarly delicate perfume. Her voice, thin for the moment with anxiety, had the quality of culture. She was a stranger; he had never heard that voice before.

'Yes. Will you come in?'

The surgery had no other light than the reading-lamp on the desk. He felt that she would have had it this way.

She wore a leather motoring coat and a little tight-fitting hat. She unfastened the coat hurriedly as though she were hot or had some difficulty in breathing. Under the coat she wore a neat blue costume. From some vague clue, he thought she was American. A lady undoubtedly, having no association with Tidal Basin, unless she was a passenger on the Moroccan boat which sailed with the tide from Shrimp Wharf.

'Is he—is he dead?' she asked jerkily, and in her dark eyes he read an unconquerable fear.

'Is who dead?'

He was puzzled; searched his mind rapidly for patients *in extremis* and could find none but old Sully, the marine store dealer, who had been dying for eighteen months.

'The man—he was brought here . . . after the fight. A policeman told me . . . they were fighting in the street and he was brought here.'

She stood, her hands clasped, her thin body bent forward towards him, breathless.

'A man? . . . Oh, yes; he's dead, I'm afraid.'

Dr Marford was for the moment bewildered. How could she be interested in the fate of one Stephens, dock labourer, of Poplar?

'Oh, my God!'

She whispered the words, dropped for a second. Dr Marford's arm went round her and assisted her to a chair.

'Oh, my God!' she said again and began to cry.

He looked at her helplessly, not knowing for whom he could frame a defence—for the dead or the living.

'It was a fair fight as far as one could see,' he said awkwardly. 'The man fell . . . hit his head on the sharp edge of the kerb . . .'

'I begged him not to go near him,' she said a little wildly. 'I begged him! When he telephoned to say he was on his track and had traced him here . . . I came by cab . . . I implored him to come back.'

All this and more came incoherently. Dr Marford had to guess what she said. Some of the words were drowned in sobs. He went to his medicine shelf and took down a bottle labelled 'Ap. Am. Arm.', poured a little into a medicine glass and added water.

'You drink this and tell me all about it,' he said authoritatively.

She told him more than she would have told her confessor. Sorrow, remorse, the crushing tragedy of fear removed all inhibitions. The doctor listened, looking down at her, twiddling the stem of the medicine glass in his fingers.

Presently he spoke.

'This man Stephens was a dock labourer—a heavy fellow, six feet tall at least. A fair-haired man. The other man was a young fellow of twenty something. I only saw him for a second when he was in the hands of the police. He had a light, almost a white, moustache—'

She stared up at him.

'Fair . . . a young man . . ?'

Dr Marford held the glass out to her.

'Drink this; you're hysterical. I hate telling you so.'

But she pushed the glass aside.

'Stephens—are you sure? Two, well, two ordinary men? . . ?'

'Two labourers—both drunk. It's not unusual in this neighbourhood. We have an average of two fights a night. On Saturday nights—six. It's a dull place and they have to do something.'

The colour was coming back to her face. She hesitated, reached for the glass, swallowed its contents and made a wry face.

'Sal volatile . . . beastly!'

She wiped her lips with a handkerchief she took from her bag and rose unsteadily to her feet.

'I'm sorry, doctor. I've been a nuisance. I suppose if I offered to pay you for your time you'd be offended.'

'I charge ten cents for a consultation,' he said gravely, and she smiled.

'How accommodating you are! You think I am American? I am, of course, though I've lived in England since—oh, for a long time. Thank you, doctor. Have I talked a lot of nonsense, and, if I have, will you forget it?'

Dr Marford's thin face was in the shadow: he was standing between her and the lamp.

'I won't promise that; but I will not repeat it,' he said.

She did not give him her name: he was wholly incurious. When he offered to walk with her until she found a cab, she declined his escort. He stood in the drizzling rain and watched her out of sight.

Police-Constable Hartford came from the direction she had taken and stopped to speak.

'They say that Stephens is dead. Well, if they will drink, they must expect trouble. I've never regretted taking the pledge myself—I'll be Chief Templar in our lodge this summer if Gawd spares me. I sent a young lady; she was makin' inquiries about Stephens. I didn't know he was gone or I'd have told her.'

'Thank you, for not telling her,' said Marford.

He was shy of P.C. Hartford, who was notoriously loquacious and charged with strange long words.

He locked the door and went back to his book, but the corruptions and permutations of Madame de Lamballe interested him no more.

Pulling up the surgery blind, he looked out into the deserted street. There was some sort of movement in progress under the shadow of the wall which encircles the premises of the Eastern Trading Company.

He saw a man and a woman talking. There was light enough from the street standard to reveal this much. The man was in evening dress, which was curious. The white splash of his shirt front was plainly visible. Even waiters do not wear their uniform in Tidal Basin.

Dr Marford went out and opened the street door as the man and the woman walked in opposite directions. Then he saw the third of the trio. He was moving towards the man in evening dress, following him quickly. The doctor saw the first man stop and turn. There was an exchange of words and a scuffle. The man in dress clothes went down like a log, the second bent over him and went on quickly and disappeared under the railway arch which crosses Endley Street, opposite the Eastern Company's main gateway.

Dr Marford watched, fascinated, was on the point of crossing to see what had happened to the inanimate heap on the pavement, when the man got up and lit a cigarette.

The clock struck ten.

CHAPTER VI

LOUIS LANDOR looked down at the hateful thing he had struck to the earth. He lay very still and the hate in Landor's heart was replaced by a sudden horror. He glanced across the road. Immediately opposite was a doctor's surgery—a red light burned dimly from a bracket-lamp before the house to advertise the profession of its occupant. He saw the door was open and somebody was standing there. Should he go for help? The idea came and went. His own safety was in question. He hurried along in the shadow of the high wall and had reached the railway arch, when right ahead of him appeared the shadowy figure of a policeman, and the policeman was coming his way. He looked round for some way of escape. There were two great gates on his right and in one a small wicket door. In his panic he pushed the door and it yielded. By some miracle it had been left unfastened. In a second he was inside, felt for the bolt and pushed it home. The policeman passed without being conscious of his presence.

P.C. Hartford was at that moment composing a little speech which he intended to deliver at the next lodge meeting, where matters of very considerable interest were to be discussed. His thoughts being so centred, it was not unlikely that he should miss seeing the fugitive.

A certain Harry Lamborn, who was by trade a general larcenist, and who at that moment was standing in the shelter of a deeply-recessed door on the opposite side of the road, had less excuse, except that his eye was on the approaching copper and that he had little interest in ordinary civilians. That night he had certain plans connected with No. 7 warehouse of the Eastern Trading Company, and he was waiting for P.C.

Hartford to reach the end of his beat and return before he put them into operation.

He watched the constable's leisurely stride, drew back still farther into the recess which afforded him freedom from observation and protection from the falling rain, and transferred a collapsible jemmy from one pocket to another for greater comfort.

Hartford could not help seeing the man in evening dress. He stood squarely in the middle of the side-walk, wiping the mud from his black overcoat. Instantly Hartford descended from the dais of Vice-Templar and became a human police constable.

'Had a fall, sir?' he asked cheerfully.

The man turned a good-looking face to the officer and smiled. Yet he was not wholly amused, for his hands were trembling violently and the whiteness of his lips was in odd contrast to his sunburnt face. And when he spoke he was so breathless that the words came in gasps. Rain had been falling; there was a brown, muddy patch on his overcoat. He looked backward, the way he had come, and seemed relieved when he saw nobody.

'Have I had a fall?' he repeated. 'Well, I think I have.'

He looked past the constable. 'Did you see the man?'

Police-Constable Hartford looked back along the deserted stretch of pavement.

'Which man?' he asked, and the other seemed surprised.

'He went your way; he must have passed you.'

Hartford shook his head.

'No, sir, nobody's passed me.'

The white-lipped man was sceptical.

'Did he do anything?' asked Hartford.

'Did he do anything?' The stranger had a trick of repeating questions and tinging them with contempt. 'He punched me in the jaw, if that's anything. I played possum.' His face twisted in a smile. 'Scared him—I hope.'

He gave a certain emphasis to the last words. Police-Constable Hartford surveyed him with greater interest.

'Would you like to charge the man?' he asked.

The other was fixing his white silk neck-cloth and shook his head.

'Do you think you could find him if I charged him?' he asked sarcastically. 'No; let him go.'

'A stranger to you, sir?'

P.C. Hartford had not handled a case for a month and was loath to let his fingers slide off the smooth edge of this.

'No; I know him.'

'There's a bad crowd about here,' began Hartford. 'A drunken, dissipated—?'

'I know him, I tell you.' The stranger was impatient.

He dived his hand into an inside pocket, took out a silver case and opened it. P.C. Hartford stood by while the man lit his cigarette, and noticed that the hand which held the patent lighter was shaking.

'Here's a drink for you.'

Hartford bridled, and waved aside the proffered coin.

'I neither touch, taste nor 'andle,' he said virtuously, and stood ready to pass on his majestic way.

The stranger unbuttoned his coat and felt in his waistcoat pocket.

'Lost anything?'

'Nothing,' said the other with satisfaction.

He blew a cloud of smoke, nodded, and they separated.

The man in evening dress came slowly to where a granite-paved roadway bisected the path before the gates of the Eastern Trading Company. The thief in the covered doorway saw him take his cigarette from his mouth, drop it on the pavement and put his foot upon it. And then, suddenly and without warning, he saw the white-faced man stagger; his knees gave from under him and he went down with a crash to the sidewalk.

Lamborn was an opportunist—saw here a gift from heaven in the shape of a drunken swell; looked left and right, and crossed the road with stealthy footsteps. He did not see Hartford moving towards him in the shadow of the wall. Lamborn flicked open the coat of the stricken man, dived in his hand and found a note-case. His fingers hooked to a watch-guard; he pulled both out with a simultaneous jerk and then saw the running policeman. To be arrested on suspicion is one thing; to be found in possession of stolen property is another. Lamborn's hand jerked up to the high wall which surrounded the company's yard, and he turned to fly. Half a dozen paces he took, and then the hand of the law fell on him, and the familiar 'Here, you!' came hatefully to his ears. He struggled impotently. Mr Lamborn had never learned the first lesson of criminality, which is to go quietly.

Hartford thrust him against the wall, and then saw somebody crossing the road, and remembered the man lying under the lamp-post as he recognised the figure.

'Doctor—that gentleman's hurt. Will you have a look at him?'

Dr Marford had seen the stranger fall and stooped gingerly by his side.

'Keep quiet, will yer?' said Hartford indignantly to his struggling prisoner.

His whistle sounded shrilly in the night. There were moments when even Lamborn grew intelligent.

'All right, it's a cop,' he said sullenly, and ceased to struggle.

It was at that moment that the policeman heard an exclamation from the stooping, peering doctor.

'Constable—this man is dead—stabbed!'

He held up his hands for the policeman's inspection. In the light of the standard Hartford saw they were red with blood.

Elk, who was at the end of the street keeping a spieling house under observation, heard the whistle and came flying towards the sound. Every kennel in Tidal Basin heard it and was drawn. Men and women forfeited their night's rest rather than lose the thrill of experience; when they heard it was no less than murder they purred gratefully that their enterprise was rewarded. They came trickling out like rats from their burrows. There was a crowd almost before the uniformed police arrived to control it.

When Elk came back from 'phoning the divisional surgeon the doctor was washing his hands in a bucket of water that the policeman had brought for him.

'Mason's at the station; he's coming along.'

'Here, Elk, what's the idea of holding me?'

Lamborn's voice was pained and hurt. He stood, a wretchedly garbed figure of uncouth manhood, between two towering policemen, but his spirit was beyond suppression.

'I've done nothing, have I? This rozzer pinched me—'

'Shut up,' said Elk, not unkindly. 'Mr Mason will be along in a minute.'

Lamborn groaned.

'Him!' he almost howled. 'Sympathetic Mason, what a night for a party!'

Chief Detective Inspector Mason was visiting his area that night, and was in the police station when the call was put through. He came in the long, powerful police tender with a host of detectives and a testy and elderly police surgeon. Dr Rudd was a police surgeon because it offered him the maximum interest for the minimum of labour. He was a bachelor, with an assured income from investments, but he liked the authority which his position gave him; liked to see policemen touching their helmets to him as he passed them on the street; was impressed by the support he received from magistrates when he declared as drunk those influential people who brought their own doctors from Harley Street to prove that they suffered from nothing more vicious than shell-shock.

He knew Dr Marford slightly, and favoured him with a cold nod; resented his being in the case at all, for the penny doctor was one of the poor relations of the profession, not the kind of man one would call into a consultation, supposing Dr Rudd called in anybody.

He made a careful examination of the still figure.

'Dead, of course,' he said.

He gave the impression that, had he arrived a little earlier, the tragedy might have been averted.

'There is a knife wound,' began Marford, 'which penetrated—'

'Yes, yes,' said Dr Rudd impatiently. 'Of course. Naturally.'

He looked at Mr Mason.

'Dead,' he said. 'I will make an examination. Obviously a knife wound. Death was probably instantaneous.'

He looked at Marford.

'Were you here when it happened?'

'Soon after,' said Marford; 'a minute after—probably less than that.'

'Ah, then,' said Dr Rudd, his hands in his pockets, his legs apart, 'you'll be able to tell us something—'

Mason intervened. He was a bald man, with a humorous eye and a deep, unctuous voice.

'Yes, yes, we'll see all about that, doctor.'

He showed no resentment at this attempt to usurp his function; was almost jovial in the face of an impertinence which was not an unusual experience when Dr Rudd was in a case.

'We'll see all about that. Doctor—'

'Marford.'

'Doctor Marford, you were here when the murder was committed or soon after: you'll be able to tell us something, I'm sure. But now naturally you're a little upset.'

Marford smiled and shook his head. 'There's nothing I can tell you, Mr Mason, except that I saw the man fall.'

'I'm detaining this man, sir.' It was Hartford, stiffly saluting, more important than a Chief Commissioner on his first case.

Mason bent down over the body and let the powerful rays of his hand-lamp pry into ugly places.

'Where is the knife?' he asked. 'We want to look after that.'

'There is no knife,' said Elk, with gloomy satisfaction.

'Excuse me, sir.' P.C. Hartford, unrebuffed, stood regimentally stiff: accuser, prosecutor and expositor all in one. 'I've got a man here detained in custody.'

Mason became aware of his humble subordinate, took him in from the rose on the crest of his helmet to the toes of his large, polished boots.

'He should be at the police station,' he said gently.

It was Elk who explained.

'I kept the man here, sir, till you arrived.'

Mr Mason put his little finger in his ear and twiddled it impatiently.

'All right,' he said. 'It's a pleasure to know that everything is being done in strict accordance with the rules of procedure. You seem to have a nice bunch of highly intelligent police officers in your division, Inspector.'

He addressed Divisional Inspector Bray, who accompanied him; but Bray had no sense of humour, and was entirely oblivious of sarcasm.

'They're a pretty useful lot,' he said complacently.

Mr Mason looked at the body at his feet, and thence to the man held between the two policemen, and back to the body again.

'No knife . . . You might search the body, will you, Elk? Help him, will you, Shale? Thank you.'

He peered round at the crowd, and there were a few who, desiring at the moment to escape his scrutiny, melted quietly into the darkness.

At any rate he had seemed oblivious of the presence of Dr Marford, who was silent in an atmosphere charged with hostility to penny doctors. Suddenly Elk lugged something from beneath the body.

'Here you are, sir.'

It was a knife-sheath, and at the moment was not pleasant to handle. Mr Mason found an old envelope in his pocket and took it carefully.

'Is the knife there?'

'No.'

Bray had joined the search party and was emphatic on the point. They had moved the body slightly.

'No knife.' Mason looked up at the high wall. 'It might have been thrown over there,' he mused.

'Excuse me, sir.' Constable Hartford froze to attention.

'Wait,' said Mason. 'Now tell me, doctor, what did you see?'

He addressed Marford, who, brought suddenly into the ambit of publicity, stammered and was ill at ease.

'I came out of my surgery'—he pointed awkwardly—'that place with the red light. I—er—heard two men fighting—I thought I heard a little altercation before then—and I went in and got my hat and mackintosh—'

'So you'd have a better view of the fight, eh, doctor?' Mason smiled blandly.

Marford could return the smile now.

'Not exactly,' he said. 'Fights are not a novelty in this particular neighbourhood. I was going out to see a case—a maternity case. When I came out I heard the commotion. The policeman was arresting a man when I came over—'

'Wait,' said Mason sharply. 'You saw two men fighting— could you distinguish them?'

'Not plainly,' Marford shook his head, 'although they were opposite my surgery.'

'Very handy for them,' said Mason. 'Was one of them this man?'

Marford could not swear. He was rather inclined to think it was. He was certain one of them was in evening dress.

'You don't know him?'

Marford shook his head again.

'I should think he's a stranger in this neighbourhood; I've never seen him here before. When I saw him lying on the ground I thought that it was a resumption of the fight I had witnessed.'

Mr Mason whistled softly, fixing his eyes just under the doctor's chin. Marford thought his collar was awry and put up his hand, but that was a practice of Mr Mason, who was sometimes called 'Sympathetic Mason'.

'Hartford.' He beckoned the constable forward. 'What did you see?'

P.C. Hartford saluted.

'Sir,' said the constable punctiliously, 'I had seen the deceased—'

A look of weariness passed across the face of Mr Mason. He was not sympathetic with loquacious constables.

'Yes, yes, my boy, but you're not in court now, you know. You needn't call him "the deceased". I don't mind what you call him. You saw him before he fell?'

P.C. Hartford saluted again.

'Yes, sir, I saw him. He stopped me when I was passing and asked me if I'd met a man he'd had an argument with. I said "No".'

'Did he describe the man?'

'No, sir,' said Hartford.

'He said nothing else?'

Hartford thought for a long time, and then repeated, as best he could remember, all that the white-faced man had said.

'You didn't meet his assailant—I mean, you weren't dreaming about the beer you were going to have for supper?'

P.C. Hartford was prepared with an indignant repudiation, but swallowed it.

'No, sir. A few minutes later, when I came back this way, I saw him lying under the lamp, and I saw another man walking away and I stopped him. Then I saw the doctor coming across. By this time I'd arrested Lamborn, who tried to run away.'

'Oh, no!' said Mason, pained.

Mr Lamborn grew voluble. He was running for a doctor, he protested.

'The man was on the ground before you touched him: is that what you're suggesting?' asked Mason.

The prisoner not only suggested but swore to this fact. He had a witness, a woman who carried a can in her hand. She might have preferred to remain anonymous, but that natural sense of justice which is the possession of poor and innocent people overcame her modesty. She was haled forward into the clear circle. She was a respectable woman. She had seen the man fall, had been a witness of Lamborn going across to him. If she had any private views as to the motive for his attentions she wisely restrained them.

Mason looked at her thoughtfully.

'What is in that can?' he asked.

There was a lid to the can. All her inclinations were against satisfying his curiosity, but she had a respect for the law and told the truth.

'Beer.'

Mason seemed oblivious of the dead man behind him, of the thief in custody, and of the very existence of secret murderers who stalked their prey on the highway.

'Beer—that's funny.' A clock chimed half-past ten. 'Why are you carrying beer about the street at half-past ten, Mrs—'

Her name was Albert. She had no explanation for the beer, except, she explained tremulously, that she was taking it home. There was a sympathetic murmur in the crowd. An anonymous revolutionary said 'Leave the woman alone!' There are always voices that offer the same advice to policemen in all parts of the world in similar circumstances.

P.C. Hartford was desperate. He had something to say—something vital, a solution which would sweep aside all the cobwebs of mystery which surrounded the pitiful heap lying under the electric light standard and yielding very little to the busy men who were searching it.

'I wanted to say, sir, that I saw this man throwing something over the wall.'

Mason looked at the wall, as though he expected it to give confirmation of this statement.

'Lamborn, you mean?' He glanced keenly at the thief and jerked his head significantly. 'Take him away,' he said; 'I'll see him at the station.'

Mr Lamborn went between two policemen, hurling back sanguinary defiance. There is something of a terrier in the habitual crook: he stands up to punishment most gallantly.

'I'll see you at the station, too, ma'am,' said Mason.

Mrs Albert nearly dropped her can in her agitation. She was a married woman with four children, and had never entered a police station in her life.

'It's never too late to learn,' said Mason sympathetically.

Another ambulance came, one of the baser kind, hand-pushed, and then a police car, with photographers, cheerful fingerprint experts and men of the Identification Bureau. Wilful murder lost its romance and passed into its business stage.

'Just plain murder,' said Mason to his subordinates as he moved towards his car. 'One or two queer features about it, though.'

And then through the crowd came a woman. He thought she was a girl, but in the cruel light of the arc lamp saw that she had left girlhood a long way behind her. She was white-faced, wide-eyed, a ghost of a woman; her trembling lips parted, for the moment inarticulate. She stared from one to the other. Dr Marford, from the shadows, watched her curiously; knew her for Lorna Weston, a lady of uncertain profession.

'Is it—he?'

Her voice, starting as a croak, ended in a wail.

'Who are you?' Mason stood squarely before her.

'I'm—I live around here.' She spoke spasmodically; every sentence seemed an effort. 'He came to see me tonight, and

I warned him . . . of the danger. You see, I—I know my husband. He's a devil! I somehow know it.'

'Your husband killed this man, eh?'

She tried to push past him, but he held her back with some difficulty, for fear had given this frail body the strength of a man.

'Steady, steady, my girl. It may not be your friend at all. What's his name?'

'Donald—' She checked herself. 'May I see him? . . . I'll tell you.'

But Mr Mason must proceed methodically, in the way of his kind, consolidating the foundations of fact.

'This is what you say, that this man came to visit you tonight, and you warned him against your husband. Now, is your husband living in this area?'

She looked at him blankly. He realised that her mind was not upon his questions and repeated it.

'Yes,' she said. There was a certain defiance in her voice.

'Where does your husband live? What's his name?'

She was moving from side to side, and stooped once to look under his arm at the still thing on the ground.

'Let me see him,' she pleaded. 'I shan't faint . . . it may not be he. I'm sure it's not he. Let me see him!' Her voice was a whine now.

Mr Mason nodded to Elk, and Elk took her by the arm and led her to where the man lay, half in and half out of the circle of light. She looked down, speechless; opened her lips but could say nothing. And then:

'Donald . . . he did it! The swine! The murderer!'

She stopped speaking. Elk felt her sagging away from him and caught her round the waist. The Tidal Basin crowd watched the drama. It was well worth the loss of a night's sleep.

Mason looked round, caught Marford's eye and beckoned him forward.

'Do you mind taking this woman to the station? I think it's only a faint.'

Dr Marford protested wearily. He and a policeman carried the woman to a closed police car and they drove off. Outside a chemist's shop at the end of Basin Street, Marford stopped the car and sent the constable to ring the night bell; but the restorative he secured did not bring the woman back to consciousness. She was still silent when he got her to the station.

Mr Mason, waiting for the return of the car, delivered himself of certain observations.

'There's murder plain and murder coloured,' he said to the patient Inspector Bray. 'This is murder plain. No music, no fireworks, no lady's boudoir, nothing sexy. A man stabbed to death under three pairs of eyes and nobody saw the murderer. No knife, no motive, no clue, no name of the dear departed.'

'The woman,' began Bray, 'talked about a devil—'

'Let's keep religion out of it,' said Mason wearily. 'Who was the man that threw the knife, and how did he get it back again? That's the mystery that's beating me.'

CHAPTER VII

QUIGLEY, crime man of the *Post-Courier* and arch-inventor of devils, telephoned through to his newspaper:

'The devil of Tidal Basin is again abroad. This slinking and sinister shadow passed unseen through deserted Endley Street and left a dead man sprawling upon the sidewalk, stabbed to the heart. Whence he came, whither he went, none knows. Under the eyes of three independent witnesses, including Mrs Albert, the wife of the night watchman at the Eastern Trading Company, Dr Warley' (names were Quigley's weak point), 'a highly respected medical practitioner, and Police-Constable Hartford, an innocent pedestrian was seen to stagger and fall. When the horrified spectators reached his side they were dumbfounded to see that he was stabbed. The identity of the murdered man has not yet been established. Who was this stranger in evening dress, wandering in the purlieus of Tidal Basin? What ruthless hand destroyed him, and in what mysterious manner did the unseen murderer make his escape? These are the questions which Central Detective Mason has to solve. Mason, one of the Big Five, was fortunately in the neighbourhood, and immediately took charge of the case. A man has been detained, but is he the devil of Tidal Basin?'

('Cut out all that devil stuff,' said the night editor as he handed the copy to a sub. 'It's been overworked.')

Elk came to the police station and into the inspector's room, where Mason was sitting, ten minutes after his chief arrived. He laid two articles on the table before the great man.

'That night watchman takes a lot of waking. By the way, he's the husband of Mrs Albert—'

'The woman with the beer?'

Elk nodded.

'I found these in the yard—obviously Lamborn threw them over when he saw the policeman.'

He enumerated his finds.

'Notebook and watch; glass broken, watch stopped at ten p.m. Swiss made, and has the name of a Melbourne jeweller on the face.'

Mason examined the watch.

'Careful,' warned Elk. 'There's a smudgy thumb-print on the back.'

Mason shifted his chair a little, and invited Elk by a gesture to draw another up to his side.

'What else?' he asked.

Elk took from an inside pocket a quantity of loose paper money and put it on the table. The pocket-case, which also contained a memorandum book, he opened, and extracted two new banknotes, each for a hundred pounds. On their backs was the stamp of the Maida Vale branch of the Midland Bank; it was a round rubber stamp, and in the centre was a date line.

'Issued yesterday.'

'If he'd got an account there—' began Elk.

Mason shook his head.

'He hadn't. You don't draw hundred-pound notes out of your own account and carry them about with you. You draw them out because you want to send them away. You couldn't change a hundred-pound note in London without running the risk of being arrested. No, these notes were drawn from somebody else's account and given to him. Which means that he hasn't a banking account of his own or they'd have been paid in. Therefore he's not in trade, or he'd have a banking account.'

Elk sniffed.

'Sounds like the well-known Shylock Holmes to me,' he said.

He was a contemporary of Mason's who had missed promotion, and his sarcasms were licensed.

'What else?' asked Mason.

'Visiting-cards—any number of them.'

Elk took them out and laid them on the table. Mason examined them carefully. There were addresses in Birmingham and Leicester and London, but a large proportion of them were the visiting cards of people who had a permanent address in South Africa.

'All the same colour,' he said. 'They've all been collected within a couple of months. That means he's been a sea voyage lately—it's extraordinary how people give away their cards to perfect strangers when they're taking an ocean trip.'

He looked at the backs of one or two of them; there were pencilled notes. One said: '£10,000 a year'; another: 'Made a lot of money in Namaqualand Diamonds; staying Ritz, London.'

Mason smiled.

'I'll give you two guesses as to what his trade is.'

He picked up a third card; this time the inscription on the back was in ink: 'Cheque stopped; Adam & Sills.'

'I'll give you one guess now. He's a crook and a card-sharp. Adam & Sills are the lawyers who do the barking for these kind of birds. That places him. Now we'll find his name. Get on to the Yard, tell 'em to call every hotel, big and small, in the West End, and find if a man has arrived there from abroad. Say that his first name is Donald. You'll find out where he came from—'

'Cape Town,' said Elk.

Mason nodded.

'I expected that. How do you know?'

'His boots are new; they've got a tag to them, "Cleghorn, Adderley Street".'

'Then make it South Africa,' said Mason.

Elk was half-way across the room when Mason shouted him back.

'Ask the bureau to give you the name, private address and telephone number of the manager of the Maida Vale branch of the Midland Bank. Wait a minute, don't rush me—tell the bureau to get on to the manager and find if he remembers on whose account two notes for a hundred pounds'—he scribbled down the numbers on a slip of paper and handed them to Elk—'were issued, and, if possible, to whom they were issued. I've got an idea we shan't discover that.'

When Elk returned, Mr Mason was sitting, chin in hand, his heavy, round face more than ordinarily blank.

'I'll see Lamborn,' he said.

Mr Lamborn was brought from the detention-room, voluble and truculent.

'If there's a law in this country—' he began.

'There isn't,' said Mr Mason genially. 'You've broken 'em all. Sit down, Harry.'

Mr Lamborn looked at him suspiciously.

'You goin' to be sympathetic?' he asked.

The glamour of legend surrounded Mr Mason. He was indeed a sympathetic man, and under the genial influence of his understanding and sympathetic heart many wrong-doers had, with misguided confidence, told him much more than they ever intended to tell, a fact which they had bitterly regretted when they stood before a jury and heard their frank-ness exploited with disastrous effect.

Mason beamed.

'I can't be wicked with you fellows—naturally I can't.' His voice was at its most unctuous. 'Life's a bit difficult for all of us, and I know just how hard it is for some of you birds to get an honest living.'

'I dessay,' said Lamborn icily.

'You never do any harm, Harry'—Mr Mason laid his hand upon the other's knee and patted it softly—'by telling the police all you know. It isn't much, because, if you knew enough to come in out of the rain, you wouldn't be thieving for a living. But this is a case of murder.'

'Nobody says I did it,' said Lamborn quickly.

'Nobody says so at the moment,' agreed Mr Mason pleasantly; 'but you never can tell what stories get around. You know Tidal Basin, Harry—they'd swear your life away for a slice of pineapple. Now let's be perfectly open and above-board.'

He leaned back in his chair and surveyed the other with fatherly benevolence.

'The constable saw you go over to this man and put your hand in his pocket, take out a pocket-book and possibly a watch. When you were detected you threw them over the wall, where they have since been found by Detective-Sergeant Elk. Isn't that so, Elk?'

'I know nothing about 'em,' said Lamborn loudly, and Mr Mason shook his head with a sad smile.

'You saw this fellow fall and you thought he was soused. You went over and you dipped him for his clock and pack.'

'I don't understand what you're talking about,' said Mr Lamborn rapidly. 'I've never heard such expressions in me life.'

'Let me put it in plain English,' said Mason gently. 'You put your hand in his pocket and took out his pocket-case and his watch.'

'That,' said Lamborn emphatically, 'is a damn dirty lie!'

Mr Mason sighed, and looked at Elk despairingly.

'What can you do with 'em?' he asked.

'I don't want none of your sympathy,' said the ungracious Lamborn. 'There's too many people in stir through listening to your smarming. I see the gentleman fall and I went over to render him assistance.'

'Medical assistance, I'm sure,' murmured Mason, 'you being an M.D. of Dartmoor and having learnt first aid at Wormwood Scrubs. Now come across, Harry. You can save me a lot of trouble by telling the truth.'

'I—' began Lamborn

'Wait a moment.' The reservoir of Mr Mason's urbanity was running low and his voice was a little sharper. 'If you'll tell me the truth I'll undertake not to charge you. I shall hold you as a Crown witness—'

'Look here, Mr Mason,' said Lamborn hotly, 'what sort of a can do you think I am? I've been treated disgraceful since I've been at this station. They stripped me naked and took all me clothes away. They haven't even a sense of decency! Give me these old duds to put on. And why did they take me clothes away? To frame up evidence by puttin' stuff in me pocket—I know the police!'

Mason sighed, and when he spoke it was very deliberately and offensively.

'If you had a little more brains you'd be half-witted,' he said. 'That's not an original remark, but it applies. There are men twice as sane as you living in padded cells. You poor, ignorant gutter scum, don't you understand that your clothes were taken away to see if there was any blood on them, and that your dirty hands were examined for the same reason? And don't you realise that a man of my rank wouldn't trouble even to spit at you if he hadn't a very good reason? I don't want you for murder—get that into your sawdust. I don't even want you for robbery. I want you to tell me the truth: did you, or did you not, dip this man when he was lying on the ground? And if you tell me the truth I'll offer no charge against you. Let me tell you this.' He leaned forward and tapped the other's knee with a heavy knuckle. 'You won't be able to understand it, but I'm doing my duty when I tell you. The whole of this case may swing upon whether you make a voluntary statement that you took this man's pocket-case out of his pocket—the watch doesn't matter—whilst he was lying on the ground, or that you did not.'

'I didn't,' said Lamborn loudly. 'I defy you to prove it!'

The chief inspector groaned.

'Take him away before I forget myself,' he said simply.

Elk gripped the arm of his prisoner and marched him to the desk.

'You fool,' he said *en route*, 'why didn't you speak?'

Lamborn snorted.

'Why didn't I speak?' he demanded scornfully. 'Blimey, look what I'm getting for saying nothin'!'

A minute later he was charged before an apathetic station-sergeant, and went noisily to the cells.

Elk came back to his chief with information that had come through whilst the charge was in progress.

'The two notes were issued on the account of Mr Louis Landor, of Teign Court, Maida Vale. Landor is either an American or has lived in America. He's an engineer, a fairly rich man, and drew out another three thousand pounds this morning—he's going abroad.'

'*Bon voyage* to him,' said Mason, in a cynical humour. 'Going abroad, is he?'

He gazed at the knife-sheath lying on a sheet of paper before him, and pointed with his little finger to ornate initials engraved on a small gold plate.

'L.L.—they may stand for Leonard Lowe: on the other hand, they may stand for Louis Landor.'

'Who's Leonard Lowe?' asked Elk, momentarily dense.

'There is no such person,' said the superintendent patiently. 'Listen, Elk—living in Tidal Basin hasn't sharpened your wits, has it? I'll be moving you to the West End soon—"C" Division. You'll shine amongst that batch of suckers.'

He got up from the table and walked heavily through the charge-room to the little apartment which the police matron used as a duty-room. On the plain truckle bed lay Lorna Weston; her face was pale, her lips colourless.

'She might be dead,' said Mason.

Dr Marford sighed, took out his cheap American watch and looked at it.

'So might be quite a large number of my patients,' he said listlessly. 'I don't know whether you're interested in the phenomena of life and death, Mr Mason—my own interest is strictly professional—but at this moment there is a lady waiting for me—'

'Yes, yes,' interrupted Mason good-humouredly. 'We forget nothing. I've arranged for your district nurse to 'phone you through to the station. We'll have to do something with this woman.'

He looked dubiously down at the still figure on the bed, moved slightly the blanket that covered her and felt her hand.

'She's a dope?' he asked.

Dr Marford nodded.

'I found a hypodermic in her bag,' he said.

'Rudd thinks she should be taken away to a hospital or infirmary.'

Marford assented reluctantly. Here was the inevitable key witness, and he was loath to leave her out of his sight.

Rudd came bustling in importantly.

'I've fixed a bed at the infirmary,' he said. 'Of course they told me they had no accommodation, but as soon as I mentioned my name—' He smiled jovially at Marford. 'Now if it had been you, my dear fellow—'

'I shouldn't have asked. I should simply have taken the case there and they'd have had to find a bed for her.' said Marford.

Dr Rudd was a little ruffled.

'Yes, yes; but that is hardly the way, is it? I mean, there are certain professional—um—courtesies to be observed. The resident surgeon is a friend of mine, as it happens—Grennett; he was with me at Guy's.'

He dropped Marford as being unworthy of his confidence, and addressed the superintendent.

'I'm getting the ambulance down right away.'

'Have you seen the man again?' asked Mason.

'The man?' Dr Rudd frowned. 'Oh, you mean the dead man? Yes. Your Mr Elk was there, searching him. I made one or two observations which I think may be useful to you, superintendent. For instance, there's a bruise on the left cheek.'

Mason nodded.

'Yes, he was fighting. Dr Marford saw that.'

Rudd was called away at that moment, and bustled out with an apology. The very apology was offensive to Mr Mason, for it inferred that investigations were momentarily suspended until the police surgeon returned.

The woman on the bed showed no sign of life. The doctor, at Mason's request, exhibited two tiny punctures on the left arm.

'Recently made,' he explained, 'but there's no evidence that she's an addict. I can find no other punctures, for example, and the mere fact that the shot has had such an extraordinarily deadening effect upon her rather suggests that she's a novice.'

He lifted the arm and dropped it; it fell lifelessly.

'When will she recover consciousness?'

Marford shook his head.

'I don't know. At present she's not in a state where I could recommend giving restoratives, but I'll leave that to the infirmary people. The resident surgeon is a personal friend of Dr Rudd's and is therefore in all probability a man of genius.'

The eyes of the two men met. Mr Mason did not attempt to disguise his own amusement.

'Fine,' he said. And then: 'Have you ever been in a murder case before?'

The doctor's lips twitched with the hint of a smile.

'Manslaughter—this evening,' he said. 'No, I have not been called in professionally. Not one doctor in eight thousand ever attends a murder case in the whole course of his practice—not if he's wise,' he added.

Mason became suddenly interested in this shabby figure with the pained eyes and the thin, starved face.

'You find living not particularly pleasant in this neighbourhood, doctor? Couldn't you work your clinic somewhere more salubrious?'

Marford shrugged.

'It's all one to me,' he said. 'My own wants are very few and they are satisfied. The clinic must be where it is wanted.

For myself, I do not crave for the society of intellectual men, because intellectual men bore me.'

'And you've no theory about this murder?'

Mason's good-humoured eyes were smiling again.

The doctor did not answer immediately; he bit his lip and looked thoughtfully past the superintendent.

'Yes,' he said quietly. 'To my mind, this case is obviously a case of revenge. He was not murdered for profit, he was deliberately assassinated to right some wrong probably committed years before. And it was not in the larger sense premeditated: the murder was committed on the spur of the moment as opportunity offered.'

Mason stared at him.

'Why do you say that?'

'Because I think it.' Marford was smiling. 'Unless you believe that this man was definitely lured to this spot with the object of killing him, and that a most elaborate scheme was formed for enticing him into this neighbourhood, you must believe that it was unpremeditated.'

Superintendent Mason, fists on hips, legs wide apart, peered at Marford.

'You're not one of these amateur detectives I've been reading about, doctor?' he challenged. 'The sort of man who's going to make the police look foolish in chapter thirty-nine and take all the credit for the discovery?'

Then unexpectedly he clapped his hand on Marford's bony shoulder.

'You talk sense, anyway, and every doctor doesn't talk that. I could name you one, but you'd probably report me to the British Medical Association. You're quite right—your theory is my theory.'

And then, suddenly: 'Do you exclude the possibility that Lamborn may have knifed him?'

'Entirely,' said the other emphatically, and Mason nodded.

'I might tell you'—he dropped his voice confidentially—'that that is the ground plan of Dr Rudd's theory.'

'He has another,' said Marford. 'I wonder he hasn't told you.'

CHAPTER VIII

MASON looked down at the woman again. She had not moved, so far as the eye could see had not even breathed, since she came in.

'She's got it locked up there.' He touched the white forehead lightly. 'No, it's an ordinary police case, doctor. Everything looks mysterious until somebody squeals, and then the case is so easy that even a poor old gentleman from Scotland Yard could work it out.'

He frowned at the woman.

'All right, shoot her into hospital,' he said brusquely, and returned to his room.

It was Inspector Bray's room really; a cupboard of a place, with a table and chair, a last year's almanac on the wall, two volumes of the *Police Code*, a telephone list a foot long—and three reprints of popular fiction. They were decently hidden from view by the *Police Code*, and Mr Mason took one down to the table and opened it.

A taste for thrilling fiction is not phenomenal in a detective officer. With this particular story Mr Mason was well acquainted, and he turned the leaves casually and disparagingly. Here was a murder the like of which never came the way of the average police officer. There were beautiful ladies involved, ladies who had their own Rolls-Royces and lived in exotic apartments; gentlemen who dressed for dinner every night—even the detectives did that. Here murder had a colour and a fragrance; it was set in scenes of beauty, in half-timbered country houses, with lawns that sloped down to a quiet river; in Park Lane mansions, where nothing less than a footman in resplendent uniform could find the dead body of his master lying by the side of a broken Sèvres vase. High politics came into the story; ministers of state were suspected; powerful cars sped seaward to where the steam cutter was waiting to carry its murderous owner to his floating den of vice.

Mr Mason shook his head, scratched his cheek and closed the book, and returned to his own murder, to the drabness of Tidal Basin, with its innumerable side streets and greasy pavements, jerry-built houses all of a plan, where three families lived in a space inadequate for a Park Lane bathroom. Silent Tidal Basin, with its swing bridges over the narrow entrance to docks, and its cold electric standards revealing ugliness even on the darkest night. People were living and dying here; one death more or less surely made no difference. But because a man who was a card-sharp, probably a blackguard, had met his just end, there were lights burning in all sorts of odd rooms at Scotland Yard, men searching records, a printing press working at feverish speed, police cyclists flying to the ends of the area carrying the wet sheets which described the dead man, and in ten thousand streets and squares policemen were reading, by the light of their electric lamps, the description of a man unknown, killed by one known even less.

The machinery was working; the wheels and pistons whirled and thundered—purposeless, it would seem, save to entertain the tall men on their lonely beats with first-hand news of tragedy.

Mason got up and walked out to the entrance of the station. A dim blue light painted his bronzed cheek a sickly hue. The street was deserted. Rain was falling steadily; every window of every house that faced the station was black and menacing.

Why he shivered he did not know. He was too serious a police officer to be influenced by atmosphere. And yet the unfriendliness of this area, all its possibilities of evil, penetrated his armour of indifference.

A queer, boozy lot of people ... A thought struck him, and he slapped the palm of his hand. There were three C.I.D. men in the charge-room; he called them and gave them instructions.

'Take a couple of guns,' he said. 'You may need them.'

After he had seen them depart, he sent an urgent 'phone message to Scotland Yard. Then he went across to where Dr Marford was standing, talking to the station clerk.

'What about this man with the white mask? You know everything that happens in this pitch. Is it a yarn, or is there any foundation for it? There used to be a man up west—had some sort of accident that upset his features—he used to wear that kind of thing.'

The doctor nodded slowly.

'I think that is the man I have met,' he said.

'You've met him?' asked Mason in surprise.

'Yes. Why he wore the mask I have never been able to understand, because there was really very little wrong with his face, except a large red scar. He wasn't exactly good to look at—but you can say that of a lot of people who don't wear masks. I've seen thousands looking worse.'

Mason scowled and pursed his lips.

'I remember the West End man. I see that some of the newspapers are recalling the fact that he was seen years ago. If I remember rightly, he lived in a top flat in Jermyn Street. He had permission from the Commissioner to go out with this thing on his face. I haven't seen him for years, but I remember him well. What was his name—West something— not Weston?'

The doctor shrugged.

'I never knew his name. He came to me about three years ago and asked for ray treatment. He was stupidly sensitive and only came after he had fixed the interview up by telephone. He's been several times since, round about midnight, and he invariably pays me a pound.'

Mason thought for a while, then went to the telephone and called a central police station off Regent Street. The sergeant in charge remembered the man at once, but was not sure of his name.

'He hasn't been seen round the West End for years,' he said. 'The Yard has been arguing about him—wondering if he was White Face.'

'Was his name Weston?' suggested Mason, but the sergeant was without information.

Mason came back to the doctor.

'Does this man live in the neighbourhood?'

But here Dr Marford could tell him nothing. The first time he had met his queer patient he had undoubtedly lived in the region of Piccadilly; thereafter he had only appeared at irregular intervals.

'Do you think he's our devil?' asked Mason bluntly, and the lean man chuckled.

'Devil! It's queer how normal people attribute devilry to any man or woman who is afflicted—the hunchback and the misshapen, the cross-eyed and the lame. You're almost medieval, Mr Mason.'

He could say very little that might assist the police, except that he no longer received warning when the man with the mask made his appearance. Invariably he came through the little yard that ran by the side of the surgery into the passage which Dr Marford's patients used when they queued up for their medicine.

'I never have the side door locked—I mean the door that goes into the yard.' Marford explained that he was a very heavy sleeper, and it was not unusual for his clients to come right into the house to wake him, and the first intimation of their needs was a knock on his bedroom door.

'I've nothing to lose except a few instruments and a few bottles of poison; and to do these fellows justice, I've never had a thing stolen from me since I've been in the neighbourhood. I treat these people like friends, and so long as they're reasonably wholesome I don't mind their wandering about the house.'

Mr Mason made a little grimace.

'How can you live here? You're a gentleman, you have education. How can you meet them every day, listen to their miseries, see their dirt—ugh!'

Dr Marford sighed and looked at his watch.

'If that child's normal he's born now,' he said, and at that moment the sergeant called him across to the telephone.

The child had been normal and had made his appearance into the world without the doctor's assistance. The male parent, a careful man, was already disputing the right of the doctor to any fee. Dr Marford had had previous experience of a similar character, and knew that for the fact that the baby arrived before the doctor came the mother would claim and receive the fullest credit.

'Half fee, as usual,' he told the district nurse and hung up the receiver.

'I used to charge half fees, but double visiting fees if I was called in afterwards. That didn't work, because the mother was usually dead before they risked the expense of calling me in. The economy of these people is excessive.'

The ambulance was ready. He and Rudd saw the woman placed in charge of a uniformed nurse, and Sergeant Elk appointed a detective officer to accompany the patient to the infirmary.

Elk was silent, and his eyes were preternaturally bright when he lounged into the inspector's room.

'This is a case which ought to get me promotion,' he said, a shameless thing to say in the presence of a man who expected most of the kudos. 'Here I've been working for years, and this is the first real mystery I've struck. More like a book than a police case. Quigley's nosing round the neighbourhood—I shouldn't be surprised if he didn't turn in a new devil. It's a good story for him.'

Mr Mason indicated a chair.

'Sit down, my poor fellow,' he said with spurious sympathy. 'What are the features of this murder which have separated it from an ordinary case of knifing?'

Elk's long arm went out, and he pointed in a direction which Mr Mason, not wholly acquainted with the geography of the station, decided was the matron's room.

'She's it!' said Elk. His voice shook. 'What happened tonight, Mr Mason? An unknown man has a fight with another unknown man, who bolts. The first fellow walks along and meets a police officer and tells him all about it. He's alive and well; obviously he's not stabbed; yet within a few seconds after the officer moves on, this fellow drops in his track like a man shot. A cheap crook comes over and dips him, and is seen by Hartford, who tackles the man. They then discover that the fellow on the ground is stabbed. Nobody saw the blow struck. Yet there he is dead—knifed, and the knife's well away and can't be found.'

Mason leaned back in his chair and closed his eyes.

'End of the first reel; the second reel will follow immediately,' he murmured, but Elk was undisturbed. That bright light in his eye was now a steely glitter. He was agitated as he had never been seen before in all the years of his service.

'Out of nowhere comes Mrs Weston. She'd warned this man he was going to be killed. She wants to be sure that it is him.'

'He,' murmured Mason gently.

'Never mind about grammar.' Elk was frankly insubordinate in his vehemence. 'She takes a look at the man on the ground and drops.'

He laid his hand almost violently upon the superintendent's arm and shook it.

'I was watching her. I knew the woman, though I didn't recognise her at first. She drops—and what do we find? She's a needler—a dope. Does that mean anything to you, sir?'

'I'm glad you said "sir",' said Mason. 'I was wondering how I'd bring you back to a sense of discipline. Yes, it means a lot to me. Now I'm going to ask you a question: does the can of beer which Mrs Albert was carrying mean anything to you, and does that can of beer associate itself in your active and intelligent mind with the disappearance of Mr Louis Landor—if that's the name of the man who fought with the dead one?'

Elk was frankly bewildered.

'You're trying to pull my leg.'

'Heaven forbid!' said the patient Mason. 'Bring in Mrs Albert. She's waited long enough to get three kinds of panic—I want her to have the kind where she'll tell the truth.'

Mrs Albert came, a rather pale woman, sensible of her disgraceful surroundings, conscious, too, of her responsibility for four children, only three of which, Mason learned, were yet born. She still clutched in her hand the tell-tale can of beer. The liquid was now flat and uninviting and some of it had spilt in her agitation, so that she brought with her to the inspector's room a faint aroma of synthetic hops. She was quivering, more or less speechless. Mason gave her no opportunity for recovering her self-possession or her volubility.

'Sorry I've had to keep you so long, Mrs Albert,' he said. 'Your husband's the night watchman at the Eastern Trading Company, isn't he?'

She nodded mutely.

'The Eastern Trading Company do not allow their night watchman to have beer?'

Mrs Albert found her voice.

'No, sir,' she piped. 'The last night watchman got the sack for drinking when he was on duty.'

'Exactly,' said Mason, at his most brusque. 'But your husband likes a drop of beer, and it's fairly easy to pass the beer through the wicket gate, isn't it?'

She could only blink at him pathetically.

'And he's in the habit of leaving the wicket gate undone every night about eleven o'clock, and you're in the habit of putting that can inside the gate?'

Her pathos grew. She could only suspect a base informer,

and was undecided as to which of her five neighbours had filled that despicable rôle.

She was not unpretty, Mason noticed in his critical way, despite the three children—or four, if her worst fears were realised.

The superintendent turned to his subordinate.

'There's the connection,' he said, 'and that is where Mr Louis Landor went—through the wicket gate. Oh, you needn't bother: I've sent some men to search the yard. But if I am any judge, Mr Landor has gone. I've already circulated his description.'

Mrs Albert, the wife of the night watchman, drooped guiltily in her chair, her agonised dark eyes fixed on Mr Mason. Here was tragedy for her, more poignant than the death of unknown men struck down by unseen forces; the tragedy of a husband dismissed from the only job he had held in five years, of the resumption of that daily struggle for life, of aimless wanderings for employment on his part—she could always go out as a hired help for a few shillings a day.

'He'll get the sack,' she managed to breathe.

Mason looked at her and shook his head.

'I'm not reporting to the Eastern Trading Company, though you might have helped a little bit if you hadn't hidden up the truth when I asked you about the beer. I blame myself for not realising that you had something to hide, and what it was. It might have made a big difference.'

'You're not reporting it, mister?' she asked tremulously, and was on the verge of tears. 'I've had a very hard time. That poor woman could tell you how hard it was: she used to live with me till she came into money.'

'Which poor woman is this?' asked Mason quickly.

'Mrs Weston.'

She had lost some of her fear in the face of his interest.

'She lodged with you?'

Elk had left the room. Mason motioned her to the chair

which the sergeant had vacated and which was nearer to him.

'Come along and let's hear all about it,' he said genially.

A bald man, with a round, amused face and a ready smile, removed all her natural suspicions.

'Oh, yes, sir, she used to lodge with me, till she got this money.'

'Where did she get the money from?'

'Gawd knows,' said Mrs Albert piously. 'I never ask questions. She paid me all that she owed me, that's all I know. I've been wondering, sir'—she leaned forward confidentially—'was it her husband or her young man who was killed?'

'Her young man was killed,' said Mason without hesitation. 'You knew them?'

She shook her head.

'You knew the husband, at any rate?'

'I've seen photographs of him in her room. They were taken in Australia—her and the two. When I say I've seen them,' she corrected herself, 'I was just going to take a look at 'em when she come in the room and snatched the frame out of my hand—which was funny, because it had always been on the mantelshelf before, but I never took any notice of it till she said one day it was her husband and a great friend. It was on the following day I took up the picture to have a look.'

'And she snatched it out of your hand? How long ago was this?'

She thought.

'Two years last July.'

Mason nodded.

'And soon after that she came into money, almost immediately after?'

Mrs Albert was not surprised at his perspicuity. She had the impression that she had given him that information.

'Yes, sir, she left me the next day, or two days after. I haven't spoken to her since. She lives in the grand part of Tidal Basin now. I always say that when people are well off—'

'I'm perfectly sure I can guess what you always say.' He

was not unkind but he was very firm. 'Now, what sort of a frame would this be in—leather?'

Yes, she thought rather that it was leather—or wood, covered with leather.

'I know she put it in her box because I saw her do it—a little black box she used to keep under her bed.'

He questioned her and cross-checked her answers, eliminating in the process all possibility that her narrative might be embroidered by imagination. Into the lives of the poor comes no other romance than that of their own creation.

He grew suddenly vague; she could not understand the questions he put to her. They seemed to have no foundation in reason. And then suddenly he touched a high note of romance. Had she ever seen a man with a piece of white cloth on his face? She shuddered pleasurably.

'The Devil . . . I've heard of him, but never seen him, thank God! It was him that done it—everybody was saying so in the crowd.'

'Have you ever seen him?'

She shook her head vigorously.

'No, an' I don't want to in my state. But I know people who have . . . in the middle of the night.'

'When they've been dreaming,' suggested Mason, but she would not have this.

The Devil was a possession of Tidal Basin; not willingly would she surrender the legend. When he showed into the charge-room a woman made tearfully grateful by the knowledge that she could go to her home and her three children, Marford was waiting to say good-night. Dr Rudd had already left.

'If you want me tonight, I shall be at my surgery. I hope I may be allowed to sleep.'

Mason had three things he wished to do at the same time—three errands on which he could trust nobody but himself. He decided to perform his first task single-handed and call back for Elk to assist him with the second.

CHAPTER IX

MICHAEL QUIGLEY was coming up the steps of the police station as Mason appeared in the doorway.

'Carrion,' said Mason pleasantly, 'the body has been removed.'

'Who is it, Mason?'

Mr Mason shook his head.

'There was once,' he said jovially, 'a medical student who was asked how many teeth Adam was born with, and he replied, very properly, "God knows".'

'Unknown, eh? A swell, they tell me?'

'He's well dressed,' said Mason in his noncommittal way. 'Go along and have a look at him. You know all the toughs in the West End.'

Michael shook his head.

'That can wait. What is this murder—a little joke of White Face?'

'Why White Face?' demanded Mason. 'Listen, Quigley, you've got a bug in your brain. White Face doesn't belong to Tidal Basin any more than your devil.'

'He's been seen here,' insisted the reporter, and Mason sighed.

'A man who wore a lump of lint over his face has been seen here. Dr Marford, in a weak-minded moment, told you. You'd see the same in the neighbourhood of any hospital.'

Michael Quigley was unusually silent.

'Oh . . . where are you going?'

No other reporter dared ask such a question, but Mason knew this young man rather well.

'You'll get me hung, Michael, but I'll let you come along with me. I'm going to see a green door and have a little independent search. Your encouragement and help will be welcome. How is Miss Harman?'

Mike almost showed his teeth.

'You can collect gossip, even if you can't collect murderers!' he snarled. 'Miss Harman is a very good friend of mine who is going to marry somebody else.'

'I congratulate her,' said Mason as they stepped out towards Endley Street. 'It must be a terribly un-romantic life being married to a reporter.'

'There is no question of my being married to anybody,' said Michael savagely, 'and you're getting under my skin, Mason.'

'Fine,' said Mason. 'Some day I'll go shooting elephants.'

They trudged side by side, cold anger in the heart of one and an idea that was growing into shape in the mind of Mr Mason. He whistled softly as he walked under the high wall of the Eastern Trading Company.

'Do you mind,' asked Michael with sour politeness, 'choosing some other tune than the Wedding March?'

'Was I whistling that?' asked the other in surprise. 'Ever noticed how like a funeral march it is? Change the time and you're there.'

It was a beast of a night; a wind had risen, with the cold of the Eastern steppes.

'Policemen and reporters,' said Mason, 'get their living out of other people's misfortunes. Has that ever struck you? Here they are!'

The 'they' were three men walking abreast towards them. They slackened their pace when Mason came into view and halted to receive them.

'We've found nothing and nobody,' said the senior. 'We searched the yard, but there wasn't a sign of a man, though there were plenty of places where he could have hidden.'

'And the wicket gate?'

'That was ajar,' replied the detective. 'Albert, the night watchman, swore that it hadn't been opened. It's against the rules to open the wicket gate unless there's a fire.'

'Maybe there was a fire,' suggested Mason. 'It's a good night for a fire. All right, you can come along with me.'

They had only a few yards to go before they came to the place where the pavement, the private yard road and the railway arch formed a triangle.

'This is where the body was found.' suggested Michael, and Mason indicated the spot.

He was still whistling when he walked to the green-painted wicket door and pushed. It was locked now. If he'd only thought of trying that door—but if there *had* been a man behind it he would have had the sense to have shot in the bolts. He must have been hiding in there when Elk was searching the yard for the pocket-case and watch. But if Mrs Albert had talked—

He confided his woes to Michael, a safe and sure recipient, for Michael Quigley knew just what not to print.

'You get that sort of thing in all these cases,' said Michael philosophically. 'And you expect it, anyway. Nobody tells the truth, because there's some twiddling little thing to hide that may bring discredit upon them. Personally, I can't understand their mentality.'

His eyes roved over the pavement.

'You searched the gutter, I suppose? There's a distinct slope to this sidewalk.'

Mason looked inquiringly at one of the detectives, but nobody could tell him anything except that the traps where storm water runs had been emptied and the mud at the bottom carefully searched, without anything of value being found.

Michael straddled the gutter, and, pulling up his sleeve, ran his fingers through the slowly moving water, groping . . .

'First shot!' he cried exultantly. 'What's this?'

Mason took it in his hand. It looked like a button or a tiny brown electric light bulb. One of the detectives put his light upon the find as it lay in Mason's hand.

'It looks to me like a capsule,' said Michael, turning it over curiously.

It was indeed a tiny capsule of thin glass, containing something the colour of which was indistinguishable.

'I seem to know the shape, too. Now where the devil have I seen those before?'

'It can go to the police analyst, anyway,' said Mason, and put it carefully in his pocket. 'Mike, you're lucky: try again.'

Michael's wet hand went through the water, but he could find nothing. And then he saw what hundreds of pairs of eyes, focused on that strip of pavement, had not seen. It lay poised upon the sharp edge of the kerb, as if it had been carefully placed there, though it must have rolled and fallen into its position through no other agent than the force of gravity. The long stone hung over the kerb: the platinum circle was so dulled with rain that it was indistinguishable from the granite on which it rested.

He picked it up, his heart thumping painfully.

'What is this?'

Mason took it from his unwilling hand.

'A ring! To think those poor, blind bats—a ruby ring! I suppose the ruby's an imitation, but it looks ruby.'

Michael Quigley said nothing. The men were swaying blurs of shadow; he found a difficulty in breathing. Something in his attitude must have attracted Mason's attention, for he looked at him sharply.

'What's the matter with you? God Almighty, you look like a dead man! It was stooping down that did it—the blood rushing to your head, eh?'

Michael knew Mason well enough to realise that Superintendent Mason was advancing an excuse for the benefit of the other detectives, and this was confirmed when he sent them left and right groping vainly through the gutters for some new clue. Then he took Michael's arm.

'Son,' he said kindly, 'You've seen that ring before, haven't you?'

Michael shook his head.

'What's the use of telling me a lie?' Mason's voice was reproachful and hurt.

'I don't remember seeing it before,' said Michael harshly. It did not sound like his voice speaking.

'Hiding up?' said Mason gently. 'What's the use? Somebody's bound to come along and blow it all. You were saying only a minute ago how silly it was to keep things from the police—twiddling little things that don't count. And you couldn't understand their mentality. Are you understanding their mentality any better?'

'I've never seen that ring before.'

It required a mighty effort on his part for Michael to make this statement. Mr Mason was by nature a sceptic and not easily convinced.

'You've seen it before and you know whom it belongs to. Listen, Michael! I'm not going to be sympathetic with you and I'm not going to try any of the monkey tricks that I use with half-witted criminals. You'll save yourself a lot of trouble and somebody else more, if you take me into your confidence. It doesn't mean that the person who owns that ring is going to be pinched, or that they're booked for pads of publicity—you know me too well for that. Hiding up, as you say, is one of the curses of the business.'

Michael had recovered himself by now.

'You'll be pinching me for the murder in a minute,' he said lightly. 'No, I don't know that stone at all. I was a little dizzy from trying to do stunts in the gutter with my head between my legs. Try it yourself and see what effect it has on you.'

Mason looked at him for a long time, then at the ring.

'A lady's ring, I should say.' He tried it on his little finger. 'And a little finger ring. It doesn't go any farther than the top of mine. That will mean publicity,' he said carelessly. 'I don't want to say anything against you newspaper men, Michael, but you certainly spread yourselves on a mysterious clue like this, and I shouldn't be surprised to find a portrait of the young lady—'

He stopped suddenly.

'Not Miss Harman?'

'No,' said Michael loudly.

'Liar,' retorted Mr Mason. 'It's Miss Harman's ring! And you knew it the moment you saw it!'

He looked at the jewel for a while, then put it into his pocket.

'This man who was murdered was a South African?' asked Mike.

Mason nodded.

'Had he come recently from South Africa?'

'We don't know, but we guess within the last week or two.'

'What is his name?'

'We don't even know that, except that it's Donald.'

His jaw dropped; his large protruding eyes opened to their widest extent.

'Whom is Miss Harman going to marry?' he asked.

'An Irishman named Feeney,' said Michael mendaciously. 'No, as a matter of fact, Mason, she's marrying me. But I've had a little tiff with her. Can I see the body?'

'Let's go together and make an evening of it,' said Mason, and linked arms with him.

Their gruesome errand lasted only a few minutes and left Michael more puzzled than ever. Puzzled and terribly distressed. There was no question at all that the man who had dropped that ring, whether it was the dead man or the murderer, was the romantic lover. He must find out the truth at all costs.

He left Mason at the police station and ran out, almost knocking down a girl who was hesitating at the foot of the station steps.

'Michael . . . Michael!' she gasped, and clutched him by the arm. 'They told me you were here. I had to see you . . . Oh, Michael, I've been a fool and I do want help terribly badly!'

He looked at her with momentary suspicion.

'How long have you been here, Janice?' he asked.

'I've just arrived. There's my car.' She pointed to its dim

lights. The shoulders of her skin coat were wet with rain. 'Could we go anywhere? I want to speak to you. There's been a murder, hasn't there?'

He nodded.

'How dreadful! But I'm glad I knew where I could find you. There always seem to be murders here,' she shuddered. 'And I've been murdered, too, Michael. All my vanity, all my pride—if it's true. And I feel that you are the only person that can bring them to life again. Where can we go?'

He hesitated. He had supplied the needs of the last edition; there was nothing more for him to write tonight, though his work was by no means done. He went back to the car. She was in so pitiable a condition that he took the wheel from her hand and drove her to Bury Street. He had never been in her flat before, so that he was a stranger to the maid who opened the door.

Janice led the way to the pretty little drawing-room and closed the door.

'Take your coat off,' he commanded before she started speaking. 'Your shoes and your stockings are all wet—go and change them.'

She went meekly, and returned in a few minutes with a dressing-gown wrapped round her, and cowered down in a low arm-chair before an electric radiator.

'Here's the cablegram I had.'

She handed him a folded paper without looking up.

'Wait! Before you read it I want to tell you. He said he had a farm in Paarl and he was very anxious to buy an adjoining property . . . and I was buying it for him and cabled out to Van Zyl, that awfully nice boy I spoke to you about, and told him to buy it. That is his answer.'

He opened the telegram. It was a long message.

'THE PROPERTY YOU MENTION IS NOT AT PAARL BUT IN CONSTANTIA ADJOINING THE CONVICT PRISON. IT IS NOT AND NEVER HAS BEEN FOR SALE. DONALD BATEMAN, WHOM YOU MENTION AS PROPRIETOR, IS UNKNOWN AS LANDOWNER EITHER

HERE OR IN RHODESIA. MY FRIEND PUBLIC PROSECUTOR IS
AFRAID MAN YOU MENTION IS DONALD BATEMAN, WHO SERVED
NINE MONTHS IMPRISONMENT AT CONSTANTIA FOR LAND
FRAUDS; TALL, RATHER GOOD-LOOKING MAN, LONG SCAR UNDER
HIS CHIN, GREY EYES. HE LEFT BY "BALMORAL CASTLE" FIVE
WEEKS AGO EN ROUTE ENGLAND. HIS FRAUDS TAKE SHAPE OF
PERSUADING PEOPLE ADVANCE MONEY BUY PROPERTY AND
DECAMPING WITH DEPOSIT. PLEASE FORGIVE IF THIS LITTLE
MELODRAMATIC. ALWAYS ANXIOUS TO SERVE. CARL.'

He folded the telegram and looked at her oddly.

And then he said in a strange voice:

'The scar under the chin. It's curious, that's the first thing
I noticed.'

She turned and looked up at him, startled.

'You haven't seen him? You told me you hadn't. When
did you see him?'

Michael licked his dry lips. Donald Bateman! So that was
his name! He walked across to her and laid his hand gently
on her shoulder.

'My dear, how perfectly rotten for you!' he said huskily. 'Isn't it?'

'Do you think that is true? That he is—what Carl says he is?'

'Yes,' he said. 'You gave him the ring, didn't you?'

She made an impatient little gesture.

'That was nothing; it had no value except a sentimental
one—which made it rather appropriate,' she added bitterly.

There was something he had to ask, something so difficult
that he could hardly frame the words.

'There are no complications, are there?'

She looked up at him wonderingly.

'Complications? What do you mean, Michael?'

She saw that he avoided her gaze.

'Well, I mean, you aren't married already . . . secretly
married, you know? It can be done in two or three days.'

She shook her head.

'Why should I? Of course not.'

He fetched a long sigh of relief.

'Thank the Lord for that!' he said. 'Are you fond of him? Not too fond, are you, Janice?'

'No. I've been a mad schoolgirl, haven't I? I've been realising it all the evening, that I didn't—love him. I wonder if you'll believe it . . . I haven't even kissed him—ugh!'

He patted her shoulder gently.

'Naturally my pride is hurt, but I haven't crashed so utterly as I should if I—well, if this thing had gone on before I found it out. You'll never laugh at me, will you, Michael?'

She put up her hand and laid it on that which rested on her shoulder.

'No, I shan't laugh at you.'

She sat gazing into the glowing electric fire, and then:

'Why did you ask about the ring?'

He made the plunge.

'Because I've been lying about it to Mason—Superintendent Mason of Scotland Yard.'

She was up on her feet instantly, her eyes wide with alarm.

'Scotland Yard! Have they got the ring? Have they arrested him? Michael, what is it?' She gripped his arm. 'You're hiding something—what is it?'

'I've been hiding something—yes. I've been hiding from Mason the fact that the ring was yours. It was in Endley Street. I picked it up myself, near the place where the body of a murdered man was found.'

'A murdered man was found in Endley Street.' She repeated the words slowly. 'That was the case you were on . . . Who was it? Not Donald Bateman?'

He nodded.

'O God, how awful!'

He thought she was going to faint, but when he reached out to catch her she pushed him back.

'He was stabbed by some person unknown,' said Michael.

'I—I've seen him. That's how I knew about the scar.'

She was very still and white but she showed no other signs of distress.

'What was he doing there?' she asked. 'He didn't know the neighbourhood; he told me today he'd never been there before in his life. Nobody knows who did it?'

He shook his head.

'Nobody. When I saw the ring I recognised it at once. Like a fool I gave myself away, and Mason, who's as sharp as a packet of needles, knew I was lying when I told him I had never seen it before. He may advertise the ring tomorrow unless I tell him.'

'Then tell him,' she said instantly. 'Dead! It's unbelievable!'

She sat down in the chair again, her face in her hands. He thought she was on the verge of a breakdown, but when she raised her face to him her eyes were tearless.

'You had better go back, my dear. I shan't do anything stupid—but I'm afraid I shan't sleep. Will you come early in the morning and let me know what has been discovered? I intended going to see Dr Marford tomorrow to ask him to let me come back to the clinic, but I don't think I can for a day or two.'

'I don't want to leave you like this,' he said, but she smiled faintly.

'You're talking as if I were a mid-Victorian heroine,' she said. 'No, my dear, you go. I'd like to be alone for a little while.'

And then, to his great embarrassment, she raised his hand and kissed it.

'I'm being motherly,' she said.

If there were no tears in her eyes, pain was there. He thought it wise of him to leave at once, and he went back to Tidal Basin to find the streets alive with police, for two important things had happened; two new phases of the drama had been enacted in his absence.

CHAPTER X

A FRAMED photograph is not a difficult object to find, and black boxes in which ladies keep their treasures deposited beneath their beds are far from becoming rarities. Mason would have liked to have Elk with him, but the sergeant had gone on to join Bray. A watch was being kept on the block in which Louis Landor's apartments were situated. Bray had telephoned through that neither Mr nor Mrs Landor was yet at home. Evidently something was wrong here, for the servant, who had returned and was awaiting admission, told Bray that she had been sent out earlier in the day, that there had been some sort of trouble between a couple that were hitherto happily married. She had been told she need not return until late. Bray had found her waiting disconsolately outside the flat, and had persuaded her to spend the night with a sister who lived in the neighbourhood.

'One thing she told me,' said Bray over the wire; 'the flat is packed with South African curios. If this girl's story is true, there are two knives similar to the one with which the murder was committed—they hang on a belt in the hall. She described the sheath exactly, and said they both had the initials of Landor, and that he got them as prizes in South America, where he lived for some years.'

'Hang on,' were Mason's instructions. 'Elk's gone up to join you. Report to me here or at Scotland Yard. I am making a search on my own.'

He had on his desk the contents of Mrs Weston's bag, including the worn hypodermic case that Dr Marford had produced. The case puzzled him, because it was old and the little syringe had evidently been used many times. And yet Marford had given it as his opinion that the woman was

178

not an addict and that it was only the second time that the
needle had been used.

There were a few letters, a bill or two from a West End
milliner. Evidently Lorna Weston, in spite of the poverty-
stricken neighbourhood in which she lived, spared no
expense in the adornment of her person. He found two five-
pound notes, half a dozen Treasury bills, a little silver and a
bunch of keys, and it was with these keys that, in company
with Sergeant Shale, he made his way to the mystery woman's
apartments.

What Mrs Albert had described as 'the grand part of Tidal
Basin' consisted of two or three streets of well-built villas.
There were several shops here, and it was over one of these,
a large grocery store, that Mrs Weston had her apartments,
which were approached by a side door and a short passage.
From this ran a flight of rather steep steps to a landing above.

The place was fitted with electric light and had, he saw, a
telephone of its own. He climbed the stairs and was staggered
to find that the landing had been painted and decorated in
the West End style. Parchment-covered walls, white metal
wall-brackets and soft-shaded lamps gave the approach to
the apartment the appearance of luxury.

The front room was the parlour, and was tastefully furnished,
and this was the case with the other rooms, including an
expensively fitted kitchenette.

Mr Mason was essentially a man of the world. He knew
that this style of living was consistent with the earnings of no
profession, reputable or otherwise. Either Mrs Weston had
a private income of her own or else—

He remembered that the woman at the police station had
spoken of her coming into a lot of money. That might be an
explanation. But why did she choose this ghastly neighbourhood in which to live?

There was a small writing-table in the drawing-room,
but a search of this—the drawers were unlocked—revealed

nothing that was in any way satisfactory to the searcher. It was in the bedroom that he and his assistant decided to make their most careful scrutiny. This was the room next to the drawing-room and the last to be visited. As soon as he switched on the lights, Mason realised that something unusual had happened. The drawers of the dressing-table had been pulled out, the plate-glass door of the wardrobe stood wide open. On the floor was a medley of garments and wearing apparel, and amidst them Mason saw the corner of a black box. He went quickly to this. It had been locked, but somebody had broken open the lid. Scattered about the floor were oddments and papers. There was no framed photograph. What he did see was a small cardboard cylinder. He picked it up and squinted through it; it was empty.

The cylinder interested him, because he knew it was the kind in which marriage certificates were kept; and however unhappy a marriage might be, that little slip of paper is one with which no woman parts willingly.

'Get the men in and we'll dust the place for fingerprints,' he said.

He had hardly spoken the words before he saw lying on the bed a pair of white cotton gloves. The intruder had taken no risks. He examined them carefully, but they told him nothing except that they were white cotton gloves which had been carefully washed, probably by their user.

When had the burglar come, and how had he secured admission? The door below had not been forced; only the black box, which, he guessed, had been in the bottom drawer of the bureau when it was found, for nothing in this drawer had been disturbed, and there was a space which such a box might have occupied.

Of clues by which he could judge the time, there was none.

'There's somebody knocking on the door down below,' said Shale. 'Shall I see who it is?'

'No, wait; I'll go.'

Mason went quickly down the stairs and opened the door. A woman was standing there with a shawl over her head to protect her from the rain. She looked dubiously at Mason standing in the light, and edged farther back. It struck him that she was ready to run.

'Is everything all right?' she asked nervously.

'Everything is all wrong,' said Mason. And then, recognising her timidity and guessing the reason: 'Don't worry— I'm a police officer.'

He saw she was relieved.

'I'm the caretaker of the house opposite; the lady is away in the country; and I was wondering whether I ought to go to the police or not.'

'Then you saw somebody go into this flat tonight?' asked Mason quickly.

'I saw them come out,' she said. 'I wouldn't even have taken notice of that if it hadn't been for the white thing—'

'What white thing? You mean, it was somebody with a white mask?' Mason snapped the question at her.

'I won't swear to who it was, but I will swear that he had white on his face. I saw it as plain as can be in the light of the street lamp. I've had toothache all night and I've been sitting in our front parlour—'

He cut short her narrative.

'When did you see this somebody come out?' he asked.

It was less than a quarter of an hour ago. She had also seen him and Shale enter and, believing that they were police officers, she had ventured to come over and knock at the door. He questioned her closely as to how the burglar had been dressed, and the description was a familiar one: the long coat that reached to the heels, the black felt hat and the white mask. He learned one characteristic which had never before been noticed: the man limped painfully. She was very sure of this. He came in no car and went away walking, and had disappeared round the corner of the block, in the direction opposite to that which the two detectives had followed on their way to the flat.

Shale came down and took a shorthand note of her statement, and then the two men returned to the flat and made an even more careful scrutiny in the hope that White Face might have left something else behind than his gloves.

'I don't even know that these won't tell us something.'

Mason put the gloves carefully into a paper bag and slipped them into his pocket.

'Then it's true, White Face *is* an institution here.'

'They all think so,' said Shalee. 'The little thieves round here glorify him!'

Mason returned to the station, a very much baffled man. He had two pieces of evidence, and these he had locked away in the station safe. He took out the ring and the capsule and brought them into the inspector's room. The garrulous Rudd would be able to tell him something about this. He opened the door and called to the station sergeant.

'I suppose Dr Rudd will be in bed by now?'

'No, sir; he rang me up a quarter of an hour ago. He said he was coming round to offer rather a startling theory. Those were his words—"rather a startling theory".'

Mason groaned.

'It'll be startling all right! Get him on the 'phone and ask him if he'll step round. Don't mention the theory. I want him to identify a medicine.'

He examined the ring through a magnifying-glass, but there was nothing that could tell him a twentieth of what Michael Quigley could have told.

'That Quigley knows something,' grumbled Mason. 'I nearly had it out of him, too.'

'What could he know, sir?' asked Shale.

'He knows who owns that ring,' nodded Mason.

The station sergeant opened the door and looked in.

'Dr Rudd went out five minutes ago on his way, sir,' he said, 'and there's a message for you from the Yard.'

It was from the Information Bureau. The mysterious Donald had been located.

'His name is Donald Bateman,' said the reporting detective. 'He arrived from South Africa three weeks ago and is staying at the Little Norfolk Hotel, Norfolk Street. The description tallies with the description you sent us, Mr Mason.'

'He's not in the hotel now by any chance?'

'No, sir, he went out this evening, wearing a dinner jacket, and said he wouldn't be back till midnight. He hasn't been seen since. He has a scar under his chin—that corresponds with your description, too—and he's about the same height as the murdered man.'

'Pass his name to the Identification Bureau,' said Mason, 'see if we have any record of him and—don't go away, my lad—post a man in the hotel. If Mr Donald Bateman doesn't return by seven o'clock tomorrow morning have his trunks removed to Cannon Row Police Station and held until I come and search them.'

He hung up the receiver.

'Donald Bateman, eh? That's something to go on. Mr Bray hasn't rung up?'

'No, sir.'

Mason strolled back to the inspector's room and resumed his examination of the ring and the capsule.

'Yes, Michael knows all about the ring or I'm a Dutchman. The young devil nearly fainted when he found it.'

'Where could the ring and the capsule have come from?' asked Shale.

'Where else could they have come from than out of Donald Bateman's pocket? You've heard all the witnesses examined: they agree that when Bateman fell he put his hand in his waist-coat pocket and tried to get something out. He probably got both these things in his hand; they rolled down the sidewalk into the gutter, and they wouldn't have been found then but for Michael. I'll say that of the kid, he's got good instincts.'

He looked at his watch.

'How far does the doctor live from here?'

'Not four minutes' walk,' said Shale, who had been sent to fetch the divisional surgeon when the murder was reported.

'Then he ought to be here by now. Ring him again.'

But Dr Rudd's housekeeper insisted that he had left ten minutes before.

'Go out and see if you can find him.'

Mason was suddenly serious. He mistrusted the doctor's theories; he mistrusted more his garrulity. A man who talks all the time and whose topics are limited in number must inevitably say something which the police would rather he did not say. He hoped he had not met a friend on the way.

In a little under ten minutes Shale came back. He had been as far as the doctor's house but had seen no sign of Rudd. It was a comparatively short and straightforward walk.

'He may be with Dr Marford. Ring him.'

But Marford could offer no explanation, except that he had been in his surgery and that Rudd had passed, tapping on the big surgery window to say good-night.

'And frightened me out of my skin,' complained Dr Marford. 'I hadn't the slightest idea who it was until I went up and looked behind the blinds.'

The distance from the doctor's surgery to the police station was less than two hundred yards, but there was another way, through Gallows Court, an unwholesome short cut, by which the distance could be cut off some fifty yards. As nobody ever went into Gallows Court, except those lost souls who dragged out their dreary existence there, it was presumable that Rudd had taken the longest route.

The lower end of Gallows Court ran out through a tunnel-shaped opening flush with and a few yards north of Dr Marford's side door. In the days when drunken sailormen from the docks and wharves were as common as lamp-posts, Gallows Court was a place of picturesque infamy. It was no longer picturesque.

A Chinaman had a tiny lodging-house there in which he housed an incredible number of his fellow countrymen. Four or five Italian families lived in another house, and other families less easy to describe dwelt in the others. It was said that the police went down Gallows Court in pairs. That is not true. They never went at all, and only with the greatest circumspection when *bona fide* cries of 'Murder!' called for their attention.

Dr Marford was one of the few people who went down that lane day or night voluntarily and suffered no harm. Did he wish, he could tell hair-raising stories of what he had seen and heard in that malodorous thoroughfare, but he was from choice a poor raconteur.

'I shouldn't think Rudd would go down there,' he said in answer to the superintendent's inquiry. 'At any rate, if you have any doubt I'll go myself.'

Half an hour passed, and at a quarter to two Mason gathered all his reserves and sent them on a search. A telephone call brought swift police launches to the water front, to the distress of the local gang that was illicitly breaking cargo when the boats arrived. But there was no sign of Rudd or message from him. Momentarily he had vanished from the face of the earth.

This was the situation as Michael Quigley found it when he arrived on the scene. He sought an interview with the superintendent and told him frankly, as Janice had directed him to tell, the story of the ring. Mr Mason listened wearily.

'Hiding up!' he wailed. 'What good did it do? Why couldn't you tell me right away—not that it would have made any difference, except that I should have known the name earlier. Yes, that's his name, Donald Bateman. We're getting warmer—hallo, doctor!'

It was Marford, who had come for news of his colleague.

'None. He's probably discovered that the murderer was an Irishman and he's gone off by the night boat to Ireland to get local colour. Sit down, doctor, and have some coffee.'

He pushed a steaming cup towards Marford, who took it and sipped painfully.

'Where he's gone I don't know, and don't care.' Mason yawned. 'I'm a weary man, and I did hope this murder was coming out nicely. If Mr Louis Landor would only come home like a good lad, we ought to have all the threads in our hands by the morning. But if Mr Louis Landor has taken his passport and his three thousand pounds in a private aeroplane to the Continent, then this is going to be one of those well-known unravelled mysteries of London that reporters write about when they're too old for ordinary work.'

The doctor finished his coffee and went soon after. His second case was due.

Mason walked with him to the door.

'Any more theories?'

'Yes, I've got, not a theory, but an absolute conviction now.' said Marford quietly. 'But for the trifling detail that I'm not in a position to supply the evidence, I think I could tell you the murderer.'

Mason nodded.

'I wonder if you are thinking of the same person, doctor?' Marford smiled.

'For his sake, I hope not.'

'Which means that you're not going to give us the benefit of your logic and deductions?'

'I'm a doctor, not a detective,' said the other.

Mason came back to the charge-room fire and warmed his hands.

'No message from Bray or Elk?'

He glanced at the clock; it was a quarter-past two. He began to have his doubts whether Mr Louis Landor would ever return to his flat.

Accompanied by the reporter, he strolled out in the direction of Gallows Court. The rain had ceased, but the wind still blew fitfully.

'And if you're writing about this place,' he said, 'don't fall into an error common to all cub reporters: that Gallows Court stands on the site of Execution Dock. It doesn't. It was named after a man called Gallers, who owns a lot of property about here, and if, instead of putting up his silly clinics, the doctor would get his rich pals to buy this area and clear away the slums, he'd be doing the world a service—and the police.'

The entry of Gallows Court looked dark and formidable. Within a few yards were the gates of the doctor's yard. It was a small courtyard, at one end of which was a shed, which he hired out to the famous Gregory Wicks, a veteran owner of a taxicab. It was in another way a most useful assembling place for the doctor, who dispensed his own medicines. Almost any evening could be seen a queue of poorly-dressed men and women lined up, waiting their turn to enter the narrow passage that flanked the surgery and to receive through a small hatch from the doctor's hands the medicine he had ordered and dispensed.

'It's more like the waiting-room of a hospital than a private surgery,' explained Michael.

Mason grunted.

'Why keep 'em alive?' he asked in despair. A wall divided Gallows Court from the doctor's yard, the houses in that by-pass being built on one side of the court only.

Mason looked up and down, and again felt that unaccountable sensation of menace.

The road was a black canyon, and the starry arc lamps emphasised the desolation. A street of tombs; black, ugly, shoddy tombs, nailed and glued and cheaply cemented together. The dingy window-glass hardly returned the reflection of the lights; no chimney smoked, no window glowed humanly. Up Gallows Court, where the door panels had been used for firewood, men and women slept in the open, huddled up in the deep recesses of doorways, slept through the rain and the soughing wind, old sacks drawn over their knees and shoulders.

As Mason and his companion picked a way over the slippery cobbles, a voice in the darkness chanted—the voice of a woman husky with sleep:

'I spy a copper with a shinin' collar. If he touches me I'll holler—P'lice!'

He never ceased to wonder how they could see in the dark.

'They're rats,' said Mike, answering his unspoken thought.

A chuckle of sly laughter came to them.

'They never sleep,' said Mason in despair. 'It was the same in my time. Day and night you could go through Gallows Court and there would be somebody watching you.'

He wheeled suddenly and called a name. From an entry slunk a figure, which might have been man or woman.

'Thought it was you,' said Mason.

(Who it was, or who he thought it was, Michael never learnt.)

'How are things?'

'Bad, Mr Mason, very bad.' It was the whining voice of an old man.

'Have you seen Dr Rudd tonight?'

Again came that eerie peal of laughter from invisible depths.

'He's the coppers' man, ain't he—Rudd? No, Mr Mason, we ain't seen him. Nobody comes down 'ere. Afraid of wakin' people up, they are!'

The chuckles came now like the rustle of a wind.

Mason stopped before No. 9. A man was sitting on the step, his back to the door, a bibulous man who slept noisily. An old hearth-rug was drawn over his knees and on top some belated wag of Gallows Court had balanced an empty tomato can.

'If it doesn't fall and wake him, old man Wicks will give him a shock if he finds him there!' said Mason.

'Uncanny, isn't it?' he said when they had emerged from the court. 'They talk about Chinamen in the East End of

London. Lord! they're the only decent people they've got in Gallows Alley, and old Gregory.'

'I wonder what they do for a living?'

'I should hate to know,' said Mason.

They came back by the way they had entered.

'I'm giving Bray another hour, and then I'm going up to the Yard.'

'I'll drive you, if you like. There's nothing more to be got here.'

The shadowy figure they had seen emerged from the opening, holding an old overcoat about his throat.

'White Face has been around tonight, they say, Mr Mason.'

'Do they, indeed?' said Mason politely.

'You don't treat us right, Mr Mason. You come down 'ere an' expect us to "nose" for you, and everybody in the court knows we're "nosing". If you treated us right and did the proper thing, you'd hear something. What's the matter with old Gregory, hey? That's something you don't know—and nobody else knows. What's the matter with Gregory?'

And with this cryptic remark he vanished.

'He's mad—genuinely mad. No, I don't know his name, but he's mad in a sane way. What in hell does he mean about Gregory?'

Mike could not answer. He knew old Gregory—everybody in London knew the man who housed his cab in Dr Marford's yard and lived alone in the one decent house in Gallows Court.

'I'd give a lot to know what that crazy man knew about him—what he was driving at.'

Mason was disturbed, irritable. A detective officer has an instinct for sincerity—it is two-thirds of his mental equipment, and the demented denizen of the court was not rambling. To speak ill, or hint suspicion, against Gregory Wicks was a kind of treason.

'Rum lot of devils,' he said, and shrugged off his uneasiness.

CHAPTER XI

THE telephone bell had been ringing at frequent intervals in the Landors' flat; the waiting detectives could hear it in the street: there must have been a half-open window somewhere through which the sound could come.

'It's Mason getting rattled, I should think,' said Elk fretfully. 'Why I came here I don't know. Madness! I get like that sometimes—just go dippy and do silly things.'

'You came here,' said Inspector Bray heavily, 'because you were told to come by your superior officer.'

Elk groaned.

'The trouble with you, Billy, is that you've no sense of unimportance,' he said helplessly.

'That doesn't sound very respectful,' said Mr Bray severely.

He wanted to be very severe indeed, but you never knew with Elk. At any moment he might force you into bringing him before the Chief Constable, and invariably when he was brought before the Chief Constable he demonstrated that he and the Chief Constable were the only people in the world who took a sensible view of the circumstances.

'How many men have you posted?' he asked. 'I don't want to give either of these two people a chance of slipping us.'

'I've posted none,' said Sergeant Elk, almost brightly. 'My superior officer has posted three, and takes all the responsibility. I ventured to suggest a different posting, but I was told to mind my own so-and-so business.'

'I said nothing of the sort,' said Bray hotly.

'You meant it,' was Elk's retort.

Bray looked anxiously up and down. He was not terribly happy, working under Mason. Very few detective officers were. And he was out of his own division, which was all wrong.

Moreover, Mason was very unforgiving when his subordinates fell into error, and this was a murder case, where no excuses would be accepted. On the whole, it was better to conciliate his sergeant, who was notoriously a favourite of the superintendent.

He stared up and down the road uncomfortably.

'If I've been a little short-tempered with you, Elk, I'm sorry,' he said almost affectionately. 'I'm so distracted with this business. Where did you say I ought to post a man?'

'In the back courtyard,' said Elk promptly. 'There's a reachable fire escape up which any healthy man or woman could climb, or vice versa.'

Elk was on the point of withdrawing a perfectly useless patrol at the far end of the street, when a taxicab turned the corner, stopped before the main door of the apartment and a woman got out. They were watching from the corner of a front garden on the opposite side of the road.

'That looks like the lady, eh? What do you think, Elk?'

'That's madam,' said Elk. 'And I've seen her before somewhere.'

She had paid the taxi and it drove slowly away. The watchers still waited.

As Inez Landor put the key in the front door they saw her turn her head and look anxiously round. She could see nobody. Her imagination had pictured the road packed with police officers. She hurried up to the first floor, unlocked her own door and went into the flat.

There was a small hand-lamp on the table, working from a dry battery, and it was this she switched on. There were four letters in the letter-box. She did not even trouble to take them out, but, taking the lamp in her hand, she went softly to the bedroom door, which opened from the hall, and looked in. Her heart sank when she saw that her husband had not returned. What should she do? What could she do? With a deep sigh, she took off her leather coat and hat and went into the bedroom, leaving the door open.

There had been a murder in the East End; she had seen the late edition bills and heard somebody speaking about it at supper—not that she ate supper, but usually, when she and her husband were both out, she arranged to meet Louis at Elford's. He had not appeared. She had waited till the restaurant closed, and had then gone on to a fashionable all-night coffee-house, where they went when he was very late. He was not there either. The time of waiting seemed an eternity. In despair she had gone home, not daring to buy the midnight sheets which were being sold on the street for fear . . .

She shivered. She wondered whether that nice doctor would say anything; the man with the gentle voice, who had been so sympathetic and who had given her sal volatile. How stupid she had been to mistake a fight between two labourers! Perhaps that was what the newspapers called murder.

She had told him so much—things she would not have told to her mother if she were living. There was hardly a step she had taken that day which she did not now bitterly regret. It was worse than folly—sheer madness, to go in search of Louis. Suppose something had happened—a fight; she dared not imagine worse. She had broadcast his motives through London.

Inez Landor drew on her dressing-gown and walked up and down the dark room, striving to settle her mind to calmness. She had had four deliriously happy years, years of dream-building. That flimsy fabric had been shivered to nothingness.

She thought she heard a sound, a step in the hall, and, opening the door, she listened. There it was again, a faint creak. There was a loose board near the hall door. She had always intended having that board replaced.

'Is that you, Louis?' she whispered.

There was no answer. She could hear the solemn ticking of the hall clock, and the far-away whirr of a motor-car passing the end of the road.

'Louis—is that you?' she raised her voice.

She must have been mistaken, then, for no answer came. She left the door ajar, and, going to the window, pulled aside the curtains carefully and looked out. A futile act, for this window looked upon the well at the back of the building.

And then she heard a faint knock. The silence in the flat was so deep that it re-echoed through the hall. She tiptoed into the hall and listened. The knock was repeated, and she crept to the door.

'Who is there?' she asked in a low voice.

'Louis.'

Her heart was beating furiously. She turned the handle and admitted him, closing the door behind him.

'Put on the light, darling.'

His voice was strained and old-sounding. It was the voice of a man who had been running and had not recovered his breath.

'Sitting in the dark? Turn on the lights.'

'Wait!'

There was a window in the tiny lobby which could be seen from the street. She pulled down the blind and drew the thick curtains across and closed her own door before she switched on the light in the hall. Save for the blue bruise under one eye, his face was colourless. Inez Landor stared at her husband with growing terror.

'What has happened?'

He shook his head. It was at once a gesture of impatience and weariness.

'Nothing very much. I have had a ghastly time. Inez, will you get me a glass of water?'

'Shall I get you some wine?'

He shook his head.

'No, darling, water.'

She was gone for a few minutes; when she returned he was looking at the knife and belt that hung on the wall. It was one

of many souvenirs he had collected in his travels—a broad
leather belt with big brass bosses, from which hung a knife
in a gaily ornamented sheath. Before this day it had meant
no more than the saddle, the lasso, the spears and the strange
Aztec relics that covered the wall.

'We've got to get rid of that somehow,' he said.

'The knife?'

'Yes, this.'

He tapped the empty frog where a second knife had been.

She did not ask him why; but what hope there was left in
her heart flickered and died. For a little while neither spoke.
There were questions she wanted to ask him which her tongue
refused to frame. She could only make the most trite and
commonplace remarks.

'I thought I heard you in the flat a few minutes ago,' she
said. 'You haven't been in before?'

'No.'

'Why did you knock?' she asked, suddenly remembering.

He licked his lips.

'I lost my key. I don't know where—somewhere.'

He drank the remainder of the water and put the glass on
the top of a little desk which stood against the wall.

'I could have sworn I heard the door close a few minutes
ago,' she said. 'I came out and called you. I heard somebody
walking in the hall.'

He smiled and his arm went round her shoulders.

'Your nerve is going. Have you been waiting here in the dark?'

She shook her head. Should she tell him? It was not the
moment for half-confidences.

'No, I have been out looking for you.'

She caught his arm.

'Louis, you didn't fight? You didn't—do anything?'

Louis Landor did not answer immediately.

'I don't know,' he said. 'Let us go into the sitting-room.'

But she pushed him back into the chair where he was sitting.

'No, no, stay here. None of these lights shows from the street.'

He looked at her sharply.

'What do you mean—none of these lights shows from the street? Is anybody outside watching?'

'I'm not sure,' she said. 'I think so. Before I left the restaurant I telephoned here in the hope that you had returned. I thought the maid was here, and didn't realise that she couldn't get in. I knew she'd gone to her sister's and I called her up. Louis'—her lips quivered—'the police have been here.'

And when he did not speak she knew—

'Has anything happened?'

Louis Landor ran his fingers through his long black hair.

'I don't know—yes—I do know, but I'm not sure how far I was involved. When I went out after him I lost sight of him, but I had an idea I should find him somewhere in the West End, and I was right.'

'You spoke to him?'

He shook his head.

'No, he was in a car with a girl—a pretty girl; some poor little fool who has fallen for him. She's a nurse who works for Marford.'

He saw her mouth open wide in amazement.

'For Marford—not Dr Marford?'

'How the devil did you know that?' he asked, astonished. 'Yes, he's got a clinic in the East End, I'm going to see her tomorrow and tell her the truth about Mr Donald Bateman. I followed them in a cab to Bury Street and then back to his hotel. I wanted the chance of seeing him alone without making any kind of scandal, but he never gave me the chance. Naturally I did not want to send my name up to his room, so I waited till he came out. There wasn't the ghost of a chance of seeing him: he went to a little restaurant which was crowded with people, but I knew that if I was patient I should pick him up and settle our little matter definitely. He lingered over his dinner and I have an idea that he was waiting for somebody.

She came eventually—rather a pretty woman. She wasn't in evening dress and her voice was rather common. When he went out of the restaurant I followed, keeping at a distance. I think he'd recognised me this afternoon. Naturally, she complicated matters: I had to wait till he dropped her. After dinner they drove away from the restaurant. I was in the gallery upstairs and could see everything that was happening. I took a taxi and followed them—they drove to a very poor neighbourhood—Tidal Basin, they call it, I think. There she went into a flat with him—it was over a shop. It was then that I telephoned to you. Darling, you didn't follow me?'

She nodded dejectedly.

'I had an uncomfortable feeling you might. You were mad!'

'I know. Go on,' she said. 'What happened then?'

He asked for another glass of water and she brought it for him.

'He came out alone, and I followed him to a street which has a long wall on one side. I was just going up to him when I saw the woman run across the road. She spoke to him for a little time and then they parted. It was my opportunity. There was nobody in sight and I came up to him—'

'He had the knife?' she interrupted, and he smiled wryly.

'I gave him no chance to use it.'

She had seen the bruise on his face but had not the courage to ask him how he came by it. It seemed so unimportant in view of the other terrific possibility.

'—Yes, I hit him. He went down like a log. I got scared. I saw somebody standing in the doorway—a doctor's place—it must have been Marford. I ran. And then I saw a policeman walking towards me. At the place where I stopped there was a big gate which had a wicket door. By some miracle it was unlocked. I got through and bolted the door. I was in a narrow yard which surrounded the warehouse. The police came and searched it but I hid behind some packing cases.'

'The police?' she gasped. 'Searched it. Is Donald—?'

He nodded.

'Not dead?' she wailed.

He nodded again.

'The police have been here?'

'Yes. They've been questioning the maid. I don't know what she has told them.'

He got up and walked to the little desk and felt in his pocket. 'I've lost my keys.'

She took a little leather case from her bag and handed it to him. He opened one of the drawers and took out a thick packet of papers.

'I suppose very few people keep three thousand pounds in the entrance hall of their flat!' His voice was now almost normal. 'Whatever happens, we'll get out of the country tomorrow. If anything goes wrong with me, you take the money and get away.'

She clutched at his sleeve frantically.

'What can happen to you, Louis? You didn't kill him—the knife!'

He disengaged her hand almost roughly.

'I don't know whether I killed him. Now listen,' he said. 'You've got to be terribly sensible about this. Even if this blackguard told everything, they can't hurt you. But I don't want you to suffer the ignominy of an inquiry—the police court and that filth.'

Her senses were unnaturally keen. She heard a sound.

'There's somebody coming up the stairs,' she whispered. 'Go into the bedroom—go quickly!'

He hesitated, but she pushed him towards the room and ran rather than walked to the door and listened. She could hear soft, whispering voices. Switching on the table lamp, she found a book and opened it with trembling hands. There was a little sewing table in the spare-room and she brought this out and had placed it near when the first thunderous knock sounded. She took one glimpse at herself in the hall mirror, used her pocket puff swiftly and opened the door.

Two men were standing there: two tall, grim-looking figures of fate.

'Who is it?' she asked.

It was an agonised effort to control her voice, but she succeeded.

'My name is Bray—Detective-Inspector Bray, Criminal Investigation Department,' he said formally. 'This is Detective-Sergeant Elk.'

'Good evening, Mrs Landor.'

It was characteristic of Elk that he took complete charge of the proceedings from that moment. He had the affability of a man supremely confident of himself.

'Come in,' she said.

'All right, Mrs Landor, I'll shut the door,' said Elk.

They walked into the hall. She noticed that neither of the men removed his hat.

She made one effort to appear unconcerned, tried to infuse a little gaiety into her voice.

'I should have known you were detectives. I've seen so many in cinemas and I know detectives never take their hats off,' she smiled.

Mr Bray would have taken this as a reproach. Elk was apparently amused, but supplied an explanation.

'A detective who takes his hat off, Mrs Landor,' he said, 'is a detective with one hand! In other words, the other hand is occupied when he may want to use two.'

'I hope you won't even want to use one,' she said. 'Will you sit down? Is it about Joan?'

It was cruelly unfair to make this implied libel on an honest and decent servant, but she could not afford to be nice.

'Don't make a noise, will you?' she added. 'My husband is asleep.'

'He got asleep very quickly, Mrs Landor,' said Bray. 'He only came in a few minutes ago.'

She forced a smile.

'A few minutes ago! How absurd! He's been in bed since ten.'

'Excuse me, Mrs Landor, did another man come into this flat?'

She shook her head.

'Do you ever have burglars coming up the fire escape?' he asked, eyeing her quickly.

She laughed at this.

'I don't even know which way burglars come, but I never use the fire escape myself! I hope I never shall!'

Elk paid tribute to the sally with a smile.

'We'd like to see your husband,' he said after a moment's consideration. 'Which is his room? Is that it?' He pointed to a door near the hall.

She had seated herself at the table where the open book was lying, her hands folded on her lap that they might not testify to her agitation. She rose now.

'No—that is the maid's room. My room is here, but I can't have him disturbed. He's not very well,' she said. 'He's had a fall.'

'Too bad,' said Elk. 'Which is his room?'

She did not answer but walked across to the bedroom door and knocked.

'Louis, there are some people who want to see you.'

He came in immediately. He was without coat and collar, but it needed no experienced observer to realise that he had been interrupted rather in the process of taking off his clothes than of dressing.

'Were you getting up, darling?' she asked quickly.

Elk shook his head reprovingly.

'I'd rather you didn't suggest anything to him, Mrs Landor. You may suggest the wrong things. That is a friendly tip.'

Louis looked from one to the other. He had heard Inez say 'detectives' under her breath, but he did not need that explanation. Inspector Bray made one effort to control the inquiry.

'I've reason to believe that you know a man who was staying at the Little Norfolk Hotel in Norfolk Street, Strand, and calling himself Donald Bateman.'

'No,' said Inez quickly.

'I'm asking your husband,' said Bray sharply. 'Well, Mr Landor?'

Louis shrugged.

'I have no personal acquaintance with anybody named Donald Bateman.'

It was here that Elk resumed charge of the examination and his superior assented.

'We don't want to know whether you're personally acquainted with him, Mr Landor. That's entirely beside the question. Have you ever heard of, or have you in any way been associated with, a man called Donald Bateman, who arrived from South Africa in the last few weeks? Before you answer, I wish to tell you that Inspector Bray and I are investigating the circumstances under which this man met his death in Endley Street, Tidal Basin, at ten o'clock last night.'

'He's dead?' said Louis. 'How did he die?'

'By a knife wound,' said Bray.

He saw the woman sway on her feet.

'I know nothing about it,' said Louis Landor. 'I have never used a knife against any man.'

Elk's eyes were roving the curios on the wall. He took a step closer, and lifting the belt from the nail, laid it on the table.

'What is this supposed to be?' He tapped the knife.

'It's a knife I brought back from South America,' said Louis immediately. 'I had a ranch there.'

'Is it yours?'

Louis nodded.

'There were two in this belt,' he said. 'Where is the other?'

'We lost it.' Inez spoke quickly. 'Louis lost it. We haven't had it for quite a long time—we've never had it in this house.'

Elk ran his finger along the belt.

'There's dust here. There ought to be dust inside this empty frog,' he said. 'If the story is true and there has been no knife here for a long time, the inside would be thick with dust. On the other hand, if your story isn't true, there was a knife here today—'

He rubbed the inside of the leather and showed his finger practically speckless.

'I dusted it myself this morning,' said Inez, and Elk smiled at her admiringly.

'Mrs Landor!' he said in reproach.

'Well, I've got to tell the truth,' she said desperately. 'You want the truth, don't you?'

She was on the verge of hysteria, near to the breaking-point which would leave her morally and physically shattered.

'You're not entitled to draw inferences without my offering some explanation. God Almighty! Haven't I suffered enough through that man!'

'Which man?' asked Bray sharply.

She was silent.

'Which man, Mrs Landor?'

Louis Landor at any rate had recovered his self-possession.

'My wife isn't quite herself tonight,' he said. 'I have been out rather late and she got rather worried about me.'

'Now what's the use of making a mystery of something that's perfectly clear?' asked Elk.

He was almost sad as he contemplated the futility of unnecessary evasion.

'Your wife knew Donald Bateman?'

Louis did not answer.

'I'm going to be perfectly frank with you. I told you we were inquiring into the murder of this man. That is our duty as police officers. We're not asking you or your wife or anybody else who is the murderer of Donald Bateman. Understand that right, Mr Landor. The only person we want is the murderer of this man! The people we don't want are those who didn't murder him, even though they know something of him. If either or both of you are responsible, I, my chief and the whole damned crowd of us at Scotland Yard will work night and day to bring you to the Old Bailey! That's treating you square. If you're not guilty, we'll do all we can to clear you.

The only thing you can give us for the moment is the truth.'

'We've told the truth,' said Inez breathlessly.

'No, you haven't.' Elk shook his head. 'I didn't quite expect you would. The truth in every case like this is hidden under a heap of rubbishy lies. What are you hiding up, Mrs Landor? It all comes down to that. You're hiding something and your husband's hiding something, that maybe doesn't matter ten loud hoots.'

'I'm hiding nothing,' she said.

'You knew Donald Bateman?'

'I don't remember him,' she said quickly.

'You knew Donald Bateman.' Elk was infinitely patient, and when she shook her head he put his hand slowly into his inside pocket. 'Well, I don't want to give you an unpleasant experience, Mrs Landor, but I've a photograph of this man—a flashlight picture taken after his death.'

She reeled back, her hands out-thrust.

'I won't look at it! I won't! It's beastly ... you're not allowed to show me things like that ... I won't see it!'

Louis's arm was round her, his cheek was against hers. He said something to her in an undertone, something which momentarily calmed her. Then he stretched out his hand to the detective.

'Perhaps I could identify this man,' he said. 'I know most of my wife's friends.'

Elk took from his pocket an envelope, and from this drew a positive that was still damp. It was not a pretty picture, but the hand which held the photograph did not tremble.

'Yes, my wife knew this man ten years ago, when she was a girl of seventeen,' said Louis.

'When did you last see him?' asked Bray.

Louis Landor thought.

'A few years ago.'

'He only arrived in England last week,' said Bray coldly.

'He may have come to England every year, for all you know,' said Louis with a faint smile. 'No, I saw his photograph.'

'What did he call himself in those days, Mrs Landor?'

She was more composed now, her voice under control.

'I knew him as Donald. He was just—an acquaintance.'

She heard Elk's murmured expostulation.

'Surely, Mrs Landor, you're not telling us the gospel truth, are you?' he asked. 'Just now you told us you'd "suffered enough from this man". You can't suffer very deeply through any man whose name you couldn't remember except as Donald.'

She did not answer.

'Can you, Mrs Landor? You're not going to tell us? He was a very close friend, wasn't he?'

She drew a long breath.

'I suppose he was. It's not a thing I want to talk about—'

'Inez! I'm not going to allow these people to think—'

Elk interrupted him.

'Never mind what we think, Mr Landor. Nothing's going to shock us—not me, at any rate. You knew this man before you met your husband, I suppose, or was it after?'

'It was before,' she replied.

'Was he anything—to you?'

Elk found difficulty in putting the matter delicately. He saw the man's face go red and white.

'You're being damned offensive, aren't you?' Louis was glowering at him.

Elk shook his head wearily.

'That's just what I'm not being. A man has been murdered tonight, Landor—and I'm anxious to put the murderer under lock and key, and it's only possible to put him under lock and key by asking all sorts of innocent people offensive questions. And when you come to think of it, there's nothing quite so offensive as stabbing a man to the heart and leaving him stiff on the paving-stones of Tidal Basin. It's a lousy place to die. Personally, I should be very much offended if it happened to me, and I'd regard any questions similar to those I am asking as being in the nature of a bouquet—in

comparison. Did you know Donald Bateman was in town?'
He addressed Inez.

'No,' she answered.

Bray interjected impatiently.

'Do you mean to tell us you didn't know that he was in
London three or four days ago?'

'No!' Her tone was defiant.

'Mrs Landor,' said Elk, 'you've been very unhappy this last
day or two; your servant told us all about it. Servants will
talk, and they love a little domestic tragedy.'

'I've not been well,' she said.

'Is it because you've seen Donald Bateman, the man from
whom you suffered?'

'No,' she replied.

'Nor you?' asked Bray.

'No,' answered Louis.

'Tonight, for instance?' suggested Elk. 'You haven't seen
Donald Bateman or the man so described?'

'No,' said Louis.

'Have you been in the neighbourhood of Tidal Basin
tonight?' asked Elk. 'Before you answer that, I must caution
you to be very careful how you reply.'

'No.'

Elk took a slip of paper from his pocket,

'I'm going to ask you a question, Landor, which I'd like
you to consider before you answer. In the pocket of the man
known as Donald Bateman were found two one-hundred-
pound notes, indicator number 33/O 11878 and 33/O 11879.
They were new notes, recently issued from the Maida Vale
Branch of the Midland Bank. Can you tell me anything about
these banknotes?'

He was silent.

'Can you, Mrs Landor?'

'I don't know anything about the numbers of banknotes—'
she began desperately.

'That's not what we're asking,' said Bray sternly. 'Have you given or sent to any person during the past week two banknotes each for a hundred pounds?'

'They come from my account,' said Louis quietly. 'I suppose I'd better tell the truth. We did know Donald Bateman was back in London. He wrote to us and said he was in great distress, and asked me for the loan of two hundred pounds.'

'I see,' nodded Bray. 'You sent them to his address in Norfolk Street by letter post?'

Louis nodded.

'Did he acknowledge receipt of the money?'

'No,' said Louis.

'He didn't even call to thank you?'

'No,' said Inez.

She spoke a little too quickly.

'You're not going to tell us the truth, either of you.' Elk's voice was rather sad. 'Not the truth about this man or this money or your visit to Tidal Basin. You've a bruise on your face—been fighting?'

'No, I hit it against a cupboard door.'

'Your wife said you fell down,' said Elk drearily, 'but it doesn't matter. Why do you keep these knives here?' He picked up the belt and dangled it in his hand.

'Why does he keep these saddles on the wall?' asked Inez impatiently. 'Be reasonable, please. They are prizes he got at a rodeo in the Argentine.'

'For what?' asked Bray.

'It was a knife-throwing competition—' began Louis, and stopped.

'Hiding up!' groaned Elk. 'Get your coat on, Landor!'

Inez Landor darted to him and caught him frantically by the arm.

'You're not going to take him away?'

'I'm taking you both away,' said Elk cheerfully, 'but only to Scotland Yard. You'll have to see Mr Mason, but you needn't worry. He's a very sympathetic man—even more sympathetic than Mr Bray.'

There was a touch of malignity in this thrust which Bray did not observe.

She did not go into the bedroom with her husband; her own coat was lying on the back of a chair. She had quite forgotten that fact—saw now the absurdity of the reading-lamp, the sewing and the book whilst this raincoat of hers testified mutely to her wanderings.

Louis came back in a very short space of time and helped her into the leather jacket.

'It's all right, we've got a police car downstairs; you needn't bother about a taxi,' said Bray, in answer to his inquiry.

He was a little huffy, being conscious that whatever result had been achieved brought him little personal kudos.

'I shan't want you to come with me, Elk,' he said shortly. 'You can help shove these people into the car and then you can come back and search the flat. Would you like to see the warrant?' he asked.

Louis shook his head.

'There's nothing in the flat that I object to your seeing,' he said, and pointed to the little escritoire. 'There's about three thousand pounds in that drawer, and railway tickets. I was leaving the country tomorrow with my wife. Give Mr—?'

'Elk's my name.'

'Give Mr Elk the keys, Inez.'

Without a word she handed the case to Elk.

As they walked through the door of the flat Bray put out his hand and switched off the light. He was a domesticated man with a taste for economy, and he acted instinctively.

'Save your light, Mrs Landor,' he apologised for his action.

The door closed and the sound of their movement grew fainter to the listening man who stood behind the locked door of the maid's room. He came out noiselessly, a dark figure, a black felt hat pulled down over his eyes, his face hidden behind a white mask.

Quickly he went to the desk, took something out of his pocket; there was the sound of breaking wood and the drawer slid out. A small pocket torch revealed what he sought, and he thrust money, passport and tickets into his pocket. He had hardly done so before he heard the detective returning, and moved swiftly towards the door. He was standing in its shadow when it opened. Elk's back was towards him when he heard a slight sound, and turned quickly. Not quickly enough. For the fraction of a second he glimpsed the white-faced thing, and then something struck him and he went down like a log.

White Face stooped, dragged the inanimate figure a little way from the door so that it would open, and a second later had slipped out of the flat, leaving the door ajar.

He ran up one flight of stairs, passed through an open window and went swiftly down a narrow iron stairway which brought him to the courtyard. There was no guard here, as he knew.

Ten minutes later one of the detectives waiting outside the house went upstairs to proffer his assistance to Elk. He heard a groan and, pushing the door open, found the sergeant in his least amiable mood.

CHAPTER XII

SUPERINTENDENT MASON boasted that he could sleep anywhere at any time. He certainly needed a considerable amount of rousing when the police car reached Scotland Yard.

As for Michael Quigley, he had never felt less sleepy in his life, and the coffee which was brought to the superintendent's room was as a stimulant quite unnecessary. It brought Mr Mason to irritable life.

His complaint was that, at whatever hour of the day or night he arrived at Scotland Yard, he was certain to find some official document waiting for his attention. There were half a dozen minutes warningly inscribed and heavily sealed.

'They can wait till the morning.' He examined the two or three telephone messages that were on his desk, but they told him nothing new. There was no news from Bray. It was a quarter of an hour later that Elk and his superior had their interview with the Landors.

Michael looked at his watch. It was too late to go to bed. He wanted to see Janice early in the morning.

'You can call back and I'll tell you anything that's going,' said Mason. 'About that ring, Michael: I'm afraid we shall have to have a little talk with the young lady. I'll make it as pleasant as possible. Maybe you can arrange for us to meet—I don't want to bring her down to the Yard, because that would rattle her.'

Michael was grateful for this concession. Ever since he had told Mason the truth about the ring, a dull little shadow of worry had rested in his mind.

'You're a pretty nice man for a policeman, Mason.'

'I'm a pretty nice man for any kind of job,' said the superintendent.

Michael strolled out on to the Embankment and up through Northumberland Avenue. He had reached Trafalgar Square and was standing at the corner of the Strand, wondering whether it would be sensible to go home and snatch a few hours' sleep, or whether to call at his club, which was open till four o'clock, when a taxicab went rapidly past him in the direction of the Admiralty gate. Midnight taxicabs either crawl or fly, and this one was moving quickly—not so swift, however, that he did not glimpse a familiar figure sitting on the box, a pipe clenched between his teeth. If he had been moving more slowly Michael would have hailed old Gregory Wicks.

'Did you want a cab, Mr Quigley?'

It was a policeman by his side; Michael was fairly well known to this division.

'No, thank you.'

'I thought you were trying to stop that driver. They take liberties, those fellows.'

Michael laughed.

'That was an old friend of mine. I suppose you know him—old Gregory Wicks?'

'Gregory, eh?' The policeman was a middle-aged man who knew his West End extremely well. 'The old fellow's getting about again. I hadn't seen him for months till I saw him the other night sleeping on his box at the corner of Orange Street. He lost a good fare that night. I wanted him to take Mr Gasso down to Scotland Yard to make a statement—I was in that case,' he added a little proudly.

Chance policemen encountered in the middle of the night can be very talkative, and Michael was in no mood for conversation. But the mention of Gasso arrested his attention.

'You were in what case?'

'The Howdah case. You know, the night they held up Mrs What's-her-name—Duval or something, and pinched her diamond chain. Naturally my name hasn't been mentioned because the case has never been into court, but I was on point duty near the Howdah Club when the robbery occurred. If anybody had screamed, or I'd heard 'em scream, I'd have been on the spot in a second. It only shows you what chances you miss because people won't behave sensibly.'

Michael gathered that behaving sensibly was synonymous with screaming violently.

'Old Gregory was about here that night, was he?'

'He had his cab about fifty yards from the club. He never joins a rank, and, knowing him, we aren't very strict. If he can find a nice quiet corner to have his snooze we never disturb him.'

Old Gregory! Then in a flash Michael remembered the mysterious words of the nondescript of Gallows Court: 'What was the matter with Gregory?'

Here was a new angle to many problems. He made a quick decision. Calling a more leisurely taxi, he drove off to Tidal Basin. Gallows Court had something to tell, and since Gallows Court never slept it might be more instructive in the middle of the night than in the broad and hateful light of day.

Shale arrived at Scotland Yard simultaneously with the telephoned news that Bray was on his way accompanied by the two people he had been sent to seek. Mr Mason leaned back in his chair and rubbed his hands. He was relieved. To find suspects quietly was more desirable than telling all the world they were wanted; for a suspect, having gained much undesirable publicity, very often proves to be perfectly innocent. Questions are asked in Parliament, and there have been cases where payment has had to be made as compensation for the wounded feelings of someone called urgently to police investigations.

Parliament had been playing too interfering a part in the police force lately. A new Commissioner had come and was taking credit for all the reforms his subordinates had forced upon his predecessor. The Home Office had issued new instructions which, if they were faithfully carried out, would prevent the police from asking vital questions. Every step

that the crank and the busybody could devise to interfere
with the administration of justice had assumed official shape.

Superintendent Mason knew the regulations by heart. One
had to know them to evade them. Like every other high official
of Scotland Yard, he lived at the mercy of stupid policemen
and the perjury of some eminent man's light o' love. But the
risk did not sit heavily upon him.

Wender, of the Identification Bureau, was ready to see him,
and he sent Shale to bring that long-suffering man with his
data.

Wender was a small, stout gentleman with a tiny white
moustache, and the huge horn-rimmed spectacles he wore
did not add any measure of wisdom to his face, but rather
emphasised its placidity. He arrived with a bundle of documents under his arm and a short briar pipe between his
teeth. He was wearing a smoking-jacket, for he had been at
a theatre when he was called to make a examination of the
few clues which had been acquired in the case.

'Come in, Charlie,' said Mason. 'It's good to see somebody
looking cheerful at this hour of the morning.'

'I'm always cheerful because I'm always right,' said Wender,
pulling up a chair and sitting down.

'Why the fancy dress?' asked Shale, who was Wender's
brother-in-law, and could therefore be flippant with his superior.

'Theatre,' said his relative briefly.

He was indeed an equable and happy man at all hours
of the day and night. Nothing disturbed him. He was, too,
something more than an authority upon fingerprints. The
range of his information was astounding.

'Before we start discussing whorls, islands and circles,' said
Mason, as he took from his pocket the capsule and laid it on
the blotting-pad, 'what is this?'

Wender took it up and turned it over between his fingers.

'I don't know—butyl ammonal, I should think. I've seen it
done up in capsules like that. Where did you find it?'

Mason told him.

'I'm not sure, of course,' said Wender, 'not having a nose that can smell through a glass case, but it's that colour. Now, what else did you want to know?'

'Is there any record of the Landors?' asked Mason.

Mr Wender shook his head.

'None whatever. That doesn't mean we haven't got a record under another name. It's a curious circumstance'—he smiled brightly—'that criminals occasionally give themselves names that they weren't born with. I took this particular job on myself,' he explained, 'because my night man is about as useful as a performing flea.' He laid the documents on the table. 'There you are.'

'Have you got the fingerprints of the dead man?'

The identification man sorted them out

'Yes. Who took them?'

'I did,' admitted Shale.

'They were of no use to me—the first lot, I mean. I had to send down and get another lot. You young officers are still rather hazy as to how to take a print.'

Mason examined the cards with their black smudges. They meant nothing to him.

'Is he known?'

'Is he known!' scoffed Wender. He sorted out another document. 'Donald Arthur Bateman, *alias* Donald Arthur, *alias* Donald Mackintosh. He's got more *aliases* than a film star.'

Mason frowned heavily.

'Donald Arthur Bateman? I know that name. Why, I had him at the London Sessions for housebreaking.'

'Fraud,' corrected the other. 'Twelve months hard labour, 1919.'

Mason nodded.

'That's right—fraud. He swindled Sir Somebody Something out of three thousand pounds—a land deal. That was his speciality. And then he was up again at the Old Bailey—'

'Acquitted,' said Wender. 'The prosecutor had something to hide up and was too ill to give evidence. There's a
conviction here at the Exeter Assizes—eighteen months, the
Teignmouth blackmail case. You won't remember that: it
was in the hands of the locals; they didn't call in the Yard.'

'Then he went abroad.'

'And died there! Semi-officially!' said Wender.

Mason read the note.

'Reported dead in Perth, Western Australia, in 1923.
Doubtful. Believed to have gone to South Africa. He's dead
enough now,' he added.

He brooded over the card.

'Blackmail, fraud, fraud, blackmail . . . he was versatile.
Married, of course . . . dozens of times, I should think.
Went to Australia; concerned with the brothers Walter and
Thomas Furse in holding up the Woomarra branch of the
South Australian Bank. Offered King's evidence . . . accepted;
no prosecution. Walter Furse eight years penal servitude,
Thomas Furse three years. Walter an habitual criminal;
Thomas, who had only arrived in Victoria from England a
month before his conviction, released after two years.'

He read it aloud.

'That's our Tommy,' said Shale. 'You remember the woman
said, "Tommy did it"?'

But Mason was reading the 'confidential'. It was written in
minute type and he had recourse to his reading glass.

'"During their imprisonment,"' he read, '"Bateman disappeared, taking with him the young wife of Thomas."' He
looked up. 'That's Lorna. "Walter Furse died in prison in
1935." Tommy's the murderer, Lorna's his wife, Bateman's the
murdered man. It's as clear as daylight. There's the motive!'

'What do we know about Tommy? Have you any Australian
records?'

Mr Wender had laid three paper-covered books on the table.
He selected one of these.

'In this office we have everything that opens and shuts,' he boasted. 'Here you are: "Strictly confidential. Record of persons convicted of felony in the State of Victoria, 1922. Published by authority"—'

'Never mind about the authority,' said Mason patiently.

The identification man turned over the leaves rapidly, murmuring the names that appeared at the head of each column.

'"Farrow, Felton, Ferguson, Furse"—here you are: "Walter Furse, see volume 6, page 13".'

He pushed the book to Mason. This collection was more interesting than most Government Blue Books, for the record of every man was in the form of a short and readable biography.

'"Thomas Furse. This man was educated in England by his brother; was probably unaware of his brother's illegal occupation when he came to the Colony. Furse was certainly an assumed name (see W. Furse, Vol. 8, p. 7), and there is a possibility that he was educated under his own name by his brother and with his brother's money, though he adopted the name of Furse when he came to the Colony. He married Lorna Weston"—'

Mason stopped reading to look up.

'"He married Lorna Weston, whom he met on the voyage out to Australia. She disappeared after his conviction. Thomas released . . ."'

He read on in silence, and presently closed the book.

'The identity of these people is now positively established,' he said. 'The motive is here for anyone who can read. Thomas goes to Australia; within a month or two he is caught for this hold-up and gets two years. Donald Arthur Bateman turns King's evidence and disappears with Lorna. Thomas comes back to England and in some way meets Donald last night. Now the only question is: is Thomas Furse another name for Louis Landor? That's what we've got to find out. If it is, then we have the case in a nutshell.'

There were one or two other documents, and he turned them over.

'What's this?' he asked. It was a large photograph of a thumb-print.

'That was on the back of the watch,' said Wender. 'Harry Lamborn, as plain as a visiting-card. Five convictions—'

'I know all about him,' interrupted Mason.

'A fine print,' said Wender ecstatically.

'You ought to have it framed, Charlie,' said Mason in his more complimentary mood. 'I shan't want you any more.'

'Then I'll toddle home to bed.' Mr Wender stretched himself and yawned. 'If I haven't brought somebody to the gallows my evening has been wasted.'

'You'll get the usual medal and star,' said Mason.

'I know,' said the other sardonically; 'and when I put my expense account in—a cab from the Lyceum to Scotland Yard—they'll tell me I ought to have taken a 'bus!'

He had left when Bray came importantly into the room.

'I've got those people.'

'Eh?' Mason looked up. He was reading again the account of Thomas Furse. No age was given, which was rather annoying, but he could put a beam cable inquiry through to Melbourne and find an answer waiting for him when he came back to the office.

'You've got those people, have you? Did you search the flat?'

'I left Elk to do that.'

Mason nodded.

'What are they hiding up?'

'That's what I don't quite know. I should have found out, but unfortunately Elk is a little difficult. I don't want to complain, Chief, but I'm placed in an awkward position when a subordinate takes a case out of my hands and starts investigating and cross-questioning, taking no more notice of me than if I were the paper on the wall!'

'He does it with me,' Mason smiled broadly. 'Why shouldn't he do it with you? As a matter of fact, you oughtn't to complain. These darned regulations about questioning prisoners are so framed that it's good to have some other officer responsible for breaking them—you can always pass the kick on to him. Shoot 'em in, Bray.'

He laughed quietly to himself after Bray had left. Elk was incorrigible, but Elk was invaluable. There was some odd kink in his mind which prevented his passing the educational test which would raise him to the dignity of Inspector. For the fourth time Mason determined to beard the Commissioners and demand promotion for his erratic subordinate.

He rose to his feet when the door opened and Inez came in ahead of her husband. She was more composed than he had expected, not quite so white. He went across the room to shake hands with her, an unusual and unexpected greeting which momentarily took her aback.

'I'm terribly sorry to bring you out in the middle of the night, Mrs Landor.' His voice was at its most sympathetic. 'If it had been an any less serious case I wouldn't have bothered either you or your husband; but here we are, all of us up and doing when we want to be in bed, in the sacred name of justice, as the poet says.'

He personally placed a chair for her. Shale put a chair for Mr Landor.

'I hope we've not alarmed you—that was worrying me.' His voice betrayed an almost tender solicitude. 'But, as I say, in a case of this character it very often happens that decent citizens are put to inconvenience.'

It was Louis Landor who answered.

'I'm not at all worried, but it is rather unpleasant for my wife.'

'Naturally,' agreed Mason understandingly.

He sat down and pulled his chair a little nearer to the desk, looking up at Bray.

'Now what has Mr Landor told you?'

Bray took out a notebook. He had kept his charges at Scotland Yard for a quarter of an hour while he had jotted down with fair accuracy the gist of the statements which they had made to him.

'Mrs Landor knew the murdered man, and Mr Landor knew him also slightly,' he read. 'The two notes for a hundred pounds found in the pocket were given to the deceased by Mr Landor, who says it was in the nature of a loan. This statement was made after Mr Landor had said that he did not know Donald Bateman.'

Mason nodded.

'Subsequently he admitted he did?'

'Yes. He also said he'd never been in Tidal Basin. Mrs Landor said that the murdered man was a very intimate friend of hers many years ago, but she hasn't seen him since. She has been married five years, was the widow of a man named John Smith. In the flat I found a belt with a place for two knives. One of the knives I found.' He put it on the table. 'The other was missing.'

Mason took up the knife and pulled it from its sheath, looked at the little gold plate with the initials.

'*L.L.*—those are your initials?'

Landor nodded.

'Where did the other knife go?'

Bray supplied the answer from his notes.

'Mrs Landor said it was lost. Both knives were presented to her husband at a rodeo competition in Central America for his skill in knife-throwing.' He closed his book with a snap. 'That is all the statement they made.'

Mason's face was very serious.

'You agree that that was what you said tonight to Inspector Bray?' and, when they answered in the affirmative: 'Would you like to amplify or correct that statement in any way?'

'No,' said Louis.

'I'd like to point out, sir,' interrupted Bray, 'that he has a bruise on his face. He said he knocked it against the door; Mrs Landor said he got it as the result of a fall.'

'Would you like to make a statement of any kind?' asked Mason.

Louis Landor drew a quick breath.

'No, I don't think so.'

'Have you any objection if I ask you a few questions?'

Landor hesitated.

'No.' The word seemed forced from him.

'Or your wife?'

Inez shook her head.

'I'll make it as easy as I can. I realise it is very trying for you. Have you ever been to Australia?'

To his surprise, Landor replied instantly.

'Yes, many years ago. I made a voyage round the world with my father. I was very young at the time.'

'Did you ever meet there or at any other place a man named Donald Arthur Bateman who, I happen to know, was an ex-convict?'

He shook his head.

'You say you have never been to Tidal Basin? If I tell you that you were recognised as having been seen in the vicinity of Endley Street fighting with Bateman, would you deny it?'

It was a bluff on Mason's part, but it came off.

'I shouldn't deny it—no.'

Mason beamed.

'That's sensible! There's no need to hide anything.' He was his solicitous self again. 'Now just forget the statement you made to Mr Bray and we'll forget it, too,' he smiled. 'You're hiding something. To save you or your wife from some imaginary danger you're implicating yourself further and further in the crime of wilful murder. Now, what are you afraid of?'

Louis Landor avoided his eyes.

'You're probably hiding something that doesn't matter two

hoots. What does matter'—he emphasised every sentence with a tap of his finger on the pad—'is that I have sufficient evidence to charge you with murder. You were in Tidal Basin; a knife similar to this—I have the sheath—was used in the murder of Bateman, and you have been paying, or have paid, money to the dead man which is traceable to your banking account. Now, why?'

Bray asserted himself.

'You're not going to stick to the story that you did it as an act of kindness—' he began, and then he caught Mason's eye, and saw there no encouragement to intervene.

'You were being blackmailed: isn't that the truth?'

'Yes, that's the truth.' It was Inez who spoke. 'That *is* the truth! I can tell you that.'

Mr Mason's nods were not ordinary nods: they were an inclination of head not unlike the reverent obeisance before the statue of a heathen deity.

'Exactly. The murdered man knew that you or your wife had committed some offence, whether against the law—' he paused expectantly.

'I'm not prepared to say,' said Louis quickly.

'You're prepared to go in the dock on a charge of wilful murder, and your wife is prepared to let you. Is that what I understand?'

She was shaking her head, momentarily inarticulate.

'Very well, then. You were being blackmailed.'

'Yes.' It came faintly from Inez.

'What had you done? Had you murdered somebody? Robbed somebody?' His jaw dropped. Into his eyes came a look of intense amusement which was particularly out of place. 'I know! You had committed bigamy!'

'No,' said Louis.

'This man Bateman was your husband.' His forefinger pointed to her. 'He was alive when you married your present husband. Isn't that the truth?'

'I thought he was dead.' Her voice was very low, but he heard every word. 'I was sure of it. I had the newspaper cutting. He told me when I saw him that he circulated the story because he wanted the police off his track for some crime he had committed in England. I swear I didn't know.'

Again Mason leaned back in his chair, and his thumbs went into the armholes of his waistcoat.

'Even Scotland Yard didn't know, Mrs Landor. I've got it here.' He tapped the pile of documents at his elbow. 'Reported dead in Australia. Good God! What a thing to worry about—bigamy! That's hardly an offence—you ought to get something out of the poor-box for that! And that's what you've been hiding up? When did you see him last?'

The eyes of the husband and wife met, and Louis nodded.

'Today,' said the woman.

'You heard he was in London four days ago,' interrupted Bray. 'Your servant said you'd been distressed for four days.'

She hesitated.

'You can answer that,' said Mason, and his permission would have been a rebuff to any other man but Mr Bray.

'He wrote—I couldn't believe he was alive.'

Bateman knew they were well off; suggested she should pay him money, threatening to publish the story of her bigamy. He arrived from South Africa penniless, having met some sharper crooks on the boat, who had taken what little money he had had when he embarked. But he had excellent prospects, he told her.

'Yes,' said Mason dryly, 'I know her name.'

He settled himself deeper in his chair and clasped his hands before him. He knew he was now coming to the really delicate part of his investigations.

'He called at your house—when?'

'Today,' she said.

'Did he call yesterday—for the money?'

She shook her head.

'No, that was posted.'

'Then what did he call about today? To thank you?'

She did not answer.

'Your husband was out?'

She was looking straight at the wall ahead of her; he saw her lips quivering.

'Was he—affectionate?'

Bray was nearest to her, and caught her before she slid to the floor.

'All right, get some water.'

There was a water bottle on the mantelpiece. Shale poured out a glassful. Presently her eyes opened and her husband lifted her into the arm-chair which Bray pushed forward.

'You needn't ask her anything more,' Landor said. 'I can tell you everything.'

'I think you can,' said Mason. 'What time did you arrive at the flat yesterday—after this man had seen your wife?'

'Immediately after. I passed him on the stairs, but didn't know who he was.'

'And yet you recognised him in the photograph?'

'I've seen him since: I've admitted that, or practically admitted it, when I said I was in Tidal Basin.'

'You found your wife very upset? She told you what it was all about?'

He nodded.

'And you went after him?'

'Yes,' defiantly.

'With a knife similar to this?'

Inez Landor came up to her feet at this, her hand on the table.

'That's a lie! He didn't go after him with a knife,' she said passionately. 'Donald took the knife—he took it from me. I'll tell you the truth. I tried to kill him. I snatched the knife from the wall. I hated him! For all the years I had with him, for all that I suffered when he was out of prison, for my baby who died because of his beastliness!'

There was a silence. Mason could hear her quick breathing.

'He took the knife from you?'

'Yes. He said he'd keep it as a souvenir, and took the sheath and put it in his pocket. You know what he wanted, don't you? He wanted me to live with him again.' Her voice rose. Mason had come round to the side of his desk and took her arm in his big hand and literally pushed her back into the chair.

'Gently, Mrs Landor. Don't get rattled. You're doing fine.' He looked round to Louis.

'You followed this man to Tidal Basin and fought with him. Did you know he had the knife in his pocket?'

'I didn't know anything about it till my wife told me on the telephone. I didn't see the knife or use it.'

'Why did you run away?' asked Mason.

Again Louis paused before he answered.

'I thought I'd killed him . . . my wife begged me not to touch him. He had some sort of heart disease.'

Mason nodded many times.

'And carried butyl ammonal in his pocket?'

'Yes,' said Inez eagerly, 'a little thing he crushed in a handkerchief and inhaled. He always carried that.'

Mason began to walk slowly up and down the room, his hands in his pockets.

'You bolted, and found a door open in the gate of the Eastern Trading Company. I call it the beer door: you won't understand why, and I can't explain. And that's all you know about it?'

'As God is my judge,' said Landor.

'You never threw a knife or used a knife?'

'I'll swear I never did.'

'Did you hear all the commotion when we were outside the gate?'

Louis shook his head.

'No, I was trying to find a way out of the yard. I didn't come back to that gate again for an hour. I was hiding part of the time and—'

'And how did—?'

Mason got so far when the door was flung violently open. Mason stared in amazement at the man who stood there. It was Elk, part of his face hidden in white bandages. He stood at the door, supporting himself by the lintel, and glared with a certain malignity at his immediate superior.

'For the love of Allah, what has happened?'

'Don't touch me,' snarled Elk, as Bray made a motion to assist him. 'I don't want anybody with a higher rank than sergeant to help me!'

He glared down at Inez.

'Did you hear anybody come into your flat before your husband returned?'

'I thought I did,' she said.

'How right you were! He was there, in the maid's room, waiting for me when I came back, and coshed me. He couldn't have got in without a key.'

'Where are your keys?' asked Mason, and Louis started.

'I lost them . . . I lost them in the fight. I didn't miss them until I was on my way back there, and then I found the broken end of the chain—look.'

He showed it: a gold chain dangling by the side of his trousers.

Elk staggered across to where Louis was standing and tapped him heavily on the chest.

'There's a desk in your hall,' he said slowly. 'Did you keep anything valuable in the top drawer—money?'

Louis stared at him.

'Stop hiding up, will you?' snapped Mason. 'What was in that top drawer?'

'Money, passports and tickets,' said Louis Landor huskily. 'I was clearing out tomorrow and taking my wife away from this man.'

'How much money?' demanded Elk.

'About three thousand pounds.'

Elk laughed mirthlessly.

'There's about nothing now! It's gone! The drawer was broken open and the money taken. I'll tell you something more, Mason.' His outrageous familiarity passed unnoticed. 'The fellow that coshed me was White Face! I'm not romancing—'

Mason interrupted him with an impatient gesture.

'Of course it was White Face. It could be nobody else but White Face. I've known that all along,' he said.

CHAPTER XIII

MICHAEL QUIGLEY had never been alone through Gallows Court by day or night. He stood hesitant at the entrance and experienced a qualm of uneasiness which was foreign to him. He looked up and down the street vainly for a policeman, and rather wished he had detained the taxi-driver. Yet Gallows Court differed from no other noisome thoroughfare; there were thousands of them in every great city, none more mysterious or sinister than the other. Two hundred years ago, when bravoes lurked in these dens, there might be another tale to tell; but here was the twentieth century; a highly organised police force, housing societies and sanitary inspectors prying into the darkest places without hurt to themselves. Not in the early hours of the morning, said a warning voice. But they would be asleep now.

It was one of Mr Mason's figures of speech that the inmates of the court never slept. But he was rather prone to exaggeration. Mike looked up at the façade of Dr Marford's surgery. The windows of the top room were open. This was evidently his sleeping-room—he had had a faint hope that the doctor would still be about. Summoning his resolution, he walked into the dark entry. There was no sign or sound of life. Every window in the court was black.

Either the storm or some human piece of mischief had extinguished the gas-lamp at the far end of the court. Groping his way along, feeling at the wall, he presently touched the door which gave into the doctor's yard. It was fastened, and he went on a little farther. Then suddenly he stopped, with his heart in his mouth. He had heard a groan, a deep, a painful groan that ended in a long-drawn 'Oh-h!'

Where had it come from? He looked around fearfully, but

could see nothing. And then he heard the groan again. It seemed to come from somewhere near him. He waited, determined to locate the sound, but it was not repeated. Instead came a soft cackle of laughter which made every hair on his head stand up. And then a hoarse voice spoke.

'Go on, Mr Reporter, nobody's going to hurt ya!'

He recognised the speaker, though he could not see him. It was the crazy man who had followed Mason and him into the street.

'Rats, ain't we? Eyes like rats,' he said. 'I heard ya! I hear everything!'

Michael edged towards the voice, and then saw an indistinguishable black mass huddled against the wall.

'I know where ya going!' The crazy unknown spoke in a thick whisper. 'Ya going to see what's wrong with old Gregory—clever! Cleverer than Mason. Here!' An invisible hand clutched his overcoat. Michael had to use all his self-control to prevent wrenching himself free. 'I'll tell you something.' The whisper grew more confidential. 'They ain't found Rudd—the police doctor. They're out on the river with their drags, raking up the old mud, but they ain't found him.'

The unseen creature laughed until he broke into a fit of coughing.

'All the busies and all the coppers in Tidal Basin lookin' for old Rudd! Do you think he's a good doctor—I don't! I wouldn't let him doctor me. Tell 'em what I say at the station, mister—have a lark with 'em! Tell 'em he's under a barge!'

Then the detaining claws released their grip.

'Blue Face is asleep down there on old Gregory's doorstep. Blue Face—not White Face.'

Again the long gurgle of laughter that ended in a paroxysm of coughing. Michael drew himself away and went on till he came to No. 9. The sleeper he had seen sat hunched up on the doorstep of Gregory Wicks, the can still balanced on his knees. His arms were folded, his head bent forward. He was snoring regularly.

Michael did not dare go back the way he had come. He went out of the lower end of the court, came round the block and found the crazy man leaning against the wall of the entry.

'Old Gregory's back—been back a quarter of an hour. An old man like him oughtn't to drive taxicabs—and I'm the only man that knows why he oughtn't! Dr Marford knows, but he's not the feller that goes snouting on his patients.'

'Snouting' meant 'nosing', and 'nosing' meant 'informing'. Dr Marford was credited with having been the recipient of secrets which it would have terrified his more opulent brethren even to hear.

'What's wrong with old Gregory Wicks? That's what I'm asking ya?'

And then, without warning, the crazy man turned abruptly and ran noiselessly through the dark entry. He must have been either in stockinged or bare feet, for he made no sound, but moved with uncanny silence. He might have been the wraith of all that was ugly and wicked in the court.

But he had told Michael one thing he wanted to know. Gregory had returned, had been back a quarter of an hour. Michael walked slowly to the police station and interviewed the sergeant.

'No, we haven't found Dr Rudd. The river police are searching. There's a chance he may have gone up west. He's got a flat near Langham Place and he may turn up there later. Mr Mason is on his way here, if you want to see him.'

'Why is he coming back?' asked Michael in surprise, but the station sergeant could or would give information on this point.

Michael was relieved: he wished for no better news, for he was desperately anxious to see the superintendent.

'Personally, I'm not worried about Rudd.' The station sergeant could drop all ceremonious titles with a sympathetic and understanding audience. 'He's a funny old chap—I don't know how old he is, but he's young compared with Methuselah. If a man's got money, he oughtn't to be messing about in this neigbourhood.'

'Has he got money?'

'Whips of it,' said the sergeant. 'An old lady, one of his patients, died and left him a packet! If he'd been a better doctor she might have been living now,' he added libellously.

He patted back a yawn.

'Yes, he's got tons of money. He owns a flat in the West End of London. Some of the Special Branch fellers from Scotland Yard tell me they often see him in the nightclubs. Thank God, a man's never too old to be silly!'

Michael, who knew the area well, had never seriously considered Dr Rudd as an individual. There are some characters who fail utterly to inspire the least interest in themselves. They are figures—men or women occupying set places, who have no existence other than the existence which is visible to their casual acquaintances. Whether they eat or drink, have home lives or private predilections, is hardly worth speculating upon. It is almost surprising to discover that they play bridge or have the gift of distinguishing between Château Lafitte and Imperial Tokay. Whatever they do that is human appears as an amazing phenomenon.

He brought Dr Rudd out of the background of his mind and tried to examine him as an entity, but he was either too tired or too bored to give this shadowy figure significance.

Mason came with Bray and Shale, and the superintendent was in his most rollicking mood. You might have thought he had risen from a long and refreshing sleep; he greeted Michael jovially.

But the news which the station sergeant gave him wiped the smile from his face.

'What?' he said. 'Rudd hasn't turned up?'

He had quite forgotten Dr Rudd, for, like Michael, he found that elusive personality difficult to place. He did not speak for a long time, but stood in front of the fire, warming his hands.

'I'm not as worried about him as I should be,' he said. 'He's a queer bird, and gets me on the raw quicker than any man I know, though I hope I've never shown it. I can't feel that he's anything to worry about.'

'I'll tell you something to worry about, if you'll give me a few minutes,' said Michael, and the superintendent looked at him sharply.

'That sounds to me like a threat. All right. Can we have your room, Bray?'

Bray looked a little sour that he was not invited to the conference. He disliked these crime reporters, and made no disguise of his antipathy. And crime reporters disliked him and maliciously spelt his name wrong if they mentioned it at all.

Behind the closed door of the inspector's room Michael revealed all his suspicions, and Mr Mason listened, making very few comments.

'I've had that idea in my mind, too,' he said. 'I'm not kidding you, Mike, or trying to jump in and take credit for your brain's work. But old Gregory Wicks is as straight as a die. I've known him since I was a boy. I was born in this neighbourhood, but don't want you to tell anybody this. Gregory's got the finest record of any cabman in London—the amount of property that fellow's restored to the rightful owners runs into five figures.'

'He limps, doesn't he?' asked Michael, and Mason's brows knitted.

'Yes, he limps,' he said slowly. 'He was thrown from the seat of a cab years ago. Of course he limps,' he went on thoughtfully. 'Now, why on earth did I forget that?'

'You told me that the man who was seen coming out of Mrs Weston's flat also limped?'

Mason nodded.

'Yes; I hadn't connected the two people. But Gregory Wicks!' He laughed. 'The idea's ridiculous! The old boy is seventy-six if he's a day, and he's the most rumbustiously straight man I know.'

'That crazy fellow in the court asked you to find out what's wrong with him, didn't he?' asked Michael quietly.

Mason rubbed his bald head.

'There are too many crazy people giving me theories,' he said pointedly. 'No, I don't mean you, Michael.'

'What about asking the doctor?'

'Marford? Must I tell him I've pulled him out of bed to confirm what a lunatic has said about one of his patients? And would he tell? That's the one thing you can't compel a doctor to do unless you get him into the witness stand, and even then the Medical Association raise a hullaboo if a lawyer goes a little too far.'

'Wake him up on some other excuse,' suggested Michael. 'After all, he may be able to help us with Rudd.'

Mr Mason thrust his hands more deeply into his pockets and rattled his loose change irritably.

'He certainly limped, if the woman witness was telling the truth. And now I come to remember it, White Face has always been a limper. That was one of the first descriptions circulated. He used to ride a motor-cycle, you remember— that rather knocks your idea on the head.'

'Motor-cyclists have been seen coming from the scene of a robbery, but nobody could swear that those particular cyclists were the robbers,' said Michael. 'The motor-cycle theory is one that everybody has jumped to, that after he did his dirty work he made his getaway on a pop-pop! When you come to think of it, motor-bikes are the most conspicuous things in London after a certain hour. Isn't it more likely that he made his grand exit on the box of a taxicab?'

'Or,' said Mason, 'is it more likely that a man with a fifty-year record for honesty, a man with a bit of money put by, with no relations or friends, no vices, a man who never goes out, has never done a dishonest thing in his life, should suddenly turn crook? And listen, Michael! You've been a witness to a White Face raid and you've read about the others. What has invariably happened? He's come into the restaurant and he's said two words—what are those words?'

'"Bail up",' said Michael.

Mason nodded vehemently.

'Exactly—"bail up"! It was an expression of the old Australian bush-rangers. It's still used by the hold-up men in Australia. Gregory's never been out of London in his life, except to drive a drunken fare into the country. The only knowledge he has of the word "bail" is that it's something to do with getting a man out of a police station after he's pinched. I'll tell you who White Face is—Tommy Furse.'

'And who in hell is Tommy Furse?' asked Michael in surprise.

'You shall have the story when it's properly cooked—at present the oven is just heating up.'

He got up quickly from his chair.

'I'll call the doctor and tell him I want to come round and see him. Or Bray can do it.'

He opened the door, shouted for the inspector, and when he came gave him instructions.

'Tell him I'm very worried about Dr Rudd and I would like to consult him.'

'As a matter of fact,' he added, when Bray had gone, 'I'm not feeling too happy about Rudd, though what Dr Marford can tell me I don't know.'

'May I come?'

'You can come, but you'd better stay outside. I can't very well introduce you into an official inquiry.'

'Anyway, he doesn't like me very much,' said Michael, with a recollection of Dr Marford's former coldness.

When the superintendent reached the surgery he found Dr Marford dressed. He had not been to bed that night, had only returned from a patient a few minutes before the 'phone message came through.

'A boy or a girl?' asked Mr Mason blandly.

'In this event it was both,' said the doctor.

He very much disliked discussing his cases, as Bray, who knew him better than Mason, was well aware.

'I'm not worried at all about Dr Rudd. I didn't like to say so before, for fear you might think I was saying something disparaging of him. By the way, I called in at the infirmary to see that woman, but as she seemed to be sleeping the house surgeon thought I'd better not see her.'

'Mrs Weston?'

Marford nodded.

'When will she be fit to make a statement?'

'Tomorrow—this morning, I should think.'

He took a whisky bottle from a cupboard and put it with a siphon on the table.

'This is all I can offer you. I keep it exclusively for my visitors. Personally, I never drink after ten o'clock in the evening.'

He had no suggestions to offer with regard to Rudd.

'He'll turn up,' he said confidentially, 'and I prophesy that he'll turn up with a headache and be quite incapable of transacting any kind of business for a day or two.'

'What on earth do you think he's done?' asked Mason, and the doctor smiled.

'I would rather not say.'

'You'd rather not say things about quite a lot of people, doctor.'

Mason helped himself to some whisky and splashed in soda.

'They tell me you could hang half Gallows Court and send the other half to prison for the term of their natural lives?'

'If I could, I should do it,' said Marford. 'Believe me, I have no sympathy with that ghastly crowd—'

'Except Gregory Wicks?' suggested Mason, and a shadow passed over the doctor's face.

'Except Gregory Wicks,' he said slowly.

'Gregory Wicks,' began Bray, 'is one of the nicest people living in this area—'

'Yes, yes, I'm sure the doctor will agree,' said Mason. 'But why not Gregory Wicks?'

'For many reasons,' replied Marford. 'He's a good fellow—'

'What is the matter with him? You attend him, don't you?'

Dr Marford smiled faintly.

'I attend a good many people, but I never say what is the matter with them, even to entertain eminent police officers.'

'There's something the matter with him, isn't there?' insisted Mason, and Marford nodded.

'Anno Domini! You can't get to the age of seventy-six without running a little threadbare. There are worn spots in men of that age, certain weaknesses, peculiar mental and physical failings which no doctor can patch. It's amazing to me that he can do what he does at his age. I've never seen him really sick or sorry—he has certainly got the loudest voice in Tidal Basin; and I can testify, for I attended the victim, that he can still deliver a blow that would knock out the average pugilist. Why are you interested?'

He stepped back from Mason and surveyed him with a troubled face.

'Do you know, Mr Mason,' he said slowly, 'I've got an instinctive idea that you've come here not to talk about Mr Rudd but to talk about this old taxi-driver. There is a half-witted man who lives in the court, whose name I forget—he used to be a shoeblack—who has an obsession about Gregory. Every time I go into the court he catches my arm and asks me what is wrong with Gregory Wicks—I wonder if he's been asking you the same thing?'

Mason was momentarily embarrassed. It did not add to his self-esteem that he should have been detected acting as a lunatic's mouthpiece.

'Well, yes,' he said, and laughed awkwardly. 'I've heard the man—in fact, he's asked me the same question. But of course

I shouldn't be stupid enough to come round in the middle of the night to pass on a crazy inquiry. I'm interested in the old boy.'

The doctor was behind his desk, leaning down on his outstretched arms, looking terribly tired. Mason found himself being thankful that he had not been born in so favourable a position that his parents could afford to educate him as a doctor.

'You'll have to ask the old man in the morning. I'm very sorry; I'd like to oblige you, Mr Mason. It isn't entirely a question of professional secrecy—I certainly wouldn't let that stand in my way with a police officer who was investigating a very serious crime—though what poor old Gregory's got to do with it I can't imagine. But I owe Gregory something more than perfunctory loyalty. He's by way of being a crony of mine, and I'm afraid you'll have to ask him yourself tomorrow.'

'He has something the matter with his face, hasn't he?'

Marford hesitated.

'Yes,' he said; 'you could describe it that way.'

And then he raised his eyes slowly to Mason.

'You will not suggest'—his lips twitched—'that the old man is your White Face?'

'I'm suggesting nothing of the sort,' said Mason hastily and reproachfully. 'Of course I'm not! I'm merely curious. That crazy fellow's got on my nerves—I'll admit it. Certainly, I'll ask Gregory himself in the morning. I'd ask him tonight if it wasn't for disturbing that mackerel who's been sleeping on Gregory's doorstep ever since midnight.'

'Is it a very red-nosed man?' asked Bray, interested. 'If it is, he's often there. I've seen him myself. I very often go through Gallows Court alone—more or less alone. A drunken-looking man with a red nose—'

'I never inspected his nose,' said Mason icily. 'It probably went red through sticking it into other people's investigations.'

'Very likely,' said Mr Bray, and Shale could only marvel at his clouded intelligence.

'Do you believe every man who wears a lint mask is a criminal?' Marford asked quietly. 'Of course you don't: you're too sensible. Any more than you believe that all Chinamen are wicked. I ask you this'—he spoke very slowly—'because the man of whom you spoke earlier this evening is coming'—he looked at his watch—'in less than ten minutes.'

'White Face?' said Mason in amazement.

'He telephoned me just before you came.'

'Tell me, Dr Marford'—Bray could not be repressed—'how is this White Face man dressed when you see him?'

Marford considered a moment.

'He usually wears a very long coat reaching almost to his heels, and a soft dark hat.'

'Black?' asked Bray eagerly.

'It may be. I've never really noticed.'

'Why is he coming this morning?' asked Mason.

'He said he would have come earlier in the night, but the streets were full of policemen. I'm telling you what he told me. It doesn't sound too good of any man that he's afraid of the police. But anyone super-sensitive as this fellow is might very easily shrink from being seen.'

'He telephoned you from where?'

'I'm not sure. It certainly wasn't our local exchange, because the calls we get through on the local exchange are always indicated by continuous ringing, and these signals came at intervals.'

He walked to the big window, drew aside the blind and looked out.

'There's somebody out there,' he said. 'Is it a police officer? No, it isn't, I see. It's the reporter, isn't it?'

'Yes.'

'Ask him to come in.'

Mason nodded to his subordinate, and Sergeant Shale went out to admit the reporter.

'If I could stop you getting a big beat I would, Michael, but this matter isn't entirely in my hands. You'll probably have to use your well-known discretion—I think I can trust you to keep out of your paper just what I want you to keep out.'

'The idea being?' asked Michael.

'White Face,' said Mr Bray, and coughed when he caught his superior's chilly eye.

'As that active and discreet officer said, it's somebody with a white face; a man who's been seen in this neighbourhood, and probably in other neighbourhoods—I think you met him at the Howdah Club. And he's due here almost at once. I don't suppose he wants to see a lot of people here'—he addressed Marford—'but you realise I'll have to ask him to give an account of himself.'

The doctor, who was arranging an instrument that looked like a huge aluminium funnel, nodded his agreement.

'As a matter of fact, he's very shy, but if I am to betray anybody in the interests of justice I might as well betray him. It isn't very admirable and I can't say that I'm very proud of myself.'

He brought the lamp nearer to his desk and turned the switch, and Mason saw a circle of green light appear on the floor. The shadows which the other lights cast ran through the circle redly. Marford turned off the lamp and explained that the current came, not from the main electric supply, but from an accumulator.

'I warn you,' he said, 'that this man may refuse to enter the surgery. It took me a long while to persuade him the last time he was here.'

'Which way does he come?'

'Through the yard and up that passage to that door.' He pointed to the door near the medicine cupboard. 'He gives me a signal—two long rings and two short ones; that was my own arrangement on account of his incurable shyness. I shall never get him in if he sees any of you.'

Mason tried the door; it was locked. The telephone bell rang at a moment when all nerves were tense. Marford sat on the desk and took up the instrument.

'. . . Yes, he's here,' he said. 'It is Dr Marford speaking . . . Better, is she? I'm glad of that . . . Certainly.'

He handed the instrument to Mason.

'The woman Weston is quite conscious and wants to come to the station to see you.'

Mason listened, giving monosyllabic interruptions. He put up the receiver and looked very thoughtful.

'She wants to come to the station. It was Elk—I thought I recognised the voice. I wonder if I could get him here in time,' said Mason thoughtfully. 'He'd be very much interested to meet White Face—he's met him once this evening.'

'There may be time—' began Marford.

A bell in the room rang shrilly and long, rang again, then came two short rings. The men looked at one another.

'That is your White Face, is it?'

Mason's voice was husky. His hand dropped mechanically to his pocket, and Bray was satisfied now: the rumour that Mason always carried a gun was true.

Michael Quigley, a silent participator, felt a little shiver run down his spine as Mason made a gesture to his two subordinates.

'Behind those curtains, you two fellows. Michael, you'd better go out into the front hall. I'll get behind the desk if you don't mind.'

'What do you want me to do?' asked Marford, as he took a key from his pocket.

'Let him in, that's all. I'll see that he doesn't get out again,' said Mason. 'You can help us by shutting and locking the door on him.'

Marford nodded. He turned the key and pulled open the door slowly. Watching him from the cover of the desk, Mason saw him smile.

'Good evening,' he said. 'Won't you come in?'

He went a little out of sight and they heard the rumble of a voice saying something which was indistinguishable. It might have been a voice that spoke behind a muffling mask.

'My dear fellow,' they heard Marford say, 'I have never promised you that I can be absolutely alone, but you have nothing to fear—come along.'

He disappeared from view into the passage and Mason held his breath. Then suddenly the door slammed; there was the sound of a bolt being drawn, and in another second:

'Help!' It was Marford's voice. 'Mason . . . Mason! For God's sake!'

Then came an unearthly scream that turned the hearers' blood cold.

Mason was on his feet instantly. He was half-way to the door when the lights of the room went out. From the passage came the faint sound of a struggle.

'Bray! Go to the front door, quick! Go with him, Shale!'

They came to the front door to find it was locked from the inside and did not yield to their frantic tugging. Mason remembered that the doctor had told him he kept that part of the premises which contained the surgery locked and double-locked, and that he invariably used the back door himself.

They stumbled back through the darkness, and as Mason picked up a chair and sent it smashing at the panel, a ray from Bray's torch glittered on the lamp.

'This works.'

He fumbled for the switch and found it, and the ghostly green circle appeared on the floor. It gave them enough light to work by. Within a few moments two panels were gone. Bray, the taller, reached through, found the bolt and drew it. There was another at the bottom, and it was some minutes before the third panel was broken and enabled them to reach this.

Bray was the first in the passage. It was empty. The door at the end stood wide open. He ran out into the yard—there was nobody in sight.

'There's blood here,' he said. 'I can't see Marford. Can you bring the lamp out?'

Shale examined the flex: there was enough to carry the ray lamp into the corridor. It revealed nothing except patches of something red and shining on the floor and walls. The doctor and his assailant had vanished.

CHAPTER XIV

To the man in the yard outside came the sound of splintering panels. White Face had no need to crank up his machine: the taxi engine was running softly. He pulled open the two gates and took a look inside the cab. On the floor was a huddled figure.

'Doctor,' said White Face pleasantly, 'I'm afraid I shall have to take you for an uncomfortable journey.'

He could have left him behind for the detectives to find, but it was most undesirable that this medical practitioner should tell his experience; for he had seen White Face without his mask.

The car ran swiftly into the street. As he passed he thought he could hear somebody trying to get out of the front door. He passed a policeman on the corner of the street; the man shouted out to him, 'Good-night, Gregory.' White Face smiled to himself.

The hands which gripped the wheel were wet and stained with the red liquid which he had poured from a bottle on to the floor and walls of the passage. He hoped it would look like blood, would at least throw his pursuers off the track until the morning.

He hadn't too much time. Mentally he calculated how long it would take Mason to telephone a description of the cab to Scotland Yard, and just how much longer time would be wasted whilst the description was being circulated through London. He gave himself a good half-hour, providing he kept to the outskirts. So he made his way northward, and in half an hour had reached the outskirts of Epping Forest. It was certain that the Yard would telephone to the outlying stations the number of the cab, and that made it imperative that he should keep to the secondary roads and avoid those key points where the Essex police patrols could establish a barrage.

With any luck he could reach the little farm undetected. It lay between Epping and Chelmsford, not a long journey if he had dared the direct route.

He came at last to a place where an uninviting country lane ran off at right angles to the road, and turned his car down this. He had to move with the greatest caution, for he had extinguished his lamps. The road was uneven, but not quite so bad as the cart track into which he guided the taxi. Here he had to move very carefully. The only thing that concerned him was whether the noise of the car in low gear would attract the attention of an inquisitive policeman, but apparently it had not.

Without any knowledge of the time, he could make a rough guess—thought it must be four o'clock. There was no sign of dawn in the sky.

He came at last to an old barn, which was built by the side of a squat and shapeless building, and, stopping the cab without stopping the engine, he got down, opened the cab door and, lifting out the unconscious doctor, laid him on the grass. Then he backed the machine into the barn and, closing the big gate of it, went back to open the door of the house. This done, he returned to the place where he had left the doctor and half carried, half dragged him into the passage.

Except for a few ugly, dilapidated articles which the previous owner had not thought it worthwhile to move, the house was unfurnished. There was a dingy carpet running the length of the hall, and in the room to where White Face carried his burden, an old sofa to which he hoisted the doctor. He stood for some time looking at his prisoner.

'It was a great mistake for you to try to set the police on me, and I hope no harm comes to you,' he said.

Lately White Face had acquired the habit of talking aloud.

He finished his examination of the unconscious man, then went out to the barn, and presently came back with a small bottle of champagne and a box of biscuits: emergency rations which he kept in a box under the cab seat.

The taxi was of no more use to him. He must make his way across country to Harwich by another means. And those means were ready to his hand. He had compiled from week to week, with scrupulous care, a list of motor excursions out of London. There was one leaving in the morning from Forest Gate to Felixstowe, and he had already decided that this was the route he would take. He would not be noticed in an excursion crowd.

The doctor was a difficulty. Almost he wished he had not brought him; but he was too dangerous to leave.

White Face drank his wine out of an old cup he found in the kitchen, poured out another cup and took it back to where he had left his charge. Placing the lamp which he carried on the table, and by the side of this the cup, White Face sat on the edge of the bed and waited. Presently he saw the doctor's eyes flicker; they opened, looked wonderingly round the room and fixed themselves finally upon the man who was sitting on the bed.

'Where is this place?' he spoke huskily.

'This place is a little farm near Romford,' said the other calmly. 'And may I tell you what your friend Mason has already guessed—that I am White Face.'

The doctor looked at him incredulously. 'You?'

The man nodded.

'Weird, isn't it? But I think you guessed it yourself and were prepared to tell your friends of Scotland Yard. I am not going to chloroform you or drug you again or do any of the things which I might do. Unless I am greatly mistaken, you will go to sleep and you will sleep for a very long time; and when you wake up you will find your way to the nearest police station. If you drive a car, I must tell you there is a taxi in the barn—I invariably use a taxi. My landlord'—he laughed at the word—'was Mr Gregory Wicks. I invariably use a taxi—Gregory Wicks's taxi. That may or may not convey something to you, but I rather fancy your mind is incapable of grasping important essentials.'

The doctor was staring at him.

'Turn on your side,' commanded White Face, and was obeyed instantly. 'Close your eyes.'

He waited a few minutes until the drugged man was asleep, and then he went out, taking the lamp with him. He made another journey to the garage, brought in a suitcase and laid out such toilet articles as he required.

CHAPTER XV

MASON had found the governing light switch and brought on all the lights in Marford's house. Bray, who had searched the yard, came back with his report.

'There's blood everywhere,' he said. 'Look at that!' He pointed to an uneven smudge near the door. 'They carried him out this way.'

'Is there any other way he could have been carried out?' snapped Mason.

In the courtyard the gates were wide open, and so were the doors of the empty garage. Gregory Wick's taxicab had gone. When they came out to the street they had heard the faint, dying whine of it as it sped westwards.

'They've got him in the cab,' said Bray incoherently. 'There must have been two or three of them.'

'Why not four or five?' snarled Mason. 'Or six or seven?'

'I only want to say,' began the aggrieved inspector, 'that one man couldn't have outed him and lifted him. I'd better call up assistance.'

The police whistle was half-way to his mouth when Mason knocked it out of his hand.

'What's the matter with the telephone?' he asked fiercely. 'I want to know who's awake in this neighbourhood, and I don't want any excuse for their being awake, either! Call every man you can lay your hands on. The reserves will be in by now.'

When Bray had gone, the superintendent made a quick search of the yard. There was an open pit surrounded by a low fencing. He struck a match, drew his own lamp from his pocket and cast the rays down. A long way below the surface of the ground he saw the glint of water. A well. How deep was it? There was something there, too, something that looked like a sack. And then he heard a voice behind him.

'Found the well?'

He looked round; it was Elk, a ghostly figure, with his white-bandaged head.

'Did you know there was a well here?'

'Yes, the winch is above your head—handle on the wall.'

Looking up, Mason saw an iron bracket.

'Something down there?' asked Elk, and peered curiously. 'Gregory's cab's gone, of course. I guessed something was happening and came round.'

The two men went up to the empty garage and made a search. There was nothing there except a few tools, a spare tyre or two and a dozen tins of petrol. They picked up the blood trail in the garage. Mason looked at these ominous stains and shook his head.

'All my ideas have gone west,' he said in despair.

'Mine have stayed strictly put, working for the good of humanity,' said Elk. 'White Face, wasn't it? And he's kidnapped the doctor—that fellow's got a nerve!'

They heard Michael's step and looked round.

'Well, are you going to interview Gregory?' he asked.

'Gregory—I presume he's with his cab.'

'Let's see,' said Michael.

They discovered that the door leading into Gallows Court was fastened with a spring lock and offered no difficulty. Elk examined this door carefully and grunted.

'As full of clues as a milkshop,' he said.

They walked quickly down the court and came to the doorway of No. 9. The sleeper still snored; the tin remained balanced on his knee.

'Whoever put that tin there were helping the police a lot,' said Mason. 'It'd break their hearts to know it, but it's a fact.'

He knocked heavily at the door, but there was no answer. After a little while he knocked again-still no reply.

'He must have gone out.'

Michael shook his head emphatically.

'How could he go in or out with that man sitting there? He must have moved him.'

The sleeper was now aroused; the tin fell noisily from his knee as he stood up, groaning, and Bray recognised him as a famous local tippler. He had been there, he said, since about— he didn't know the time; he thought it was about half an hour after the public houses had closed. He could not remember anybody passing, either going in or out. Mason knocked again.

Gallows Court was alive now—alive with dark shapes that had melted out of the walls, silent things that just looked and gave no evidence of their humanness. Curious watchers, eager to see somebody, something happen. If they had chatted amongst themselves Michael could have borne their presence, but they were terribly silent, edging nearer and nearer.

Then suddenly the upper window of No. 9 was raised creakily.

'Who's that?'

It was old Gregory Wicks's strident voice, unmistakably so.

'I want to see you, Gregory.'

'Who is it?'

'Superintendent Mason. You remember me?'

The old man cogitated.

'I don't know no Superintendent Mason. There used to be a young feller called Sergeant Mason a few years ago.'

'A good few, Gregory,' said Mason with a chuckle. 'I'm Sergeant Mason. Come down and let us in.'

'What do you want?' asked the old man cautiously.

'I want to have a talk with you.'

The man above hesitated, but after a while he put down the window and Mason heard his feet descending the stairs. The door opened noisily.

'Come on up to my room,' he said.

There was no light in the house save the lamp which the police brought, nor in his little sitting-room.

'Come in and sit down. Here's a chair, sergeant—superin-tendent, eh? Gosh! Time goes on!'

'Haven't you got a lamp?'

The question seemed to embarrass the old man.

'Lamp? Well, yes, I've got a lamp somewhere. You'll find it in the kitchen, mister. There are three of you, ain't there? My eyes are not as good as they used to be, but I sort of heard three lots of feet on the stairs besides mine.'

It was Michael who went downstairs and found the lamp half filled with oil. He lit it, fixed the glass chimney and carried it carefully up the stairs into the room where the three men were. And then, to Mason's surprise, he said:

'I couldn't find your lamp anywhere, Mr Wicks.'

This in face of the fairly bright light he carried in his hand. The old man smiled.

'What do you call that you've brought into the room?' he said. 'Put it on the table, young man, and don't try to take liberties with me.'

The look of chagrin in Michael's face brought joy to Superintendent Mason's heart.

'Now sit down, everybody. What do you want to know?'

'Have you been out tonight, Gregory?' Mason asked.

Gregory felt his scrubby chin.

'For a little while,' he said cautiously. 'I always pop up to the West End. Why?'

'Does anybody else drive your cab?'

'I've let it out before now,' said Gregory. 'I'm not so young as I was, and an owner-driver has got to live, and he can only live if he works his machine all the time.'

'Who takes your car out?'

The old man did not answer, and Mason repeated the question.

'Well . . . my lodger takes it out.'

'The man who lives downstairs?'

'That's right, sergeant—I mean, superintendent. Bless me life, fancy you being a superintendent! I remember you getting your first stripe.'

Mason patted him gently on the knee.

'Of course you do. And I remember summonsing you for using abusive language and the magistrate dismissing the charge.'

Gregory gurgled with laughter at the recollection.

'I was always a hard one to get the better of,' he said smugly.

'Where is your lodger now?'

Again the hesitation.

'Out, I suppose. He usually goes out at night. Rather a nice young feller. Very quiet. He's about thirty-five, and he's had a lot of trouble: that's all I know about him.' Then, in sudden alarm: 'He's not been in trouble again?'

'Oh, that's the kind of trouble, is it?' said Mason. 'Gregory, where is your badge?'

Now, a cabman's badge is an almost sacred thing. It is to the driver what marriage lines are to a woman. The effect of the question on the old man was extraordinary. He fidgeted in his chair and rubbed his chin.

'I've put it away somewhere,' he said lamely.

'Gregory, where is your badge? If you've been out tonight, you must have been wearing it,' said Mason. 'As a matter of fact, you haven't been out tonight; you haven't been out any night for months; you know that, old pal.'

Again he pressed the old man's knee affectionately, and this time his sympathy was genuine.

'You know why you haven't been out. The doctor knows.'

'He hasn't told?' said Gregory quickly.

'No, I've told myself. You knew there was a lamp came in the room because you could smell it, but you couldn't see it, Gregory—only dimly. Isn't that true?'

The old man shrank back.

'I've been a licensed cabman for fifty-five years, Mr Mason,' he pleaded.

'I know. I hope you'll be a licensed cabman all the days of your life. Only you mustn't drive cabs, Gregory—when you're blind!'

He saw the old man wince, and cursed himself for his brutality.

'I'm not exactly blind, but I can't see very well.'

The blustering Gregory Wicks had suddenly become an oddly pathetic figure.

'My eyes are not what they were, Mr Mason, but I never like to admit it. I've had my licence and badge all these years, and naturally I didn't want to part with it; so when this young lodger of mine, who's been in trouble and couldn't get a licence, said he'd like to take out the cab, I—well—I lent him my badge. That's an offence, I know, but I'm willing to take my medicine.'

'Then you've never seen your lodger?'

'No, I haven't seen him; I've heard him. He comes in sometimes; I hear him moving about; and he pays me regularly.'

'How do you know he's thirty-five, and a nice young man who's going to be married?'

'I heard he was—a friend of mine told me.'

They left him bemoaning the loss of the thing which was more precious to him than any other possession—the stamped licence that had been issued every one of the fifty-five years of his active life, and which might never be issued again. Mason went downstairs and tried the door of the lower room. The lock was not difficult to pick—did not, if they had known, require picking at all, for the key of the upstairs room fitted both doors. In five minutes it swung open and Mason went in, followed by Bray, who carried the oil lamp.

There was a bed in one corner, but evidently it had not been slept in for a long time: the blankets were folded, the pillow was without cover. The floor had a large square of carpet in the centre, and that, with a table, a chair and a square mirror over the fireplace, seemed all that the room contained, until

Elk began to test the mirror and found that it hid a roughly hewn hole in the wall, large enough to take a heavy steel box.

'This will tell us something,' said Mason.

The lid opened squeakily, and he stared down into the interior at what it contained.

It was a short, stout knife, the blade stained and smeared red. Carefully he picked it out and as carefully laid it on the bare table.

'Here is the knife that killed Donald Bateman,' he said.

CHAPTER XVI

ONLY one man in the court had ever seen Gregory's lodger, or would admit they had seen him. At the very hint of an inquiry the crowd that filled the court melted back into the walls again; only the crazy, nameless man remained.

'Didn't I tell you? Didn't I tell you?' he almost screamed when he caught sight of Mason. 'You and the reporter fellow—what's wrong with Gregory, eh? *I* knew!' He tapped his nose. 'I'll bet the doctor knew, but he wouldn't squeak. Here!' He detained Mason. 'Is it true that they got the doctor? . . . Somebody'll be murdered if they touch him! Everybody in Gallows Court will go and find the man and bring him in here and put him down into a cellar, and put clay in his mouth and tear little bits off him till he dies!'

The awful face grinned up at the superintendent.

'In which case,' said Mason, 'I shall come and do a bit of pinching myself, and somebody else will die. No, I don't know who has taken the doctor.'

'I heard him—shouting, screaming something awful. And then the cab went out,' whispered the man. 'If we'd known it was the doctor we'd have been after 'em.'

'What is this lodger like?'

The man shook his head.

'A tall feller—that's all I know. Seen him once or twice go in and out, generally at night; but I've never seen him any closer than that. He didn't sleep there—old Gregory thought he did, but he didn't.'

This was so near to the conclusion that Mason formed that he was inclined to listen to other opinions with respect, but Shoey—as they called him—said no more.

There was one good quality about Inspector Bray: he was an

excellent telephonist. Before Mason left the surgery, Scotland Yard knew all about a taxicab No. 93458—its colour, its appearance generally and the direction it had taken. And Scotland Yard knew all about the missing Dr Marford and the chauffeur who lived with old Gregory Wicks.

That busy printing press at the Yard worked furiously to carry the news to the outermost beat, and the early workers straggling into the City saw police cyclists disregarding all speed rules.

Lorna Weston sat in the infirmary hall waiting for the ambulance which was to take her to the police station. A pallid, shaken woman, her eyes weary and heavy, she barely noticed or heard the laborious platitudes of Police-Constable Hartford, who sat by her side—all the more laborious because he had decided that her condition was due to excessive indulgence in alcohol, and had set himself the task of opening her eyes to the evil that men (and women) put in their mouths to steal away their brains.

One of the policemen who came with the ambulance gave a fragmentary and generally inaccurate résumé of what had happened to Dr Marford. P.C. Hartford clicked his lips unhappily.

'It only shows, Mrs Weston, what drink will do to a man,' he said. 'They were probably all drinking together up at the doctor's surgery, and naturally something happened. It's never too late to turn. Take me: five years ago there wasn't a man who loved a glass of beer more than myself. I used to call myself a moderate drinker, but was I? No man who drinks can be a moderate drinker. Then one day I was induced to take the pledge, and look at me today!'

She did not look at him. She hardly heard him. If she had looked, she would have realised that if there had been any improvement in P.C. Hartford's appearance, he must have looked very dreadful in his moderately drinking days. But she heard nothing except a buzz of voices that had been going on all night—whispering, buzzing voices that came from another planet; and there was a little pain in her left arm which irritated her; and through all her confusion of mind and dread, formless reality which could not be reduced to any dimensions or advanced into clear perspective.

When she spoke it was mechanically to repeat:

'I want to see the Chief of Police. I must see the Chief of Police.'

She repeated this monotonously. Part of the mechanism of her reason was working; some tremendous motive power impelled a demand of which she was not conscious. She had little flashes of complete understanding; knew she was sitting on a hard form in a long and dimly-lit corridor, with bare, discoloured walls. In the next second she was sitting in an arm-chair in a small room, which was so light that it hurt her eyes; and a different lot of people were around her.

'Why did the infirmary people let her go?' asked Mason, in despair.

'I want to see the Chief of Police,' she said. 'I want to make a statement.'

'So you've told me a dozen times, my dear,' said Mason, patting her hand. 'Now wake up. You know where you are—I'm Superintendent Mason.'

She looked at him searchingly and shook her head.

'Where's the matron?' asked Mason. 'Oh, here you are, Miss Leverett. Let her lie down; give her some coffee. Where's that damned—oh, there you are, Bray! Is there any report?'

'None, sir,' said the inspector. And then, painfully: 'I don't think I can stand much more, sir. I shall have to go to sleep. After all, I'm only human.'

'You're not human at all'—Mason was distinctly offensive—'you're a policeman. You haven't been awake twenty-four hours, and you'll certainly be awake another twenty-four; the first forty-eight hours are the worst.'

'My own belief is,' said Bray, 'that this fellow drove the cab straight into the Thames—'

'Yes, yes, I'm sure he did,' said Mason soothingly, 'or into the British Museum, possibly. You might put an inquiry through.'

Inspector Bray considered this.

'I shouldn't think they'd go to the British Museum, sir—' he began.

Mason pointed to the door. He felt that another ten minutes of Inspector Bray would reduce him to a state of imbecility.

He returned to the inspector's room, now littered with a medley of articles which had been removed from the 'lodger's' home. There were one or two very important documents which he had found in a tin case, which had been half filled with platinum settings. Searching the box he found tweezers, awls and instruments of the jeweller's art by the dozen. White Face had himself removed the stones from their settings—the wonder is that he had not disposed of the platinum. He must have felt himself perfectly safe under the aegis of old Gregory, whose very honesty was the lodger's best credential.

A diligent search had been made for evidence of firearms, and, as a matter of precaution, to the circulation of the description of the wanted man had been added the warning: 'May carry a pistol.' But there was no proof that he carried anything of the sort. Neither cartridge nor cartridge box was found and, except for the knife, no arms whatsoever.

In the bottom of the cupboard they had unearthed a cardboard box bearing a Lyons label, which was filled with bundles of white cotton gloves, and in another part of the room half a dozen squares of twill into which eyeholes had been roughly cut. To the edge of each was fastened a strip of whalebone and a piece of elastic; the whalebone kept the mask rigid, and the elastic obviously fitted over the ears. Except for the eye-holes they might have been parts of the hangman's ghastly equipment.

White Face was well found in all matters pertaining to dress. There were two new long black coats, obviously of foreign make, three pairs of rubber goloshes, only one pair of which had been used and, most curious of all, a dummy automatic pistol. It was the kind that is used in theatres, was made of wood, and was a lifelike representation of the real article. Until he had picked it up in his hand and had felt its lightness, Mason had been absolutely certain that it was the real thing.

In his own mind he was convinced that White Face had no other weapon and that this was the gun he carried on his unlawful occasions, the weapon which had cowed crowded restaurants and nightclubs, and had reduced porters and waiters to trembling jelly.

Elk was half dozing in the room when Mason entered. 'Do you know what I think, sir?'

'You thinking, too?' growled Mason. 'All right, I'll buy it.'

'There's one man who is going to get White Face acquitted. You can look at it any way you like, but it comes back to the same thing. You couldn't work a conviction against him—if Lamborn sticks to his story.'

'Oh!' Mason's face fell. 'Lamborn—that's the pickpocket. H'm!'

He pondered on the matter for a long time.

'You're quite right, Elk,' he said at last. 'In the face of what that dirty little thief has said it would be very difficult to get a verdict. When I say "we couldn't", we mightn't. It's a shade of odds how the jury would take it.'

'The jury,' said Mr Elk oracularly, 'is a body or institution which gives everybody the benefit of the doubt except the police. Juries don't think; they deliberate. Juries—'

'Don't let us get clever,' said Mason. He went out through the charge-room (where he borrowed a key), down a passage lined on one side with yellow cell doors, and stopped before No. 9, pulled back the grating and looked in. Mr Lamborn was lying uneasily on a plank bed, two blankets drawn up over his shoulders. He was awake, and at the movement of the grating lifted his head.

'Hallo, Lamborn! Sleeping well?'

The thief blinked at him, swung his legs clear of the plank and sat up.

'If there's a law in this country, Mason, you're going to get fired out of the force for this what I might call outrage!'

'Invincible soul,' said Mason admiringly.

He put the key in the lock and turned it.

'Come out and have some coffee with me?'

'Poisoned?' asked Lamborn suspiciously.

'A little strychnine—nothing serious,' said Mason.

He conducted his prisoner along the corridor, handed over the key of the cell to an amused gaoler and ushered Lamborn into the little room. At the sight of Elk's bandaged head the prisoner brightened visibly.

'Hallo! Had a coshing?' he asked. 'Prayers *are* answered sometimes! I hope you're not seriously injured, Mr Elk?'

'He means,' interpreted Elk, 'that he hopes I'm fatally injured. Sit down, you poor, cheap, butter-fingered whizzer.'

'I shouldn't like to see you killed—flowers ain't cheap just now.'

Lamborn sat, still smirking, and when the inevitable coffee was brought, half filled a cup with sugar.

'Got the murderer?' he asked pleasantly.

'We've got you, Harry,' said Mr Mason in the same tone, and Lamborn snorted.

'You couldn't prove anything against me, except by the well-known perjury methods of the London police. I dare say you'll put half a dozen of your tame noses in the box and swear me life away, but Gawd's in his heaven!'

'Where did you learn that bit?' asked Mason curiously.

Lamborn shrugged his shoulders theatrically.

'When I'm in stir I only read poetry,' he explained. 'The book lasts longer because you can't understand it.'

He sipped noisily at his coffee, put down the cup with a clatter and leaned towards Mason.

'You haven't got a chance of convicting me. I've been thinking it out in the cell.'

Mason smiled pityingly.

'The moment you start thinking, Harry, you're lost,' he said. 'It's like putting a cow on a tightrope. You're not built for it. I don't want to convict you.'

His tone changed: he was so earnest that he carried conviction even to the sceptical hearer.

'All I wanted then, and all I want now, is that you should tell the truth. Have you ever known me to take all this trouble to get a little whizzer a couple of months' hard labour? Use your sense, Lamborn! Does a Superintendent of Scotland Yard, one of the Big Five, come down here to Tidal Basin and waste his night trying to get a conviction against a poor little hook like you? It would be like calling on the Navy to kill an earwig!'

Mr Lamborn was impressed. The logic was irresistible. He rubbed his chin uneasily.

'Well, it does seem funny,' he said.

'Funny? It's ludicrous! There must have been some reason why I wanted you to tell me this, and some reason why I should promise to withdraw the charge against you. You're wide, Lamborn—as wide as any lad in this district. Use your common sense and tell me why I should take all this trouble if I hadn't something behind it.'

Lamborn avoided his eyes. 'It does seem funny,' he said again.

'Then laugh!' growled Elk.

The man was not listening; he was frowning down at the table, obviously making up his mind. He made his decision at last.

'All right, guv'nor, it's a bet!'

He put out his hand and Mason gripped it, and that grip was a pledge, an oath and a covenant.

'I dipped him—yes. I saw him drop and I thought he was soused. I went over and I was knocked out to find he was a swell.'

'He was lying on his side, his face away from the lamp, wasn't he?' asked Mason.

The man nodded.

'Just tell me what you did—one moment.'

He raised his voice and called for Bray.

'Lie down there, Bray.' He pointed to the floor. 'I want to reconstruct Lamborn's petty larceny.'

Mr Bray looked with some meaning at Elk.

'Elk can't lie down because of his head,' said Mason irritably.

Bray went down on his knees and stretched himself, and Lamborn stood over him.

'I flicked open his coat—so. I put my hand in his inside pocket—'

'Left side or right side?' asked Mason.

'The left side. Then I hooked his clock—his watch, I mean—with my little finger—like this.'

His hands moved swiftly. There happened to be a pocket-case in Mr Bray's inside pocket. It also happened to contain the photograph of a very pretty girl, which fell on the floor. Bray retrieved it quickly and made a wrathful protest.

'And he's married!' was Elk's shocked murmur.

Bray went very red.

'All right, you can get up.'

Taking a sheet of paper out of a drawer, Mason began writing quickly. When he had finished he handed the sheet to Lamborn, who read it over and eventually affixed his sprawling signature to the statement.

'Why did you want to know, guv'nor?' he asked. 'What's my robbery got to do with the murder?'

Mason smiled.

'You'll read all about it in one of the evening papers—I'll try to arrange that your photograph's published.'

Elk laughed hollowly.

'What's the matter with his fingerprints?'

'But why do you want me to tell, Mr Mason?'

Mason did not explain.

'Release this man, Bray. Mark the charge "withdrawn". You'll have to attend the police court tomorrow morning, but you needn't go into the dock.'

'It's the only part of it he knows,' said Elk *sotto voce*.

Lamborn shook hands forgivingly with the chief and with Elk.

'One thing, Harry,' said Mason, and the released prisoner paused at the door. 'You'll be given back all your possessions except the jemmy we found in your pocket. I didn't tell you, but I was putting a felony charge against you in the morning— "Loitering with intent". Congratulations!'

Lamborn made a hurried exit from the police station. Until morning came he lay in his bed, puzzling to find a solution of the strange philosophy of Superintendent Mason, and could discover no answer that was consistent with his knowledge of English police methods.

CHAPTER XVII

LAMBORN had hardly left before the superintendent came into the charge-room hurriedly and the police reporter heard his name called.

'Michael, this young lady of yours—what was she at the clinic?'

'I believe she acted as Marford's secretary,' said Michael, surprised. And then, anxiously: 'You're not going to see her tonight, are you?'

Mason was undecided.

'Yes, I think I will. Somebody ought to be told about the doctor—I mean, somebody that matters. Besides, she may give us some very valuable help.'

'What help could she give you?' asked Michael suspiciously.

Mason rolled his head impatiently.

'If you imagine I'm waking her up in the middle of the night on any old excuse for the sake of seeing her in her négligée, you're flattering me. I'm out to find all the threads that lead to and from everybody who has played a part in this crime,' he said. 'I want to know who were Marford's friends, who were his enemies, and I can think of nobody else who can tell me. She can, because she worked with him, and Elk's got an idea that he was sweet on her.'

'Rubbish!' said Michael scornfully. 'I don't suppose he ever looked at her twice.'

'Once is enough for most men,' said Mason. 'Are you going to take me up and introduce me?'

When they were huddled up under heavy rugs, for a cold wind made an open car a death trap, Michael gave expression to his fears.

'It's going to be a terrible shock to Janice—Miss Harman.'

'Call her Janice: it sounds more friendly. Yes, I suppose it is. Marford is a fellow who got a lot of affection and sympathy without asking for it.'

'His body hasn't been found?'

Mason shook his head.

'And it won't be, in spite of the blood. If he'd been dead, White Face would have left him, wouldn't he?'

It was the first encouraging statement Mason had made.

Bury Street was lifeless when the car drew up before the flat, and it was a quarter of an hour before they could arouse the porter. Mason identified himself, and the two men climbed up to the first floor.

The maid was a heavy sleeper; it was Janice who heard the bell and, getting into her dressing-gown, opened the door to them. The first person she saw was Mason, whom she did not recognise.

'Don't be worried, Miss Harman. I have a friend of yours with me.'

And then she saw Michael and her alarm was stilled. She took them into the drawing-room, went off to wake her maid (there was something old-ladyish about Janice, Michael decided), and came back to the drawing-room to learn the reason for this visitation.

'I'm afraid I've got rather bad news for you, Miss Harman,' said Mason.

Invariably he adapted his tone to the subject of his speech, and he was so melancholy that she thought he could have come only on one subject, the murder of Donald Bateman.

'I know. Mr Quigley has told me,' she said. 'You want to ask me about the ring? I gave it—'

He shook his head.

'No. Dr Marford has disappeared.'

She stared at him.

'You mean—he is not hurt?'

'I hope not,' said Mason. 'I sincerely hope not.'

It was remarkable to Michael that this man, whom he had regarded as a stout, unimaginative and fairly commonplace officer of police, could tell the story with such little offence, and suppress so much without losing any of the main facts. She listened: the news was less shocking than that of Bateman's death, but it left her with a deeper heartache, for Marford was one of the ideals which experience and disillusionment had left undisturbed.

'The trouble is, we know nothing about the doctor or any of his friends, and we don't know where to start our inquiries. You were his secretary—?'

'No, not his secretary,' she corrected. 'I kept the accounts of the clinic, and sometimes of the convalescent home, and I was helping him to get Annerford ready—he has been trying for a year to open a tuberculosis institute for the children of Tidal Basin.'

'Where is Annerford?' asked Mason, and she told him and described the work which the doctor had set himself to do.

He had planned greatly, it seemed; had, in one of the drawers of his desk, blueprints of a princely building. His appeal to the wealthy public was already typewritten, and he had discussed with her many of the details.

'Now, Miss Harman,' said Mason, 'you know the people of the clinic. Is there anybody there who had a grudge against the doctor, or did he have any great friend there—man or woman?'

She shook her head.

'There was an elderly nurse and one or two occasional helpers. The staff at Eastbourne consisted of a matron and a nurse. He was trying to raise money to enlarge these homes,' she said; 'it was always a source of distress to the doctor that the places were understaffed, but they cost an awful lot of money.'

'There was nobody at any of these places—the clinic, the home at Eastbourne or at Annerford—who was in the doctor's confidence?'

She smiled at this.

'Not at Annerford. No, I know of nobody. He had no friends.' Her lip quivered. 'You don't think . . . any harm has come to him?'

Mason did not reply.

'Did Bateman have any friends?' he asked.

She considered the question.

'Yes, there was a man who came over with him from South Africa, but he never mentioned his name. The only other person he seemed to know was Dr Rudd.'

Mason opened his eyes wide. 'Dr Rudd?' he said. 'Are you sure?'

She nodded. She told him the story of the dinner and Bateman's perturbation when he had seen the doctor, resplendent in evening dress.

'That certainly beats me. Where could he have met Rudd?' said Mason. 'All gay and beautiful, was he—the doctor, I mean? Yes, I knew he knocked about a little bit in the West End, but I didn't realise—h'm!'

He looked down at the carpet for a long time, deep in thought.

'Yes,' he said suddenly. 'Of course. I understand now. Naturally he didn't want to meet Rudd.'

He looked at Michael quizzically.

'Are you going to stay to breakfast?' he asked, and Michael returned an indignant denial.

'You'd better go down to Tidal Basin and wait for me. I'm only calling at Scotland Yard to check up a few dates; I'll be with you in an hour. I'm sending a police car back—you can use that.'

White Face waited patiently for daylight. He had changed his clothes, and the suit he wore now would attract no attention when he lined up at Forest Gate for his char-a-banc ticket to the coast. Once or twice he went in to see his unwilling companion, and on each occasion found the doctor sleeping peacefully.

From his pocket he took an evening paper which he had not had time to read before. There was quite a lot about White Face, of course. He was a star turn in those days. Great authors, who catered exclusively for the intelligentsia, stepped down from their high pedestals to speculate upon what one called 'this amusing malefactor'. The Howdah affair was still topical. There was a revival of the 'Devil of Tidal Basin'; some gross plagiarist had attempted to revitalise the myth, but it needed Michael Quigley's skilful touch to make it live.

He dropped the paper on to the table, walked out into the open and stood listening. From far away he could hear the sound of distant motor-cars, and whilst he stood there, he saw a white magnesium rocket, probably a Verey light, flame in the air and die. So the police had put on the barrage! He knew that signal. A suspected car had been seen, and the white flare was the order to the nearest police control to stop and search it. Ingenious people, the London police, in their quiet untheatrical way. Very difficult, very dangerous to fool with. And yet they were not men of education—just common policemen who had raised themselves out of the rut, established their own little hierarchy, and attained by some extraordinary method a complete efficiency.

He did not despise them nor did he fear them. The odds against his escaping were twenty to one—there was enough of the gambler in him to fancy his chance.

No man who was wanted, and whose photograph was procurable, had ever escaped from England. Perhaps some did, but the police never admitted the exceptions.

As he came back along the passage he heard a faint voice call from the open door of the darkened room.

'Can I have some water, please?'

He carried a glass in to the doctor, who drank it and thanked him.

'You're in considerable danger, my friend. I hope you realise that?' said the voice from the sofa weakly.

'My dear doctor, I have been in danger for quite a long time—go to sleep, and don't worry about me.'

He waited till he heard the doctor's regular breathing, and then came out, closing the door softly behind him.

Danger! It had no significance for White Face. He feared nothing, literally and figuratively feared nothing. He did not regret one act of his life; regretted least of all that which had sent Donald Bateman into nothingness. Perhaps Walter would not have approved, but then Walter was weak—a daring man, but weak. White Face approved his own deed, which approval was more important than self-glorification.

Poor old Gregory! As for the doctor, he would put water and some kind of refreshment ready to his hand. In the morning he would be well enough to drive the taxi to the nearest police station.

Only one regret he had, and that he did not allow his mind to rest upon. But to give up life was an easy matter if necessity arose; with life one surrendered all aspirations.

He had finished his shaving, using cream instead of soap and water, when he heard a footstep in the passage. The doctor, then, was awake; that was unfortunate. He took one step towards the door when it opened. Mason stood there; an untidy Mason with his hat on the back of his head and his overcoat unfastened.

'I took the liberty of coming through a back window; most of them are open,' he said. 'I want you, of course.'

'Naturally,' said White Face. There was no tremor in his voice. 'You'll find the doctor in the next room. I don't think there's very much the matter with him.'

He held out his hands, but Mason shook his head.

'Handcuffs are old-fashioned. Have you got a gun?'

White Face shook his head.

'Then we'll step along,' said Mason politely, and guided him by the arm into the darkness outside.

Stopping to despatch his men to look after the doctor, he led his prisoner to where the police car was waiting.

'You weren't seen, but you were heard,' he explained.

White Face laughed.

'A taxicab in low gear is a menace to the security of the criminal classes,' he said lightly.

CHAPTER XVIII

THERE was a complete dearth of news when Michael Quigley reached the station. Negative reports are never sent to minor stations, and the absence of anything positive was sufficient to indicate that the search for the missing taxicab had so far been fruitless.

To kill time he wandered up and down the streets, revisited the scene of the murder, would have gone again to Gallows Court for news, if Gallows Court had not come out to meet him.

Michael was turning over the mud in the gutter with the toe of his boot when he saw the odd figure of the crazy man crossing the road. This strange apparition had one curious (and welcome) characteristic. He avoided the light, and no sooner had he come within the range of the arc lamp, than he halted and half turned away from its searching beams.

'Come over here, reporter! I've got something to tell you.'

'You can tell me your name to start with.'

The oddity chuckled.

'I ain't got a name. My parents forgot to give me one.' (This astounding statement, Michael discovered later, was true.) 'People call me anything they like—Shoey, some of 'em, because I used to black shoes.'

'What have you got to tell me?' asked Michael.

'He took the doctor away.'

He said this in a hoarse whisper.

'Who—White Face?'

Shoey nodded violently.

'I've got all the rights of it now. He took him in his cab—he was layin' there on the floor and nobody knew.'

He doubled up with silent laughter and slapped his knees in an agony of enjoyment.

'That makes me laugh! Mason don't know! All these clever busies from Scotland Yard, and they don't know that!'

'What are the "rights of it"?' asked Michael.

Sometimes, Mason had said, this strange creature was nearer to the truth than a saner man.

'Elk knows.'

The man without a name stuck a grimy forefinger into Michael's ribs to point his remark.

'That fellow's wider than Broad Street. Elk! I'll bet you he knowed all the time! But he likes to keep things to hisself until he's got 'em all cleared up. I've heard Bray say that—Bray's got no more brains than a rabbit,' he added.

Somebody was walking along the sidewalk towards them.

'That's him!' whispered the ragged object and melted across the street.

Bray was at such a distance that it seemed impossible for anybody to recognise that it was he. It appeared that he was walking off a grievance.

'As soon as this affair is over I'm going to put things straight,' he said aggressively. 'Mason really shouldn't do it! You understand, Quigley, that an officer of my rank has his position to uphold; and how can I uphold it if important inquiries are placed in the hands of subordinates? Insubordinates, I call 'em!'

'What's Elk been doing now?'

There was no need to ask who was the offender.

'Mason is a good fellow,' Bray went on, 'one of the best men in the force and one of the cutest. It you ever get a chance of dropping a hint that I said that, I'd be obliged, Quigley. You needn't make a point of repeating the conversation, but just mention it accidentally—he takes a lot of notice of what you say. But he's altogether wrong about Elk. Evil,' he went on poetically, 'is wrought by want of thought as well as want of heart—'

'Shakespeare?' murmured Michael.

'I dare say,' said Bray, who had no idea that American citizens wrote poetry. 'Mason does these things thoughtlessly. I told him I was willing to cross-examine this woman as soon as she came round and was in a fit state to talk. But no, Elk must do it! Elk knows her, apparently. But I ask you, Quigley, is it necessary to know a person before you question 'em? Was I properly introduced to Lamborn—there's another scandal; he's out on bail!'

To shorten the length of the grievance, Michael suggested that they should walk back together to the station. They arrived at an interesting time for Inspector Bray, because Lorna Weston had decided to talk.

She had refused to go into the inspector's office, and was seated in the charge-room, the bandaged Elk towering over her. Michael could see that it was not his but Bray's presence which brought that demoniacal frown to the sergeant's face when they appeared.

'All right, let's have all the press in, Bray,' he said savagely. 'Won't you come into the private office, Mrs Weston?'

'No, I won't.' The pale-faced woman was determined on the point. 'I'll say what I want to say here.'

'All right,' said Elk grimly. And to Shale, who was the stenographer of the party: 'Get your book. You're known as Lorna Weston,' he began, 'and you're the wife of—?'

She had parted her lips to speak when Mason came in briskly; behind him came two detectives and between them walked their prisoner.

Lorna Weston came up to her feet, her eyes fixed upon the smiling man who stood between the two guards—unconcerned, perfectly at his ease, not by so much as the droop of an eye betraying consciousness of his deadly peril.

'There he is! There he is!' she shrieked, pointing at him. 'The murderer! You killed him! You said you would if you ever met him, and you did it!'

Mason watched the prisoner curiously, but he made no response.

'It wasn't for me you hated him. It wasn't because he took me away from you—it was because of your brother who died in prison.'

The man nodded.

'It was because of that,' he said simply. 'If he could be brought to life and I were free, I'd kill him again.'

'Do you hear him?' she shrieked. 'My husband—Tommy Furse!'

'Call me by my real name,' said the other. 'Thomas Marford! It is a pretty good name, though it has been borne by some pretty bad people.'

He turned smilingly to Mason.

'You won't want this lady, I think? I can tell you all you wish to know, and I will clear up any point which may seem to you to be obscure.'

Michael Quigley stood petrified, unable to speak or move. Marford! This self-possessed man ... White Face ... hold-up man, murderer ... He must be dreaming. But no, here was the reality.

Marford, as unemotional as the crowd of detectives who stood around him, was twiddling his watch-chain, looking half amused, half pityingly at the shivering woman who called herself his wife.

He was evidently considering something else than his own position.

'I hope Dr Rudd will feel no ill-effects from his unhappy experience,' he said. 'As I told you earlier in the morning, I don't think he will suffer anything worse than a headache, which he can easily remedy. He has been in my garage all the night. You see,' he was almost apologetic, 'Rudd had a theory, which was to me a very dangerous theory on the lips of a rather loquacious and not terribly clever man. His view, which he was developing most uncomfortably, was that there was only one person who could possibly have killed Bateman—and that was myself! He thought it was a huge joke, but it wasn't

a joke to me; and when he called in at my surgery on the
way to the station to put his ideas before you, I realised at
once that I was in considerable danger. I realised more than
this,' he added calmly, 'that my life's work was done, that my
clinic and my convalescent home and my new rest-house at
Annerford—how did you find your way to Annerford Farm,
by the way? But perhaps you wouldn't like to tell me—were
things of the past, and that I must save myself at all costs.'

He looked round and caught Elk's eye and shook his
head sadly.

'I had to do it, Elk. I'm terribly sorry. You're the last man
in the world I would have hurt.'

To Mason's surprise, Elk grinned amiably.

'I don't know anyone I'd rather take a coshing from,' he
said handsomely.

'You were a dangerous man, too,' smiled Marford, 'but I
couldn't give you a whisky and soda with a little shot of drug
in it, as I gave to Dr Rudd. Just enough to put him under for
a few minutes. What I did then was to dope him and put him
in the garage. I was afraid he had betrayed me later, when I
heard him groaning. You probably heard him groaning, too;
I think you mentioned the fact to me?'

He addressed the reporter, and Michael remembered the
noise he had heard as he had moved through Gallows Court
in the dead of the night.

'There is one other matter I'm concerned about—how is
old Gregory? I'm afraid he's taken it rather badly.'

He talked fluently enough, but with a little slur in his voice.
It was the first time Mason had noticed that he had an impediment of speech which caused him to lisp a little.

'I'm rather anxious you should take my statement now.'

Mason nodded.

'I must caution you, Dr Marford—I suppose you are a
doctor, Marford?'

Marford inclined his head.

'Yes, I am qualified: lay anything to my door but the charge of being a quack! You can confirm this by a visit to my surgery, where you will find the certificates.'

'I have to warn you,' Mason went on conventionally, 'that what you now say may be taken down and used at your trial.'

'That I understand,' said Marford.

He looked at his wife; she had approached more closely to him; her dark eyes were blazing with hate; the straight, white mouth was bloodless.

'You'll hang for this, Tommy!' she breathed. 'Oh, God, I'm glad—you'll hang for it!'

'Why not?' he asked coolly, and, turning on his heels, followed Mason into the inspector's office.

'A nice woman,' was his only comment on his wife's outburst. 'Her loyalty to her unfortunate friend is almost touching—but then, loyalty invariably is. I cannot let myself think about poor Gregory Wicks.'

He was sincere: Mason had no doubt of it. There was no cynicism in his tone. Whatever else he might be, Thomas Marford was not a hypocrite.

Mason offered him a glass of water, which he refused.

He sat down by the side of the writing-table; his only request was that somebody should open a window, for the room was unpleasantly crowded. And then he told his story. He did not refuse a cigarette, but through most of the narrative he held it and its many successors between his fingers and only occasionally raised it to his lips.

'Are you ready?' he asked, and Sergeant Shale, who had opened a new notebook, tested his fountain pen and nodded.

CHAPTER XIX

'ONE always tries to find a beginning to these stories,' said Dr Marford, 'and usually one chooses to enumerate the virtues and describe the splendid domestic qualities of one's father and mother. That I do not purpose doing, for many reasons.

'My brother and I were left orphans at an early age. I was at a preparatory school when Walter went out to Australia to try his luck. He was a decent fellow, the best brother any man could wish to have. The little money that came to us from the sale of my father's practice—oh, yes, he was a doctor—he put in the hands of a lawyer for my education. He hadn't been in Australia long before he found work, and half his salary used to come to the lawyer every month.

'I don't know what date his criminal career began, but when I was about fifteen I had a letter from him, asking me to address all future letters to "Walter Furse". He was then in Perth, Western Australia. His full name was Walter Furse Marford. Naturally, I did as I was asked, and soon after larger monthly sums came to the lawyer and were very welcome, for I had been living practically without pocket money, and my clothes were the scorn of the school.

'By this time I was at a high school, or, as they call it in England, a public school, which I shall also refrain from mentioning, because every public school boy has a sneaking pride in his school. One day the lawyer came to see me. He asked me whether I had heard from my brother, and I told him I had not had a letter from him for four months. He told me that he was in a similar case, but that, previous to my brother's ceasing to correspond, he had sent a thousand pounds. But all the lawyer's letters asking how he would like this money invested had been unanswered. I was a little alarmed, naturally, because I had a very deep affection for Walter, and realised, as I had grown older, just what I owed to him. I was to go to a hospital and take up the profession of my father—it was my brother's money which made this possible.

'The mystery of Walter's silence was explained when I received, in a roundabout way, a letter which had been sent to a friend of his, and which was by him transmitted to me. It was written on blue paper, and when I saw on the heading the name of an Australian convict prison I nearly fainted. But it was the truth: Walter hid nothing in the letter, though in justice to him it contained no cant of repentance. He had been arrested after holding up a bank, where he and his gang had got away with nearly twenty thousand pounds. He asked me to think as well of him as I could, and said that he was telling me because he was afraid the authorities might trace me, and I should hear from some unsympathetic person the story of his fall.

'I will tell the truth. After the first shock I was not horrified at the revelation. Walter had always been an adventurous sort, and at my age I had that touch of romanticism which exaggerates certain picturesque types of crime into deeds almost worthy of a Paladin. My reaction to the blow was that I felt an increasing love for the man who had made such sacrifices and had taken such risks in order to fit his brother for membership of a noble profession.

'I exalted him above all men, and I yet do. But for the burden which my education and living imposed upon him, he could have afforded to live honestly, and I know, though he never told me, that I and I alone was responsible for his entering into the crooked path.

'The letter which I sent to him was, I am afraid, rather disjointed, and had in it a suggestion of hero-worship, for when he was released from prison he answered me very straightly; pointed out that there was nothing admirable in what he was doing, and that he would sooner see me dead than go the way he had gone.

'I worked like the devil at the hospital, determined to justify his sacrifice, if it could be justified. From time to time he wrote me, now from Melbourne, once from Brisbane, several times from a town in New South Wales, the name of which I cannot at the moment recall. Apparently he was going straight, for there were no delays in his letters; he told me that he was thinking of buying a "station", that he had already acquired a house and a few hundred acres in the hope to extend these by the purchase of other land.

'It was in this letter that I first heard of Donald Bateman. He said that he had met a very clever crook and had nearly been caught by him in connection with a land deal, but that a mutual friend, who had been in prison with Walter, had made them known to one another, Bateman had apologised, and they were now chums.

'Bateman apparently made his money out of persuading innocent purchasers to put up a deposit on imaginary properties, but he did a little other crook work on the side, and was one of the best-informed men in Australia on one topic—the security and deposit of banks. He himself was not a bank robber, but he supplied the various gangs with exact information which enabled them to operate at a minimum risk. Usually he stood in for his corner—by which I mean—'

'I know what you mean,' said Mason.

'As soon as my final examinations were over Walter wanted me to come out to Australia and stay with him for six months, to discuss future plans. He asked me if I would mind adopting the name of Furse. He said he could arrange to get me my passport and ticket in that name. The only awkward point about this arrangement was that my examinations finished on the Friday, I was to leave for Australia on the Saturday, and I could not know the result of the exams, except by letter. I arranged, however, with the manager of the bank which carried my account to have the certificates addressed care of the bank and for him to send them on to an address which my brother had given me. I had to invent a family reason why I was calling myself Furse in Australia, and he seemed satisfied.

'The work at the hospital grew increasingly hard. The last days of the examination came, and on the Friday I handed in my final papers with a heartfelt sense of thankfulness. The results would not be known for some weeks, but I had a pretty good idea that I had passed except in one subject. As it happened, my highest marks were for the subject in which I thought I had failed!

'The next morning, as happy as a child, I drove off to St Pancras and Tilbury, and on the Saturday afternoon was steaming down the Channel, so excited that I hardly knew what to do with myself.

'The boat had a full complement of passengers. I was travelling second class, because, although my brother had sent the first class fare, I wanted to save him as much as possible, and second class on a P. & O. steamer is extraordinarily comfortable.

'This particular ship was crowded with people, the majority of whom were bound for India and quite a number for Colombo. We dropped the Indian passengers at Port Said or Suez—I'm not sure which—and now that the dining-room was thinned out and there was space to walk about the decks, one began to take notice of one's fellow passengers.

'I had seen Lorna Weston the day we left England, but I did not speak to her until we were passing through the Suez Canal, and then only to exchange a few words about the scenery.

'It was at Colombo, where we both went ashore, that I came to know her. She was very pretty and vivacious, and was, she told me, travelling to Australia to take a position as nursery governess. Looking back from my present age, I can see that, if I had had more experience of life, I should have known she was much too young for the job, and should have guessed, what I later knew, that she was going out in the hope of finding easy money.

'I told her very little about myself, except that I was a medical student, but for some reason or other she got it into her head that I was a wealthy young man or had wealthy relatives. She may have got this idea because I was travelling second from choice, or because I had a lot of money in my possession—I had a couple of hundred pounds in notes which I had managed to save from my allowance. I had an idiotic idea that it would please Walter if I handed him back this colossal sum, as it appeared to me, out of the money he had so generously sent me.

'If you know anything about ship travel you will understand that it takes no more than a few days for an ordinary friend-ship between a young man and a girl to develop into a raging passion. We were not five days out of Colombo when, if she had asked me to jump over the side of the ship, I should have obeyed. I adored her. I loved her, and she loved me. So we told each other. I'm not complaining about her, I'm not reproaching her, and I don't want to say one single word that's going to make life any harder for her, except that I must tell the truth to explain why she was living in Tidal Basin.

'She only loved one man in her life, and that was Bateman. I say this without bitterness or hatred. She probably loved the worst man she has ever met or is ever destined to meet. It is not necessary for me to tell you what happened during the remainder of the voyage. I had moments of exaltation, of despair, or heroic resolve, or terrible depression. I wondered what Walter would say when I told him that at the outset of my career, before I was in a position to earn a penny, I had engaged myself to a girl who had been a perfect stranger to me when I went on board.

'He came down to the dock to meet me, and I introduced him to Lorna, but I did not tell him of my intentions until we were back in the hotel where he was staying and where he had rented a room for me. To my surprise, he took it very well.

'"You're a bit young, Tommy, but I'm not so sure that it's a bad thing for you. If I had married I mightn't have made such a fool of myself. But don't you think you could wait for a year?"

'I told him there were imperative reasons why we should marry almost at once, and his face fell.

"'She told you that, I suppose? She may be mistaken."

'But I couldn't argue the matter, and after a while Walter agreed.

"'I'm going through a pretty bad time," he said. "I've been speculating on the Stock Exchange, and I've lost quite a lot of money racing. But things will take a turn soon, and you shall have the best wedding present that money can buy."

'How bad was his financial position I only discovered by accident. He had sold his little property and for the moment was without occupation. His prison life had naturally brought him into contact with all sorts of undesirables, but so far he had resisted their solicitations, and had steered a straight path.

'Walter was not a strong character. Viewed dispassionately, he was a weakling, because he invariably took the easiest route. But he had the heart of a good woman, and I can't help feeling that again it was to make some provision for me that he fell back into his old ways. In fact, I am sure of it. His wedding present to me was five hundred pounds, and it didn't make me a bit happy, because I had read in the papers that a country bank had been stuck up the day before and a considerable sum of money had been stolen. In fact, I taxed him with it, but he laughed it off.

'It was a few days after the wedding that I made up my mind. I left Lorna at the hotel and went in search of Walter. I found him in a restaurant which was also a bar, and that was the first time I met Donald Bateman. Bateman went out, and I took this opportunity to put forward my proposal, which was no less than that I should share a little of his risk.

"'You're mad," he said, when it dawned upon him what I meant.

'I suppose I was. But if I were to analyse my motive from the standpoint of my experience, I should say I was no more than stupidly quixotic. He wouldn't hear of it, but I insisted.

'"You've been taking these risks for me all these years. You've suffered imprisonment. Every time you go out on one of your adventures you stand the risk of being killed. Let me take a little of it."

'Bateman came back at that moment, and I realised he was well in Walter's confidence. I tried to put the matter hypothetically to Bateman, without betraying myself and Walter, but it was a fairly childish effort, and he saw through it at once.

'"Why not, Walter? It's better than taking in any of these roustabouts—Grayling or the Dutchman. Besides, he's a gentleman, and nobody would imagine he was a member of a gang of crooks."

'Walter was furious, but his fury did not last long: he was, as I say, weak, though I'm not blaming him, for, if he had refused, I believe I should have gone off and stuck up a bank of my own out of sheer bravado.

'We all three went back to the hotel, and I introduced my wife to Bateman. He was a good-looking fellow in those days and terribly popular with women; the worse they were the more was the fascination he seemed to exercise. Although I was only a kid, I could see she was tremendously attracted by him, and the next day, when I went out with Walter to talk matters over with him, I came back to find that Bateman had lunched with her, and thereafter they hardly left one another. I wasn't jealous; I'd got over my first madness and realised that I'd made a ghastly mistake.

'Naturally, I didn't want any complications with Bateman, who I knew was married and had left his wife in England. As a matter of fact, he was married before he met and married the present Mrs Landor—the lady who came to my surgery on the night I killed Bateman and told me, to my amazement—however, that can wait.

'Walter at last agreed that I should stand in and help him with the robbery of a country bank which carried a considerable amount of paper currency, especially during weekends. The job was to be done "two-handed", as we say, and Bateman, of course, took no part in the actual hold-up, but was the man who spied out the land, supplied us with all particulars as to the movements and habits of the staff, and could discover, in some way I've never understood, almost to a pound how much cash reserve a branch office was holding.

'It was a little town about sixty-five miles from Melbourne, and Walter and I drove out overnight in a motor-car and stayed with a friend of his till morning. Naturally I was wild with excitement, and I was all for carrying a gun. Walter wouldn't hear of this. He never carried firearms, the only pistol he used being a dummy—that was a lesson I never forgot.

'"You're either going to murder or you're not going to murder," said Walter. "If you're going out to rob, a dummy pistol's as good as any. It's its persuasive power and its frightening power that are important."

'He was a man of extraordinary principles, and held very strong views on criminals who used firearms.

'"It's the job of a bank official to defend his property, and if you kill him you're a coward," he said. "It's the job of a copper to arrest you, and if you shoot at him you're a blackguard."

'But he had no especial affection for the police; no faith in them; and before we went out, he had insisted on my having all my pockets sewn up with strong pack-thread.

'"You only want a handkerchief, and you can carry that in your sleeve," he said.

'I didn't see why he took this precaution, until he explained that it was not unusual, if the police caught a prisoner, to slip a gun into his pocket in order to get him a longer sentence. I don't know whether this was true. It may be one of the yarns that crooks invent and believe in.

'We carried our dummy pistols in a belt under our waist-coats. You'll find all the particulars of the raid we made upon the branch bank, in a little scrap-book in my bedroom. It was successful. At the appointed minute we entered the bank with white masks on our faces; I held up the cashier and his assistant with my dummy pistol whilst Walter passed round the counter, pulled the safe open—it was already unfastened—and took out three bundles of notes. We were out of the town before the police had wakened up from their midday sleep.

'We came back to Melbourne by a circuitous route, and I'll swear there was nobody in the town who would have recognised us or who could have identified us in any way. That evening the Melbourne papers were full of the robbery, and announced that the Bank of Australasia were offering five thousand pounds for the arrest of the robbers, and this was supplemented by a statement issued on behalf of the Government, through the police, that a free pardon would be granted to any person, other than one of the perpetrators, or any accomplice, who might turn King's Evidence. Walter was worried about this notice. He knew Donald Bateman better than I.

'"If he gets the reward as well as the pardon, we're cooked," he said, and when he put through a telephone inquiry to the newspaper office and heard that the reward was to go to anybody, accomplice or not, he went white.

'"Go and find your wife, Tommy," he said. "We've got to slip out of this town quick! There's a boat leaving for San Francisco this afternoon. We might both go on that. I'll see the purser and we can travel in different classes."

'I went to the hotel, but Lorna was out; the porter told me she had gone with Mr Bateman to the races, and I returned to Walter and told him.

'"Maybe he won't see the offer until after the races are over. That is our only chance," he said. "You'd better leave her a note and some money, tell her you'll let her know where she can join you."

'Returning to the hotel, I packed a few things and wrote the note. When I walked out of the elevator into the vestibule, the first person I saw was Big Jock Riley, Chief of the Melbourne Detective Service. I only knew him because he'd been pointed out to me as a man to avoid. I'll say this about him—he's dead now, poor chap!—that he was a decent fellow. I knew what was going to happen when he came towards me and took the suitcase out of my hand and gave it to another man.

'"You'd better pay your bill, Tommy," he said. "It will save everybody a lot of bother."

'He went with me to the cashier, and I paid the bill, and then he took me to a taxi and we drove to the police station. The first person I saw when I got in was Walter. They'd taken him soon after I had left, and I learnt that I had been followed to the hotel, and they had only waited until I had collected my kit before they arrested me. That was one of Riley's peculiarities, that he made all crooks pay their hotel bills before he arrested them. They said that his wife owned three hotels in Melbourne, but that is probably another invention.

'The police found most of the money—not all, for Walter had planted four thousand pounds, and had paid two thousand to Bateman, which Bateman returned when he found he was going to get the five thousand reward.

'Bateman was the informer, of course. He hadn't gone to the races: he was sitting in another room at the police office when we were brought in, and he came out to identify us. Walter said nothing; he didn't look at him. I think he must have had a premonition that this had been his last day of freedom, he was so utterly broken and dejected. But I met Bateman's eyes, and he knew that if ever he and I met, there would be a reckoning. Is that melodramatic? I'm afraid it is.

'There's very little to tell about the court proceedings. The prosecution was fair, and we were sentenced, Walter to eight years and I to three. I never saw Walter after we left the cells until I was taken to the prison hospital where he was dying. He was too far gone to recognise me. Riley was there; he'd come to see if he could get any information about the four thousand that was cached. He told me, while I was waiting to be taken back, that if I would tell him he would get me a year's remission of my sentence. I was so utterly miserable that I was on the point of telling him, but I thought better of it, and told him only half the truth.

'There was two thousand planted in one place and two thousand in another. I needn't tell you where, but one was a respectable bank. I told him the hardest, and I believe he went away and recovered it, because within a week I had my order of release. Riley never broke a promise.

'I hung around Melbourne for a month. I didn't have to look for Lorna: I knew she'd gone—you get news in prison— and that Bateman had gone with her. That didn't worry me at all. I was certain that Bateman and I would meet sooner or later. It's curious how Walter's warning always stayed with me. I have never owned a pistol in my life, and even in my most revengeful mood I never dreamt of buying one.

'The police left me alone when I came out. Riley may have suspected that there was more money to collect, but probably he wasn't bothering his head about that. I had had all my English letters sent to a certain address in Melbourne, and when I went to this place I found a dozen old bills, receipts, letters from hospital friends, and a long envelope.

'Sometimes when I was in prison I used to wonder what had been the result of those examinations, but after a time I ceased to take any interest in them. It seemed that whatever honest career I had had was finished. I should be struck off the Medical Register on conviction, and that was the end of my doctoring. I didn't realise that the Australian authorities knew nothing of "Marford"—knew only Tommy Furse—and it was only when I opened the envelope and took out the stiff parchment certificate that the truth dawned on me. In England I was Dr Marford, a duly and properly qualified medical man. I could begin practice at once. A new and wonderful vista was opened, for I was terribly keen on my work, and had determined to specialise in the diseases of childhood.

'I collected the two thousand, and after a reasonable interval left Australia for England, travelling third class as far as Colombo and transferring to first class from that port. It was a little too sultry in the steerage, and I could afford better accommodation. I stopped off in Egypt; I wanted to break completely all association with Australia, to snap the links of acquaintanceship formed on the ship which might extend to somebody who knew me and my record. In Cairo I presented my credentials to the British Minister, obtained a new passport in place of one which I said I'd lost, and travelled overland through Italy and Switzerland, arriving in London at the end of September.

'My intentions were to buy a small practice, and I had no sooner arrived in London than I called on an agent, who promised me very considerable help, said he had the very thing for me, but who proved to be worse than useless, submitting propositions which I could not afford to buy or country practices which I knew I could not keep. Country people are very conservative where doctors are concerned, and do not trust any medical man until he has grown a white beard or lost his eyesight.'

'I decided to build up a practice of my own in London. I had fifteen hundred pounds left of my money, and by a system of strict economy I knew I could live for five years without a patient—three years if I carried out my big plan, which was to establish a sunlight clinic for babies. I have always had a natural enthusiasm for work amongst children. I love children, and if I had not been interrupted by Donald Bateman and my wife, I should within a few years have opened a great institution, which would have cost twenty thousand pounds to build and ten thousand a year to maintain. That was my ambition.

'It is common knowledge that I opened a surgery in Endley Street and started my practice as cheaply as any practice has ever been founded. From the first I was successful in obtaining patients. They were of the cheapest kind, and required nineteen shillings back for every pound they spent, but it was interesting work, and in a burst of enthusiasm I arranged to open my first clinic at the farther end of Endley Street. I reckoned that by the practice of the strictest economy I could live on the earnings from my practice, and that the money I had so carefully hoarded could keep the clinic running for two years.

'And then one day a thunderbolt fell. A woman walked into my consulting-room. At the time I was at my desk, writing a prescription for a patient who had seen me a few minutes before. I saw her sit down without looking at her; and then, as I asked, "What can I do for you?" I looked up—into the eyes of Lorna Marford, my wife!

'I had forgotten her. That is no exaggeration. Literally she had passed out of my life and out of my memory. I had half forgotten Donald Bateman. For a moment I did not recognise her, and then she smiled, and my heart felt like a piece of lead.

'"What do you want?" I asked.

'She was very poorly dressed and shabby-looking, and was lodging at that time with a Mrs Albert. She was, she told me, three or four weeks behind with her rent.

'"I want money," she said coolly.

'"Isn't there a man called Bateman?" I asked.

'She laughed at this and made a little gesture. I knew from that that she was still fond of him, and that he'd left her.

'"Bateman's gone. He and I have not seen each other for over two years," she said.

'She told me the kind of life she had been living, how she had been forced into a slum by sheer poverty. I felt sorry for her—I find it very easy to be sorry for women. But I remembered also that she had taken her share of the blood money, and had probably helped in our betrayal. There were a lot of little happenings that I remembered afterwards in prison which gave colour to this view. And I remembered Walter, dying in a prison hospital, so friendless, so lonely, so heartbroken.

'"You'll get no money from me," I said. "You had your share of the reward, I suppose?"

'"I had a bit of it," she answered coolly. "Not so much as I deserved. The police would never have found your white masks but for me."

'Her coolness took my breath away. I got up from the table and opened the door.

'"You can go," I said, but she did not stir.

'"I want a hundred pounds," she said. "I'm sick of living in poverty."

'I could only look at her; I was speechless.

'"Why should I give you a hundred pounds, supposing I had it?"

'"Because," she answered slowly, "if you don't give me a hundred pounds I shall tell somebody that you are an ex-convict. And then where will you be—doctor?"

'From that day onwards she blackmailed me. Within three months I had only half the money that I had put aside for the clinic, and I had committed myself to twice as much: ordered lamps, beds, structural alterations, and had practically placed myself under an obligation to buy the premises in five years' time.

'If I could have got her to leave the neighbourhood I might have had some respite; but though I was giving her a big sum every week, and she could have lived in comfort in the West End, she insisted, when she changed her lodgings, upon taking rooms locally, and upon these she spent a sum equivalent to my yearly income.

'Why she refused to live somewhere else I did not know. It puzzled me, until one day there flashed upon me the solution. She believed that sooner or later I should meet Donald Bateman—she wanted to be on hand to watch every movement of mine, so that she might save her lover. She may have had a premonition. That phenomenon is outside the ambit of my knowledge. I am a physiologist; mental and psychic phenomena I know nothing about.

'It seemed there was not one chance in a million that I should ever see Donald Bateman again. Suppose he came to London, what likelihood was there that he should come to such an out-of-the-way spot as Tidal Basin? And yet I had met with some odd coincidences. The very first doctor I met, when I came to the place, was Dr Rudd—and I had heard Bateman speak of Rudd. Rudd had been prison doctor at a county gaol where Bateman had served two years' hard labour! I remembered the name and the description the moment I saw him. It is quite possible that he also saw the doctor in London, but of that I know nothing. He hated Rudd, who had been the cause of his getting extra punishment for malingering whilst he was in prison, and he often described him—unflatteringly, but, I must say, faithfully.

'The demands from the clinic increased with the growth of my ambition. I was desperately hard pressed for money. On the one hand, by the legitimate expansion of my experiment, on the other by the increasing demands from Lorna.

'I don't know what gave me the idea; I rather think it was the pathetic distress of old Gregory Wicks when I told him that he could never take out his cab again except at the gravest risk to himself and to the community. He was nearly blind, and his misery at the idea of surrendering the licence he had held for fifty-five years touched me. I thought how useful a taxicab might be, and how easily one might make up as Gregory. One thought suggested another, and when the idea took definite shape I was thrilled by the prospect.

Isn't there a legend of an old highwayman who robbed the rich to give to the poor? That would not have amused me; but to take toll of those wealthy people who had ignored the appeals I had hectographed and posted broadcast, and use the money to extend my clinic—that was a fantastic but a fascinating thought.

'I don't think I was ever completely happy until I began my raids. I planned everything, spent nights in the West End, observing, timing and arranging my first coup. I invented, for the benefit of Gregory Wicks, a fictitious convict who could not obtain a licence, but who was a good and careful driver. I took lodgings for him in Gregory's house, and the old man was delighted. It is not true that he never allowed another man to take out the cab. He is colossally vain of his own individuality, poor old fellow, and the idea that somebody would go out looking very much like him, ply for hire and keep alive the traditions of his taciturnity and his hardihood appealed to the simple man. Only one stipulation he made, and it was that his substitute should place himself under a solemn vow to return any lost property he found in the cab. He was inordinately proud of his record.

'The first raid was ridiculously simple. I took my taxicab to the vicinity of a restaurant where smart people go to supper, and, walking boldly into the hall, I held up the room with a dummy pistol and got away with the jewels of a large, florid woman. I have no regrets. She is probably not starving, for I left on her person considerably over ten thousand pounds' worth of diamonds.

'The underworld had given me its confidence. I knew a receiver in Antwerp and another in Birmingham, with whom I could place the stones, and the first coup gave me enough money to completely re-equip the clinic and to open my Eastbourne convalescent home.

'But I had reckoned without Lorna. She had read an account of the stick-up, and it so happened that, unknown to me, she had witnessed my return. She came the next morning and demanded her share. Subsequently I gave her nearly a thousand pounds. I should have hated her if I was not a philosopher. It was much easier for me to pretend she had no existence.

'The second and third raids were as successful as the first. I paid Lorna her share. She was now the talk of the neighbourhood, with her smart dresses. She paid visits to the West End in hired cars and was probably living more expensively than she had ever lived in her life.

'If I had any qualms about the work on which I was engaged, they were caused by my association with a girl who shall be nameless. I seldom spoke to her. She was largely a creature of dreams: her sweetness and her purity were all the more transcendent in contrast with the character of my wife.

'Of Bateman I had seen nothing. I had no idea that he was in England and that Lorna had met him by accident in the West End and had asked him to come down and see her. The first mention of him I had came one night when I was visited at my surgery by a lady who was under the impression that her husband had been engaged in a fight and had killed his assailant. She was hysterical, and in her hysteria she took me into her confidence, told me of a man who was blackmailing her, mentioned his name—Donald Bateman! When I heard it the room seemed to spin round. Bateman was in England—was in that very neighbourhood! Imagine the devil that took possession of me.

'She grew calm when I assured her that the two men who had been fighting were labourers from the docks, and she went away, leaving me in a kind of passive delirium. I was almost incapable of thinking reasonably. The old loathing for the informer had come back to me. I could see, as plainly as though he were before me, the pinched face of my dying brother. It came back vividly and seemed to reproach me, that I had let it pass from my mind. Yet all in me that was sane told me that it was impossible that I could do anything, that it was unlikely I should ever meet Bateman. Could I go wandering round the streets of London looking for this blackguard? I should know him, of course: he had a knife scar under his chin—a woman did that in Australia. It had only just healed when I arrived in Melbourne.

'I was still thinking over things after Mrs Landor had left, when I heard voices on the other side of the street. It was raining, and that had driven the crowds away and left Endley Street empty. I saw a man in evening dress, and I saw a woman run across to him. He had been to her flat, and apparently had left something behind. I knew Bateman suffered from angina pectoris, and invariably carried a phial of butyl ammonal to be used in case of emergency. Apparently he had left this behind at Lorna's flat. I heard him thank her. And then I saw them looking across the road towards me, and knew that she had already told him who I was. He did not dream that I was as well aware of his identity!

'He sent her back; didn't move till she was out of sight; then he began to walk on slowly, and I was preparing to follow, when I saw a man come up to him—it was Landor— heard a few words, and then saw Landor lash out and Donald Bateman fall. He was always a tricky sort of fellow, and it was a favourite dodge of his in a fight to pretend he'd been knocked out. In this way he saved himself from further punishment. It succeeded with Landor, for after a while he walked quickly away, and I lost sight of him.

'I still hesitated as to what I should do. I knew P.C. Hartford was on his beat, saw the flicker of his helmet as he passed under a distant street lamp. I could do nothing now.

'And then Bateman got up, dusted himself and began to walk the way that Hartford had come. I saw the man and the constable talking together, and Hartford came on. He didn't come far; presently he turned round, and at that moment Donald Bateman dropped as if he'd been shot.

'I knew exactly what had happened: he had a heart attack. My professional instincts urged me forward, but at that moment a figure crossed the road and crouched over the fallen man—and Hartford had seen him. He went back, quickening his stride, and I followed. As I came along the pavement I saw something lying at my feet. It was a broken key-chain, attached to which was a bunch of keys. I picked it up and put it in my pocket. The man who was searching Bateman's pockets was a well-known local thief named Lamborn. He, too, saw the policeman and started to run, but before he could go far Hartford had grabbed him.

'While they were struggling, I came up. Then I saw, lying by the side of the man I hated, a sheath knife. It had evidently fallen out of his pocket. I had to make my decision quickly. There he lay—the liar, the traitor, the wronger of women, the man who had killed my brother. I don't remember taking the knife from its sheath or using it. He never moved—must have died instantly.

'The struggle between the policeman and the thief was subsiding. I slipped the red knife into my pocket. There was excuse for the blood on my hands—I was a doctor handling a murdered man. Nobody questioned me or suspected me. A policeman brought me a bucket of water to wash my hands. I didn't regret it long. I do not regret it now. I am glad I killed him—proud I killed him!

'Then came Rudd, an imbecile theorist; but even imbecile theorists sometimes and by accident hit upon solutions with diabolical accuracy. And Elk suspected. I knew he suspected me from the first. But the real danger threatened when Lorna came on to the scene. Her woman's instinct had told her something was wrong. She had heard that a man had been murdered, pushed her way through the crowd, and went whimpering over the man who had made her what she was, if indeed she was not born with more than her share of original sin.

'She didn't see me in the crowd. I knew she was going to speak, and wondered how I could stop her. Fortunately, nature intervened and she fainted. I was asked to take her to the station. It was the opportunity I could have prayed for. We got her into the car and drove a little way till we came to a chemist's shop, and I sent the policeman who accompanied me to wake up a chemist. He had hardly gone before I slipped a hypodermic syringe out of my pocket. It was one I kept loaded, and had prepared for a maternity case. The drug was working by the time the policeman came back with a restorative, which certainly would not restore her. I waited my opportunity while she was in the matron's room, and gave her a second dose—enough, as I thought, to keep her quiet for the rest of the night. It was easy to explain her condition when I put the hypodermic syringe and its case in her bag. I would have given her a third shot, and called at the infirmary for that purpose, but the house surgeon would not allow me to see her.

'To dispose of her was one thing, to silence Rudd another. I heard he'd gone home to bed. I was amazed when he tapped at my window on his way to the station and came in with this astounding theory—astounding in him because it was true.

'"The man," he said, "must have been murdered between the time the policeman arrested Lamborn and the time I said he was stabbed." He was working on the same grounds as you, Mason. If Lamborn had told the truth at first your task would have been simplified. Obviously, Bateman could not have been stabbed when the little thief picked his pocket, or his pocket-book and Lamborn's hands would have been covered with blood. That was Rudd's theory, too. He jokingly accused me of being the murderer, and pointed out certain stains on my coat which could not have been there had I not been by the body at the moment of killing.

'Rudd had to be silenced at all costs. I invited him to drink a glass of wine with me—he preferred whisky and soda. Getting his attention fixed on my new ray lamp, I doctored his drink. Curiously enough, he detected nothing wrong, though he had very little time to detect anything, for he was on the ground in ten seconds. I served him as I had served Lorna—carried him into the garage and left him there.

'I had to get away: I knew that was imperative. But to travel needed money, tickets, passport—things I did not possess. And then, standing near the door of the inspector's room, I heard that Landor had a large sum of money in his flat. This was my only chance. I went home, got out the taxi and drove to a road at the back of Landor's house. I guessed that the place was under observation, but I was desperate. Happily, there was a fire escape and up this I went.

'I had the keys of Landor's flat—I had picked them up on the night of the fight. I had to take my chance—wasn't even sure whether the flat was on the first or the second floor. But I had luck. Landor's name was on a brass plate, and I opened the door and went in. I had hardly closed the door behind me when I was startled to hear a woman's voice asking if I was Louis. I have a memory for voices, and I recognised it instantly as the lady who had called at my surgery that night. I kept quiet, fearing that at any moment she would come out and put on the lights. But she went back into her room and I crept along, looking for a hiding-place. There was a small room which, from its furnishing, was, I guessed, a maid's room. I got into here; the key was on the inside and I turned it. Landor arrived two minutes afterwards; and then, to my embarrassment, I heard Elk and Inspector Bray. Again I was fortunate: the detectives left with the Landors and gave me a few minutes to get the money and tickets—though neither these nor the passport could have been of much use to me. They had been located for me by Landor, who had told the detectives what was in the drawer.

'I had hoped to take the money and make my getaway before Elk returned, but he came back too soon, and the life-preserver, which was the only weapon I carried, had to be employed. I can't say how sorry I was to strike down a man whom I have always regarded as a friend.

'And there was another danger, I discovered when I got back to the surgery. Rudd was returning to consciousness. I heard him groan as I went along the yard to give him a second injection, and I wondered who else had.

'There was one chance of getting away, but when I had finished my preparations and had brought the car to the back door I was rung up from the police station with the news that Mason was on his way. I knew my last minute of safety had arrived, and on the spur of the moment I invented the forthcoming visit of the man with the white mask. I planned it all out, sprinkled the passage with a bottle of beef extract, which would look like blood in artificial light, tested the switches and oiled the bolts outside the door, between the time the detectives left the station and arrived at the surgery.

'I still had to get out, but I had arranged that, too. There is on my desk a bell-push which rings in the passage, and which I use as a signal for the next patient to come in. I waited my opportunity and rang the bell, using the signal which I had said White Face invariably used. Thereafter it was easy; to hold an imaginary conversation with somebody in the hall was a simple matter. To slam suddenly and lock the door, pretend that I had been attacked, switch out the lights and get away in the cab, occupied a few minutes. I had already put Rudd there, since I dared not leave him behind.

'I made, as you know, for the farm-house I had bought, and which I intended turning into a home for tubercular children. Perhaps some philanthropist will carry on the good work.

'I don't think there is anything more that I can tell you. If there is, I shall be able to supply any deficiency.'

CHAPTER XX

Dr Marford stretched back in his chair, a smile on his weary face.

'Tired, doctor?' said Mason.

He nodded.

'Very, very tired,' he said.

'I never knew you had a lisp before?'

The doctor ignored the question.

'Tell me, how did you find me at Annerford? Oh, I know.' He smiled. 'You interviewed poor Miss Harman, and she told you that I had another institution and naturally you went there.'

Mason nodded.

'You have no questions to ask me?'

Mr Mason considered.

'I don't think there is anything I can ask you, doctor. You won't tell me the names of the two fences who bought the diamonds you stole?'

Marford shook his head slowly, laughter in his eyes.

'That would be unprofessional, wouldn't it?' he said.

'That crazy man in the court—did he know?'

'He's a very good guesser. I sometimes think he's psychic,' said Marford. 'Every time I met him he used to give me just the oddest, understanding look.'

'I was talking about your lisp just now, doctor. I've never noticed it before,' said Mason again.

'I haven't a lisp'—Dr Marford stretched himself luxuriously in his chair—'and I haven't any impediment of speech. But, you see, I recognise inevitabilities, and for the last hour and a half I have had in my mouth—it is now between my teeth—a little glass phial of cyanide of potassium—'

Three detectives flung themselves upon him, but it was too late. He shuddered slightly; a spasm of pain passed over his face, and he stiffened. There was no other movement.

Mason looked at him in admiration.

'Game, eh?' he said huskily. 'By God, how game!'

He turned abruptly and walked across to the charge-room, and came, bare-headed, into the street, to breathe the sweet air of morning.

The day was breaking.

THE END